PRAISE FOR CHRISTOPHER REICH

Once a Thief

"A stylish, jet-propelled thriller full of intriguing characters and surprising twists. Simon Riske is a character I'll want to meet again."
—Jeff Abbott, *New York Times* bestselling author of *Blame*

"Reich paints his characters in broad strokes, much in the manner of Ian Fleming in the James Bond novels, giving us the big picture and letting us fill in the small details from our imaginations. In fact, comparison to the James Bond novels is apt in many ways: the dashing spy, the snappy dialogue, the glamorous locales (in this case, Corsica, the French Alps, and Switzerland, among others). An entertaining escapist adventure."
—*Booklist*

"*Once a Thief* is a good read and moves at a good clip. Reich's readers who are fans of his previous Simon Riske books will enjoy this one and will look forward to Riske's next adventure."
—New York Journal of Books

"The exotic locales and plot twists, not to mention enough action to keep you turning each page, make *Once a Thief* an enjoyable experience."
—Bookreporter

"Heart pounding . . . Reich combines great action with surprises readers won't see coming. One doesn't have to care much about cars or high finance to enjoy this cinematic thriller."
—*Publishers Weekly*

"Intricately plotted."

—*Kirkus Reviews*

The Prince of Risk

"*The Prince of Risk* is a terrific thriller, written by a guy who knows what he's doing. Check it out. I think you'll love it."

—Steve Berry, #1 bestselling author of *The Lost Order* and
The Patriot Threat

"*The Prince of Risk* will knock your socks off. Christopher Reich seamlessly weaves the high-stakes world of hedge funds and international terrorism into a frightening, big-time thriller that pulls you into his world and rockets ahead like a runaway train. Reich knows how to deliver and does."

—Robert Crais, *New York Times* bestselling author

"At the moment I'm reading a great new financial thriller by Christopher Reich, *The Prince of Risk*. One thing Doug Preston and I love to do in our books is come up with scary but credible near-future scenarios— and crafting just such scenarios is a talent Reich has in spades."

—Lincoln Child, *New York Times* bestselling author

The Palace

"In Reich's entertaining third Simon Riske novel . . . Simon has less success with this operation than with the one in Amsterdam, and he's soon on the run. Appealing supporting characters ex-Mossad agent Danni Pine and top-notch financial reporter London Li come to his aid. An unexpected closing twist promises exciting developments to come. Clever, sophisticated Riske stands out in the crowded action-hero field."

—*Publishers Weekly*

"On a mission to free his friend, Riske winds up in a cat and mouse chase with a skilled assassin. Simon Riske novels feature nonstop action in vividly rendered international locales, and this third in the series delivers on both counts. Stylish escapism."

—*Booklist*

"Simon Riske returns for another high-octane ride . . . Riske is a likable character, a nice blending of quick wit, a misspent youth, and better impulses; he's not above picking a pocket or stealing a Ferrari, but he's on the side of the angels."

—*Kirkus Reviews*

Crown Jewel

"A stylish international thriller . . . Reich's solid tradecraft and nonstop action are humanized by the hint of a relationship of the heart."

—*Booklist*

"An entertaining sequel . . . Reich infuses his narrative with numerous plot threads that seem separate but end up satisfyingly intersecting for a suspenseful ending. Readers will want to see a lot more of Riske."

—*Publishers Weekly*

"Simon Riske returns for another car-studded adventure . . . Monaco, fast cars, rich women, bad Bosnians—what more is there?"

—*Kirkus Reviews*

The Take

"It's *To Catch a Thief* meets Jason Bourne."

—Jeff Abbott, *New York Times* bestselling author of *Blame*

"Make sure your seat belt is fastened and your tray table is up: this is one hard and fast battle royale. Tension, turmoil, and drama ooze from every page. There's not a wasted word in this high-octane game changer."

—Steve Berry, #1 bestselling author of *The Lost Order* and *The Patriot Threat*

"A fast, wild ride with no less than the balance of power in the Western world at stake."

—*Parade*, Books We Love

"*The Take* is a slick, elegant, and gripping spy thriller of the first order. With a brilliant heist, a twisting web of secrets and intrigue, and an adrenaline-fueled plot, Reich whisked me out of my world and into his from the explosive first pages. Simon Riske is my favorite kind of hero—flawed, dark, and utterly intriguing. Fabulous!"

—Lisa Unger, *New York Times* bestselling author of *The Red Hunter*

"A beautifully constructed heist is only the beginning of this spectacular thriller, which sets thief versus thief, spy versus spy, and even cop versus cop. *The Take* is dazzling fun that surprises to the last page, with a hero who deserves an encore."

—Joseph Finder, *New York Times* bestselling author of *The Switch* and *Judgment*

"There's plenty of action, interesting bits of tradecraft, and well-sketched locales in London, Paris, and Marseille. Best of all is Reich's succinct prose style."

—*Booklist*

"Likable, rascally, and suave, Riske is as distinctive as Reich's other series lead, Jonathan Ransom."

—*Publishers Weekly*

"Reich's stylish and action-packed thriller introduces an appealing new protagonist . . . Recommend to fans of Daniel Silva."

—*Library Journal*

"*The Take* is impossible to put down: nonstop action, a mysterious letter, and a fascinating, complicated, and sexy hero whose tool bag of wit and strength helps him fight his way through the dangerous back alleys of glittering European capitals. An engrossing thriller."

—Christina Kovac, author of *The Cutaway*

"An out-of-control joyride for those who like their heroes flawed, scarred, and on the edge. Reich has created an irresistible character that will leave readers both wincing and cheering with every page."

—Kyle Mills, #1 bestselling author of *Fade* and *Rising Phoenix*

MATTERHORN

ALSO BY CHRISTOPHER REICH

Simon Riske Series

The Take

Crown Jewel

The Palace

Once a Thief

Dr. Jonathan Ransom Series

Rules of Deception

Rules of Vengeance

Rules of Betrayal

Stand-Alone Novels

The Devil's Banker

Invasion of Privacy

The First Billion

The Prince of Risk

The Runner

Numbered Account

The Patriots Club

MATTERHORN

CHRISTOPHER
REICH

THOMAS & MERCER

Published by Thomas & Mercer, Seattle

www.apub.com

Amazon, the Amazon logo, and Thomas & Mercer are trademarks of Amazon.com, Inc., or its affiliates.

ISBN-13: 9781662516542 (hardcover)
ISBN-13: 9781662516535 (paperback)
ISBN-13: 9781662516559 (digital)

Cover design by Laywan Kwan
Cover image: © Jens Schouten, © Ferdinand Rio / Shutterstock;
© Christoph Wagner, © Arte Index / Getty Images

Printed in the United States of America
First edition

MATTERHORN

CHAPTER 1

Valais, Switzerland

"So, it's true?"

They sat at a table in the frigid room, their breath sending clouds of vapor into the dark. "Why are you surprised?" she asked.

He unscrewed a thermos and poured a cup of hot tea, handing it to her. "Even for her, it's . . . I don't know."

"Too far?"

"Insane." His name was Will Dekker. He was twenty-nine but looked older, his features creased, skin weathered. For the past five years, he had served as an officer in the Central Intelligence Agency's Directorate of Operations.

"You don't know her." Marina Alexandrovna Zhukova was a few years older, with blonde hair and blue eyes, her sharp Slavic cheeks streaked red from fatigue and exposure to the cold. She was Russian, a captain in the SVR, her nation's foreign intelligence service.

"But why?"

"There's no *why*," said Marina. "There is only *because*. Because they can. Because they want to. Because no one will stop them."

Outside, the wind howled, buffeting walls of century-old pine.

Marina slipped a stainless steel ring off her finger. "Hercules. It's all here."

Will picked up the ring and expertly snapped it open, revealing a miniature USB drive. He had no idea what had been required to obtain the information it contained. The risks she'd taken, the individuals she'd compromised . . . or killed. "Thank you. I mean, *we* thank you."

A smile. "The noble servant."

"Well, I mean—"

She put a hand to his lips. "Don't . . . it's why I love you." Will snapped the ring closed and slid it onto his finger.

Marina leaned forward, eyes locked on his. "Give it to someone you trust."

"Marina, come on."

"Will," she said, with authority. "Listen to me."

He looked away. There had been rumors about a mole at the highest levels of the Agency for years. He never knew what to make of them. Were they an excuse to rely on when ops went south, or was there really something there? To his mind, it was a complication he didn't need. "You're sure?"

"I'll have a name in a few weeks," she said.

The sun's first rays fought past the shutters. There was a rusted first aid cabinet on one wall. A footlocker marked **SOS** filled up a corner.

Marina stood, rubbing her hands. "You need to move fast," she said. "This is happening now."

Will rose to his feet, his chair skidding over the floorboards. "Stay. A few minutes, at least."

"In this romantic spot? I'm tempted. Are you going to woo me with a warm Clif Bar?"

"Coconut chocolate chip," he said, slipping a hand around her waist. "Your favorite."

"I was crazy to even come."

Will pulled her to him. She looked the same as she had when they'd first met years ago in Chamonix. Lean, eager, capable. A force then and now. He studied her face: her eyes, her nose, the faint scar running from the corner of her mouth to her jaw. There were so many things he wanted to say. He was angry at the risks she took. He feared for her safety. He loved her.

Things that people like them didn't discuss. He kissed her lightly, then stepped away, grabbing his rucksack and throwing it over a shoulder.

"Wait." Marina dug into her pocket and handed him a small photograph.

"She's grown," said Will.

The girl in the picture was three years old with straight blonde hair, soft blue eyes, and a look that promised the photographer a hard time.

"I'm teaching her English," said Marina.

"Already?"

"It's the best time."

"She looks like you."

"Take another look," said Marina. "You."

Will studied the photo. Yes, she did. "May I?"

"It's for you."

Will slipped the photo into his pocket. "Let me bring you out."

"Not yet."

"Marina, they're going to know who did this."

"Soon. I told you. I still have something to do."

"You've done enough."

"Trust me."

"For Katya." He took her in his arms again and kissed her, feeling her chapped lips and the warmth behind them. "For me."

Marina considered this, her eyes studying his.

A moment passed. Her soft gaze vanished. Her body stiffened. She pushed him away. "What is it?" he asked.

Marina's eyes climbed the walls as if tracking something beyond them. "Listen."

Will heard it too. A low, ominous rumbling. The sound grew louder, more distinct. In seconds, it hardened into a steady, rhythmic pounding.

A helicopter.

Will dropped his rucksack to the floor, opened a compartment and pulled out a pistol. A Glock 19. It had belonged to his father. He moved to the door, chambering a round.

"Put on your ruck."

Marina zipped up her parka and threw the pack onto her shoulder. "Ready."

Will opened the door and stepped outside onto the narrow concrete band surrounding the Solvay Hut. The hut, a single-room log cabin at an altitude of 13,200 feet, was perched on a shelf of ancient rock halfway up the Hörnli Ridge of the Matterhorn.

At Will's feet, the mountain fell away sharply, a three-thousand-foot vertical drop to the Zmutt Glacier. A view to make the strongest stomach tumble and palms sweat. The wind was fierce, steady from the north. Clouds carpeted the valley, running to every corner of the horizon. Italy to the south. Switzerland to the north. France to the west. Only the surrounding peaks were visible, stone and snow sentinels thrusting out of the gray fleece. Breithorn, Castor, and Pollux closest. Farther away, Monte Rosa and Dent Blanche.

Marina followed close behind. "Do you see it?"

Before Will could answer, a bullet struck the hut inches from his head. Splintered wood tore at his cheek. He spun and saw the helicopter approaching from the east, at eye level. It was an Aérospatiale Écureuil, the compartment door open, a sniper inside, legs dangling over the landing skids.

Will raised his pistol and fired, first at the sniper, then higher at the engine cowling. The shots were ineffectual. The chopper was moving too fast, the wind too strong, buffeting the craft and playing with the flight of his bullets.

Will ducked behind the wall as a fusillade blasted shards of wood from the hut.

"Get down as fast as you can," he said. "I'll do my best to keep him away. Once you're past the Moseley Slab, he'll have a harder time keeping close to the face."

Marina touched his cheek. "I told you."

There was no doubt as to her meaning. It was his side that had betrayed them. "Hurry," he said.

The helicopter swooped overhead. Will raised the pistol and fired. Sparks flew from the airframe. Marina lowered herself off the ledge, feet finding a rock outcropping below. A last look.

"Go," said Will.

Still, Marina hesitated, her eyes locked on his.

A bullet struck her neck, shearing flesh and muscle. She let go of the rock, her hand clutching the wound.

"Marina!"

Will threw himself headlong across the ledge. A second bullet struck her chest. He heard her breath escape her lungs. He scrambled to reach her, arms outstretched. Marina's eyes lost focus. Her hands fell to her side. For a moment, she teetered, seemingly hanging in space. Then she was gone. Into the abyss.

Will rolled onto his back. The helicopter hovered above him, rotor wash blasting grit and gravel into the air. Fast ropes dropped from the open compartment. Two men clad in black rappelled from the aircraft, automatic weapons strapped to their torsos. Will took aim and shot the man on the left. Three rounds to the chest. The commando released the rope, his head falling below his feet, still attached.

Will fired at the cockpit. The windscreen cracked. The pilot dropped the chopper's nose and fell away to the east, out of range.

Will climbed to his feet. He stared down the mountain, trying to sight Marina's body. Far below, two climbers ascended skillfully. Their presence, he knew, was not a coincidence.

Rapid strides took him to the rear of the hut. The rock rose vertically, a rugged slab, fifty feet high, with a thick fixed rope bolted along its length. Hand over hand, he walked the wall. Reaching the top, he stood on a mound of dirt, slurry, and granite. Above him, the rock assumed the form of a great thorny spine, plates of every size and shape protruding at odd angles. The pitch was not quite vertical, but never far from it. An arm's length to his left and right, the rock fell away. Thousands of feet of air stood between him and the valley below. And always, the wind. The demon wind.

He climbed with his hands and feet in concert, never losing hold of the rock, his steps fast and focused, his breath disciplined, more adrenaline coursing through his blood than he could remember. A high-octane mixture of rage, loss, and the untamed lust for revenge. His world narrowed to the great gray mass in front of him. He saw no farther than an arm's length above him, a foot or two below.

He arrived at a second section of fixed rope, this one longer, more demanding. His path narrowed to a crooked, impossibly steep staircase of loose rock. He wasn't aware how long he had been climbing. The helicopter had departed. The wind was too chaotic; visibility was deteriorating.

He reached the top of the fixed ropes and scrambled across a tightrope ledge, leaping from stone to stone. The mountain changed its personality once again. Above him rose a broad field of snow and ice, impossibly steep, and beyond that the summit ridge. He dug his boots into the snow, nearly running up the expanse. No axe to steady himself. Eyes watering, desperately out of breath.

A statue stood near the top. A four-foot wooden totem, scarred by the ages. It was Saint Bernard, patron saint of alpinists. No climber passed without touching his head and requesting benediction.

Will fell to a knee. He allowed himself a look behind him. Disconsolately, he saw the colorful jackets of the climbers in pursuit. The thought came to him that he might not get off the mountain alive. He needed to take necessary measures.

And then, he was up, moving again. One hundred steps delivered him to the summit ridge. The wind blew harder, howling in his ears.

To the east, the sun crested the cloud bank. A blazing disk almost too bright to look at. A narrow track led to the great iron cross standing at the very peak.

Will crossed the band of snow warily. It had been weeks since a climber had taken the path. The snow was hard and slick as ice. Without crampons, it would take nothing to slip. A look to his left. A four-thousand-foot vertical drop to the glacier below. He decided he would descend the southern face to the Italian side of the mountain.

Just then, a man approached from the far side of the summit ridge. Tall, parka unzipped at the neck, no helmet, blond hair. Will recognized him instantly.

"I came up the Lion Ridge," said the man, shouting to be heard. His name was Ilya Ivashka. He was Russian and, like Will, an agent in the employ of his country's intelligence service.

"A more challenging climb," said Will. "Mac preferred it."

"The harder, the better," said Ilya.

"That sums him up," said Will.

"A shame we lost him."

"Is that what you call it?" said Will. "A shame?"

"These things happen in our line of work." Ilya stopped ten paces away, placing a hand on the cross. "Hello, Will."

"Ilya. Long time."

"Eight years?"

"Ten. Maybe twelve. We did that climb in the Dolomites. You, me, and Mac."

"Sassolungo. A good day."

Will regarded the man, a friend once, perhaps more than a friend. No longer. Now an enemy. More than an enemy. "I won't give it to you."

"Too late for that."

Ilya looked past Will, raised a hand, and shouted some words in Russian. Will spun. The climbers he'd seen earlier stood fifty feet away.

"Will, please. Hand it over and we can all go back down the mountain."

"Have a beer for old times' sake."

"I don't see why not."

"And Hercules?"

"It stays where it belongs. With us."

"Don't think so."

"Hardly the time for a principled stand," said Ilya. "You tried; you failed. We all live to fight another day."

"And Marina?"

"She was a traitor."

"So are you."

"I was always Russian."

"I'm not talking about your country."

"Of course you're not."

"You were his best friend."

Ilya stepped closer. In no apparent hurry, he pulled a pistol from his parka and waved it lazily. "Hercules. Now."

Will glanced behind him. The other climbers had moved closer. Both held pistols, raised and aimed at his back. There would be no catching up over beers. The pleasantries were a ruse; the sly, easygoing banter, a deception.

Will was surprised how quickly it had come to this. He shook his head, knowing what had to be done. Dammit. Why did it have to be over so soon?

He studied the skyline, admiring the peaks, allowing himself to be thrilled one last time.

His mouth was dry. It was difficult to swallow. He thought of his daughter. He flushed with shame that he didn't know her—and anger that he never would. He hoped that one day she would learn what had happened to her mother and father, that she might understand. Sometimes there was only the hard way.

Will grinned. "Remember what he used to say? 'It ain't gonna get any easier just looking at it.'"

Ilya nodded. He smiled, only for the smile to disappear a moment later. "Don't!"

"See ya."

Will Dekker stepped off the mountain and plummeted to the rocks below.

CHAPTER 2

Zinal, Switzerland

The cows had left a week earlier.

Robbie Steinhardt directed the stream of water into the last stall, gripping the hose with both hands as he washed the mud and straw and manure into the drain. He advanced the length of the enclosure, obstructing the flow with his thumb to drive away the stubborn patches of shit and dirt and whatever else had accumulated inside a barn high on an alp in the Val d'Anniviers over the course of a summer.

Robbie turned off the water and examined his work, making sure that the stalls were as clean as the day the concrete floor was poured. He was solid and broad in the beam, an inch under six feet tall, his posture not what it used to be. Spending hours each day with a pitchfork and shovel tossing hay and silage didn't help. His hair was as thick and wavy as ever, more gray than black these days. The same went for his beard, as coarse and tangled as a bramble bush. Which left only his eyes to study to get a sense of the man. They were large and so dark as to be nearly black. Eyes that stared into a person's soul. Eyes that told you he'd seen a few things in his years. As always, he was dressed in corduroy trousers and a flannel shirt, his Wellingtons caked in muck.

"Not bad," said Robbie to the empty barn as he dragged the hose to the spool and wound it up. People had a hard time guessing his age. Sixty-five? Seventy? Older? There was no questioning his constitution, however. No one on the mountain worked harder. He tramped up the hillside soon after dawn and stayed until the work was done. A few boys from the village helped now and then.

Mostly, he was on his own, notwithstanding the dairymen who did the milking. It was by choice. He was not a man who wanted company.

Robbie turned the hose to his boots and sprayed off the mud. Another summer come and gone, he thought wistfully. The cows made the journey up from the valley in June and went back down in late September. Their annual return occasioned a parade, each cow given a large bell, the farmers wearing traditional Bündner shirts and floppy hats, leading the procession down the main street. Villagers lined the path, waving small flags, cheering heartily. How many processions had he seen? Eight? No, nine, since he'd arrived.

It was lunchtime when Robbie closed the barn door. The barn itself was a hundred years old and looked it: wooden walls stained black by sun and rain, a gently sloped, shingled roof, a stone foundation. He used his shoulder to fit the door into place, then lowered the padlock.

"Till next year, then."

Robbie walked up a modest rise to a modern, low-slung concrete building that housed the dairy. The operation boasted sixty cows, all Brown Swiss. Each produced ten gallons a day, give or take: a total of six hundred gallons. The milk was high in fat and protein, ideal for cheese.

Each evening, Robbie loaded the milk, stored in one-hundred-liter canisters, onto a wagon and drove it into town to be sold to artisans lower in the valley.

He opened the door. "Ready?"

A slim Black man wearing a white work coat darted from the back room. His name was Martin. "Just need to shutter the windows. Give me a minute."

"But only one," said Robbie.

"Hot lunch date?" asked Martin. "Frau Bolliger has an eye out for you."

"*Quatsch*," said Robbie. Nonsense.

Martin was Eritrean, a refugee granted asylum when he was a boy. It was his first summer on the alp. Robbie knew little about him, other than that he'd fled the country after his parents' death. Somehow life had led him to Zinal and a job running the dairy. Maybe the only person, thought Robbie, whose path here was more unlikely than his own.

"I've seen her visiting you. Always stopping by the barn to say hello. She's not bad for sixty. Better watch out."

Robbie rolled up a sleeve and pointed at his watch. He was not a fan of small talk. "It's been a minute."

He walked outside to wait.

Martin emerged a while later. He led Robbie to the loading area at the rear of the building. A dozen stainless steel milk canisters stood next to the back door. "Empties," said Martin. "Can you bring up the wagon?"

The "wagon" was a farm utility vehicle: tight cab, short flatbed; electric, naturally.

Robbie had seen bigger golf carts. He walked back to the barn, and drove the wagon to the dairy. Martin struggled to pick up a canister, needing both arms and considerable effort to hoist it into the truck. Robbie patted him on the back. "Get in."

"Sure?"

"You haven't gotten any stronger since yesterday." Robbie grabbed a canister in each hand and flung them onto the flatbed.

Martin crossed his arms. "Show-off."

———

It was a bumpy ride down the mountain. The alp—the traditional name for a barn high in the mountains—rested on a gentle slope at eight thousand feet. The village of Zinal sprawled across the narrow valley far below, cradled by steep, craggy peaks rising vertiginously to fourteen thousand feet, magnificent busts of rock, ice, and snow. A dirt track wound down the hillside, twin rails intermittently visible in the tall grass.

After a glorious summer with too much sunshine and too little rain, fall had arrived in an indignant mood. From one day to the next, temperatures dropped twenty degrees. Blue skies were a pleasant memory. Storms battered the mountain, dusting the surrounding peaks with snow and filling the glacier-fed streams to overflowing. The only constant was the cold, swirling wind.

"Vacation plans?" asked Martin.

"Excuse me?" Robbie wasn't used to conversing with Martin. Their rides were normally silent, taciturn affairs.

"Vacation? Going anywhere?"

"Ah, vacation, of course."

It was customary to take time off at the end of one season and before the beginning of the next.

Robbie shook his head. He hadn't left the village since he'd arrived, let alone the country. The Swiss, however, loved their vacations, and loved talking about them even more. He knew of no nationality that traveled as much. The farther, the better. In fact it seemed to Robbie that a destination's desirability was determined by its distance from home. Thailand, a twelve-hour flight, was an easy stretch. Botswana and the Okavango Delta, fourteen hours, merited serious consideration. Lately, Patagonia, a twenty-hour jaunt, had become the rage. If there were a resort at McMurdo Station in Antarctica, thought Robbie, it would be overrun by Swiss.

"I'm heading to the States," said Martin. "You've been?"

Another shake of the head. It was Robbie's most frequent form of communication.

"Never?"

"Never," said Robbie, looking out the window.

"California," said Martin. "Yosemite. I hear fall is the best time of year to visit. The leaves are turning, and there are no tourists."

"Except you."

"Well, yes," said Martin. "But not many of me."

"I wish you a nice trip."

Martin bowed his head in thanks. "I saw a film about the fellow who climbed that rock without any ropes. Three thousand feet straight up. One mistake and that's it. *Auf Wiedersehen.* See it?"

"I did not."

"It's streaming. I'm sure you can find it."

Robbie nodded uncertainly. He didn't stream.

"You ever do anything like that?" Martin asked.

"What?"

"Climbing. You look like the type."

"Oh?"

"When you were younger, I mean."

"*Younger?*" said Robbie, aggrieved. For a moment he'd forgotten just how old he was. "No. No climbing. I like to keep my feet on solid ground."

Martin looked out the window. They'd reached the meadow at the southern end of the village. He gazed at the imposing peaks that cradled the valley. Zinalrothorn. Weisshorn. The Bellos. "We have mountains at home," he said. "Big mountains. The Emba Soira in the southern highlands. Nine thousand feet. It is a large rock shaped like a camel. I have never read about anyone climbing it. Instead, we must all go to the military to support our dictator. My country prefers fighting instead of climbing." He looked at Robbie, his eyes wet. "May I tell you something, Herr Steinhardt? I am sorry my parents were killed. But I am glad I came to Switzerland."

Robbie looked at the young, eager man seated beside him. So much of life still ahead. A feeling of kinship stirred inside him. He placed a hand on his shoulder. "I am glad, too, Martin."

——

Robbie unloaded the canisters at the dairy's business office on Poststrasse, then parked the truck in the subterranean garage. Martin helped him cover the vehicle with a tarpaulin. Together they walked to the bus stop. Robbie noted that Martin had grown pensive. He knew the feeling. There was a certain melancholy when summer ended and it was time to come down from the alp. A sense of time passing, of fleeting freedom. The dread of a return to the real world, whatever that might be. A foreboding, even. The weather didn't help. Another cold, cloudy day, rain coming and going.

They reached the bus stop. Robbie checked the timetable. "Twenty minutes till your bus," he said. "Time for a coffee?"

Martin hesitated. The two had seen each other every day since June, and this was the most the old man had ever spoken to him. "Yes, all right," he answered.

Robbie led the way to a café nearby. They ordered at the counter inside. Espresso for Martin. Tea for Robbie. Each was served with a small chocolate. They took the hot beverages and sat at a table by the window.

Robbie looked at Martin. He guessed his age to be thirty. He had an angular, expressive face, ancient semitic bloodlines evident, teeth an orthodontist would kill to get his hands on.

"You have a family," said Robbie.

Martin pointed to his wedding band. "Two children. A girl and a boy."

"It will be an expensive trip to California."

"I told them 'no Disneyland.' They hate me."

Robbie drank his tea, peering out the window.

"And you," said Martin. "Family? Children?" Robbie shook his head.

"No Mrs. Steinhardt?"

Robbie shook his head.

"Never?"

"Never," said Robbie. "Lucky for her."

Martin finished his espresso, wiping his mouth with a napkin. "May I ask you something?"

"Yes."

"You're Swiss."

"I am."

"I know that, obviously . . . but where are you from originally?"

"What do you mean 'originally'?"

"Sometimes I hear an accent. Maybe it's because I didn't learn the language until I was older. I can always pick out a foreigner."

Robbie stared at Martin. Perhaps he'd been wrong to befriend him. He saw the yellow PTT bus approaching. "Ah, here it is." He finished his tea, then stood and walked outside.

The bus came to a halt. Martin extended a hand. "Till next June."

Robbie shook his hand. "Enjoy Yosemite. I hear it's beautiful."

"One day you'll go," said Martin, climbing onto the bus.

Robbie did his best to smile. No. He would not go to Yosemite. He would stay here. In Zinal. He had no choice. His life depended on it.

CHAPTER 3

Zinal

Robbie lived at the north end of the village, a two-kilometer walk. He followed the bus's path along the Route of Five 4,000s, named for the four-thousand-meter peaks surrounding the village. A stream ran beside him, the glacial water milky white, roaring loudly, jumping its banks.

Zinal was a resort town. It depended on skiing in the winter and hiking and mountaineering in the summer. Even so, it had never done much to compete against its more famous neighbors. It didn't have any fancy hotels or restaurants like Gstaad. Nor did it host World Cup ski races or professional golf tournaments like at Crans-Montana. While the surrounding peaks were known to alpinists, there were none to rival the Matterhorn, which towered over Zermatt thirty kilometers east as the crow flies. For the past hundred years, a thousand souls had called it home, never more. It was off the beaten track in the best possible way.

Robbie walked slowly, hands in his pockets, taking time to see what was in the shop windows. Sprecher Sport was offering new Raichle ski boots at five hundred francs a pair. It was never too early to peddle winter merchandise. Wyss Jewelers was having a sale on Raymond Weil timepieces. Robby was perfectly happy with his Casio G-Shock. Flora's Boutique displayed a collection of racy lingerie. A black brassiere for two hundred francs and even more for accessories he didn't quite recognize. Maybe there was more to his neighbors than he realized.

Robbie lifted his eyes from the suggestive merchandise and studied the reflection of the street behind him. Across the road, a stout, gray-haired man in a Shetland sweater walked his wire-haired terrier. Rolf Roth and his dog, Strick. A young redhead passed in the opposite direction on her bicycle. Vreni Zurbriggen, who ran the kiosk. After eight years, Robbie knew everyone in town, and everyone knew Robbie. It was the people he didn't know who were of interest. He made it a point to pay attention to visitors.

Reaching the end of what passed for the town's commercial district, he stepped into the bakery. A small, officious man wearing a red apron stood at the counter. "*Grüezi*, Robbie."

"Hannes."

Robbie studied the breads on offer. He didn't really know why. He bought the same thing every day. "One *Zopf*, four *Gipfeli*."

Hannes Schmid was already gathering the rolls. He placed them in a paper bag, which he set on the counter. Robbie placed a ten-franc note on the tray.

"Eleven francs," said Schmid. "Just like yesterday."

Robbie fished in his pocket for a one-franc piece. "Thief," he said, dropping it into Schmid's palm.

"Cheapskate," said Schmid.

———

The Chalet Ponderosa stood alone on a forested hillside at the end of its own private lane a few hundred meters off the Poststrasse. The chalet had been built in the 1930s. Three stories. A steep roof. A rustic stone chimney. Upper floors built entirely of wood, all of it stained black by the sun and weathered by too many hard winters. The window boxes on the second and third floors were Robbie's pride, overflowing with geraniums, violent shades of red and maroon.

"My retirement home" was Robbie's stock answer to his neighbors when he'd arrived one day out of the blue.

But that wasn't enough. They wanted to know more about him. This was Switzerland. They wanted to know everything. Where had he grown up? How had he made his career? What about his family? What was his favorite football team? What did he eat for breakfast?

He had prepared his answers. They were brief. To the point. Unembellished. And true, as far as anyone cared to prove them. An entire life's history woven from his imagination. Or, as he'd been taught long ago to call it, "Cover."

Robbie collected his mail and passed through the gate. He was thinking of Martin from Eritrea, chastising himself for not having made an effort to get to know him earlier. He had his reasons. They were sound reasons. Still, he had enjoyed talking to him. They had more in common than he would have suspected. At the least, they both enjoyed films about climbing.

Distracted, Robbie stumbled and dropped his mail and the bag of bread. He looked down to see an arc of black rubber cable protruding from the ground. He fell to a knee. A look over his shoulder to make sure no one was watching. He reburied the cable and took care to cover the pressure plate as well. The plate was set to forty pounds. Dogs were fine. People were not.

Standing, he tamped down the loose dirt with his boot. There.

Robbie stooped to pick up his letters, yesterday's newspaper from Zürich, and his bread.

He asked himself how he'd missed the cable in the morning. The answer was easy enough. It was the same reason he'd broken down and spoken with Martin. It wasn't just that he was out of practice. It was worse. He'd been hiding for so long he'd finally stopped caring.

Robbie walked to the front door, eyes scanning the eaves, checking on the miniature CCTV cameras bolted into the rafters. He slid his key into the door, turned it to the left, then thumbed the fob in his pocket. The triple dead bolts retreated as one.

Inside, he placed the bread on the side table, then entered his study. He tossed the mail onto his desk. A large, fat tabby cat lay asleep in his chair.

"Mine," said Robbie, in English, lifting the cat off the chair, ruffling his fur, then setting him on the floor. The cat was not amused. He left the room in search of calmer quarters.

Robbie sat down and sorted through the mail. A utility bill, a solicitation, and, last, a letter addressed to "Robert A. Steinhardt." His name and address were written in neat cursive script. A check of the postmark. Yesterday, the thirtieth. A postal frank from the Zinal office. He slid open the top drawer and rummaged for his letter opener. He found it wedged beneath the grip of his pistol. Deftly, he opened the correspondence and extracted a piece of stationery. He unfolded the paper slowly. A single black hair lay in the crease. The page was blank. This did not surprise him.

He took a new envelope from the drawer, refolded the paper, and placed it inside.

Choosing a pen, he wrote his name on the envelope, this time in block capital letters. He affixed a stamp then tossed the envelope into the outbox. Done.

Robbie picked up the bread and wandered into the kitchen. He turned on the TV, a decades-old Siemens with an antenna, then made himself a sandwich. Ham, cheese, mustard on two slices of the fresh *Zopf*. A last beer was tucked into a corner of the fridge. Budweiser. American, not Czech.

He sat down to eat, occasionally glancing at the TV. The sound was low. On the screen, a helicopter flew past the lower flank of the Matterhorn, a body basket hanging below it. He grimaced. Another accident. He'd stopped counting how many people lost their lives on the mountain each summer. Still, it was late in the season to be climbing. By October, the mountain was all but closed.

The TV cut to a reporter standing in front of the Zermatt police station. Robbie turned up the volume in time to hear the reporter sign off.

Robbie took his sandwich and beer into his office. He found his copy of the *NZZ*—the *Neue Zürcher Zeitung*—and scanned the front page. Bank profits were up. The Aletsch Glacier was receding. Saudi Arabian diplomats were visiting Bern. His eyes grew heavy.

A buzzer woke him.

He bolted to his feet, opening the desk drawer, fingers wrapping around the steel crosshatched grip. A Beretta. Slim. Accurate. Good for close-in work. A monitor on the shelf showed a woman walking down the front path. Trim, wearing a wide-brimmed hat, carrying a large plate in both hands. Could it be?

The doorbell rang.

Robbie looked at the monitor more closely. It was her. He dropped the pistol and closed the drawer. No need for that . . . *yet.*

Robbie walked to the front door, his gait faltering with each step, his shoulders slumping.

A breath, then, "Showtime." He opened the door. "Frau Bolliger. A surprise."

"Irene, please."

An attractive woman in her seventh decade. Graying hair. Sparkling blue eyes. An admirable figure showcased in stylish sportswear.

"Irene." Robbie made no effort to invite her in. Martin had not been lying. Once a week, she passed by the alp. She made a point of seeking out Robbie to say hello. Robbie replied courteously, if tersely. He was fine. Yes, it was a beautiful day. He hoped to see her again soon. Such was the extent of their relationship. Until now.

"Basler Läckerli," said Irene Bolliger, extending the tray of cookies covered in transparent wrap. "They were my husband's favorite."

Robbie's eyes went from Irene to the cookies and back to Irene. He stepped forward and accepted the gift. "Thank you . . . *Irene.*"

Irene knitted her hands, her head dodging to either side of him, angling for a look inside the chalet. Robbie didn't budge.

"There's a concert this evening at the Gemeindehaus," she said. "Local boys. Music. Dancing."

"Very nice," said Robbie. "Seven o'clock."

"Seven, yes."

"If you're not otherwise busy."

"Music. Dancing. Very nice."

"And?"

How long had it been since he'd gone out? Months? Years? "I'll be there," said Robbie, to his surprise.

"Perhaps we can walk over together," said Irene Bolliger. Now she was going too far.

"Seven," said Robbie. "At the Gemeindehaus." He closed the door.

CHAPTER 4

Bern, Switzerland

Ilya Ivashka was a poor driver, but he did not lack in confidence.

It was 4:00 p.m. Traffic in the Swiss capital was heavy. He'd enjoyed a long, boozy lunch on the terrace of the Hotel Bellevue Palace and lingered over a third kirsch with his coffee. Now he was late.

To his credit, it was a working lunch. Ilya and his favorite client: himself. Ilya had required counseling after his encounter in the mountains the day before. He wasn't shaken. Ilya was never shaken. He was occupationally depressed. Self-medication, he had learned from extensive experience, proved an effective remedy.

Ilya crossed the Nydegg Bridge, pulling into the opposing lane and driving around a city tram. He was due at the embassy in ten minutes. Not likely. He steered his car through the congested streets, running red lights, leaning on his horn. If he failed to arrive on time, it wouldn't be for a lack of trying.

Ilya Alexandrovich Ivashka, fifty-four years old, unmarried, born in the state of Maryland to Russian parents (researchers at the National Institutes of Health), amateur alpinist, veteran of the United States Marine Corps, recipient of the Silver Star and Purple Heart, decorated member of the Central Intelligence Agency's National Clandestine Service, and most recently, defector to Russia, currently serving with the rank of major in the SVR, or Foreign Intelligence Service. He was, it went without saying, no longer an American citizen.

Ilya spun the wheel and turned right onto Brunnadernrain. The embassy was located nearby in a leafy residential quarter. At the sight of the first linden trees, he slowed his speed to the posted limit. He did not wish to draw attention to himself. No one enjoyed informing on their colleagues more than a Russian. It was something in their blood. A thousand years of being shit upon had etched malice into their DNA.

And I myself, thought Ilya, am no exception.

The road narrowed, barely wide enough for one car to pass another. He saw the black wrought iron gates a block ahead. Luck was with him. He found a parking space. No one needed to see his car, a new Land Rover Defender. Servants of the Russian state drove ZiLs at home and the cheaper-model BMW when abroad. They did not drive luxury English SUVs that cost two hundred thousand francs. His defection had not come cheaply.

The embassy sat on top of a grassy knoll in its own private park in a renovated three-story Victorian mansion that had once belonged to one of Bern's wealthiest families. Ilya waved at the guards and passed through the gate. Inside, he took the stairs to the second floor, slowing in front of a full-length mirror to adjust his collar and shoot his cuffs. The climbing gear was gone. He wore a tailored navy suit, Italian loafers, and a shirt from Sulka of Paris. Fifty-four years old and he hadn't lost a hair, even if a few had gone gray. He didn't mind the wrinkles.

He'd earned them. He fished in his jacket for his flask. A nip of Russian courage and he was ready.

A uniformed guard stood at the end of the corridor. "Phone."

Ilya dropped his phone into the woman's hand. Standard procedure before entering a SCIF—a Sensitive Compartmented Information Facility. It peeved him, nonetheless. Rules, to his mind, were for the other fellow.

The guard stowed the phone in a locker and handed Ilya the key.

"*Spasibo*," said Ilya, with a lingering glance. She wasn't bad underneath that awful tunic and cap.

The guard unlocked the door.

To all appearances, the SCIF was a conference room. There was a sleek wooden table, six chairs, pads of stationery at each seat. A Russian flag stood in one corner, the former Romanov flag in the other, its double-headed eagle looking to the east and west for enemies. Ilya's attention, however, was squarely on the television monitor that covered the wall. More specifically, on the uniformed female officer seated at her desk and eyeing him with what could politely be called professional disdain.

"And you," said the woman. "Not a scratch."

"It was a little dirty," said Ilya. "But good riddance all the same."

Colonel Alexandra Zaitseva, chief of Directorate 6 of the Foreign Intelligence Service, picked up her cigarette and inhaled. "I don't care about Marina Zhukova. I do care about Will Dekker. You killed an American agent in one of the few countries that tolerate our presence."

"In fact," said Ilya, "he killed himself."

"Before you could retrieve Hercules."

"We don't know for certain that she gave it to him."

Zaitseva stubbed out the cigarette, then rose and circled her desk. She was fifty-something years old and formidable, hair more silver than blonde and pulled into the tightest of buns. She was built like a steel rail with a posture to match. Blue eyes with a hint of Mongol cast. Sharp cheekbones. A daughter of the steppe.

"Don't insult me," she said. "Of course she gave it to him." Ilya said nothing. Of course she had.

"Under no circumstance," Zaitseva continued, "can the Americans be allowed to obtain evidence tying us to the coming action."

"I'll check the body," said Ilya.

"Frankly, I'm reluctant to give my permission."

Ilya looked her in the eye. They'd slept together several years ago. A rough encounter, to be sure. He'd felt as if he were in training all over again. It had been one order after another the entire night.

He stepped toward the door. Could he please get the hell out of here? "Are we done, Colonel?" he asked with formality.

"Not quite."

Ilya noted more than the usual pique in her voice. He put himself on guard. She was not someone he wanted pitted against him. "Yes, Colonel."

"You were friends once," said Zaitseva.

"Excuse me?"

"You know who I'm talking about."

"We climbed together," said Ilya.

"And served in the same unit."

"Yes." They'd both been snipers, Force Recon, then MARSOC, before being recruited by the Agency.

"Practically brothers, I'm made to understand."

"I did my job."

"That remains to be seen."

"He's dead," said Ilya, fed up. "What more do you want?"

"You traded loyalties once," said Zaitseva. "It's natural to question if there might be a second time." She leaned closer still, so that he could see the web of wrinkles bracketing her eyes, the dried lipstick on the thin, cracked lips, the nicotine stains on her teeth. So close that he could feel her presence from a thousand miles away. For a moment, he was certain he even caught the foul cigarette smoke that permeated her uniform.

"Find what Marina Zhukova stole," said Colonel Zaitseva. "And bring it to me. *Quickly.*"

CHAPTER 5

Zinal

The secret to keep from losing his mind was activity.

During the summer, Robbie worked as a hired hand at the alp—formally, the Brunner Farming Collective AG—seeing to the barn and cows. It was a full day's work. Up at 4:00 a.m. Home at 6:00 p.m. Plenty of tasks to dull his thoughts. During winter, he drove a snowcat to groom the pistes and performed the general maintenance required to keep the lifts running. During the nether months between seasons—April, May, October, and November—he trekked into the mountains. Weeklong journeys into the backcountry where he could camp beneath the stars, hunt, and pretend the rest of the world did not exist.

The days weren't the problem. It was the nights that constituted his greatest threat.

Specifically, the hours between 6:00 p.m. and midnight. Hours he had to fill before his mind grudgingly granted him five or six hours of respite. Hours that required tasks to prevent him from thinking about all he had left behind. Career. Children. The woman he'd loved. Everything.

And to keep from thinking about the man who had wronged him and how he would pay him back.

Robbie designed courses for himself to complete his incomplete education. Forced marches through ancient history, astronomy, anatomy and physiology, botany, and biology. He taught himself languages: Italian, Spanish, French. He became a connoisseur of cinema. A cineast. Godard, Fellini, Truffaut. He was acquainted with all the greats. (Of course he streamed.) Finally, there was exercise. Nightly competitions in calisthenics, grudge matches versus the pull-up bar, epic rides on his exercise bike.

Lately, he had taken to jigsaw puzzles. No better way to lose yourself for a few hours than to dive into a table littered side to side, top to bottom with nearly identical pieces.

And so it was that at 5:00 p.m., Robbie Steinhardt was bent over a table in his upstairs rec room working on a five-thousand-piece monster that, when completed, promised him a favorite Ansel Adams photograph of Yosemite Valley.

He had lied to Martin about never having visited the States. He had lied about never having been to Yosemite.

He had lied about not being a climber.

Robbie lied about most things, beginning with his name.

He fished around for a piece with a smooth edge, a little shading in the upper corner, light below. The puzzle's frame was almost complete. The upper-right-hand corner was coming along nicely. There was Half Dome in the distance. Bridalveil Fall closer. His fingers skipped over the pieces. He was searching for a piece of Vernal Fall, a spot halfway up the trail beside it, where there was a bench not ten feet from the plummeting water.

Fifteen years ago, on a sunny summer afternoon, he'd stopped there to eat lunch with his son. Peanut butter, banana, and honey on wheat bread. The nectar of the gods. The memory was so strong he could feel his boy's shoulder touching his.

"How many pitches will we need, Dad?"

"Ten should do it."

"Ya think?"

The boy turned to him. His hair was cut short, the same wine black as his own. Fourteen and already taller than his father. He could see the boy's apprehension, the fear hidden behind his exuberant smile. They were going to climb Half Dome, just the two of them.

Robbie dropped the puzzle piece. He closed his eyes, banishing the memory.

Reminiscing was forbidden. *Verboten*, in his adopted country's language. The past was enemy territory.

He lifted his head and looked out the window. The clouds had rushed away to the south. The late-afternoon sky was painted a faint blue, darkening rapidly as the sun dipped below the Rothorn. He checked his watch. It was nearly 6:00 p.m.

Robbie hurried to the bathroom. He gave himself a "navy shower"—sixty seconds hot, thirty seconds cold—drying himself as he walked to the bedroom. His wardrobe had not changed in eight years. He found a pair of gray slacks and a chambray shirt far back in the closet. He decided against a jacket, ditto for a tie. Still, it would be cold after dark. He pulled his Basque shepherd's sweater off the shelf. It would do.

He turned on the television as he finished dressing. CNN was broadcasting a story from the Middle East. Syria, Lebanon, Gaza. More fighting. More lying. More chaos. He wasn't listening. The region had survived just fine without him.

He changed the channel to the local news as he dashed into the bathroom. He brushed his hair and groomed his beard. It was getting too dark again. He found the box of hair dye. No time now, but tomorrow. There were two bottles of cologne in the medicine cabinet. He wondered if fragrance remained . . . well, "fragrant," after so many years. He unscrewed the cap, sniffed. His eyes watered. A resounding no. A thought occurred to him. Was it possible he'd liked that smell when he was younger?

He caught a glimpse of himself—*his real self*—in the mirror. He laughed. It felt good. Something on the television drew his attention.

". . . seventh fatality on the Matterhorn this season."

Robbie looked over his shoulder. It was the report from earlier. He watched as an Air Zermatt helicopter flew low over the base of the mountain, the rescue basket ferrying the unfortunate alpinist dangling below it. Who the hell climbed in October after the first snow? He turned up the volume.

". . . the victim was thought to be climbing alone when he fell to his death yesterday morning. Authorities have identified the man as an American, William Andrew Dekker, age twenty-nine. Dekker worked as an executive in the IT sector for a multinational corporation in Lausanne. According to reports, he was climbing without proper safety measures at the time of the accident."

Robbie's knees buckled. He staggered, throwing a hand to the dresser to keep from collapsing. His vision blurred. Somehow, he managed to remain standing.

He turned the channel, checking the news from Geneva and Ticino. Then back again.

He saw nothing more about the accident.

He left the bedroom and walked downstairs, one hand on the wall in case he needed it.

Had he heard correctly? Could there be another Will Andrew Dekker? Also an American, also a climber, also twenty-nine years old, who worked in Lausanne? If so, was he also a vice president at Tradepoint Data?

Robbie reached his study and fell into his chair. He brought up the local papers on his laptop. First, *Blick*, the Swiss scandal sheet that trafficked in rumors, misfortune, and tragedy. He found the story halfway down the page. Horu's Latest Victim, read the headline, with a blurred photo of a body lying on the rocks. *Horu*—the locals' nickname for the Matterhorn.

He found similar articles in *Le Matin*, *Tribune de Genève*, and *24 Hours*. In each, his experienced eye found too many troubling phrases:

... fell from the summit ridge, apparently alone.

... amid reports of strange activity on the mountain.

. . . residents spoke of a helicopter flying in the area at
dawn.

None had a picture of Will.
Finally, the *Tages-Anzeiger*, Zürich's daily paper. There it was.
A picture. His boy.

———

Will was gone.
Robbie remained in his study, seated in the dark.

He'd spent his career learning to ignore emotion, or, at least, to
deflect it. An instructor at the Farm, a psychologist, had taught him
to acknowledge his feelings (no matter how painful), then to imagine
placing them in a box, sealing it with tape, and storing it in the attic,
or some other safe place to access at a later time.

He'd been taught to carry out assignments, to obey instructions,
to see a task through from inception to execution without questioning.
Often, he had his own feelings about a job.

Usually, those feelings were about methods and means, not about
any underlying morality. Rarely did he question his orders. Success
required commitment. There was no place for hesitation, for questioning. For emotion.

It was that training that had allowed him to survive in the mountains away from everyone he knew and loved for eight years.

Robbie stood to examine the photographs on his shelf. One showed
a little boy and girl standing on the beach. Another showed Will in his
baseball uniform with an attractive blonde woman—Abby, Robbie's ex.

It was Abby who'd left. It was back in the late nineties and early
aughts. A time when covert meant covert, even from your family. She
knew he worked for the government but didn't ask more. To the kids, he
was a government official of some stripe, attached to an obscure agency

traveling the world on his country's behalf. The problem was the travel. He was never home. They divorced when he was thirty.

His eye moved to a more recent picture, taken maybe fifteen years earlier. He picked it up and held it under the light so that he might see it more clearly.

The picture had been snapped at the base of Half Dome the day of Will's first multipitch climb. Will was gazing up at the wall, and you could read the full gamut of emotions on his face. Excitement, incredulity, fear. It was that moment before you started. One minute you were standing on a hill of scree and loose rock, the next you were ascending a vertical granite face.

Robbie closed his eyes. He was there. Yosemite. "Seriously?" Will had said, looking back at him.

"Scared?"

"Shouldn't I be?"

"That's up to you."

Will returned his attention to the rock, placing his palm on the stone as if calming an animal. He laughed nervously, probably at the realization that there was no going back.

"It ain't gonna get any easier just looking at it." Robbie's favorite saying.

"Guess not," said Will. The smile faded. Something in his face hardened.

"Ready?"

"You bet, Dad."

Reminiscing is forbidden.

Robbie put the picture back on the shelf. He opened the bottom drawer of his desk, grabbed a mobile phone still in its packaging. He ripped off the plastic cover and powered it up. He knew the number by heart. The call went to voice mail.

"Hey, this is Will. I'm out of the office for a few days, getting my spirit recharged in the mountains. If it's important, leave a message. Peace out."

Robbie ended the call, then hit Redial. He listened to the message again. And again. Fuck *forbidden*.

Tears ran down his cheek. He sobbed. Will was gone.

After a while, he got a hold of himself. He wiped his eyes. The phone was still in his hand. He removed the SIM card, snapped it in half, and dropped it in the trash.

He picked up his own phone and scrolled through the contacts. He stopped at the letter *J*. There was only one entry.

JAYCEE

His thumb hovered over the Send button.

CHAPTER 6

Zürich, Switzerland

Every European city had its sleazy district, the concentration of city blocks where anything goes. Sex shops, strip clubs, bars, bordellos (licensed and not), drugs if you knew where to look. A part of the city frozen in an earlier, analog era.

In Hamburg, it was the Reeperbahn.

In Paris, Pigalle.

In London, Soho.

And in Zürich, it was the Langstrasse, a four-block area just one kilometer from the Hauptbahnhof. Ilya Ivashka thought of it as his private office while visiting Switzerland.

It was 11:00 p.m. The evening's festivities were off to an unenthusiastic start. A stream of middle-aged men patrolled the sidewalk, braving the chill night air and a smattering of rain. Ilya stopped at an outdoor grill and bought a bratwurst. He ate half, dipping it liberally in his favorite Thomy mustard. Spicy, but not too. Chewing, he surveilled the passing faces to be sure no one was following him, then tossed the sausage into the trash and crossed the street. His destination was a nightclub, **Go Go '79**, as advertised by a bloodred neon sign.

The door stood open. An older woman occupied a stool inside, a beaded curtain behind her. "Hello, handsome," she said. Bleached blonde, with gobs of mascara, a surgically enhanced bosom.

"Hello back," said Ilya, palming her a fifty-franc note as he kissed her cheek.

"Is that all I get?" She gave him a welcoming squeeze in an unwelcome spot.

Ilya winked. He'd rather put his cock in a Cuisinart. He passed through the curtain into a dimly lit lounge. Gloria Gaynor at full volume serenaded the guests. Low tables formed a semicircle around a runway. Business was slow. A spotlight illuminated the lackadaisical efforts of a topless dancer twirling around a pole. He'd seen men go to the firing squad with more enthusiasm. He tucked a twenty-franc note into her G-string. "How 'bout a smile, *Schatzi*?"

"Fuck off." Well, he'd tried.

Ilya continued past the runway, pushing aside a velvet curtain and traversing a corridor that led to the private rooms. A look into the first: a customer receiving the house special, head lifted toward the ceiling, gasping like a fish out of water. The second room was unoccupied. Ilya passed it and entered the next one. A well-dressed man sat on the velour banquette. There was an ice bucket, a bottle of Stoli, and two shot glasses.

"This is a new low," said Detective Andre Berner of the Zürich police. He was forty, with thinning hair and a push broom mustache.

"You miss the point," said Ilya, grabbing the bottle by the neck and pouring himself a drink.

"What's that?" said Berner.

"It's so bad, it's good." Ilya drank the shot and set the glass on the table. "*Nastrovje.*"

"If you don't mind," said Berner. "It's late."

Ilya slid onto the banquette. "The climber killed on the Matterhorn yesterday."

"I read about it. An American."

"Where did they take him?"

"Excuse me?"

Ilya poured himself a second drink. "His body. Where is it?"

"I'm a homicide detective," said Berner, "not a tour guide. How should I know?"

Ilya downed the vodka, considering the cop's response. He decided he didn't like it. Not one bit. Not after what he was paying Berner. Fast as lightning, he took the man's face in his hand and slammed his cheek onto the table.

"The climber's name was Will Dekker. He was the son of a close friend. Find out."

CHAPTER 7

Gorky Park, Moscow, Russia

In Moscow, the first snow was falling. The pale flakes fell lazily from the night sky, painting a glistening carpet on the knolls rising from the banks of the Moskva River.

"Don't worry so," said the little girl. "She's with my father."

Nadia Smirnova slipped her phone back into her pocket. Twenty-four hours late and not a message. "I'm not worried, Katya. I'm sure you're right."

"She misses him. She told me."

"Of course she does." Nadia followed the little girl as she pedaled her tricycle along the asphalt path. Beside them, the famous Gorky Ferris wheel turned slowly, its cars empty.

In fact, Nadia was very worried. Marina Zhukova had been due home last night on the Alitalia flight from Milan landing at Sheremetyevo at 9:00 p.m. The flight was on time, but she was not on it. More troubling, Nadia's text and voice messages had gone unanswered. Marina had vanished.

It was nearly 11:00 p.m. A biting wind skipped off the river. Nadia turned her face up and felt a snowflake land on her cheek. Barely October and winter had arrived for its seven-month stay. She pulled her jacket tightly around her, then knelt to adjust Katya's cap. The child's nose was red, her cheeks warm and rosy despite the cold. "But shall we go home now? It's very late."

"One more time round," said Katya Zhukova. "I want to see the carousel."

"One more time," said Nadia. "Then home to bed."

"Mama will be home by then. I'm sure of it."

"Me too." Nadia smiled uneasily as they made their way toward the carousel.

This really wasn't her problem. Her mother was Katya's babysitter. Her mother, a sixty-one-year-old teetotaler and retired Aeroflot flight attendant who'd looked after Katya since the day she was born. But her mother was in the hospital. Yesterday morning, she'd come to her flat, Katya in tow, complaining of stomach pains. "I'll only be a few hours," she'd said, before leaving for the emergency room.

By afternoon, she was in a private ward awaiting surgery for an inflamed gallbladder and acute pancreatitis. Nadia had spoken with her this morning before the operation. She'd sounded confused. Her only advice had been to "wait until she was home." Nadia didn't know if she meant Marina or herself.

"Arctic terns fly forty thousand kilometers each year," said Katya. "Did you know that?"

"What?" Nadia stirred from her thoughts.

"From Greenland to Antarctica and back."

"Really?" said Nadia, a bit mystified. "That's amazing." It wasn't the question. She didn't know the first thing about terns, arctic or otherwise. Nothing mysterious about that. It was the child. Just three and she sounded like a college professor.

Nadia was twenty-five, unemployed, an aspiring hairdresser who'd barely made it out of high school. Sometimes she thought her life was already behind her. Once she'd been a promising gymnast, then a promising painter, then a promising singer. None of them had panned out.

Nowadays, she took classes at the local Y, learning to cut hair, and even that wasn't going well.

Yesterday, she'd nicked the ear of a fellow student. She'd had no idea an ear could bleed so much. One more mistake and she was out.

Nadia followed Katya and her tricycle around a copse of birch trees and down a slope to the river. The brightly lit onion domes of the Kremlin peeked from around the next bend. The snow grew heavier. The wind snarled. Someday, she promised herself, she would live in a country where winter did not begin in October and end in May. Portugal sounded nice. Or Bali. Or Mexico. Anywhere but Russia.

They came to the carousel. The lights were doused. In the gloom, the horses took on a sinister cast. The caretaker was chaining the entry. He gave Nadia a nasty look. Children should not be out so late.

"Ready to go home?" asked Nadia. "I'll make you a hot cocoa once you're all tucked in."

Katya nodded eagerly. "Mama will."

———

Marina Zhukova's flat on Tverskaya Ulitsa was small but modern and, to Nadia's eye, the height of luxury. Scandinavian furniture, an enormous flat-screen television, granite countertops, and a refrigerator large enough to climb into. If Nadia had known diplomats earned so much money, she would have studied harder in school.

"Hello, Mama," shouted Katya the moment Nadia opened the door, dashing into the apartment.

"Hello, Marina," said Nadia, sharing in the child's excitement. For a moment, she allowed herself to believe that Marina Zhukova had returned. That she'd simply forgotten to call to let her know.

Katya emerged from her mother's bedroom, her face downcast. "She's still with Father."

Stubbornly, Nadia checked her phone. Nothing. No text. No voice mail. More stubbornly, she dialed the woman's phone once again. After one ring, it went to voice mail.

"You've reached Marina. Leave a message."

"Hello, Marina. It's Nadia. Katya and I just got home after a walk to the park. She couldn't sleep. I'm sure you're having a wonderful time."

Katya stood at her feet, tugging on her jacket. "Please, I want to talk to her."

"It's only a message."

"Please."

Nadia gave her the phone.

"Mama, it's me. I know you're with Daddy, but please come home. Nadia is very worried about you. I saw her crying this afternoon. You told her you'd be home last night. It isn't very nice to make someone so frightened. I'm not worried at all. I know everything is fine." She paused to gulp down a breath and drag a sleeve across her nose. "I told Nadia about the arctic terns. Now we're going to have some cocoa and I'm going straight off to bed. Please come home soon."

Katya ended the call and handed Nadia the phone. "I lied," she said. "I told Mama I wasn't worried. I am."

Just then, Nadia's phone rang.

"It's her," shouted Katya. "She heard you!"

Nadia checked the screen. Not Katya's mother. Her own, Svetlana Smirnova. "Hello, Mother. Are you all right?"

"I'm fine," said Svetlana Smirnova, as dry and unemotional as ever.

"The operation, it went well?"

"Don't worry about me. I said I'm fine. I received your messages. Is Marina home yet?"

Nadia looked at the little girl, eyes glued to her. She smiled and patted her head. "Excuse me," she whispered, then walked into the kitchen. "No, I haven't heard from her. Nothing. No calls. No texts."

"You're sure?"

"Of course," said Nadia, with irritation.

For a moment, Svetlana Smirnova did not speak. Nadia could hear her labored breathing. "Mama . . . are you okay?"

Again, a pause. Nadia didn't like the sound of her mother's voice. She was always reserved, detached even. Tonight, Nadia heard something else. Fear.

"Mother?"

"Leave the apartment at once. Don't pack anything. Take Katya and go to my flat."

"Leave? What do you mean? It's midnight."

"Be quiet and listen," said Svetlana Smirnova. "There's a book on my bedside table. A biography of Stalin. There's a letter inside the back cover. It will tell you where to go and what you must do."

"Mother, I don't understand. You're scaring me."

"Nadia, for once, do as I tell you. Get out of Marina Zhukova's apartment this minute. Go to my flat. Read the letter. Do you understand?"

"Yes."

"Go now."

Nadia made no effort to leave. The last thing she wanted to do was abandon the warm, safe apartment. It came to her that she knew very little about Marina.

"Who is she, Mother? Who is Marina Zhukova?"

"Go, Nadia. Hurry!"

CHAPTER 8

Zinal

A new reality.

Robbie Steinhardt slid into a seat at the back of the postal bus. He was the sole passenger and placed his rucksack on the seat beside him. The driver closed the door and followed the Poststrasse north, their destination the city of Sierre, a winding thirty-kilometer descent of the Val d'Anniviers. It was 8:00 a.m. For the first time in a week, the sky was clear, the wind calm. Robbie was dressed for a day of hiking, or *Wandern*, as the Swiss called it. He wore a sturdy, royal blue windbreaker, dark pants, Scarpa boots that had carried him to the summit of every four-thousand-meter peak in the Valais, and his Vuarnet sunglasses, tucked into his hair.

The bus rocked gently as it crossed a bridge over the Mottec, the milky glacial stream tumbling below. It was his first journey in eight years. In Zinal, he was safe. A small village tucked away at the end of a remote alpine valley. No train service. A constabulary of four charged with policing all the villages in the area: Grimentz, Chandolin, Saint-Luc. He had selected his refuge with care. A largely forgotten town to ensure that he remained largely forgotten. But those considerations were no longer in play. Safety was no longer paramount. He needed an answer.

What had Will been doing on the Matterhorn alone during the first week of October, climbing without safety equipment—"free soloing," one paper had claimed—amid claims of strange activity in the region?

The postal bus arrived in Sierre at 9:00 a.m. An underground shopping arcade led from the bus terminal to the train station. Robbie stopped in the restroom and proceeded to the rear stall. He removed his jacket, turned it inside out—trading blue for red—and slipped it back on. He dug a Rossignol ski cap out of his pack and pulled it low over his ears and forehead. He removed his boots and inserted lifts to add an inch to his height, and, more importantly, to alter his gait, even if slightly. He exchanged his Vuarnets for mirrored Revo wraparounds. Last, he removed his walking poles and extended them to the proper height. The beard stayed. All these changes made him, in the eyes of the security cameras and the algorithms that analyzed the images they captured 24-7, 365 days a year, a different man.

The train to Zermatt via Visp departed at 9:12 a.m. At the ticket office, he purchased a roundtrip fare, second class. The fares, he noted to his chagrin, had doubled in eight years. He made his way to the proper track, keeping close to other travelers. "Shadowing," they'd called it eons ago in his new officer course.

Be part of the crowd.

A lone wolf gets noticed.

And the cardinal rule: *Don't stand out.*

The train lumbered into the station, **Matterhorn Gotthard Bahn** painted boldly on the cars. The sight of the red cars, the sounds of the wheels groaning, the general hubbub provoked a slew of fond memories and, less fondly, put him in mind of how much he had missed.

Robbie ambled over to the kiosk and spent time scanning headlines from papers across Europe as the passengers alighted. Casually, he counted the CCTV cameras mounted throughout the station. Street entrance. Above the tracks. On the departures board. They were everywhere.

The feeds went to the regional transportation authorities, local and cantonal police, and all fire and rescue services. Additionally, they were tied in to a federal image bank that could be accessed by the Swiss Federal Intelligence Service (FIS).

Who spies on spies? Robbie knew the answer firsthand. Spies spy on spies.

He had noted the proliferation of digital and surveillance devices on his ride down the mountain. Not just the mushrooming of cell phone communication towers, but the widespread introduction of license plate recognition systems, traffic cams, radars governing speed and conduct, and, he suspected, additional cameras situated to cover any areas the first ones missed. And all that, of course, did not include private surveillance. Home and office security systems, cameras built into doorbells, hidden in alleys, covering every square inch of sidewalks.

Combine the images gathered by the government with those collected by private security systems, and you'd be able to follow an unsuspecting citizen every step of the way from Lugano to Geneva. "Big Brother is watching" was no longer a chilling slogan. It was an undisputable, ubiquitous, and unchallenged fact.

Robbie spotted a group of tourists approaching the train. He left the kiosk and melted into their ranks, joining them as they boarded. The car was nearly full. He advanced down the aisle, casually scanning the passengers' faces. He had no reason to believe he was being followed or that he was in jeopardy. It was too soon for that. All the same, he did his best to memorize as many faces as possible. Call it a training exercise. Better yet, a retraining exercise. Time to get the lead out.

He found a seat at the back of the car beside a young woman. He placed his rucksack between his feet and kept his gaze directed out the window as the train left the station. For twenty minutes, the train moved east toward the Grimsel Pass, at the far end of the Rhône Valley, the sights all the more beautiful for his not having seen them in far too long.

"*Alle Billette, bitte.* Tickets, please."

Robbie handed the conductor his ticket, barely glancing up. He didn't want the man to take note of his face. ". . . I do remember an old man with a thick, gray beard and expensive sunglasses."

"*Nächste Halte, Visp*," a female voice announced over the loudspeaker. "*Prochain arrêt, Visp.* Next stop, Visp."

There was a five-minute stop. Then, the train shunted onto a southbound track and began the leisurely climb to Zermatt, elevation 5,310 feet. It was a sunny morning. The tracks ran parallel to the banks of the Matter Vispa, beside dense pine forests and broad meadows, hardly seeming to climb at all. The motion was calming, reminding him that he'd barely slept the night before. He forced himself to sit up. He pinned his shoulders to the seat back and thought of Will. Good thoughts.

"Excuse me, sir." Someone was shaking his shoulder. "Sir, we've arrived. May I get out?"

Robbie woke with a start. It was the woman, his seatmate. Around him, passengers stood in the aisle, taking their bags down from the luggage rack. The woman stared at him impatiently.

He hadn't merely dozed off. He'd slept soundly for forty minutes, not stirring during stops in Randa and Täsch.

He picked up his rucksack and stood. He was not off to a good start.

———

Two Jeep Grand Cherokees sat parked in front of the Zermatt police station across the Bahnhofplatz. Both black with diplomatic license plates. This is odd, thought Robbie.

Zermatt was an automobile-free town. Trucks and trade vehicles were allowed for a few weeks in May and October, but that was all. He peeked in the front windows as he passed. He saw a copy of the international *New York Times*, a venti Starbucks in the cup holder, and a box of Altoids.

Americans.

The reception area inside the police station was a small, antiseptic room, benches set against the wall, posters of the Matterhorn and the Gornergrat Railway, linoleum floor, fluorescent lights. A CCTV camera spied from a corner. Robbie kept his head angled to the floor as he approached the desk sergeant's window.

"Good morning, sir." The desk sergeant was young and chirpy, with well-scrubbed cheeks. The worst crime she'd witnessed, Robbie guessed, was the theft of a baby's ice cream cone.

"Steinhardt, Robert." He announced himself in Zermatt fashion: family name first. "I believe my wallet was stolen."

A clipboard glided beneath the window. "Please fill out these forms."

Robbie fumbled with the clipboard, eyes scanning the back office. A few empty desks. A door at the far side stood ajar. He glimpsed several individuals walk past: dark suits, short haircuts. "Perhaps it was yesterday," he said to the desk sergeant. "Or the day before."

"Once you're finished, I'll have an officer speak with you."

Robbie retreated to a chair facing away from the camera. Beside him, a door led to the interior of the station. He took his time filling out the questionnaire. He could hear voices coming from behind the door. After a minute, he stood and asked the sergeant for a new pen. She opened a drawer, looking for one. He could hear the voices more clearly. English with a Swiss German accent.

". . . gunfire was reported . . . some kind of operation."

". . . details to remain confidential, Lieutenant." An American.

"Please," said the desk sergeant, handing him a new pen. "Here you are."

Robbie ignored it. One of the Swiss was talking again. ". . . give us some idea what was happening . . . this is our country, not yours."

"Sir, your pen?"

"May I use the restroom?" asked Robbie.

"At the end of the hall."

A buzzer sounded. Robbie passed through the door into the heart of the station. A corridor led past the reception. To his right, there was a door marked **KONFERENZZIMMER**. Conference room. A heated discussion was taking place inside.

"Look, we've got to claim the body." One of the Americans.

"Of course," responded a Swiss. "But an autopsy must be performed beforehand."

"He fell. What are you expecting to find?"

"This is federal procedure." It was the Swiss again, and he was upset. Rules were not to be trifled with. ". . . considering the circumstances."

Robbie had stopped walking. What circumstances? What gunfire? Why did the Americans want the information to remain confidential? Were these the "strange happenings" the newspapers had referred to?

"We realize this is an irregular request," one of the Americans said. "We'd consider it a favor."

A door at the end of the hall opened. A trim, diminutive man in a gray suit and knit tie stepped out of the men's room, still buckling his belt. Robbie continued past him. "*Entschuldigen Sie, bitte,*" he said in Swiss German.

"*Natürlich.*" Another Swiss. Maybe forty. Quick, perceptive eyes. Gun beneath his left arm. Expensive shoes. Not a speck of the dust that coats a shoe within ten steps of arriving in a mountain town. A federal agent from Bern.

Inside the bathroom, Robbie washed his hands, glancing at his watch, willing the seconds to pass more quickly. *Some kind of operation. Details to remain confidential. Reports of gunfire.*

The words rattled around Robbie's brain.

But my son is an executive with a multinational IT firm. What operation are you talking about?

A sense of disorientation passed over him. He wasn't sure what he'd expected to discover, but it wasn't a powwow between US diplomats and the FIS.

It was a climbing accident, for God's sake. Not an international incident. Or was it?

He quashed a violent urge to throw open the door of the conference room, draw his pistol, and start asking questions. What the hell had happened on that mountain?

The meeting was disbanding when Robbie left the restroom. He waited as five men and women filed into the hall. The Americans were easy to spot. Two men and a woman. The men wore penny loafers, blazers with gold buttons, button-down shirts. They might as well have stepped straight out of a Brooks Brothers catalog. The woman was dark haired and officious, the notebook under her arm bearing the seal of the US Department of State. The Swiss were local badges dressed in uniform: pale-blue shirts, navy pants, hiking boots. No sign of the Fed.

Robbie followed them into the reception, then out of the building. He hadn't forgotten about his "stolen wallet." He just didn't care. Give him an F for tradecraft. He'd blame it on shock.

Outside, a few clouds threatened an otherwise sunny day. A steady breeze lent the air a chill. He pulled a pair of sunglasses from his breast pocket and put them on. They were not the pair he'd worn earlier. To look at, they were Wayfarers, horn rimmed, fat arms, green lenses.

The Americans clustered near their vehicles, engaged in a post-mortem. Robbie walked past, taking a moment to look at each closely, offering a polite *"Grüezi."* They ignored him. No one paid attention to an old man.

The woman was on the phone.

"Dekker is at the hospital in Sion," she was saying.

"What's left of him." Her colleague was medium height, had reddish hair, and was built like a fire hydrant.

"Show some respect, Gilroy," said the second man. Tall, Asian, with a buzz cut and a thick, muscled neck.

"We can pick up the body from the morgue this afternoon. Thank you, sir." The woman ended the call and spoke to her colleagues. "After all that bullshit, I need a drink, but I'll settle for a coffee."

Robbie continued past them and turned the corner at the far side of the station. He did not see the member of the Swiss Federal Police exit the building in urgent conversation with a tall, sturdily built blonde woman dressed in a navy pantsuit. Whatever he was saying appeared to concern her.

"Thank you, Peter," she said, shaking his hand. "Let's keep this between us for now."

"Of course, Jane," said Peter Kleiner, deputy director of the DAP. "You have my word. But, Jane, I'll need something. And soon."

"I'm not sure how to respond just yet." Her name was Jane McCall. She was a member of the US Intelligence Community, or IC, and had been sent to investigate the death of William Andrew Dekker.

Kleiner shook his head apologetically. "Let's hope I'm not right."

CHAPTER 9

Zermatt, Switzerland

The Snow Café was a new, hip establishment catering to the tastes of the younger crowd who flocked to Zermatt in winter and summer. The snowboarders and BASE jumpers and paragliders. It sat on the corner of Wiestistrasse, meters from the river, windows and doors opened to allow in the fresh air and the sound of rushing water.

Robbie found a table by the entrance and powered up his laptop. A server handed him a menu. The specialty of the house was sushi, something he hadn't thought of for eight years.

Today's featured item was a spicy tuna roll. Price: forty francs. Forty bucks, more or less. "Ham and cheese," he told the server. "And some water. From the tap."

Robbie set his sunglasses next to the laptop, squinting to locate the download button atop one of the arms. The sunglasses did double duty as a camera with a Zeiss lens and a powerful microprocessor. When he'd been issued them, they were state of the art. These days, you could probably buy a pair at Walmart for ninety-nine dollars. Pretty much the cost of two spicy tuna rolls.

He AirDropped the pictures of the American diplomats into his photo app and then moved the mouse over an icon depicting a blue magnifying glass above the letters C-AI. C-AI stood for "Clearview AI," the world's most powerful commercially available facial-recognition program. It worked by scraping photographs from millions of websites, among them Facebook, YouTube, Instagram, and Venmo, to name only a few.

One after another, Robbie dragged a photo of each diplomat he'd encountered at the police station into the C-AI browser. A flurry of pictures streamed past too quickly for him to focus on individual faces, except to note a general similarity to the snaps he'd taken in front of the police station. Ten seconds later, he had three names: Evan P. Gilroy, James Kee-yun Chen, and Julie Farrar.

Robbie opened a new tab and brought up Google. First at bat: Evan Gilroy. Bang.

LinkedIn said Gilroy worked at the US Department of Commerce. Graduate of Wheaton College. A specialist in bilateral trade, stationed in Geneva.

Next up: James Kee-yun Chen. LinkedIn popped up first again, identifying Chen as working for the Office of the US Trade Representative, Geneva. There was a link to the USTR website. Not interested.

Last, but not least: Julie Farrar.

Robbie read the search results. No, he thought. It can't be. "Julie Farrar. Vice president. Tradepoint Data, Lausanne." Tradepoint Data, where Will Dekker was also a vice president.

He pulled up the Tradepoint website. A bold blue home page. "Tradepoint, world leader in IT solutions for the financial and banking sectors."

Robbie looked away. He'd read dozens of articles about Tradepoint since he'd learned his son had taken a job there. He'd googled pictures of its headquarters, read up on its executives. It was a real company with real clients and a real balance sheet.

But it was also something else. A front for American intelligence efforts.

The server arrived with his sandwich and a glass of water. Robbie took a sip of water and forced himself to take a bite. He drew a breath and returned his attention to the laptop. He opened a VPN, then accessed the Tor Browser, linking him to the dark web, where he typed in an untrackable URL. The screen went black except for a rectangular white log-on box. No username required. Just a password. Eighteen letters, numbers, and symbols assigned to him and only him.

Robbie typed in the password. He had used it too many times to ever forget.

They called it "Cerberus," and Cerberus was the official personnel directory of the US Intelligence Community. Everyone who worked for one of myriad agencies under the intelligence umbrella—CIA, NSC, DIA, DHS, NGA, and on and on—was listed in its pages.

Evan Gilroy did not work for the Department of Commerce.

James Kee-yun Chen did not work for the US Trade Representative. Julie Farrar did not work for Tradepoint Data.

They might be attached to the US embassy in Bern, but he doubted that too. Robbie was fairly certain that they all worked for the same three-letter agency where he'd toiled for all too many years. The grand-daddy of them all. The Central Intelligence Agency.

Still, Robbie did not enter any of their names into the query bar. It was not worth jeopardizing his hard-won anonymity, and possibly risking his life, to confirm his suspicions. These three meant nothing to him.

Robbie drummed his fingers on the table. Decision time.

Until now, his actions had been a calculated gamble that he could leave his cozy hideout to gather some information about his son's death with only a moderate fear of discovery. While he'd consciously chosen to abandon what had proven a safe haven, he had not yet engaged in any actions that would, in and of themselves, bring him to the attention of the people he'd striven to avoid. Not just avoid, but fool. The people who thought him dead.

With one tap on the keyboard, he would change all that. Somewhere, sometime, someone would without any question be made aware that an agent presumed dead for eight years had logged on to a top secret database. And not just any agent. A man who had been accused of treason against the government of the United States of America.

Somewhere was Fort Meade, Maryland, the headquarters of the National Security Agency.

Sometime was between one and five seconds.

And *someone* was a junior cybersecurity analyst whose sole responsibility was policing that database.

Here's what would happen: "Excuse me, sir," the junior cybersecurity analyst would inform his superior. "Something popped up that might be of interest."

"Is that right?" His superior would take a look, spot the code name "Scylla," and feel his ulcer flare up before contacting his counterpart over at the Central Intelligence Agency. "Hey, Bob, got something here you need to take a look at."

His counterpart over at the CIA would then contact the human resources professional in charge of the National Clandestine Service. "We have a possible level two breach of security. Scylla is alive."

Inexorably, word would climb the ladder that Scylla had logged on to Cerberus. Scylla, last seen climbing into a Peugeot taxi on the rue Leclerc in Beirut seconds before an IED blew it into smithereens.

Any doubt about the accuracy of the report would be dispelled as soon as they learned the subject of the inquiry. William Andrew Dekker. Scylla's son.

And then?

Hard to say. They'd come after Robbie once. Quietly. Without warning. Using deadly force. He'd escaped, but barely. He'd killed the man sent to kill him. Eight years had passed since. Eight quiet years. Not a peep. He was dead, after all. Dead men tell no tales.

One guy might think that was enough and let him slide. Another might not. It all depended on who was in charge.

Robbie bet on the second guy.

They'd come after him again. Count on it.

Robbie stared at the screen. Enough hypothesizing. It didn't matter who was running the show. He'd made his decision the moment he'd left the Chalet Ponderosa. He was done hiding. He was going to see things through no matter the consequences.

Decision time.

Robbie hit Send. His password remained active. In a split second, he was on Cerberus's home page. He typed in his son's full name. "William Andrew Dekker." He hit Return.

Boom! Bad news traveled fast. And even faster on the internet.

Robbie was looking at a photograph of his son standing beside an American flag, hair cut short, wearing a dark suit, white shirt, striped tie. It was the standard photo taken upon completion of the new officer course at Langley.

WILLIAM ANDREW DEKKER. BS. GEORGETOWN UNIVERSITY. FIRST LIEUTENANT, UNITED STATES MARINE CORPS.

Robbie felt as if he'd been punched in the gut. The kid had followed in his footsteps.

Climbing, the Corps, the company. Stupid sonuvabitch. Robbie's reaction wasn't surprise, but anger. *Why?*

And then something more sinister. *How?*

Sons of people like Robbie, of men with work names like Scylla, who'd been hunted down for acts deemed traitorous to the republic, were not normally invited to join the Central Intelligence Agency.

Unless . . .

An explanation came to Robbie. It was an explanation that pleased him, perhaps even cast him in a more positive light.

They'd finally come around to his point of view. They believed him. They'd admitted their error. He was not guilty of treason, or any other crime for that matter. Allowing his son to join was proof that bygones were bygones.

With a rueful smile and a shake of the head, Robbie discarded it. How vain. How wrongheaded. How flat-out ignorant. There was a rule: if you wanted to believe something was true, you damned well already knew it wasn't.

So, then, how?

For now, Robbie didn't have the answer.

For the hell of it, he typed in the others' names. Gilroy, Chen, Farrar. All of them were spooks. Field officers in the Directorate of Operations, informally known as the National Clandestine Service.

There it was.

Will hadn't slipped and fallen while climbing without safety measures. At the time of his death, he'd been operational. He'd been on the run. He'd been moving fast, no time to worry about his safety. He was KIA.

The fog of eight years of inaction vanished. Robbie saw things as clearly as his last day on the job. There was a reason Gilroy, Chen, and Farrar were anxious—desperate, even—to get the body. Will had something they wanted. At the time of his death, he was in possession of confidential information. Ours? Theirs? What did it matter?

The Americans believed it was essential they get it back. Robbie meant to beat them.

———

Like most alpine railroad stations, Zermatt's was open air. A steel roof the length of a football field sheltered the tracks and quais, a shopping arcade, and the offices of the Schweizerische Bundesbahnen, or SBB. No trains were presently in the station. A smattering of passengers milled about, killing time. A look to the departures board. The next train for Visp left in thirty minutes. Robbie hurried to the ticket window, reviewing his options, ruing his lack of an automobile.

At that moment, two black Jeeps sped down Mattenstrasse across the Bahnhofplatz, headed out of town. Robbie knew their destination.

The Kantonsspital in Sion. His options had dwindled to one. He needed a car.

Robbie broke into a jog, rushing into the street. So much for shadowing and not drawing attention to himself. He ran to the north end of the terminal and crossed the tracks to a long-term employee parking lot. He counted four vehicles, three of them covered by tarpaulins. There was a Fiat sedan. Too new. Impossible to hot-wire a car with an electronic transmission. He lifted the tarpaulin off the second. A Škoda. Thirty years old with two flat tires. Next was a VW Golf. Again, too new. The last car boasted a sleek silhouette. He lifted the tarp, recognizing the horizontal grille that covered the rear-mounted engine. A Porsche 911, circa 1995. This, he could work with. He slid the tarp off the car, then moved to the driver's window. Stick shift. An odometer reading over eighty thousand kilometers.

Robbie slid off his jacket and wrapped it around his elbow. A look in both directions.

Even on a blustery October day there were too many people around. He crouched and drove his elbow into the window. A second blow and the glass buckled.

He pushed the window into the car and unlocked the door. It took another few seconds to get rid of the glass. He swept it off the front seat and climbed in. He located the ignition, yanked the wires clear, and used his teeth to scrape off the PVC sheath. He depressed the clutch, then wrapped the wires together and touched the gas. The engine roared to life. Like all Porsches, it was too loud. The fuel gauge stood at half. He rapped his knuckles on the dash for good luck, then shoved the gearshift into first.

A minute later, he was driving down the Mattenstrasse out of Zermatt. He passed the old cement works, and the road widened into a proper highway. A look in the rearview mirror: no one.

Maybe he'd gotten away scot-free.

He floored it, taking the curves aggressively, eyes trained for the Americans and their Jeeps. He dropped down a long, gradual slope and entered Täsch, the first town in the valley. He tapped the brakes, keeping his speed beneath the limit. Another look in the rearview mirror. If the police weren't after him by now, they weren't coming.

The town behind him, he accelerated wildly. Traffic was light, and he passed cars with abandon. The speed was exhilarating. A tonic. The thought came to him that for the first time in far too long, he had a purpose—a mission, even. It was not the mission he wanted. Like it or not, it was his.

He rounded a curve overlooking the next town, Wildi. His fingers tightened on the wheel.

He leaned toward the windscreen. The vista gave way to a broad grassy plain a few hundred feet below, the highway cutting across it. And there, two black vehicles. The Americans.

Robbie downshifted to third and pressed the pedal to the floor. Time to reel them in.

CHAPTER 10

Bürgenstock, Switzerland

The Grand Hotel Bürgenstock sat atop a steep mountainside thirty kilometers south of Lucerne, a sleek, ultramodern hostelry gazing down on the waters of Lake Lucerne below. The hotel had begun life more than a hundred years earlier as a refuge for the throngs of hiking-mad tourists—English, German, even the odd American—who had invaded the country at the end of the nineteenth century. With its central location, the hotel promised convenient access to the majestic Mounts Rigi and Pilatus, nearby. For those who didn't relish a challenging excursion, endless foothills carpeted by grass and colorful flowers lay just outside the front door.

A spa was installed. The hotel added a new wing. It built an outdoor elevator, the Hammetschwand Lift, the highest in Europe. It added one star, then another. Though it could not boast the hot springs and curative baths of its older, snobbier rivals across the border in Baden-Baden, it offered its own menu of muesli, massage, and the unquestioned restorative powers of the Swiss alpine air.

But Ilya Ivashka, stealing up a back stairwell at 10:15 a.m., had not come to the Bürgenstock for a spa treatment. His visit was of a professional nature. He'd come to speak with a prominent scientist attending the annual meeting of the International Association of Research

Chemists. His appointment, if it could be called that, was with this year's keynote speaker, Dr. Ashok Mehta, professor at the University of Cambridge, retired chairman of Imperial Chemical Industries, and holder of a dozen infamous patents.

Mehta worked for Ilya. For the past five years, he'd supplied Russian intelligence with the fruits of his labor. His most recent discovery was of particular interest to Ilya, to Colonel Zaitseva, and now, due to the conniving of Marina Zhukova, to the United States.

Ilya made his way to room 615. He pressed a skeleton card against the magnetic reader. The lock yielded. Inside, he filched a vodka from the minibar and dropped onto the couch. He sent a text to Mehta. Five minutes later the door burst open. Mehta entered, visibly distraught.

"Ashok, how are you?"

"Who let you in?" Dr. Ashok Mehta swept past Ilya, making an anguished survey of the suite, pulling back curtains, poking his head into the bathroom, opening closets.

"Don't worry," said Ilya. "I'm alone." As if he needed assistance to kill the man.

"I told you to call me when you arrived," said Mehta.

Ilya Ivashka offered an insincere shrug. "I'm sorry. It's what we do. You see a locked door and search for your key. Me, I break in. Tell me, are all your conferences in five-star hotels?"

Mehta put down his briefcase. He was a compact man attired in a dove gray suit, seventy-odd years old, with jet-black hair combed back over a broad forehead, rimless glasses perched on an imperious nose. "You promised," he said, ignoring the question. "I was a fool to believe you."

Ilya kicked his feet up on the lacquered coffee table. If Mehta was a fool, it was because he'd accepted a payment of $5 million from a Russian intelligence agency and didn't think there would be any unpleasant consequences. "What is it, Ashok? What's bothering you?"

"They know," said Mehta.

"Who?" said Ilya, playing dumb. "Who knows what?"

"The Americans. They visited me. They had questions."

"Be specific," said Ilya. "Who exactly visited? And when?"

"One of their agents. The day before yesterday. He bumped into me during cocktail hour downstairs."

"Thirty, maybe thirty-five? Tall, dark hair, cagey?" Will Dekker, RIP. Had to be.

Mehta sat down opposite him. "You know him?"

"In a sense," said Ilya.

"He tried to pass himself off as an academic. He was interested in my recent discoveries. He wanted to know how I'd altered ethyl S–phospholi-debenzene. VX—"

"Please, Ashok. I know what it is."

Mehta leaned closer. "He asked if I'd taken my work further."

"Meaning?"

"You know what he meant. It's what you paid me to do."

Ilya sank lower in his chair. *Weaponize it.* He didn't need to say the words out loud. "And we paid you to keep quiet about it."

"I did."

"Are you sure?"

"He asked about its efficacy in water. I told him it was impossible."

"It is," said Ilya. "As far as anyone knows."

"Why is he curious? About that of all things? Water."

"It's his job to be curious. Like it's mine to break into your room to make certain no one sees us together."

"I think they're following me," said Mehta.

"You've seen them?"

"No, not exactly."

"Then?"

"I can just feel it. Something's off."

"Perhaps we should switch jobs," said Ilya. "You seem to have a knack for this kind of thing."

"Don't patronize me."

"Nonsense," said Ilya, with a laugh. "No one's following you. In fact, I'm ready to wager you won't be seeing the American again."

Of course, there was nothing nonsensical about it. If Will Dekker suspected Ashok Mehta of selling a weaponized version of VX gas capable of being spread through a water system, you can be damned sure that he and his colleagues would put Mehta under a microscope. Now that Dekker was dead, the risk was multiplied tenfold.

"What if they kidnap me?" said Mehta. "They do that, you know. Rendition."

"You're a seventy-year-old research scientist, not an Islamic terrorist. Please, Ashok. Give them some credit."

"What do you mean?"

"They'll shoot you dead before they kidnap you."

Mehta did not appear to find the remark humorous. "If you use what I gave you, everyone will know the source. I may as well be dead right now."

"No one plans on using it," said Ilya. "The game is all about possession. It's about having something the other side doesn't. It's the perception that counts. The ability to make them ask: 'What if?'"

Mehta rose. He poured himself an orange juice from the minibar. "What now?"

"Let me think." Ilya stood and made his own tour of the suite, if for different reasons. He noted that the window was unlocked. Easy enough to toss him out. But no. Mehta's murder would draw attention. It would have to be an accident. Possibly, suicide. Ilya stuck his head into the bathroom. The glassed-in shower could wash clean an entire family. He would have preferred a bathtub. Hard to drown beneath a rainwater showerhead.

He caught a glimpse of himself in the mirror. Harried. Fatigued. A man in a bind. What now? The answer was right there in his eyes. Reckless, but what other choice was there?

Ilya realized that Mehta was right. The Americans probably were following him. Catch him and Mehta would blab. One slap and it would all come pouring out.

Ilya slid the stiletto from his pocket and wandered back into the living area. Mehta had moved to the far side of the room, his eyes darting this way and that, all too fearful.

"'What now?'" said Ilya, soothingly. "I'll tell you. We sit tight."

"And the Americans?"

"I'll take care of them."

Ilya tightened his grip on the stiletto, taking Mehta's measure. He liked to insert the blade between the third and fourth ribs, angle it upward, give it a little oomph to puncture the pericardium. It was over like that.

"You'll protect me?" said Mehta.

"That's why I'm here." Ilya smiled, approaching the scientist.

"You promise?" A step closer.

"Trust me, Ash—" Ilya's phone rang. He looked at the screen. Andre Berner. Zürich police. Ilya turned his back and answered the call. "Detective."

"You didn't tell me he was a spy," said Andre Berner.

"You didn't ask."

"People are paying attention to this."

"It was an accident."

Berner scoffed. "Is that so?"

"Where is he?" asked Ilya.

"Sion. The Kantonsspital. You'll find him in the morgue."

"Noted."

"Where are you now?" asked Berner.

"None of your business."

"Have it your way," said Berner. "But just so you know, Dekker's people are on their way already. Good luck."

Ilya ended the call. He checked his watch. Sion was a two-hour drive. He slid the stiletto back into his pocket. Another day then. "I'm sorry, Ashok. Have to run. You were right to call. I'll have my men check the surroundings. Don't stray too far unless you want to end up in a CIA black site in Morocco."

"No?" said Mehta. "Really?"

"Really."

CHAPTER 11

Sion, Switzerland

Robbie passed the Americans coming out of Visp, merging onto the A6, the highway that ran the length of the Rhône Valley. One Jeep stayed behind him; the other headed north toward Kandersteg and, he guessed, onward to Bern and the US embassy. He kept his speed well above the limit. Within minutes, he'd left the Jeep far behind. Twice he felt a flash of light on his retina. Radar equipped with a camera to capture a car's license plate and its driver's identity. In a week, the owner of the Porsche would receive an infraction from the police asking him to pay a hefty fine. With any luck, it would be the first he'd heard of his car being stolen.

An hour later, Robbie arrived in Sion. The hospital was a broad tower of unadorned concrete wedged between two apartment buildings on the southern boundary of the city. A directory was posted inside the main entrance. **Morgue. Ground Floor. East Wing.**

The halls were lightly trafficked. Nurses and doctors passed him without interest. He followed markers to the east wing. The morgue sat at the end of the corridor. A sign hung from the ceiling, directly above the head of a uniformed guard. In Robbie's experience, the bodies of civilians killed in climbing accidents did not warrant protection.

He turned down a corridor and located a supply closet a little too close to a nursing station. He stopped at a drinking fountain, then unmistakable. The name "Katya" was written on the flip side. Was the mother Russian? Ukrainian? German, perhaps?

A granddaughter. Something else he'd missed.

Robbie was not sure how to process this. Sadness, of course. A child forced to grow up without a father. But something more. She carried his blood and was, therefore, in some way, his responsibility. He took the photograph and tossed the wallet back onto the table.

Robbie studied his son's personal effects. Other than the phone, there was no device that might hold sensitive or confidential information. No thumb drive, microfilm, CD. Yet, the Americans' actions indicated that they believed otherwise. How else to explain their urgent pleas to the Swiss police? To their minds, Will had been in possession of something important. Vital, even. As far as Robbie could tell, that something was missing.

The guard moaned and began to stir.

Robbie returned everything to the bag and replaced it on the tray. He touched his fingers to his son's head. He told Will he loved him and slid him inside the cold locker.

Robbie turned off the lights and left the morgue.

Closing the door, he shot a look down the corridor. A slim man in a suit rounded the corner, walking in his direction. Robbie headed the opposite way. He'd glimpsed the man for less than a second. Dark suit. Open collar. Confident stride. A man with a plan. All that he'd picked up in the blink of an eye. It was another detail, however, that captured Robbie's attention: the man's thick blond hair, combed off his forehead and, as usual, cut too long and tucked behind the ears.

Ilya.

CHAPTER 12

Sion

Despite his name, Ilya Ivashka was American. His parents had emigrated from Russia in the 1970s and taken American citizenship. He himself was born in Bethesda, Maryland, and grew up in an upper-middle-class suburb of Potomac. He played Little League, Pop Warner football, and soccer. He attended Dyson School and Willtown Prep. He enjoyed vacations in Rehoboth Beach and Stowe, Vermont.

His only ties to the old country came during annual pilgrimages to visit his grandparents in Kursk. The Iron Curtain had not yet fallen. Their home was a three-room apartment in a grim industrial block. He slept on a cot in the living room. Each morning he watched his grandmother remove her dentures from a glass next to the kitchen sink and loudly, painstakingly, fit them to her gums. Breakfast was black bread with margarine and milk coffee. There was no orange juice, no cereal, no MTV to entertain him while he devoured his Frosted Flakes. He was not impressed.

Mornings were spent learning Russian with his babushka, or grandmother. For three hours, they sat head-to-head at a card table in the family room. His babushka would take his cheeks and mouth in her bony fingers and force him to pronounce the words correctly. *Po-zhau-shta.*

She was just sixty, yet to his eye she might have been one hundred. Her hair was gray and stringy. Fat hung in great folds from her arms. She limped angrily around the apartment with the help of a crutch. All the while one cigarette after another dangled from the corner of her mouth. Belomorkanal. Hollow tube at one end, tobacco loosely packed in cheap paper on the other. A *papirosa*, they called it. The smell was foul.

When he was twelve, he stole one and sneaked out later that day to smoke it. After three puffs, he became violently ill, coughing, retching, overcome with dizziness. He hadn't touched a cigarette since.

Afternoons were his own. He escaped to hills nearby with local boys, who, naturally, thought the world of him. A real-life American. The stuff of legend. There was a quarry and a schist wall thirty feet high they'd take turns climbing. No one made it to the top, but somewhere a seed was planted. Ilya liked the freedom that came with being alone in the wilderness, the thrill of hanging off a slab of rock. He liked the feeling of being in charge, of knowing that whatever happened depended on him alone. A captain of his fate.

It was not until he was a junior in high school that he began climbing at home. It began on a school trip to New Hampshire. One afternoon, they traveled to Cannon Cliff in the White Mountains. A confidence-building exercise. The students were going to learn to rappel down a rock face.

Ilya watched transfixed as the instructor lectured the group of twenty students, explaining how he would fashion a seat out of a rope and secure them to a safety line and how they would lower themselves a hundred feet to the ground below. The instructor was a regular guy, a little shorter than Ilya, skinny, with long black hair and pale-blue eyes. There was something about him, however—steadfastness, confidence, reliability, whatever it was—that Ilya admired. After five minutes, everyone in the class was ready to trust him with their lives, Ilya included.

The first few students rappelled down the cliff without incident. All you had to do was lean back and trust the rope until you were perpendicular to the rock, then simply walk down it, your speed governed by how quickly you let the rope pass through your fingers. Easy enough, thought Ilya, after he'd reached the bottom.

Of course, there was an incident. Marli, the theater chick, let go of the rope halfway down, tumbled a few feet, and ended up dangling upside down on the safety rope with her head below her feet. Ilya still remembered her screams.

In no time, the instructor—his name was Mackenzie, "Mac" for short—rappelled down the rock and helped Marli get sorted out. He replaced the rope on her shoulder, showed her once again how to place her left hand high, her right hand behind her, loosely clutching the rope, controlling her descent.

When they got to the bottom, Mac climbed up the vertical face like a spider. "You see that?" one of Ilya's friends had said. "Badass."

"I don't know," said Ilya. "Not so hard."

A chorus of hoots. "You couldn't do it."

Ilya felt all eyes on him. He thought of the thirty-foot chunk of rock he'd fooled around on in Kyiv. Never once had he made it to the top. This was a sheer granite face, three times as tall and nearly vertical. It didn't matter. A challenge had been issued. He was funny that way. It was always the world versus Ilya, and Ilya was eager to prove the world wrong.

He was climbing before he knew it.

He found a handhold, then a place for his foot. The first steps were easy enough.

Everywhere he looked, he found a spot to grab on to, a surface wide enough to accommodate a foot. He wasn't sure when he stopped hearing his classmates' voices. It wasn't as if he'd made a conscious decision to tune them out. One moment he heard them, the next it was just him and the rock.

At some point, he looked down. Everyone appeared remarkably small. It was only then that he took note of how high he had climbed. Forty feet? Fifty? Far higher than the quarry outside Kyiv. High enough, he realized, with an instantaneous and overwhelming dread, that were he to fall, he would die.

One moment Ilya felt confident and relaxed, effortlessly ascending the granite face. The next he was hugging the wall, cheek pressed against the cold stone, scared to death. One second his palms were dry as chalk, the next, wet as water. He couldn't move. He was frozen to the spot.

And then a voice. "Hey, kid, you got it."

It was the instructor, Mac. Ilya didn't move. If anything, he held on more tightly.

"You already did the hard part," said Mac. "I wished you'd asked me. I would have roped you up. Usually, that's the idea. But listen, right now, it doesn't matter. You're golden. Keep coming up."

"I don't want to fall," said Ilya.

"You're not going to fall," said Mac. "I promise." He laughed. It wasn't a mocking laugh but a laugh among friends. Maybe among equals. "Take a breath, lean out from the rock, and look up. There's a hold above your left hand. Grab it, then move your right foot on top of that round bulge by your knee. Can you do that?"

Ilya inched his head back. The handhold was where Mac had said. He took a breath. He extended his arm. His fingers found the flat surface. He identified the foothold beside his knee. Up went his foot. "Now what?"

"Look around you. All I see are handholds. Get your butt up here." Ilya didn't move. The fear had come back. He was paralyzed. "You don't think I'm *that* much better than you," said Mac.

Ilya felt the words sting. The instructor wasn't better than him. He'd just had more practice. Ilya gazed at his classmates. All eyes were trained on him. No one said a word. They were frightened. They thought he might not make it. They believed he might fall. Something about the idea bugged him. He felt humiliated, and humiliated was way worse than scared.

Ilya released a hand and waved. "Relax," he called. "I'm just checking out the view."

And then, strangely, the fear left him, and he was climbing. Mac the unshakable was right. There were holds everywhere. Ilya felt as if a crane were hoisting him up the cliff. He climbed quickly and gracefully with calm and confidence.

A minute later, he was staring at the instructor's outstretched hand. Ilya ignored it and pulled himself over the lip, jumping to his feet.

"That wasn't so bad, was it?" asked Mac.

Ilya waved to his classmates, then looked at the instructor. "Again."

———

Inside the hospital, Ilya turned the corner and spotted the sign for the morgue. An empty chair was positioned beside the door. Just then, a doctor emerged from the room and walked in the opposite direction, away from him. A few moments later, Ilya reached the morgue. He opened the door warily, poking a head inside.

A security guard lay on the floor. He was moaning, moving his limbs with difficulty. Ilya entered the room and stepped over him. He hurried to the drawers, found Will Dekker's name tagged to one. He looked back at the guard, recalling the doctor who'd just left. An older man with gray hair and a beard.

Whoever he was, Ilya realized, he was not a doctor. He was the enemy.

CHAPTER 13

Sion

Robbie continued down the corridor, certain that Ilya Ivashka was watching him.

Ilya: godfather to his children.

Ilya: once a friend, more than that, even. Ilya: who'd stuck a dagger in his back.

Ilya: who he'd dreamed of killing a thousand times over.

Robbie heard the footsteps behind him slow, the door to the morgue open . . . then close. He broke into a run. Reaching the end of the corridor, he threw open the exit to the street.

A stiff breeze cooled the hallway. Instead of leaving the building, he retraced his steps and entered the stairwell. He ran up four flights, stopping on the second floor landing.

By now, Ilya would have discovered the incapacitated guard. That was enough. He wouldn't need to check the morgue any further. He would know it was the old man in the lab coat he'd observed leaving the morgue who was responsible for the guard's condition and that if there was something of value to be found among Will's belongings, he'd taken it.

A moment later, Robbie heard the ground floor door open. He'd been foolish to think Ilya would fall for his ploy. The man had always had a sixth sense about this kind of thing.

Ilya's presence signaled something more. He'd come for the same thing as the Americans, whatever it might be. The conclusion was inescapable. Whatever had happened on the Matterhorn, Ilya Ivashka, a ranking agent in the employ of the SVR, was involved. For the moment, Robbie didn't need the details. Ilya had played a role in Will's death. To Robbie's mind that made him responsible. Ilya had killed his son.

Robbie listened with all his being. He imagined Ilya craning his neck inside the stairwell, eyes narrowed, scenting his prey. No time to dally.

As quietly as possible, Robbie opened the door to the fourth floor. In contrast to the ground floor, the hallway bustled with activity. Painted on the wall were the words **MRI** and IMAGING. He walked as quickly as possible without running. A sign marked **X-RAYS** hung above a door. He entered the office and walked past the reception desk into a narrow corridor, passing one examining room after another, offering a courteous smile to everyone he encountered. Somewhere behind him, a woman shouted, "Excuse me! Excuse me, can I help? Sir? Sir!"

Ilya.

Robbie turned left and spotted a sign for the main hallway. He pushed through the door and broke into a run, tearing off his white jacket—it had become a liability, a bull's-eye on his back—and tossing it into a trash bin. There was no longer any point in trying to hide. This was a race, and Ilya had always been faster than him. The man was a jackrabbit over a short distance.

Robbie came to the end of the hall. Which way? Right? Left? He had no idea where he was. He went left. Fewer people. The doors to either side were locked. At the end of the hall, he turned left again, into a broader, well-trafficked corridor. Ahead, he saw the large windows that looked out the front and back of the building. It was harder to run here. He dodged in and out, the sight of an old man moving so vigorously drawing wary, frightened glances.

Behind him, a cart overturned. Glass shattered. A woman cried out, *"Con!"* Asshole. Ilya had never been one to finesse things.

An alarm sounded. A Klaxon repeated every second. A voice blared from the loudspeaker: "This is a police alert. There is an emergency in the building. Please shelter in place."

Robbie ran to the window. He unfastened the lock and with both hands raised it. He poked his head out. There was a narrow ledge, maybe six inches wide, and directly above him, maybe ten feet, another. To his right a drainpipe ran from the roof to the ground.

He climbed out the window and positioned himself on the ledge facing inward, weight on his toes. It was ninety feet to the pavement. He raised a hand over his head and touched the ledge above him. Then, he extended an arm toward the drainpipe, fingertips straining. Too far. He glanced inside the hospital and caught Ilya rounding a corner, running toward him.

Robbie directed his gaze upward, drew a breath, and jumped. His fingers grasped on to the ledge just as Ilya's lunged for his ankle. He kicked the hand away and awkwardly pulled himself up. He got to his feet. There was no ledge above him, only the overhanging eaves of the roof. He tried the window. Locked. Then he extended an arm toward the drainpipe. It hadn't moved any closer in the last thirty seconds. He inched to the side of the ledge. A last glance down. He met Ilya's eyes, saw the surprise blossom. A curious smile. Disbelief, but only for a moment. Then rage.

Robbie leaped to his right and managed to grab the drainpipe. He slipped an inch, and another, then caught himself, hands holding firm. He wedged the toe of a boot beneath the pipe and shimmied up, hauling himself over the eaves and onto the roof. It was all coming back to him.

He looked over the edge. Ilya was following, as adept as ever. He'd never been much at leading, but once you set a route, he wasted no time following.

Robbie ran across the roof. The door leading to the emergency stairs was locked. He didn't want to go back inside anyway. Too many people had seen the old man with the thick beard running through the halls.

He continued to the edge of the roof. Another building pressed against the hospital. It was a ten-foot drop to the roof. He vaulted the precipice, arms flailing to keep his balance. He landed poorly, toppling onto his side, his hip absorbing too much of the impact. He stood, shaken, and trotted to the far side of the roof. An alley and thirty feet separated him from the next building.

He spun. There was no door anywhere leading downstairs. He returned to the edge and looked over. This was a residential building. Laundry lines extended from some of the windows.

Elsewhere, air conditioners rested upon window ledges, propped up by sturdy supports, some iron, some wooden.

Maybe.

He peered over his shoulder in time to see Ilya land expertly, dropping and rolling like they'd been taught at jump school. Ilya rose. He held a pistol in his right hand.

Another look over the side of the roof. "Maybe" was his only choice.

Robbie lowered himself from the roof, his feet positioned more or less above an air-conditioning unit. A six-foot drop. A lot farther to the ground. He let go. He landed neatly, knees bent, weight forward. The air conditioner groaned but held firm beneath his weight.

The nearest unit was one floor down and one window over. There was no way to lower himself and swing over. He had to jump. He measured the distance and leaped. He landed off-balance, one boot sliding off the unit. He fell onto his belly, clutching the air conditioner with both hands.

"Are you crazy?" Ilya poked his head over the roof. He craned his body outward and aimed his pistol. He didn't fire. Instead, he hauled himself over the lip and dropped onto the air conditioner.

Robbie maneuvered himself over the edge of the air conditioner, taking hold of the iron supports beneath it and swinging into the air. Another unit rested on its own supports one floor below. He steadied himself and dropped. The air conditioner sagged and tilted backward. Robbie lost his balance. The air conditioner held, but momentum had him. His boots slipped off the unit. His butt slammed onto the air conditioner. Helpless, he toppled off it and fell ten feet to the sidewalk, rolling into the street.

A horn blared. He heard a car screech to a halt, felt a breath of air. He struggled to his feet, seeing stars. A black SUV was stopped barely a foot away. He placed his hands on the hood to steady himself. An Asian man sat behind the wheel, staring daggers at him. A blonde woman with dark sunglasses was seated in the rear. Robbie's eyes returned to the driver, taking note of his sturdy neck.

Dazed, Robbie stepped back from the vehicle. A Jeep. The Americans.

CHAPTER 14

Rhône Valley, Switzerland

"Jet lag getting to you?" asked Jimmy Chen, ten minutes earlier, as he entered Sion.

Jane McCall glanced up from her paperwork and met the driver's eyes, looking at her in the rearview mirror.

"No more than usual," she said, yawning as if on cue. "This job is all about putting out fires. Go here, go there. When they ask you to be a supervisor, Jimmy, take my advice: run in the opposite direction."

"Gotcha, boss."

Chen guided the car along the highway, heading west down the Rhône Valley. They passed crumbling medieval châteaus perched atop bold hills and meadows planted with saffron, blazing yellow. The sky was an impressionist's dream: lazy clouds wandering across a pale firmament. Yes, it was beautiful. No, Jane couldn't care less.

Six months earlier, she'd been promoted to regional supervisor of Western Europe / Switzerland, Austria, Northern Italy. If it sounded like a position for IBM, not the CIA, it wasn't far from it. Her job was to oversee a network of covert operatives, pass on instructions from the Directorate of Operations, monitor their progress, and offer any necessary assistance. It was up to her to decide what "necessary" entailed. A covert operative's primary responsibility was to gather information. A supervisor's primary responsibility was to collect, collate, and forward that information to the appropriate parties. And yes, she had a quota to fill.

"I'm sorry," said Jimmy. "Really."

"Thank you," said Jane. "I'm not sure I believe it. Will was the indestructible one."

"What do you think happened?" asked Jimmy. "Or am I not allowed to ask?"

"Of course you're not allowed to ask," said Jane. "You're my body man. You're not cleared for this stuff."

"Forget I asked."

Jane patted him on the shoulder. "Chill," she said. "I was joking. I think I can trust you after all the shit we've pulled together."

"Bagram. Helmand. The Kush. Hard to believe it's been seven years."

"For you, maybe," said Jane. "I was on the last plane out. Now, *that* was a clusterfuck."

"Didn't everyone know they wouldn't fight?" asked Jimmy. "The Afghans, I mean."

"Define 'everyone.'" Jane looked out the window. Thinking about Afghanistan made her angry.

Jane Margaret McCall was thirty-one, divorced, no children, an "Agency widow," and proud of it. She was also a jock. Five-ten in her gym socks. A childhood spent on the playing field. Soccer, softball, field hockey. These days, it was rucking when she had the time. Stick a thirty-pound slab of iron in her rucksack, put on her boots, and hit the trail. She was never happier than when she was outside, preferably attacking a steep slope somewhere deep in the wilderness.

She'd joined the Agency straight out of Williams, where she'd hung around long enough to earn a master's degree in French literature and to realize that Flaubert didn't really float her boat. By chance, she saw an ad in the paper and applied. The CIA advertised. Go figure. At least, that's what she told others.

She'd spent the better part of her twenties, and now her thirties, flying in and out of Bagram Air Base. Her work mirrored the country's failed policies. First, she'd been attached to civilian-military teams, traveling from village to village in the care and protection of people like Jimmy Chen, trying to convince women to convince their husbands that they could trust the United States. It was a tall order.

Her next assignment was out of the embassy in Kabul, political risk analysis, interviewing players on every side—the provincial governors, the warlords like Haqqani, and the bad boys fronting for the Taliban—and trying to fashion a solution to bring them all to the peace table.

That didn't go well either.

Finally, she'd been stationed at Eagle Base, the CIA's secretive compound a few miles outside Kabul, selecting high-value targets for "night soldiers" like Jimmy Chen and his fellow SEALs to take out. Her work put her in mind of a slogan popular during the Vietnam War. "Join the army. Travel to foreign lands. Meet exotic people and kill them." Just substitute "CIA" for "army." It was the only job she'd performed to her superiors' complete satisfaction. She came out with a promotion, a desk on the fourth floor—one below the DDO, director of the Directorate of Operations—and a serious case of PTSD.

"Everyone in the Agency knew they wouldn't fight," she continued, answering Chen's question. "I'm pretty sure we spread the word. The problem was that by then, everyone had been lying for so long to so many people, no one believed what anyone had to say."

"Sounds about right," said Chen.

"There was no good solution," said Jane. "We just chose the worst of the bad ones. End of story." She stole a look at the speedometer. "Can't you make this thing go a little faster?"

"It's my ass if we get a speeding ticket."

"I'm thinking claiming Will's body is a priority."

"You don't have to pay the fines."

"On second thought," said Jane, "maybe you will make a decent supervisor."

Chen glanced over his shoulder. "So, what happened up there? You know, on the mountain."

"It was a crash meet. Will was running an agent. Marina Zhukova. There was more to their relationship, but that's strictly off the record."

"Yes, ma'am."

"She was bringing out some intel. A Russian op possibly involving the use of a WMD. Something went wrong."

"Why up there?"

"They met climbing a few years ago. Maybe it was their happy place."

"What happened to her?"

"Don't know. Her body hasn't turned up, and we can't ask the police."

Chen steered the Jeep off the highway and into the city. "For what it's worth," he said, "we liked having you cover our six over there."

"From a few hundred miles away," said Jane.

"You would have come if they'd let you."

"Damn straight, Jimmy. In a heartbeat."

"Your ops always panned out," said Chen. "The bad guys were where you promised. We never lost a man on one of your ops."

"You angling for a citation?"

Chen sneaked a look over his shoulder. "Always."

He turned down a side street, following signs to the hospital. "Watch out!" shouted Jane.

A blur fell through the air, just ahead of the car and to the left. It was a man. He landed on the pavement and rolled into the street, directly in front of them.

Chen pumped the brakes. The car lurched to a halt. Jane's laptop went airborne, as did what was left of her Americano. She threw up her hands in time to keep her face from slamming into the headrest, sparing herself a broken nose.

"Jesus," she said. "What the hell?"

She looked up. A grizzled old man with a beard that could have belonged to Robinson Crusoe stood in front of the car, his hands on the hood. The next moment, he was gone, sprinting across the street.

Yes, *sprinting*. Jane was astonished by his agility. Old men did not run like . . . well, *like that*. Knees high, arms pumping, shoulders pinned forward as if he were a cornerback closing in for the kill.

"You okay?" asked Chen.

"Think so," said Jane offhandedly. She was still locked on to the old guy. He was motoring. At the end of the block, he turned into an alley and disappeared. "Did you see—?"

A body landed on the hood of the Jeep. The noise was terrific. Chen shouted in surprise.

It was a man. He lay supine, arms splayed. Before Jane could wonder where he'd fallen from or what the hell had just happened, the man rolled off the hood. He was middle aged, fair, angular, dressed in a dark suit that she immediately recognized as quality.

The man stepped back, peering at them as if they were to blame. He looked directly at Jane.

And she looked at him. Jane's stomach dropped.

The man stumbled away from the car and ran off in the same direction as the old man. "Follow him," said Jane, rattled.

"Which one?" said Chen.

"Both of them!"

Chen put the car in gear and took off up the street. The man who moments ago had been a hood ornament ducked down the same alley as the old guy. Chen pulled the wheel right to follow, then slammed on his brakes. The alley was too narrow for the Jeep to enter.

It didn't matter. By then, the men were nowhere to be seen.

CHAPTER 15

Avenue Général Guisan, Sion

Ilya reached the end of the alley and bent double, catching his breath. His ribs hurt like hell. His head felt like he'd been struck with a baseball bat, and his knees were as stiff as oaks. No part of him, however, as wounded as his ego.

A dead man had bested him.

It didn't bother Ilya that he'd been outrun. It was the fact that Mac had gotten to Will ahead of him.

A dead man had bested him. It wasn't the first time.

He'd bested him when he stole Ava.

He'd bested him when he was chosen to lead Simba.

He'd bested him when he disappeared in Beirut. Killed by a car bomb. No body. Or one that was nearly impossible to identify.

And now here, today, in Sion, he'd bested him again. Not a dead man. Not any longer.

Ilya straightened up, wiping the sweat out of his eyes. He staggered forward, knowing that his life and everything about it had changed. He'd figure out what to do about it later. Right now, he had other concerns.

Like it or not, Ilya had to assume that the "old man" had found what Marina Zhukova had given to Will Dekker.

And so?

And so, Ilya had to get it back before Colonel Alexandra Zaitseva found out. "Mac," he shouted at the top of his lungs. "You sonuvabitch. You're alive!"

———

It was over.

Robbie Steinhardt stared into the mirror, hands clutching the porcelain sink. Sweat ran down his face, carving ugly, grayish tracks on his cheeks. An eyebrow hung askew. At some point, he'd lost a contact lens; one eye was blue, the other black. There was a scrape on his cheek that looked worse than it felt.

Thankfully, the public lavatory in Parc Général Guisan was empty. He couldn't let anyone see him like this. He looked like a madman. An *Amokläufer*, the Swiss called people like him, literally meaning someone running amok.

He recalled the Klaxon sounding inside the hospital. To his fevered mind, it had sounded like the alarm on a submarine. *Dive! Dive!* There were cameras all over the hospital. He wasn't worried about the police. He was worried about the Americans. About the Asian man with the neck of steel and the woman in the back seat. Once they got their hands on the video files and started zooming in and manipulating the pixels and fed the images into their proprietary facial-recognition software— software a hundred times more powerful than Clearview AI—they could identify anyone.

He turned on the faucet, splashed water over his face, and wiped away the makeup he applied every morning. It wasn't to make his skin appear brighter, healthier, but the opposite: to give it a wrinkled, leathery texture. He dabbed his cheek with a paper towel and dried his face.

It was over.

Eight years, two months, ten days. His exile had come to an unwanted, unexpected, and unceremonious conclusion.

Robbie removed the remaining contact lens and flicked it down the drain. More carefully, he peeled off the false eyebrows, sewn into his own, and tossed them into the trash.

He left the restroom and crossed the park.

Yes, he said to Ilya. You're right. I'm still alive. And I'm coming for you.

CHAPTER 16

Kantonsspital, Sion

She'd seen the body. The official from the coroner's office had made her look.

"Yes, it's Will Dekker," Jane McCall said, even as she kept her eyes half-closed. She'd signed the necessary paperwork to have the body transferred to US custody, wondering all the while why the present tense was used to address a dead man. What's a body without its soul? He *was* Will Dekker. He *was* twenty-nine years old. He *was* a good field officer. Not great.

Impossible to be great after so few years on the job. But good. Ambitious. Dependable. Loyal. She'd trusted no one more.

He was, on the other hand, a great climber. He'd conquered the Eigernordwand and the Dent Blanche and the Aiguille du Midi. He was not the type to fall from the summit of the Matterhorn. The Matterhorn, he'd once told her, was the easiest big peak for an experienced alpinist to summit and the hardest for a beginner.

Jane had known about the meet with Marina Zhukova, if vaguely. Will was that way. He kept things to himself until he was certain of the facts. He blamed this tendency to secrecy on his upbringing. There'd been too much deception and uncertainty during his childhood.

Still, she'd questioned the location. The Solvay Hut? Really? Wasn't that a little out of the way?

To which Will had answered that he deserved to have a little fun. His last words to her were "Don't worry."

So how had he fallen?

As importantly, where was *she*? Where was Marina Zhukova?

It was 4:00 p.m. From the morgue, they trooped down the corridor to the elevator bank next to the reception. There were four of them: Jane, Jimmy, the chief of hospital security, and a lieutenant from the *police municipale*. They were in the French-speaking part of Switzerland now, the boundary somewhere west of Sierre.

The lieutenant held the elevator for them to enter. *"Suivez-moi, s'il vous plaît."*

Jane spoke French and thanked him for his hospitality and professionalism. The officer nodded, and she noted the appreciation in his eye. An American who spoke a second language fluently was rare enough. One with good manners rarer still.

The elevator took them to the second floor belowground. Their destination was the hospital security office. Thirty-six monitors covered one wall. There was a map of the hospital floor by floor on another.

The man assigned to guard the morgue was waiting for them. He sat in a corner, head bowed, a compress held to his neck. When he glanced up, it appeared that he'd been crying. Embarrassment, thought Jane. Not pain.

"He was an old man," the guard said. "He had a stethoscope. I thought he was a doctor."

"No one's blaming you," said Jane. She held the bag holding Will's belongings beneath an arm. The Swiss authorities had compiled a list of all items removed from the body. Item number three was "One (1) iPhone (green)." The phone was not in the bag. Nor were any of the usual devices favored by Jane and her ilk to convey confidential information from one spot to another. No flash drives, thumb drives, documents of any size or shape, etc. etc. had been found on the body.

"Can we take a look?" she asked.

Silence as they watched footage of the "doctor" walk past the morgue, then return wearing a lab coat and gain entrance. Jane noted the way he kept his head inclined toward the floor, his face angled away from the camera. A man who knew he was being watched and did not wish to be identified. The "doctor" exited exactly three minutes and ten seconds later—noted by the time stamp flashing on the bottom of the screen—walked to the end of the corridor, threw open the exit, then turned and ran to an interior stairwell.

"I know him," said Jimmy Chen. "That's the first guy. The one who fell in front of the car."

Jane shot him a withering glance. Put a lid on it.

The chief of hospital security pointed to the monitor. "The second man also entered the morgue. It seems that they just missed each other."

Jane stepped closer to study the images of the second man who'd entered the morgue. He was blond, fit, well dressed. Time inside the morgue: less than fifteen seconds.

"Can you replay this?" asked Jane.

The chief of security rewound the tape.

Again, she watched the blond man enter the morgue, then leave seconds later, bolting down the hallway to the exit. He opened the door, looked outside—but only for a moment—then retraced his steps and entered the stairwell.

Conclusion: it was the "doctor" who stole the phone.

One more thing: Unlike the "doctor," who did his best to keep his face hidden, the second man made no such effort. At some point, prior to entering the stairwell, he stopped and looked directly into the camera. He might as well have been sitting for a passport photo.

It was the man who'd fallen onto the hood of their car, whose eyes she'd met and recognized faster than she'd ever have thought possible. She could no longer tell herself otherwise. It was Ilya. The last of the great traitors, after Hanssen and Ames and Pollard.

Of course the Russians wanted what Will had on his person. The question was, Who was the old man? Why had he taken Will's phone? And why was Ilya chasing him?

"Jesus Christ," said Jane under her breath. Chen began to speak, then apparently thought better of it.

Jane turned her attention to the chief of security. "Anything more?"

"Just this," he said. "Fifth floor. Corridor C. It was taken after the alarm was sounded."

A long shot of a broad hallway. The "doctor," once again without his lab coat, opened a window, stuck his head out, looked around, then climbed onto the ledge.

A minute later, the blond man did the same. "Where," asked the chief of security, "did they go?"

CHAPTER 17

Moscow Oblast, Russia

"Bring him in," said Dr. Leonid Mirin to his assistant.

"Who is he?" inquired Colonel Alexandra Zaitseva. "A Ukrainian?"

"Hardly," said Mirin. He was a short, bluff man in a lab coat and bow tie, seventy, with a vain man's perfectly trimmed beard and fashionable Italian designer eyeglasses. "One of our own. A deserter. After all, we wouldn't want to be accused of war crimes."

"Certainly not," said Zaitseva, sternly. She did not appreciate Mirin's sense of humor.

The two stood inside the laboratory of the Borodin Research Institute, situated deep in a birch forest on the shores of a scenic lake seventy miles northeast of Moscow. The institute was named for Alexander Borodin—the Alexander Borodin—who considered himself first and foremost a doctor and chemist, and only then, a composer. *Prince Igor*, his operatic masterpiece, paled in comparison to his preparation of methyl bromide from silver acetate.

Like Borodin, the institute harbored competing natures. Research was only part of its mandate. The other, and far more secretive, one involved the manufacture of the world's deadliest chemical weapons. Sarin, VX, Novichok, among others. And today, something new and even more lethal.

The laboratory was a modern, shiny, well-scrubbed space. Gray floors, gray ceilings, gray work surfaces, all lit by halogen bulbs. Zaitseva's attention was not on the lab or the profusion of sophisticated equipment but on the room adjacent to them and separated by a glass wall. In contrast to the lab, the room was sparsely furnished with only a chair and a table.

"You people," said Mirin, irritably. "Always in a hurry."

You people meaning *spies.*

"The nature of our work," said Zaitseva. "We are forced to be nimble."

"Not a word we're familiar with," said Mirin. "Neither is 'reckless.'"

Zaitseva refused to be baited. Marina Zhukova's betrayal had left her no choice but to accelerate the timetable for Hercules. For the moment, she needed his help. She placed a hand on Mirin's arm. "I appreciate you meeting our new timetable."

"It was difficult, but . . ." Mirin offered a shrug and an eye for her bosom. "For you."

"Thank you again, Leonid." Zaitseva smiled. There was a reason she had not worn her uniform.

"We are also anxious to see the fruit of our efforts," said Mirin, mollified. "It's about time someone puts our expertise to advantage. What's the use of having a fast car and never taking it out for a drive?"

"I couldn't agree more," said Zaitseva. To herself, she added: But first, we shall see about your expertise.

Alexandra Maria Zaitseva was born to Ivan and Mariana Zaitseva, peasants from Lvov. More importantly, as concerned her destiny, she was the granddaughter of a hero of the Soviet Union, her nation's highest military honor. The recipient was not her grandfather but her grandmother and namesake, Alexandra Maria Zaitseva, known to history as the "Angel of Stalingrad."

In the third year of World War II, 1942, one year after the launch of Barbarossa, the invasion of Russia, Nazi Germany led by Adolf

Hitler had brought the full fury of his military to bear on the city of Stalingrad, an industrial and transport hub of three million souls on the banks of the Volga River. For nine months, the battle raged. Hundreds of thousands of lives were lost on both sides. No combat was so brutal or so consequential. If Stalingrad fell, so, too, would Mother Russia.

Into this battle came Alexandra Maria Zaitseva, nineteen years old, five feet tall, an apprentice midwife and expert markswoman. As a child, she'd accompanied her father, a hunter, on weekend treks to fill the family pot. Mostly they shot hares but occasionally deer and antelope. He taught her all he knew.

A volunteer, she arrived on the front line with her father's rifle and two weeks' training. No attention, however, was paid to her skills as a markswoman. Alexandra was put into the line as a member of the infantry, and for months she engaged in the day-to-day street fighting that made Stalingrad the bloodiest battle of the war. It was her own initiative that brought her talent to her superiors' attention.

For weeks, a German sniper had been shooting the officers in her sector, the Piotrov neighborhood of Stalingrad. One after another was killed. No one had been able to spot the sniper, let alone kill him. So devilish was his marksmanship that he was given the nickname "Satan."

Alexandra decided to take the job upon herself. Armed only with her father's rifle—no scope, no binoculars, no spotter to help her—she ventured alone into enemy-held territory and, like a dormouse, burrowed into the collapsed ruins of the embattled city. Day after day, she moved from one hiding place to another, lying motionless beneath the rubble. Watching.

Waiting.

Finally, she spotted him.

At first, it was a random glimmer. A shaft of sunlight refracting off glass. Blessed with perfect eyesight, Alexandra discerned movement inside a ruined flour factory one hundred meters away. A hint of field gray. A flash of boot leather. Slowly, patiently, she brought her rifle to bear, inching the iron barrel through a gap in the rubble, balancing it on a wooden spar. She laid her cheek on its stock and placed the sight on a very small square of daylight.

He was there. It was not a question of seeing him, but of instinct.

She did not move for an hour, then two. Not a muscle. For a while, she thought herself mistaken. He wasn't there. Her imagination was acting up, playing tricks on her. Still, she waited, as mute and immovable as the mountain of shattered stone that sheltered her.

Then she saw it.

A patch of field gray. Boot leather. A uniform. It was him. It was "Satan."

At that moment, she moved. Had she adjusted her boots? Tilted her head? She never knew.

Across a distance of one hundred meters, she saw the barrel of a rifle poke through the debris, the sun's rays refracting off a scope. The rifle was aimed at her.

But Alexandra was ready. Her rifle remained in place. The sight remained fixed. She did not panic. With preternatural calm, she squeezed the trigger as her father had taught her. *"Slowly, Sasha, slowly. As if you are giving your babushka a hug."*

She saw the bullet hit before she heard the report. A puff of smoke appeared. In fact, her target's uniform was ever so slightly singed by the white-hot round. "Satan" rolled down the slope of rubble, his Iron Cross visible at his neck. She fired a second time to make sure that he was dead.

It was Alexandra's first kill as a sniper.

Months later, on the day General Paulus offered his surrender to Marshal Rokossovsky, January 31, 1943, Alexandra recorded her last kill. Two hundred forty-one German soldiers dead.

Now, eighty years later, Russia was again at war. Again, the attack came from the West.

From Nazis and socialists and degenerate forces bankrolled by amoral capitalists hell bent on spreading their devil's lifestyle to the Rodina. Drugs, sodomy, homosexuality, wild Negroid wailings.

It was Colonel Alexandra Zaitseva's turn to step up. To place herself in the path of seemingly superior forces. It was her turn to repay the sacrifices of her blood relatives and to earn her place in the pantheon of Russian heroes.

———

The door to the adjacent room opened. Two uniformed soldiers, members of the elite Rostov engineering division, escorted a lone man into the room. The man was in his twenties, short and slight, with dark eyes and a week's stubble, his head shaved. He wore the black-and-white-striped uniform of the Russian prison system. Strangely, he did not appear to be frightened. If anything, he appeared to be perfectly calm. As he sat, he smiled, lifting a hand in greeting, pulling the chair to the table, and adopting the prize pupil's perfect posture.

"What did you tell him?" asked Zaitseva.

"Before the conflict he was a student at Moscow State University," explained Professor Mirin. "A PhD candidate in molecular biology. He thinks this is a job interview. If he can convince us of his skills, he will be released from prison."

"Can he see us?"

"Why not?" said Leonid Mirin. "This isn't a police station. But hear us? No." He punched a button to activate the intercom. "Mr. Shvets, please fill out the questionnaire in front of you. Take your time."

The prisoner, Shvets, slid the papers toward himself and picked up the pen. Before starting, he glanced over his shoulders. The guards had left the room. More secure now, he gave his attention to the form.

"And you were able to meet our request?" Zaitseva asked.

"Forty gallons," said Mirin. "We divided the agent into two containers. Easier to carry that way. May I ask the target?"

"An urban conglomeration," said Zaitseva.

"Population?"

"Greater than five million."

"A large number," said Mirin, eyes widening.

"You said it would be enough."

"My God, Colonel, how many do you wish to kill?"

Zaitseva's answer was a smile to rival the Cheshire Cat's. A lot, said her smile. As many as possible.

The agent was called Zeryx. Mirin described it as "a little sarin, a little VX, and a little something even nastier." With the crucial assistance of Dr. Ashok Mehta, it had been weaponized for use against the enemy of their choosing.

"The secret," said Mirin, standing much too close to her, "is to add it to the water supply rapidly. All at once. Let it diffuse over time. Peak efficacity is in the first twenty minutes."

Twenty minutes will be more than sufficient, thought Zaitseva. The target is not a city of five million but a city of twelve million.

"I promise that you will hear about it on the news."

"A success, for once," said Mirin. "The people will be surprised."

"For both of us," added Zaitseva, the threat cloaked in velvet. Failure, too, would be shared.

Mirin drew his assistant aside and whispered urgently in her ear, something about double-checking that the cameras were turned on. Zaitseva searched for them, without success.

"In the power outlet and one of the halogens," said Mirin. "We try to be discreet." Still, Zaitseva couldn't find them.

"Finished," announced Shvets, holding up the questionnaire like a victory banner.

"Thank you," said Leonid Mirin. "Please relax. Have some water."

Shvets placed the papers in front of him. He did not pick up the glass and take a drink. He sat in his chair, hands clasped. To Zaitseva's eye, he might have been a statue.

"You should have offered him some herring," she said.

"Why not caviar?" retorted Mirin. "With minced onion. Chopped egg whites. Give away our hand entirely." He cleared his throat. "Patience, Colonel."

A minute passed. Mirin stuffed his hands in the pockets of his coat, shifting his weight from foot to foot. Zaitseva, by contrast, didn't move a muscle. She kept her eyes on the prisoner, arms crossed over her chest, if only to keep the lecherous chemist from ogling her.

It had been her idea to visit the institute. She was an intelligence officer, which meant she was trained to be suspicious. She was a Russian, which meant it was in her blood to expect the worst. And she was a woman, which meant she trusted no one. Alexandra Zaitseva did not plan to go into battle without the utmost assurance that her armory was intact and functioning properly. On a more private and lurid note, she wanted to see how the nerve agent worked.

"Maybe you should reconsider the caviar," suggested Zaitseva.

Mirin knew when he was beaten. "Maybe you are right, Colonel."

They shared a chuckle. Oddly, neither saw Shvets take a drink of water. It was the cough that drew their attention back to him.

Shvets's mouth stood open. He still held the glass, and for a moment it appeared as if he wanted to take another sip. He coughed a second time. The cords in his neck became pronounced. His eyes were opened wide. His eyeballs seemed to expand, forcing themselves out of their sockets.

The glass exploded as his hand involuntarily crushed it. He shot to his feet and began to tremble, the trembling amplifying into a grand mal seizure. Milky, aerated froth spilled out of his mouth. A terrible moan issued from his throat.

Mirin leaned closer. "Ten seconds from—"

"Shut up," said Zaitseva, transfixed.

The prisoner fell to the floor, writhing. His arms flew out from his sides. His head arced backward. His jaw was agape, spasming muscles forcing it wider than it ever had been. A plume of vomit erupted from his mouth, a single violent rush.

Then he was still.

For a moment, neither spoke. It did not seem that such frenzied activity could have come to such a sudden, final halt. Zaitseva was disgusted and exhilarated in equal measure. It worked. Oh yes, it worked.

"As I was saying," continued Mirin, clearing his throat. "Ten seconds from ingestion to death."

"How much did you put in?" asked Zaitseva.

"Excuse me?"

"How much of the VX solution? The Zeryx?"

"Five drops," said Leonid Mirin.

"And how many drops are in forty gallons?"

"Millions."

CHAPTER 18

Zinal

Robbie was moving fast.

The drive to Zinal passed in a blur, ninety kilometers in the blink of an eye, or more accurately, forty minutes by the Porsche's analog clock. It was risky to drive a stolen car, but he had no choice. He was no longer an escapee or an exile. He had reported back to the real world. He was an operator in full operational mode.

It was a new man who parked the Porsche up a logging road a kilometer from his chalet, or rather, the old one—meaning his former self, a field officer with twenty years' experience, the last ten running dirty operations with the Special Activities Center and then, dirtier still, pioneering the Rovers.

It was this man who dashed through the forest, leaping over fallen logs and dodging tree stumps. He pulled up at the edge of his property. Dusk was falling. It had been raining, and water dripped from the branches above him. He pressed himself against a pine, keeping still. There was no possibility that anyone could be watching his home, not yet. But that's what you always thought until you were proven wrong, and then it was too late.

He waited another ten minutes to be safe. The sun dipped below the Rothorn. Shadows grew longer. The smell of wood fire filled his nostrils. He circled the house once more, then broke from the forest, jogging to the back door. A pin light glowed green. He unlocked the door, hit the fob, and let himself in. It was 6:00 p.m.

Somewhere, Ilya was trying to find him.

The consulate in Geneva was closest, but it was little more than an administrative office. He'd have gone to the embassy in Bern. If Robbie recalled correctly, the Russians had a decent setup—an entire ELINT room with trained staff who would only have gotten better over the years. If the Russians were anything like the Agency, they were tied in to all of Switzerland's domestic surveillance systems. Everyone hacked everyone else. That's just how it went. Cybersecurity was a perpetual rearguard action. You were constantly thwarting one attack after another. There was no question of winning, just battling to maintain the status quo ante.

Robbie ran upstairs and turned on the shower. He allowed the water to get hot, stripped, and climbed beneath the jets. He found his special shampoo and massaged a large dollop into his scalp, waiting a minute before rinsing. As the water rushed from his head, he imagined he could see the gray going with it. Take off the parka, the sweater, and the T-shirt, and behold, he was a powerfully built man. Not a sixty-year-old or a seventy-year-old, but an athletic fifty-six-year-old male in peak condition. His shoulders were broad, the heads of his deltoids rounded, well defined. His lats cut an elevated ridge along his rib cage. His biceps were the size of softballs, and he could still see his abs, though, he admitted, that might be wishful thinking.

On his best day, he could knock out twenty pull-ups. Last month, angry at the world and inspired by a documentary he'd seen about CrossFit, he'd fired off one thousand push-ups in ninety minutes. The secret was to only do four reps at a time.

"USMC" was tattooed on one shoulder, with an Army Ranger tab below it, because marines weren't allowed to wear insignia from other services on their uniforms and Ranger school was a beast. A dagger decorated his other shoulder, the words "Dulce et Decorum Est" below it. Blood dripping from the dagger accented the gothic script. He'd left off the words that completed the verse: "Pro Patria Mori." How sweet and fitting it is to die for one's country.

At various points along the line, he'd taken two bullets. One, from a handgun at close range, had passed directly through him, nicking his large intestine and obliterating a kidney. The second was from an automatic weapon, probably an AK-47, though he hadn't been able to ask the shooter. (It was Syria, and he was fairly certain a Hellfire missile from a friendly Black Hawk had taken him out shortly afterward.) The bullet had entered his hip, nicked his pelvis, then tumbled diagonally upward through his torso, exiting below his left arm. That one had hurt and had cost him ten days in Bumrungrad International Hospital in Bangkok, which was where scrubbed agents went to get better. "Scrubbed" meaning agents whose identities had been meticulously erased from the internet and who couldn't be seen in American military hospitals.

"Dad was in a car accident" was the line he'd fed his kids upon his return home. At the time, he hadn't seen a reason for them not to believe it. When Will spied the wounds, he'd asked in horror, *"What happened? Did the steering wheel go through you?"*

Robbie turned the shower to cold. Two minutes at fifty degrees Fahrenheit. The water turned to needles. He concentrated on his breathing. The pain dissipated after a while. He relaxed. Maybe he enjoyed it.

He turned off the water and toweled dry.

A look at himself in the mirror. "So long, you old bastard. Good friggin' riddance."

He started with the beard, electric clippers trimming it close to the skin. Then, he lathered his cheeks and neck with soap and shaved it off entirely. There was a scar on his jaw that resembled claw marks, courtesy of an al-Qaeda hothead who was pretty good with a blade. The rest of his face looked the same—jaw solid enough, flesh still hugging bone—but so pale it was almost blue.

He dug out a pair of scissors and went to work on his hair. He was no stylist. Short was the only option. He came out looking like a marine on graduation day from Basic.

Robbie dropped the scissors and sized up the stranger in the mirror staring back at him.

Black hair cut to the scalp, a little gray at the temples. His own gray. Taut skin. Blue eyes as steady as ever. A moment to get used to it. He'd just gotten twenty years of his life back.

He checked his watch. Six forty-five p.m. Somewhere, Ilya was looking for him.

Robbie dressed in record time. Jeans, T-shirt, sweater. Back to the bathroom to load up his shaving kit. Toothbrush, toothpaste, razor, brush. And finally, a few goodies from the bad old days. A vial of Benzedrine, a.k.a. bennies, a.k.a. go pills. A second vial chock full of Percocet and OxyContin—hillbilly heroin—for those times when the job demands you give it just that little extra. He checked the expiration date. A grimace. He hoped the painkillers hadn't aged as poorly as his cologne.

Downstairs.

A door in the kitchen led to the cellar. It was the only door in the house he kept locked. He rummaged in the cutlery drawer, scowling as he dug the key out from beneath the butter knives. He unlocked the door and turned on the lights. A flight of creaky wooden stairs descended to a dim, low-ceilinged space, colder by five degrees, redolent of damp earth and cement. Crates of beer, fresh and empties, stood against one wall. There was a washer and a dryer, and a clothesline just in case. And there, looking lonely, an empty homemade rack meant to hold the vintage wines he'd promised to collect one day.

Across the room was a massive steel door, seven feet by seven feet, fourteen inches thick, built into a concrete wall and held open by a sturdy iron latch. On the wall beside it was an air ventilation system complete with an antigas filter. It was his home's *Schutzbunker*, or air-raid bunker. The name was a polite euphemism, a less frightening way of saying "fallout shelter."

Sometime at the height of the Cold War, Swiss parliamentarians had decided that it would be a good idea for homes to include a room on the ground floor, or preferably beneath it, where a family could gather in case of nuclear attack. Switzerland might not rank high on anyone's list of enemies, but its neighbors to the north, west, and south—Germany, France, and Italy—did, and boasted many plum targets, several within spitting distance of the border: Milan, Munich, and Lyon, to name three.

Robbie hit the light switch, lowering his head as he stepped over the threshold. The bunker was a single room, concrete walls painted white, measuring twenty feet by thirty. Not one to waste space, he'd turned it into a kind of private lair—part workshop, part man cave, part library. It was the only room in the chalet that gave away its occupant's true identity. There was a Pearl Jam poster and one of Royal Robbins making his first assault on El Capitan. Another of soldiers in fatigues, faces blacked up, carrying a rubber raiding boat. THE FEW, THE PROUD, THE MARINES. Hell, yes. His Sony boom box sat on the floor next to a stack of his favorite paperbacks. Only the classics: Deighton, Forsyth, and Clancy.

The workshop took up the right half of the room. Bench, table, tools hanging on the pegboard wall. Over the years, he'd built most of the furniture in the house. His first efforts were . . . well, first efforts, and ended up providing most of his kindling over the course of a winter. Over time, his skills grew. The desk in his study, his dresser, the dining table and chairs—all came from his own hands.

A vice on the worktable held a German Sauer 202 hunting rifle. He'd attached a Leupold Mark 8 scope. Ostensibly, the rifle was for hunting springbok and other high mountain sheep. In fact, he'd given up hunting long ago. These days he put the rifle to more benign use. After downing a few beers, and maybe a few kirsches to go with them, he'd come to the cellar—murder on his mind—put the rifle to his shoulder, and pretend to sight in on a certain man with angular features and blond hair worn too long. Robbie might spot him in a city, the countryside, or maybe a back alley in Beirut. Crosshairs squarely in the middle of Ilya's smug face, he'd ever so slowly depress the trigger. *Bang!* To date, he'd yet to miss.

Robbie's desk was pressed into a far corner. He dropped into his chair and placed Will's phone in front of him. He turned it on. Nothing happened. He unwound a paper clip and used it to free the SIM card. He snapped the card into a smart card reader attached to his laptop. Lines of code filled the screen, marching upward at ever-increasing speed. It was all Greek to him.

Hopeless.

He shut off the laptop and replaced the SIM card in the phone.

He had an idea who might be able to help him. It was a crazy idea. But in the course of a day, his world had gone crazy too. There was no more right side up. There was only sideways.

He leaned to his left and freed the bottom drawer. It had been closed for so long he needed to give it an unceremonious tug that nearly dislocated his shoulder.

Reminiscing is verboten.

No longer, buddy. Reminiscing may save your ass.

He dug out his old address book, a high school graduation present. His parents had started it for him, writing in the names and contact information of family and close friends. He'd kept it up, adding new and old acquaintances. At some point—post-9/11 and pre-iPhone—it had assumed a kind of hallowed status. He decided he didn't trust the digital domain with his most private information. He knew firsthand how vulnerable even the most secure files had become. Passwords, encryption, two-step verification; all of it was window dressing. Potemkin protection. If someone wanted something badly enough, they'd find a way to get it.

And so, he'd confided her information to the address book. For his eyes only. He opened it to the letter *A* for Attal. Seeing the name sent a painful shiver down his spine. What might have been. Country code 972 for Israel. City code 3 for Tel Aviv. 1251 Beit Eshel Street. A tiny apartment overlooking the old town of Jaffa. The Clock Tower. The Christian church. And beyond it, the sea. The apartment sat above an Arab café, the smell of coffee and pastry wafting up at all hours. The bed sagged, but in just the right way at just the right moment.

Attal, Ava. He didn't need to check the number. After all this time, he still knew it by heart.

He grabbed his navy kit bag and freed the drawstring, yanking open the mouth. He spun in his chair and dialed in the combination of his gun locker, which resembled an old stand-alone steel safe. He kept a half dozen weapons inside. He pushed aside the Uzi and removed his Glock 19. Noise suppressor. Three magazines. For good measure, he grabbed a box of bullets. Jacketed hollow points. Man-killers.

He threw everything into the kit bag, then rolled his chair away from the desk. He got to his knees and peeled back the carpet. He punched a six-digit combination into the floor safe, then pressed his thumb to the biometric scanner. The Bank Steinhardt. He pulled out packets of currency at random. Three times ten thousand Swiss francs. Three times ten thousand euros. Three times ten thousand dollars. Ninety grand total, however you wanted to call it. The money went into the kit bag.

A last look. Plenty left for an *even rainier* day.

A leather dossier leaned against a wall of the safe. He opened it flat on the desk. Inside was a selection of passports. Some were even real. US diplomatic passport? No. German? Sure. Canadian? Always a safe bet.

He spotted the envelope tucked inside a fold. He dumped the contents onto the desk. Identifications, government and otherwise. United States Armed Forces. US Department of State. Commonwealth of Virginia driver's license. All were authentic, if not in chronological order. Even one from high school.

All bore the same name: Mackenzie David Dekker.

He selected the most recent ID. It was nine years old, but the man in the black-and-white photo looked remarkably like the one he'd seen in the mirror a few minutes ago.

"Mackenzie David Dekker." He spoke his name aloud. The act made him wince, as if he were ripping the bandage off a wound.

Mackenzie David Dekker. Father of William Andrew Dekker. There. Already better.

Part of the trick was forgetting the past. Not just the last few years. Or the time spent serving his country—the time that had gotten him into this mess—but all of it. Easier said than done. A person, he'd learned during his alpine exile, was defined by the sum of his memories. As long as the memories existed, so did he. It turned out that Mac cherished all his memories. Good and bad. Sweet and bittersweet. The triumphs and failures. Births and deaths.

He rummaged through the pile of identifications. His mind drifted back to past days.

Sights, sounds, emotions.

Finally, relief. He no longer needed to fight them.

Somewhere he was a nine-year-old riding horses on the family farm in the rolling hills outside Harpers Ferry. A Virginia gentleman in the making. His favorite was Apache, an Appaloosa pony, as gentle as he was swift. As far as he could remember, his first real friend.

Somewhere he was a ten-year-old finding his father asleep in a horse stall, a bottle of bourbon in one hand, his .45 Colt Combat Commander in the other. It was the sidearm his father had carried into combat at Khe Sanh and other places Mac couldn't pronounce.

A cold winter's night. Mac covered him with his rain slicker and watched him shiver and shudder and call out. Part of him still in Vietnam.

Somewhere he was a fourteen-year-old joyriding in his father's Ford pickup, two of his buddies up front, four more riding in the flatbed. The first day of summer vacation. FM radio blaring full blast. All of them hollering for all they were worth. Good times ahead . . . until he'd lost it going round a bend, skidded off the road, and blown two tires. By some miracle, no one was hurt. No one, that is, except Mac, who got twenty lashes with the black belt when his father found out.

The next night he took the pickup out again. So there, Dad.

Somewhere he was a seventeen-year-old senior skipping high school graduation to go rock climbing in Georgia. His first taste of freedom. His first experience with a woman.

Skinny-dipping in the Chattahoochee River. Sipping wine coolers. Sleeping with a naked woman in his arms. So this was being a man.

Somewhere he was a nineteen-year-old marine PFC, fresh out of boot camp at Parris Island, dressed in his olive Class A's, granted emergency leave to serve as a pallbearer at his father's funeral. One night his daddy hadn't fallen asleep in the stalls. Maybe he hadn't drunk enough bourbon. Maybe too much. The war had claimed another casualty. Captain Montague Mackenzie Dekker. "Monte." The last marine killed at Khe Sanh.

It was an open casket. His father had requested to be buried in his dress blues with his medals. Silver Star. Distinguished Service Cross. Purple Heart with three bars. A hero.

Mac woke from his reverie. Suddenly he realized why Will had followed in his footsteps.

Because Mac had done the same.

He gathered up the IDs and slipped them back into the envelope. He kept one for old times' sake. Red-and-white-laminated plastic. The size of a credit card. The picture showed a young man with shaggy hair, corduroy jacket, cheap necktie. *Is that a mustache?* Expiration: 2002. And across the top, the name of his employer. "Central Intelligence Agency."

Time to go back to work.

———

One more thing.

A stop in his study before leaving. Mac turned on a light and sat at his desk. He held his phone with one hand, extending his arm. Time for his first official selfie. Why not make it a video?

Mac cleared his throat and pressed his thumb against the glowing red button. A moment for the sonuvabitch to get a good look at him. "Enjoying yourself?" he began.

Thirty seconds later, he ended the recording. He needed a minute or two to fix things just right, then he was out the door. He hit the fob, locking the door, then turned and ran straight into a woman.

"Irene," he said, more surprised than she was.

Irene Bolliger stood as if nailed to the ground. She looked him up and down, and he could see her mind trying to piece things together. *This man looks like Robbie Steinhardt, or maybe like Robbie used to look. He sounds like him. But this man is much younger, and dare she say it, vitally attractive.*

"Sorry I missed the dance," said Mac.

Still, Irene Bolliger made no sound, her eyes locked on his.

He kissed her politely on both cheeks. There was no time to explain. "Goodbye, Irene."

He stepped to one side to walk around her. In that instant, Irene Bolliger took his face in her hands and kissed him. Not politely on both cheeks. It was the other kind of kiss. Square on the lips and held for a second too long.

Afterward, Mac drew a breath. He retreated a step, then made his way past the fence and onward to the main road.

Irene Bolliger watched him leave, feeling quite unlike herself. Whoever the man was, she hoped he returned.

Reluctantly, she lifted her hand in farewell. "That's not all you missed," she said.

CHAPTER 19

Bern

Ilya Ivashka was searching for Mac Dekker.

He stood at the shoulder of an infosec (information security) specialist in the embassy's operations center, two floors belowground. It was a smaller room than he remembered. Desks against three walls, monitors all over the place, a raft of fluorescent lights hanging from the ceiling. Terrible ventilation and the pungent reminder that Russians needed to take more showers. It was nearly 8:00 p.m. A skeleton crew remained on duty.

"Traffic cams," ordered Ilya.

"Where?" The infosec specialist was a junior SVR officer on his first posting abroad. Like all the new recruits, he was some kind of computer genius, and he looked the part. All knees and elbows and a teenager's blotchy complexion. His name was Mikhail, but he'd informed Ilya that he preferred Mike.

"Here," said Ilya. "Switzerland."

"What city?" demanded Mike.

"Zermatt," said Ilya. "To start with."

According to Detective Berner of the Zürich police, the Americans had visited the police station there to inquire about Will Dekker. It made sense that Mac would begin at the same spot. Mac, who was alive.

"No cars there," said Mike.

"Even better," said Ilya. "Show me the train station."

Silence. A nervous rustle and adjusting of the shoulders. "I can't execute an illegal tap without authorization," said Mike.

"What do you mean 'without authorization'? I'm here."

"From a superior . . . um, I'm sorry."

Ilya crouched so he could look Mike in the eye. It was clear he had no clue who Ilya was.

Alas, fame was fleeting. Lesson learned, though it caused a problem. Authorization came from the head of station, who would note the request and report it to SVR headquarters in Yasenevo. Anything with Ilya's name on it would be flagged and forwarded to Colonel Zaitseva. He couldn't have that.

"Humor me," said Ilya. "No one's around. I'm sure you have a line already in place." Meaning the Swiss Federal Railways networks had been hacked long ago and could be accessed with the touch of a key.

"Of course we do," said Mike. "We own the Swiss."

"Well, then."

"You're asking me to disobey protocol. I can't do that. I need authorization."

"You want authorization?"

Mike nodded.

"Okay then," said Ilya. "You have it."

"Really? I do?"

Ilya yanked his pistol from his waistband and pressed the barrel against Mike's forehead. "Right here," he said, all business. "Signed by Comrade Glock-ski."

Mike nodded. "Zermatt."

"This morning," said Ilya. "Shall we begin with all trains arriving between eight and eleven?"

Ilya pulled up a chair as Mike went to work. In moments, the monitors above his desk had come to life with images of passengers disembarking from the red cars of the Zermatt Glacier Express. A chyron with the time stamp ran across the bottom of the screen. Several times Ilya ordered Mike to freeze the images so he could study a face or to rewind on the chance that he'd missed something.

"Stop," said Ilya, rising from his chair. There was Mac Dekker, alighting from a train that had arrived at 9:43 a.m., his face partially hidden beneath a red ski cap and sunglasses. "Zoom in. That's the one."

"You're certain?"

Ilya said he was. "What train is it?"

"The 8:58 from Visp," said Mike.

"Check Visp station. Find where he transferred from."

"But—"

Ilya tapped the barrel of the pistol against Mike's cheek. "Do I need to introduce you to Comrade Kalashnikov?"

Mike drew a square around Mac's face, copied the image, and entered it into an AI-assisted software program that compared Mac's face against those recorded by all surveillance cameras in Visp station. "Between?"

"8:20 and 8:53," said Ilya. Mike entered the parameters.

"Got him," said Mike, less than sixty seconds later. "Arrived in Visp on a local train with stops in Sierre, Sion, Martigny."

There on the screen was Mac Dekker disembarking from a train in Visp station at 8:49 a.m. "What station shall I check next?" asked Mike.

Ilya patted him on the shoulder. Finally, he was getting with the program. "None of them."

"Pardon me?"

Ilya pointed at the image of Mac Dekker. "Zoom in if you can."

Mike rewound the feed. Zooming in required that the software enhance the pixels to avoid blurring. The moment the older man entered the frame, Mike froze the image and dragged it to a photo enhancement file, then cropped the image until the man occupied the entire frame.

"Closer," said Ilya, his nose nearly touching the screen. Mike continued zooming in.

"There." Ilya pointed to a name tag attached to Mac's rucksack. "You have one minute to give me that name."

Mike needed only fifteen seconds. "Robert Steinhardt," he said. "Poststrasse 7, Zinal."

CHAPTER 20

US embassy, Bern

"It was a simple debrief," Jane began. "Will wanted it off the books."

"Off *my* books," said Cal Thorpe, CIA station chief, Switzerland.

"She was his agent," said Jane. "His call."

"My country," said Thorpe. "My call."

Eleven p.m. A SCIF on the top floor of the embassy. Jane, Jimmy Chen, and Calvin McWhorter Thorpe sat around the conference table, fluorescent lights flickering overhead, diet sodas, chips, and candy bars lying around for nourishment. It was just like Langley.

Thorpe perused the dossier Jane had prepared, occasionally taking a sip of coffee from his mug, the emblem of his Ivy League law school emblazoned on the side. "Marina Alexandrovna Zhukova," he said, "Directorate Six. Counterintelligence. Captain. She was his agent?"

"For three years," said Jane.

"Ah," said Thorpe. "His agent."

Jane kept quiet. She'd erred. And she'd done it with premeditation. She'd okayed a meet on a superior's territory, and she hadn't told him. Had she broken any rules? Not officially. There was no codicil stipulating that she had to tell Thorpe about the meet. But unofficially? Oh yeah. It just wasn't done. Not these days. Not after all the seminars on sharing and inclusion and stovepiping. The US Intelligence

Community was one big, happy, and cooperative family. The Agency was a turf-free zone.

"This was their first meet on Swiss soil," said Jane.

"I'm feeling so much better." A flash of Thorpe's hazel eyes above his glasses. A glimpse of his shark's smile.

Cal Thorpe, forty-seven years old, Morehouse College, Yale Law, twenty years plus with the Agency, tight with the deputy director, a career in high gear. What had she been thinking?

Thorpe had spent a few years on Wall Street straight out of law school before getting religion and entering government service. He still had the Wall Street look. Tailored suits. Hermès ties. Belgian loafers. Family money, and he didn't bother hiding it. He was tall and graceful, always moving a half step slower than everyone else. The world could wait for Calvin Thorpe. His nickname back at Langley was "Silk." He approved.

Switzerland was his first posting overseas. He'd built his career as a desk man. Legal affairs. He was the one who wrote the briefs exculpating the Agency's actions. "The insertion of American personnel on Syrian soil did not break any international laws because . . ." or "Agent XYZ's actions against enemy combatants was not in contravention of United Nations code XYZ because . . ." Jane wasn't sure how he'd managed to jump to her side of the fence, but jump he did, and with both feet.

She went on: "Zhukova came to him last month about an op named Hercules. Something the czarists in Yasenevo cooked up. The ones who thought Ukraine was a good idea. Bare bones, it involved a new bioweapon. She was bringing out proof."

"In development?" asked Thorpe.

"Completed," said Jane. "Pending deployment."

"Target?"

"Unknown."

"Timing?"

"Unknown."

Thorpe took off his eyeglasses and fixed her with a damning stare. "A Russian bioweapon capable of killing thousands. An op called *Hercules*. A crash meet in a neutral country so a captain in the SVR could bring her controller proof. Yes, I see. Just the kind of thing to keep to yourself."

Jane chose her next words carefully. "Will has always been wary about who he can trust . . . given past history."

"Given past history," said Thorpe, "it seems that he should be pretty damn forthcoming. One wouldn't want to infer anything . . . *given past history*."

"No, sir," said Jane.

Thorpe shook his head as if she were quite possibly the dimmest bulb on the planet. He replaced his glasses. "Continue."

"Zhukova believed that if we knew about it—about Hercules—the Russians couldn't use it."

"No deniability," said Thorpe.

"Exactly."

"So, she sets a meet halfway up a four-thousand-meter mountain?"

Chen spoke up. "She was a climber. It's how they met. Cover."

Jane nodded. "Something didn't go as planned. Swiss police received reports of gunfire in the area."

"On the Matterhorn? Who reported it?"

"Villagers," said Chen. "Locals. Sound travels a long way in the mountains."

"From our resident climbing expert," said Thorpe.

"Four hops downrange in the Khyber Pass," retorted Chen, cheeks flushing. "Ought to count for something."

Thorne squared his shoulders and sat up. "I'm sorry, Mr. Chen, if I disparaged your service. It was not my intention."

Chen smiled, lips pressed against his teeth. Jane was relieved he didn't slug the man.

"All we know," she went on, "is that Will died from a fall at around the time he was supposed to be meeting Marina Zhukova."

"And her? Zhukova?"

"Unknown," said Jane. "Possible sighting of a body on the north face. Lots of snow on that side. Ice. Crevasses."

"At the airports? Geneva, Zürich, Milan? Any other port of entry or departure?"

"Nothing."

Thorpe frowned as he made a notation in the margin of Jane's report. He didn't like loose ends. No legal opinion had been issued giving Zhukova permission to disappear. "Reports of her back in Moscow?"

Jane shook her head. For all intents and purposes, they had to assume that she, too, was dead.

"So, the question is," said Thorpe, still writing: "Did Will fall before or after taking possession of the information Zhukova smuggled out?"

"My guess is after," said Jane. "We went to claim his body this afternoon. There was nothing on him. His phone was missing."

Thorpe looked up. "I'm not following."

"The Swiss gave us a list of all items found on the body at the time of death. There was nothing about flash drives or anything like that. Will's phone was on the list. When we arrived, it was missing. Someone got there before us."

"Two people, actually," said Chen.

Thorpe shifted his gaze between them. "Got there before you? Two parties?"

"Correct," said Jane. "Who were looking for the same thing as us."

Thorpe dropped his pen onto the table. "Did everyone know about the meet but me?" A look to the heavens. A sigh. "I so preferred it when spying used to be secret."

Jane explained what had transpired in the hospital, fusing the guard's testimony and the images captured by the security cameras.

"A chase through the hospital," said Thorpe, after she'd finished. "Culminating with both men exiting the building through a fourth floor window, not to be seen again. I thought defenestration went out in the Middle Ages."

"Actually," said Jane, "we did see them."

"You and Mr. Chen?"

"Before we entered the hospital," said Jane.

"Before?"

"We didn't know it at the time."

"One fell in front of our vehicle," said Chen. "The other onto the hood."

"Jumping from the roof, no doubt," said Thorpe. "Was one wearing a cape?"

"It appeared that they descended by way of exterior air conditioners," said Jane. "Jumping from one to another."

"Go on," said Thorpe, growing unhappier by the second.

"I recognized one of the men," said Jane. "The recording from the security cameras confirmed it."

"Someone you know?"

Jane took a breath. This, she knew, was not going to go over well. "Ilya Ivashka."

"*The* Ilya Ivashka?" said Thorpe.

"Yessir."

"Last rumored to be seen eight years ago, boarding a jet to Moscow with a briefcase full of secrets. *That* Ilya Ivashka?"

Jane said yes. She knew about the rumors too. Everyone did. "I'm guessing whatever Hercules is, he's involved."

Thorpe resumed scribbling notes in his copy of the dossier. "What about the other one? Know him too?"

"I didn't get a good look," said Jane. "Older male. Beard. Dark eyes."

"And you, Mr. Chen? Did you get a good look?"

Jimmy Chen shook his head. "All I know is that I've never seen an old man run so fast. Like fuckin' Usain Bolt. Excuse me, freakin' . . . I mean—"

"You're allowed to say 'fuck' in front of me, Mr. Chen. I may not be a SEAL, but I have heard one or two expletives in the past." Then to Jane: "I assume that you've got the video from the hospital."

"Yes. The quality's spotty, but—"

"Send me a copy. I'll make sure it gets cleaned up."

"Yessir," said Jane. "For now, however, I'd like your permission to go after Ivashka."

Cal Thorpe drummed his pen on his legal pad. He gazed at Jane for a long while, eyes narrowing as if he were trying to game out a problem. He shifted his attention to Chen. "Mr. Chen, get the fuck out."

Chen left the SCIF.

Cal Thorpe opened a can of soda, took a sip, winced, and set it back down. "Tough couple of days," he said. "It's never easy to lose an agent."

"No," said Jane. "It isn't."

"And now this."

"Hard to believe, I know."

"Oh, I believe you," said Thorpe. "Your reputation precedes you. Jane McCall. No nonsense. Gets things done. Not afraid to break a few rules . . . but only when necessary. 'Act first, explain later.' I can dig it. And listen, I appreciate you reading me in about Marina Zhukova."

Jane couldn't tell if he was being sincere or patronizing. "Like you said, it's your turf. I apologize for not having done so sooner."

"Here's the thing," said Thorpe, leaning closer, speaking in a confidential tone. "Isn't all of this getting a little personal? A little messy?"

Jane was ready for the question. She'd been answering to superiors her entire career. "Ten agents disappeared after Ivashka went over. Our entire network in Syria and Lebanon. We owe them."

"That's not what I'm talking about," said Thorpe.

Of course he wasn't, thought Jane. "Does it really matter either way?" she said, the voice of reason. "I'm here. I can do the job."

"I don't question it. Not for a second. Like I said, your reputation precedes you."

"No nonsense," said Jane. "Count on it."

Thorpe sat back, studying her and letting her know it. "All right then," he said, this time with conviction, finally joining the team. "Go ahead. Find the sonuvabitch."

"And?"

"And what?" asked Thorpe.

Jane wanted more. Finding him wasn't enough. Not by a long shot. "What then?" she asked. There was no mistaking what she had in mind.

"I can't give you that authorization," said Thorpe.

"He's here. We can get to him."

"Take this one step at a time," said Thorpe.

"One step at a time?" said Jane. "Are you kidding me?"

"Jane."

"This is our chance. We can't let Ilya Ivashka get away."

"We won't."

"And when I find him?"

"Bring him in," said Thorpe. "We question him. You yourself said he's involved with Hercules."

Jane didn't take the request seriously. Bring him in? *Really?* "And if circumstances don't allow it?"

Thorpe drew a breath, calming himself. "We are not a hit squad, Jane," he said. "We are not the Rovers, even if present company wishes we were. That's done and over with, and Ilya Ivashka is one of the reasons. Are we clear?"

Jane didn't answer. She couldn't. The next words out of her mouth might end her career.

"I'll need a verbal confirmation," said Thorpe.

"Yessir, we are clear."

A finger raised in warning. "Remember this is my turf. Nothing happens without my okay."

"Yessir."

"Cal."

"Yes, Cal."

"Good," said Thorpe. "Get the hell out of here. You look like you could use some sleep." Jane pushed back her chair and stood, feeling her joints crack.

"And Jane," said Thorpe. "This is not about revenge."

CHAPTER 21

Zinal

The clock on the Land Rover's dash read 1:47 a.m.

Ilya slowed the car and stopped next to the blue placard announcing he'd arrived in Zinal. Any vehicle driving through town this late at night would rouse suspicion. He checked his Maps app, then backed up and turned onto a dirt road leading into the forest. He cut the motor fifty meters in and hopped out. The air was cool and damp, the scent of pine and beech stinging his nostrils. Mountain air.

Ilya pulled his knit cap over his head and zipped up his jacket. He moved to the rear of the vehicle and opened the hatch. A travel bag sat inside. He unzipped it and removed his pistol, chambered a round, then attached a noise suppressor.

A last check of the map to memorize the route to Herr Robert Steinhardt's chalet, Poststrasse 7, Zinal. A ten-minute walk, but he'd do it in seven. He'd parallel the river running to his right and then come at the house from the woods behind it. A broad lawn surrounded the house on all sides. A free-fire zone if he'd ever seen one. If Mac was waiting, Ilya wouldn't stand a chance.

Ilya locked the car and set off. There was a half moon. In no time, his eyes adjusted to the dark. He wasn't tired. Not in the least. He'd been up going on twenty hours. He'd driven back and forth across the country three times. He'd bruised a rib and knocked himself senseless falling off a building. No matter. He was pumped, jacked on adrenaline and the prospect of imminent danger. He was downrange all over again.

He broke into a jog and before long found himself running headlong through the trees, faster than was either safe or necessary. The fact was that he'd been drifting the last few years.

Upon his arrival in Moscow, they'd given him a medal. The commendation had said something about "securing the country's influence in the Middle East." More specifically, he'd given them the Agency's playbook for Syria and Lebanon. They owed him. The SVR couldn't be seen to treat him poorly. He was the example to lure the others. "Betray your country. We'll make you rich and take care of you for the rest of your life."

At first, Zaitseva and her minions at Yasenevo hadn't known what to do with him. For a few years, he hung around headquarters, doing half-assed analyses of this issue and that, penning psychological portraits of his former bosses, basically wasting everyone's time. No one wanted to send him back out. Too risky, especially to a country in the West. He was on every spy agency's most-wanted list.

The problem was that Ilya was antsy. He was like a working dog. He needed to be given a job or else he started acting crazy. Tearing up shoes, running around in circles, that kind of thing. In his case, it was drink, drugs, and women.

He'd always been a field guy. In the Corps, he'd been a sniper. He missed the first Gulf War, but saw action when the shit hit the fan in Yugoslavia and then big time in Iraq. Soon after, he was with the Agency, attached to the Special Activities Center, the paramilitary wing of the organization. No business suit required. He was inside the country nine months before the war, sneaking around with Mac, convincing Iraqi generals to lay down their arms and surrender when the fighting started. It wasn't difficult. Mostly, they just bribed them. A handshake and a fistful of dollars. He was in and out of the country for ten years afterward. Ugly times. Not bribing. Killing. The Israelis called it "targeted assassination." Even that sounded bad.

Finally, Zaitseva found a role for him. Not as a field guy, per se, an agent, but as an agent runner. A controller. More specifically, one attached to run Americans the SVR had turned. To his surprise, there were plenty and across all levels of the Intelligence Community, government, and industry. It was one of those agents who had tipped Ilya off about Marina Zhukova. It was only because Will Dekker was a seasoned alpinist that Zaitseva had ordered Ilya back into the harness. An agent once more.

Ilya arrived at the edge of the woods. He crouched by a tree, gathering his breath, and stared at the Steinhardt chalet. The place was dark, no lights burning anywhere. It was an exposed dash across ten meters of open lawn. If Mac was inside, he'd be waiting. He was always the better shot, not that a great deal of skill was needed from this distance. But Ilya didn't think he was there. Mac was a mover. He wouldn't hang around his house waiting for Ilya. If that's what he'd wanted, he'd have confronted him outside the hospital. No, Mac wasn't home. He was up to something. He had his kid's phone, maybe something more. He was operational.

At least, Ilya hoped so.

With a breath, he left the forest and ran across the lawn. He kept low, eyes on the back door.

He wasn't sure why he was worried. It would be a headshot, and he wouldn't feel a thing anyway.

Ilya made it to the door. He tried the knob. Locked. He put a few bullets into the frame, dumdums that flattened on impact and tore the wood apart. It still needed a little help. He rammed the door with his shoulder. The lock gave way. So much for the element of surprise.

Inside, he stood with his back against the wall, listening. The house was still. He checked the hallway. No activity. He moved to the foot of the stairs and swung around, pistol raised.

Nothing. He gave up trying to be quiet and bounded up the stairs. The place was deserted. He could feel it.

He walked down the hall, peeking into each room. He wasn't sure what he was looking for. Partly, he just wanted to get a feel for his old friend. He came to Mac's bedroom. There were some clothes scattered across the floor. Ilya recognized the parka from that afternoon. He checked the pockets and found a bus ticket and a receipt from a café in Zermatt. The bed was made in the military fashion. If Ilya had a quarter, he could bounce it sky high off the blankets.

Mac was still Mac. Good to know. He checked a few drawers. It made him feel foolish. He didn't need to see the guy's socks and skivvies.

In the bathroom, Ilya found a box of hair dye and some weird cosmetic crap for your skin. There was hair in the sink and in the wastebasket. Lots of it. Mac wasn't an old man any longer.

Ilya went back downstairs. He was looking for Mac's lair. No way the guy could pretend to be Robbie Steinhardt 24-7. This was Switzerland. Only one place made sense.

The door to the cellar was unlocked. A trap. Still, what choice did he have?

Ilya pushed open the door and jumped back, just in case. All quiet. He turned on the lights and descended the stairs. Mac had turned the cellar into a workshop. Ilya stopped to admire a beautifully polished rifle held in a vice. He crossed the floor and ducked his head as he entered the air-raid shelter.

Bingo. Mac's lair.

Ilya looked around the place, taking in the posters, the boom box, Mac's precious books.

He remembered that Mac never went anywhere without a paperback in his ruck. The last book Ilya had read for fun was his *Weekly Reader*.

He dropped into Mac's chair. The desk was neat as ever, nothing out of place. Mac had left his laptop there, and Ilya noted that it wasn't quite closed. He nudged it with the pistol as if checking if it were alive.

His eyes rose to the corkboard above the desk, covered with photographs. Nearly all were of Mac and his family. Will. The kids at the beach. Birthdays. Graduations.

And there in the top-right corner, *something else*.

Two bearded, emaciated climbers sitting cross-legged on a portaledge attached to some vertical face—El Capitan by the color of the granite—and smiling like idiots. Ilya and Mac. The dynamic duo. Boys really, not yet men. And yes, it was El Cap. Freerider or the East Buttress, two of their favorite routes.

Ilya freed the pushpin and peeled the photo off the board.

"A long time ago in a galaxy far, far away," he said aloud, bringing the photo closer. He was wearing a red North Face T-shirt, sleeves torn off. Hair pulled into a ponytail.

Face sunburned, nose peeling. But it was what Mac was wearing that jogged his memory. A dark-green T-shirt, much too clean—essentially new—with a single word printed across the chest. MARINES.

That was the day, Ilya remembered, like a bolt out of the blue sky. The day that had set into motion everything that was to come.

"It was your fault," he whispered bitterly, hurling the accusation across the decades. "All of it."

July 14. His nineteenth birthday. Ilya remembered it vividly.

He and Mac were living out of a battered panel van on the floor of Yosemite Valley, subsisting on ramen, jerky, peanut butter, and bananas. "Dirtbags" was what they called guys (and girls) like them and their way of life. It was all about the climbing. Nothing else mattered. Just the chance to get onto the rocks and prove something. The name was a badge of sorts, not really of honor but, well . . . *something*.

As Ilya stared at the photo, he felt himself being drawn back in time. He could hear Mac's confident voice as clearly as if he were standing beside him.

"We can't do this forever," Mac had said, sitting on that portaledge a thousand feet above the valley floor.

"Why not?" Ilya asked, much too innocently, as it turned out.

"It's not enough," said Mac.

"It's enough for me."

"I need something more."

"Go ahead," said Ilya. Mac always wanted to do more. Nothing new about that. It was Ilya's job to sit back and watch.

"I did," said Mac.

Ilya shot him a look. Only then had he realized that Mac wasn't just spitballing, mulling their options out loud.

"Did what?" he asked warily.

"Joined up," said Mac, tugging at his forest green T-shirt. "Marine Corps."

"What?" said Ilya. "I thought it was like some kind of joke."

"No joke," said Mac. "I'm due at Parris Island, South Carolina, in September. I could have gone to San Diego, but I wanted to be closer to home."

"Why?" Ilya stammered. "I mean, why the marines? Do they even take people like us?"

"My dad was a marine," said Mac. "My grandfather did some shit in World War Two. In Switzerland or Germany. You know, behind enemy lines. He was some kind of spy."

"You never told me that."

"OSS," said Mac. "Office of Strategic Services. Figure it's in my blood."

"For real?"

Mac nodded.

Ilya cupped his hands to his mouth and spoke in a low, ominous voice. "Luke . . . it is your destiny," he said, before breaking out laughing.

"Something like that," said Mac, much too seriously.

"I can't believe this," said Ilya. "The Marine Corps. Wow."

"'The few, the proud,'" said Mac. "Sounds like us. You should come."

"Me?" Ilya shook his head, taken aback. "I'm Russian."

"You were born in the States. You're American by birth. They'll take you."

"You asked them?"

Mac nodded. "If I can do it, so can you."

"No way, man," said Ilya. "I don't want to kill anybody." He gave him his best Michael Jackson. "'I'm a lover, not a fighter, Paul.'"

"The war's over," said Mac. He was referring to Desert Storm, the multinational operation to remove Saddam Hussein from Kuwait. "We can do some cool stuff. Rappel out of choppers, shoot machine guns, float around on big-ass ships."

"I don't know," said Ilya, but already the hook had taken.

For the past year, the two had been inseparable, more or less joined at the hip, driving around the western United States. Moab, Arches, Boulder, Yosemite. He'd never had a closer friend.

There was more, though. When they were on the rocks, when each held the other's life in his hands, they experienced some kind of communion. With nature. With each other. In some way, they became a single person. One goal. One will. One identity. The thought of Mac leaving . . . *of leaving him behind* . . . didn't sit well. In fact, it made him queasy. He needed a minute to realize that it scared him.

"How long?" asked Ilya.

"Four years," said Mac. "If we play our cards right, we'll be in training for two. It'll be fun."

"Fun?" said Ilya. "Running around with a shaved head and a fifty-pound pack on our back. Yeah, right."

"Hell, yes." There he was. Rah-Rah Mac. "I don't know," said Ilya.

"I love you, man," said Mac, socking him in the arm. "But there's more out there. More than ramen and PB&Js. More than skinning our knees on a slab of rock and sleeping on a leaky air mattress. For both of us. Time to go get it."

"Marines? Really?"

Mac looked out over the valley, eyes focused squarely on the future. "You know what they say? The marines. Semper fidelis."

"What's that? Italian?"

"Latin, dummy," said Mac. "It means 'always faithful.' Semper fi. Like you and me, bro." He put out his hand. "We'll have each other's back. Just like always. You in?"

Ilya tossed the photo onto the desk, upset with himself. Even after all this time, he couldn't help but feel that jolt of adrenaline, that spurt of youthful enthusiasm. Anything was possible.

Fucking Mac. It was his fault.

It was then he saw another photo, and he came right back to the present.

There, nearly hidden, were Ilya, Mac, and a striking woman with dark hair and a deep tan. The three were standing in the desert, an airstrip really, as evidenced by the tip of a fighter jet's tail, visible in the corner. Ilya's eyes, however, were on the woman. Her. *Ava.* The one that got away. He was surprised at how angry he still was. Bitch.

Even so, Ilya snagged the photo and stuffed it into his pocket.

He returned his attention to the laptop. It was, he knew, a present from Mac. For a moment, just before he opened it, he wondered if there might be a way for Mac to have booby-trapped it, to replace the hard drive with some C-4 and send his old friend Ilya to kingdom come.

He flipped up the screen anyway. No explosion.

"Enjoying yourself?"

Ilya jumped as the screen came to life.

"Long time, buddy," said Mac Dekker, staring back at him. "Getting a little slow. Then again, you don't have me to push your ass up the hill."

The beard was gone. So was the gray hair. It was the real Mac, hair cut short, eyes intense as ever, jaw clenched too tightly. The Agency's poster boy.

". . . did you really think I'd let you get rid of me? Surprise, surprise, I'm still here. I never forgot what you did. To Frank Logan. To the Agency. To me. To my family. I had to put all that away so I could protect them. That's over now. Hear me? You killed my boy. I'm coming for you."

Ilya closed the laptop. He shook his head and said, "Sure you are." He tried to laugh but couldn't. His mouth was too dry.

Only an idiot would want Mac Dekker coming after him.

CHAPTER 22

Hauterive, Switzerland

Calvin McWhorter Thorpe—Yale man, HBCU grad, finalist in the national mock trial competition, high scorer on his college basketball team, homecoming king at Robert E. Lee Academy in Appomattox, Virginia, owner of sixteen bespoke Zegna suits and an equal number of John Lobb shoes—a.k.a. Silk, paced the floor of his living room, faster than he'd ever paced before. One peek at his manic step, one whisper of his near-frenzied state, and he could kiss his nickname goodbye. Silk did not sweat through his Turnbull & Asser shirts. Silk did not tear at his manicured fingernails. Silk did not allow a little stress to leave him gasping like an asthmatic without his inhaler.

Cal took hold of a high-backed chair with both hands and stopped his frenetic activity. He needed to sit, to take a few deep breaths, to just "chill" and think things through. But the idea of sitting, of doing nothing, of "chilling," left him physically ill.

With great effort, he found a way to his liquor cabinet and poured himself three fingers of Johnnie Walker Blue. He wasn't a drinker, not in the old-fashioned sense, but a little scotch wouldn't do him any harm. In fact, it might restore some small measure of sanity to his recently upended life. He put the glass to his lips and drank the amber liquid, all of it. His eyes watered.

He gasped. But after a few moments, he felt better. At the least, he no longer wanted to vomit.

Slowly, he turned his head back toward the flat-screen monitor mounted on the opposing wall. The tech boys at the embassy had done their job. They'd cleaned up the video from the Sion hospital's security cameras. They had washed away the snow, enhanced the brightness, and refined the focus. It wasn't HD, not by a long shot, but no one could call the picture quality "spotty."

Cal picked up the remote control and started the video from the beginning. It wasn't a question of punishing himself. Rather, it was a matter of forcing himself to believe his eyes. He was a rational man. An empiricist. Facts were facts. Truth was not subject to interpretation. *It is what it is.* And so, it followed that he did not believe in ghosts.

And yet, at that very moment, he was looking at one.

Cal watched the old man in the lab coat enter the morgue and exit a few minutes later. Ilya Ivashka appeared, but he didn't care about Ilya. He cared about the old man. Cal watched him throw open the exterior door, then turn and rush to the stairwell. He was a pro, no doubt about it. Look how he kept his head angled away from the camera. But even pros slip up. There was a moment when he raised his head a fraction, canted his jaw. It was enough.

For an instant, you could see his face. Cal hit Pause.

Control in hand, he approached the screen. The tech boys had made sure he could zoom in. He enlarged the face until it filled the entire screen. Not satisfied, he moved closer still and looked past the beard and the hair, past the tangled eyebrows and the wine-black eyes. He saw past all of it.

"Jesusfuckingchrist."

Cal continued to stare at the monitor.

There was no doubt who he was looking at. He was looking at a ghost.

CHAPTER 23

Minsk, Belarus

Nadia Smirnova arrived in Minsk at dawn. Katya lay asleep on the back seat of the battered Ford Escort, her little body sprawled half-on, half-off, a wool blanket covering her. Nadia checked the directions and left the M1 motorway at Privolnyi, continuing north on the E271, which became Partizanskiy Prospekt. Minsk was in Belarus, but so far, it looked the same as Russia. She drove along broad boulevards, past lovely parks, and soon was in the city center. Traffic became as congested as at home in Moscow. She passed a large square and several majestic government buildings. The road ran parallel to a river. In another hour, they reached the northern suburbs. This was an industrial part of the city. There were no more majestic buildings, only square, gray factories and decrepit redbrick warehouses. The air smelled like burnt rubber and exhaust.

They'd left Moscow early yesterday morning. Nadia had done as her mother instructed. She'd taken Katya to her mother's apartment and found the book about Joseph Stalin. The letter was where her mother had said, and she'd read it through three times. Nadia was one person when she opened it and another after she'd finished reading. For one thing, she was $5,000 richer, which was more money than she'd ever had in her life.

The letter read:

Dear Svetlana,

If you are reading this, it means that I am not coming back. I think you have known for some time that I am not a junior officer in the trade secretariat of the Ministry of Foreign Affairs. Junior officers do not leave the country at a moment's notice and return a week later at two o'clock in the morning with a black eye and a broken wrist. I will tell you who I am and what I do in a moment. First, I wish to thank you from the bottom of my heart for the love and affection you have shown our little Katusha. I lost my mother at a young age. I never knew what a mother's love meant until I had Katya and learned firsthand how to express it. Your care, good humor, and discipline have helped Katya become the independent, intelligent firecracker she is. Svetlana, thank you.

Now comes the difficult part: I work for the SVR and serve with the rank of captain in the Directorate of Counterintelligence. This means that I am what people call "a spy." (To me, it is just my job.) But this is not my secret.

For many years now, I have been dissatisfied with our government. Specifically, I believe that the man who has ruled our country as a dictator for the past twenty-four years is corrupt, and more than that, mad. Should actions not be taken to end his rule, Russia, a country I love dearly—MY Russia—will cease to exist. I cannot allow that. And so, I have pledged my service to the United States of America.

If I do not return, it is because my activities have been discovered. I am either in custody or I am dead.

Please forgive me. Not as a Russian, for I know I am doing the right thing. But as a mother, for having forced such a profound responsibility upon you. I never wished to hurt my daughter. The price she will pay for her mother's beliefs is dear. She is the patriot, not me.

Svetlana, Katya cannot remain in Moscow, or in Russia, for that matter. It is our government's way to punish the family of so-called traitors. At the least, she will be sent to a school for orphans. I fear worse. Katya has a father in the West. His name is Will Andrew Dekker. He lives in Geneva, Switzerland. I am compelled to tell you that he is an officer of the American Central Intelligence Agency. You must take Katya to him. (His phone and address are listed below.)

Please peel back the end plate of this book. You will find five thousand US dollars. You may use it for your expenses. Please know that this journey is not without danger. You must not fly, as my name will surely be on a watch list. If I might suggest, please travel to Minsk. I have a colleague who will help with travel documents and may provide a safe route out of the country. (Vilnius is only 180 kilometers to the west.) His name is Pyotr. Call him. You are to say that you are a friend of his brother, Konstantin, and that you are coming for a short visit. He will understand.

Please follow these instructions closely. Katya's life depends on it. Thank you.

With love, Marina

Nadia shivered, thinking of her new responsibility. She didn't know if she was a patriot, or even what it meant to be one. All she knew was that Katya was in danger and it was her job to see that the girl reached her father. After that, she didn't know what she would do. At the least, however, she would no longer be in Russia. Switzerland wasn't Bali, but it was a start.

Katya stirred and in a minute was sitting up, rubbing sleep from her eyes. "Where are we?"

"Minsk. It's a big city like Moscow."

"Have you spoken to my mother?"

"Not yet," said Nadia.

Katya looked out the window. She didn't ask any further questions, and Nadia feared that somehow the little girl was preparing for the worst. Nadia didn't know what to tell her, because she knew so little herself.

"I'm hungry," said Katya.

"Me too," said Nadia. "I'm sure our friend will have a nice breakfast waiting for us."

"What is his name?"

"Pyotr. He is a good friend of your mother's."

"Maybe he will know where she is," said Katya.

"Maybe," said Nadia. "Let's keep our fingers crossed."

Katya smiled. "And our toes!"

CHAPTER 24

Zürich

She took his breath away, just as she had the first time he'd seen her all those years ago.

Ava Attal stood at the tram stop, briefcase in hand, dressed formally for work in her new formal posting. Skirt, hose, blazer beneath a stylish trench coat. A hundred bucks said the coat was from Burberry. Ava liked nice clothing. Her hair was lighter than he remembered—no longer the sun-dappled chestnut brown—but with tasteful blonde streaks and cut to her shoulders. Her face was thinner, the cheeks sharper, the lines at her eyes more firmly entrenched. The green eyes hadn't changed, however, nor had her Roman nose. Her lips were a bold crimson. A surprise. In the field, she never wore lipstick. It wasn't her looks, though, that caught him off guard, that stabbed him beneath his armor and threatened his well-planned defenses. It was her bearing, the way she stood so confidently, shoulders strong, jaw raised to face any challenge, gaze directed toward the coming tram. Go ahead, she told the world silently. Try it. See what happens.

Eight years later and still the force he'd loved deeply, madly, and now, he knew beyond doubt, forever.

The tram rang its bell as it approached. Mac waited until she had boarded and taken a seat. He jumped on as the doors closed. He remained in the stairwell for a moment, watching from over her shoulder as she removed a tablet from her briefcase and got down to work.

He took notice. This was not a social visit.

Mac slid into the seat facing hers. Ava glanced at him swiftly. Her eyes returned to the tablet, but only for a second. Slowly, she lifted her head. She looked at him, and he looked back. Mac could see the shock wave pass through her, her pale skin grow paler yet. A gasp that even she could not stifle.

"Will is dead," he said softly. "My Will. Ilya killed him."

She stared at him uncertainly, and he imagined the foundations of her world teetering, and her with them.

"Did you know Will was in the business?" he continued.

"Of course I knew," said Ava Attal.

"When?" asked Mac.

"When what?"

"When did he join?" He had to keep her talking, focused on the present.

"Four years ago," said Ava. "No, three." Her hands were shaking. Mac took the tablet so it wouldn't fall. "I claimed your body," she said. "Your ring. Your watch."

"Listen to me," said Mac. "Ilya killed him. If not him, one of his thugs. Will was on the Matterhorn. There must have been a meet. Ilya was looking for something Will had."

"Mac."

"I managed to get his phone. Will's."

"Mac!" There it was. The voice he knew. Commanding, steady, with a touch of gravel. Her eyes were clear. The hands no longer shook. "Eight years ago, I stood by your grave as you were lowered into the ground. Now here you are in front of me. Alive."

Mac nodded, never taking his eyes off hers. There would be time for an explanation later. It was the apology that worried him.

The tram slowed. Ava took the tablet and placed it in her briefcase. "This is my stop."

———

He followed her up the street, a step behind and one abreast. She walked north on Talstrasse, past a travel agency with pictures of Thailand in the window, and turned into an alcove with a sturdy glass door—bulletproof, he saw at once—and heavy steel handles. A polished brass plate on the wall advertised the BANK MEIER. Ava unlocked the door and entered the building without looking behind her. She crossed a dim vestibule to a door also marked BANK MEIER, and below it, on a smaller plaque, ISRAELI CONSUL GENERAL. She punched a six-digit code into an alarm pad, then laid her thumb on a biometric reader. The door clicked loudly, and she pushed it open.

Lights came to life in a small, elegantly appointed waiting area. Ava unlocked a door across the room.

"Come in," she said.

The office was spacious and modern, with a sitting area to the left and a sleek desk opposite. Dark carpeting. Paneled walls. Photos of Mount Scopus, the Damascus Gate, and the Wailing Wall to provide the proper history.

Ava set her briefcase on her desk and removed her trench coat, hanging it on a coatrack, then walking around Mac, as if he, too, were a piece of furniture. A moment to open the blinds. Not much to see. An alley and the rear of the office building behind them. She sat at her desk, sliding the chair uncomfortably close before clasping her hands and placing them on the glass surface.

"Mackenzie David Dekker."

"Hello, Ava."

"You took me by surprise. It won't happen again. I'm sorry about Will. I heard about it on the television. They said it was an accident."

"No," said Mac.

"You got here quickly."

"I live here."

"Here . . . you mean in Switzerland."

"Zinal."

Ava considered this. The muscles in her jaw tightened. Alive . . . and so close. She needed a few moments. "All this time?"

"Yes."

A smile, the opposite of amused. "Nice place to spend your death."

"Quiet," said Mac. "Out of the way."

"You never thought about reaching out?" she asked.

"Every day."

"We were together," said Ava. "We wanted a future."

"I didn't have a choice," said Mac. "That's how it had to be."

"You could have warned me. Given me some indication that you were alive."

"No," said Mac, too firmly. "I couldn't. That's not how the game works."

"Game? Is that what this is?"

"You know it is."

Ava shook her head and sighed. "Yes, I do."

They stared at each other for a while. What was painful, then awkward, grew uncomfortable.

Mac placed Will's phone on the desk. "I can't get in."

Ava picked it up, looked at it this way and that. She stood. "Come with me."

———

They left the building through a side door and proceeded down the alley to Selnaustrasse, veering left and crossing a short bridge. Below them, mist rose from the river like a bog. Bankers, phones to their ears, hurried past, gray men in gray suits.

"Why are you so surprised he joined the Agency?" asked Ava, slowing to walk beside him.

"He didn't know what I did . . . not what I really did."

She smiled briefly. "You still believe he thought you were what . . . a traveling salesman?"

"A contractor for the State Department," said Mac. "Putting up new buildings. Inspecting old ones."

"You really think you look like a guy that checks if the air-conditioning is working?"

"Everyone needs air-conditioning," said Mac.

Ava shot him a look. Please. "How many inspectors get blown up by a car bomb in Beirut?"

Mac started to answer, then thought the better of it. He'd told so many lies, fashioned so many half truths, been away so often, he didn't know what exactly his children had thought he'd done for a living.

"Mac, it was only a matter of time until they found out," said Ava. "Kids are always smarter than we think. I'm sure they must have suspected."

Mac frowned. Not the answer he'd hoped for.

Before he could respond, Ava was ducking into a bakery on the corner. The counter was jammed two deep with customers. The room was warm, richly scented of fresh bread, jams, cheese, and coffee. None of the staff batted an eye as Ava passed through the swinging door to the bakery proper. Mac followed.

A stout, bearded man, sleeves rolled up, apron stretched over his ample belly, retrieved a pallet of baguettes from the oven.

"Save one for me," said Ava, in *Schweizerdeutsch*.

"Five francs," replied the baker. "Same as everyone."

"What about family?"

"Five francs!"

Mac eyed him with suspicion. Any chance he was related to Hannes the baker in Zinal?

To her left, Ava opened a door painted navy blue with the letters **WC**. Instead of a water closet, stairs descended to a dim, dank basement. Ava crossed a concrete floor to a second door, this one unmarked except for the biometric reader set into the frame at eye level. She placed her right eye to the glass shield, waited a moment, then opened the door.

It was a bare-bones hacking lab. Laptops, hard drives, and mobile phones lay scattered across a large wooden table. The room was unoccupied except for one man seated with his back to them at a desk dominated by three flat-screen monitors. All Mac could see of him was a head of curly red hair, a yarmulke, a wrinkled T-shirt, and a half moon rising unapologetically from his pants.

"Whatever you're looking at, Itzak, turn it off," said Ava. "And make sure your trousers are zipped up."

The man named Itzak spun in his chair. "Very funny," he said, waving at the monitor to show them he was studying pages of computer code. "Though I do have some friends who find this exciting in a very strange way."

"Itzak, meet Mac."

Itzak stood, one hand to pull up his pants, the other to shake. "Cohen."

"Dekker."

Itzak studied his hand as if it had been mangled. "One of your friends from Shin Bet?"

"Him? He wishes. Mac's an old friend." Ava handed him Will's handset. "See what you can do."

"What happened to it?" joked Itzak. "Get run over by a tank?" He looked between Mac and Ava for a laugh. "What? Did I say something?"

"Fix it," said Ava. "It's important. Think 'your career.'" The smile left Itzak Cohen's face. "Yes, Colonel."

"That means now."

"I'll do what I can," said Itzak. "The handset's toast. I need to run a full diagnostic."

"Text me when you're done."

CHAPTER 25

Bern

Jane McCall passed through the doors of the US embassy in Bern, catching a glimpse of herself in the mirrored glass. She did not like what she saw. Her hair was a mess, dark circles rimmed her eyes. She needed a blowout, a facial, and 500 cc of Botox, not necessarily in that order. More urgently, she needed a good night's sleep.

She passed through security and punched the button for the elevator, stifling a yawn. She wasn't sure what had kept her awake. Jet lag, the gallons of coffee she'd consumed, or her simmering anger at not being allowed to do her job.

Ilya Ivashka was in Switzerland. It wasn't a matter of simply finding him but of putting him in the ground. Six feet under, to be precise, and with extreme prejudice. She knew her clichés as well as anyone. It seemed to her that once her superiors found out, they'd unleash the hounds of hell to get him. He might not be bin Laden, but bin Laden wasn't an American who revealed names of men and women composing the CIA's two most important networks of covert agents in Syria and Lebanon. Ivashka was walking free in a neutral country. He was fair game.

The Rovers might have been disbanded, but there were plenty of others more than capable of carrying out the mission, Jane included. She didn't have the training, true. She worked from behind a desk. Her bosses couldn't drop her a hundred klicks inside hostile territory to take out a bad guy and exfil unseen and unscathed. But she had something the others didn't have. Motivation.

Forget Thorpe and his turf. Jane barely stopped herself from spitting out the words. It was about revenge. For Will, for her family, and for her country. She sure as hell hadn't joined the Agency for the competitive salary and first-class travel accommodations. The Four Seasons Hotel did not have bedbugs and sheets with suspicious stains. She'd joined because she bled red, white, and blue. So sue her.

Jane rode the elevator to the second floor belowground. A marine sentry stood nearby as she exited.

"Phone, electronic devices, laptop," he said.

Jane placed her phone in a plastic basket to be stowed in a locker. The marine handed her the key and punched a button to unlock a steel door.

The operations center was a large, low-ceilinged, aggressively lit room. A SCIF within a SCIF. A half dozen analysts sat around a horseshoe desk crammed with flat screens of every size and shape. Monitors on the walls broadcast live feeds from various European cities. Jane recognized the gallery of the Duomo di Milano, the Tuileries Garden in Paris, and the Hotel Danieli in Venice. All were static posts keeping tabs on one target or another.

"Jane! Down here!"

Jane made a beeline for a familiar face. "Hannah, we have eyes on our Russian colleagues, don't we?"

Hannah Irving was fifty, short, whippet thin, a longtime hand who'd given up chances of advancement to remain in Switzerland with her wife and children. "Here? You kidding? Bern is Spook Central Station."

"The embassy?"

"Twenty-four seven."

"Archived?"

"Five years, last I checked."

Jane grabbed an empty chair and sat down. "I came to the right place."

"What do you need?"

"Last seventy-two hours."

"I can do that," said Hannah. "Make my life easier if you tell me who we're looking for."

"Male. Six feet tall. Blond hair. Slim."

"Sounds like half the embassy staff. Got a name? We can cross-check traffic against photos we have on file."

"No name," said Jane.

Hannah shrugged. No skin off her nose. "You want to fast-forward through seventy-two hours of tape? Be my guest."

No, Jane did not want to spend the better part of her day playing stop and go with the archived surveillance feed. Likewise, she did not want to spend the next ten years in Leavenworth for passing along top secret information. "Give me a minute, then check your email."

Jane left the ops center and retrieved her phone. She opened the photos app and scrolled back in time. Way back, until she found the one she was looking for. She accessed the Tor Browser, brought up an anonymous, untraceable email account, attached the photo, and sent it to Hannah. File under "attribution unknown."

When she retook her seat in the ops center, Hannah Irving was looking at a photograph of a rangy, blond man in climbing gear, his face tanned a deep brown by the mountain sun. "Cute," said Hannah. "One of theirs?"

"Something like that," said Jane. "It's twenty years old."

"Doesn't matter," said Hannah. "The software maps the face. Distance between eyes, nose, and upper lip, stuff like that. I'll need some time. Hour, tops. If I get anything sooner, I'll ping you."

"Appreciate it."

"And Jane . . ."

"Yeah?"

"I know who this is," said Hannah, sotto voce.

Jane leaned closer. "No, Hannah. You don't."

———

Jane McCall left the ops center and took the elevator to the fifth floor. The door to Cal Thorpe's office was closed. His assistant sat grim faced at his desk, mesmerized by his cell phone.

"I thought TikTok was supposed to make you laugh," said Jane.

"This isn't Tik—" The assistant stopped midsentence. Use of the TikTok app was banned on all government-issued devices. TikTok was owned and operated by the Chinese Communist Party. Its purpose was not to entertain the world's teens with short, amusing videos of songs, dances, and silly pets but to vacuum up any and all personal and private data from the users' mobile devices. "Mr. Thorpe isn't in."

Jane checked her watch. It was after 9:00 a.m. "An off-site?"

"On his way," said the assistant, shoving his phone into his desk drawer. "Between you and me, he sounded a little iffy."

"*Iffy?* How?"

The assistant pulled a face. It was up to Jane to decide. "Good to know."

Jane stopped by the fourth floor and spoke to Jimmy Chen, telling him about her visit to Hannah Irving. "I'm getting a coffee. You?"

"I'm good," said Jimmy.

Jane left the embassy and walked to the kiosk at the end of the block. She purchased a cappuccino and a chocolate croissant. *"Heisse, bitte."* Hot, please. The diet would have to wait. She did not, to her credit, buy a pack of cigarettes, which was her go-to when she was this stressed. It was not due to any act of willpower. It was because cigarettes in this country were so god-awful expensive. Fifteen bucks for a pack of Marlboros? Really?

She took her coffee and croissant to a table. The sky was gray, spitting rain. Cars drove past, spraying grit and gravel. She buttoned her coat and carefully dipped the croissant into her coffee. Of all mornings to arrive late to the office and hungover, this is not the one, she mused angrily. Or was Thorpe avoiding her? She reminded herself to keep her lips buttoned. Chain of command was a real thing. Switzerland was Thorpe's turf. Any ideas about speaking truth to power were not just misplaced but also suicidal.

She swallowed the last of her croissant and washed it down with a gulp of coffee. Her phone rang. Peter Kleiner from Swiss intel. "*Grüezi*," she said, stifling a burp.

"We found her," said Kleiner. "Rather, a guide did. Rescue teams recovered her body a few hours ago."

"Marina Zhukova?"

"Who else?"

"Good," said Jane. "Now we know."

"The furthest thing from it," retorted Kleiner. "Jane, we have a problem."

"I'm listening."

"She was shot twice by a large-caliber weapon."

"Oh, God," said Jane. The news felt like a punch to the gut.

Kleiner went on: "There were already questions about the gunshots heard that morning. Our journalists are as dogged as any others. My agency is not practiced at covering up information. We'll have to come clean."

"How long can you give me?" asked Jane.

"Twenty-four hours."

"Peter, come on."

"Six people saw the body. From what I hear, it made quite an impression."

"Can you sequester them?"

"Could you?"

It was a stupid question, and Jane knew it. She ran through the coming repercussions. Marina Zhukova's death was a matter for the local and federal police. Her identity would be scrutinized. In no time they'd learn she was a Russian agent. More questions would be asked about Will. In short order, it would be discovered that he'd worked for the Central Intelligence Agency. Cue a full-fledged investigation. Joy!

Closer to home, Will was Jane's agent, therefore it was Jane's screwup. She would have to leave the country. Most probably, Ilya Ivashka would have to leave as well. There would be no chance of finding out what he was doing . . . of learning the details of the weapon Marina Zhukova had smuggled out of Russia. There would be no possibility of stopping a pending terrorist attack.

"Twenty-four hours?" she asked. "That's it?"

"I can't muzzle the news organizations longer than that," said Kleiner. "And you . . . any progress?"

"I may have something soon."

"Jane, come on."

"Twenty-four hours."

"Keep me in the loop."

"Thank you, Peter."

As she ended the call, the phone buzzed. Hannah Irving. Jane kept the phone to her ear. "Yeah?"

"Got him."

———

"Let it spool."

Jane stood at Hannah Irving's shoulder, eyes glued to the monitor as they studied the entry to the Russian embassy. The time stamp indicated the date as two days earlier. A blond man in a dark suit passed through the wrought iron gates and jogged up the main stairs. Ivashka.

"Your guy?" asked Hannah.

"That's him," said Jane.

"He visited again yesterday. Check it out."

A second camera showed Ivashka leaving the embassy and walking to a car parked a short distance away.

"In plain sight," said Jane, as Hannah froze the picture. "Can we get a read on his plates?"

Hannah tapped a few keys, and the image of the car grew larger. "ZH99901." Land Rover Defender. Much too showy. "Nice wheels."

"Wait," she added. "Registered to the Russian Ministry of Foreign Affairs."

"Are we tapped into the license plate recognition database?"

"Roger that."

"Run it," said Jane, feeling as if she were already a step closer, imagining her finger on the trigger, a blond head in her sights. "I want to see where he sleeps at night."

CHAPTER 26

Zürich

"Spill," said Ava.

She sat beside Mac at a corner booth on the first floor of the Confiserie Sprüngli, the elegant café overlooking the Bahnhofstrasse. It was early on a weekday. The bankers had already left. Half the tables were empty, the others taken by women of a certain age. All were dressed to the nines, patiently sipping their espressos and nibbling croissants, a few talking on their phones in hushed tones.

"The last time I saw you was Tel Aviv," said Ava. "It was November. The day after your birthday."

Friday the thirteenth. Mac remembered the day. He'd relived it a hundred times, a thousand.

Lunch by the sea. Fresh fish. Mussels in garlic butter. Two bottles of white wine from the Jezreel Valley that they'd sworn were as good as anything from France, or California, for that matter. She had lived in a flat a few blocks away in the old city. Three rooms above an Arab coffee house. A battered rattan fan that turned slowly over her bed. A straw mattress that sagged in all the right places. They had played the radio to drown out the arguing from the patrons below. Brazilian cool. Stan Getz's "Desafinado." It had been hot for November. They had kept the windows open. A breeze had delivered warring scents from a faraway world: brine from the sea, honeyed almonds, exhaust from the camions navigating the narrow streets.

"We were going to quit," he said, recalling the promise he'd made while lying beside her, resting on an elbow as he ran a hand through her hair. "Once and for all."

"Majorca," said Ava. "You were going to write."

"Thrillers," said Mac, then a laugh. As if. "The next Frederick Forsyth."

"Why not?" said Ava. "If not you, then who?"

She still believes, thought Mac. For him the dream had died long ago. "Majorca," said Mac. "I had a home picked out."

"You did?" There was a catch in her voice. She hadn't known.

"On the south side of the island. Near Manacor. You could see the water."

Ava lowered her eyes. He sensed a shudder passing through her. He didn't know it would be this painful. For her or for him.

"Do you remember the last thing you said to me?" she asked.

"Yes." Mac tried to speak more, but the words caught in his throat. Sharp as barbs. He'd gone as far as he could go.

The server arrived. Ava ordered a *Kaffee Crème* and a soft-boiled egg. Mac asked for a Passugger water with lemon. For a while they sat without speaking, hostages to their stolen promises.

"And so," she said. "November." The sentimental lilt had left her voice. This was a debrief. Only the facts.

"November." Mac had been waiting to tell someone what had happened for eight years.

Why did she have to be the first?

———

"Simba was over," he began.

Operation Simba. Swahili for "lion."

Supposedly, names for operations were chosen randomly and with no consideration or reference to their objective. Not in this case. "Simba" was spot on. Lions were their targets. A systematic program of targeted assassination to identify, locate, and eliminate the chieftains of the Islamic State of Iraq and the Levant, known familiarly as ISIL, or better yet, ISIS. Ava and her counterparts at Mossad supplied the intel. Mac, Ilya, and the Rovers supplied the firepower. One hand pointed. The other hand chopped.

Simba ran for fourteen months. The plan called for Mac and Ilya to play hopscotch—one man's turn, then the other's. Mac made ten hops to Israel. A week of prep in Tel Aviv, followed by a week downrange in Syria, Northern Iraq, or the Kurdish borderlands. It was all very surgical. Night drops. Laying up at a distance. Shots taken from a thousand yards or more. The enemy was far away. A hazy figure in their scopes.

Ava ran the briefings from a conference room below runway 29 of the air force base in the Negev. Five minutes after meeting her, he knew. She was the one. He'd found her. He was divorced ten years by then. In that time, there were several women, several earnest attempts at building a relationship. None took. The running excuse was that his work prevented it. But that's all it was: an excuse. When you find the right one, Mac discovered, anything was possible. The fact that Ava knew what he did . . . that she did the same, more or less . . . cemented things.

It turned out she felt the same.

So, one week a month for a year. That's all they had. Those were the rules. So be it, and make the best of it. Mac and Ava spent every moment together. Work, sex, sleep, repeat. Finally, at the tail end of his forties, he'd discovered what love was all about.

"We were in Aleppo," said Mac. "Simba was over. We'd decimated their leadership. It was a success. High fives all around. At the last minute, we got tasked to exfil the CIA station chief, Frank Logan. The city was a madhouse. Control changed block to block. Hashemites loyal to Assad were one place. The insurrectionists somewhere else. The Wagner Group of mercenaries kind of everywhere. It was ugly.

"Ilya and I flew in on a Black Hawk, just the two of us, armed to the teeth. Full-on Rambo.

"Logan's local support were all dead when we arrived. He was alone, no protection, working like a banshee to destroy all the sensitive crap, bashing hard drives, burning paperwork. We were on our own. We helped him for as long as we could. Artillery fire was coming down helter-skelter. A shell took out the building next door. Our driver was freaking out. Finally, we had to scram. We got Frank Logan outside, hauling a pack filled with stuff we absolutely had to keep. That's when he did it."

"Ilya? Did what?"

"Turned," said Mac. "Went over. At first, he refused to get into the truck. We had the usual Hi-Lux with twin thirty-cals bolted to the flatbed. I'm standing there yelling for him to get in, mortar fire landing a block away, and he just stares back, looking at me funny. 'I'm not going,' he says finally. I asked him what he was talking about. Ilya looks at me and says, 'You don't always get to win.' 'Win what?' I ask him. 'Everything,' he says.

"Just then I see a truck packed with Wagner mercs rolling in. Ilya is waving to them and talking to them in Russian.

"That's when the dime dropped. He was going over to the Russians. Back to his parents' country.

"At that point, everything went sideways. Ilya shoots our driver dead. He asks Frank Logan for the pack with all the classified info. Logan tells him no. Ilya shoots him, then aims his M4 at me and tells me to drop my weapon. I think about it for about a second, and I drop the weapon. Ilya jumps into the truck with the Russians. He was laughing, really happy with himself. He says, 'They're never going to believe I did this alone.' And like that he's gone. I didn't understand what he meant till a couple of days later."

"Why would he go over to the Russians?" asked Ava.

Mac looked at her. She didn't know, even after all this time. "He had his reasons."

"Money?"

"I'm sure that was part of it."

"How much?" she asked.

"Five million up front," said Mac. "Same amount they paid me."

"You?"

"Ilya and his handlers set me up. Some very nice work. A numbered account at a bank in Liechtenstein. Easy-to-follow paper trail. He knew I'd never join him, so he made sure he took me out of the game. I never stood a chance."

"No one believed you."

"They flew me directly to a black site in Beirut. Locked me up for a few days. Brought in a hotshot from Langley to interrogate me. Specialist in terrorist finance, money laundering. Three days with no sleep. The same questions over and over again. 'How could I not have seen this coming?'"

"You were his partner."

"Lifelong friends," said Mac. "Turned out he'd been planning it for months. He sold his house, his motorcycles, moved into an extended-stay motel in Falls Church. The signs were everywhere. How could a close friend miss them?"

"Because you weren't looking," said Ava.

"Not in a million years," said Mac. "I was with you even when I wasn't." He laughed bitterly. "Try telling that to a guy who wants your skin."

"But you had twenty years in. Friends at Langley?"

"Didn't matter. Twenty-four hours after Ilya defected, the Russians had rolled up all of our networks in Syria and Lebanon. I don't know how many died. A lot. Langley needed someone to hang this on."

"Mac Dekker."

"It always came back to Ilya. They just couldn't believe he could pull something like that off on his own."

"And the car bomb?"

"People like me . . . like us . . . we know too much. After so many years in the harness, come on. Once they decide that you can't be trusted, that you're a liability, it's over."

"They came for you?"

"Yeah. Said I could go home. Laid on a plane to fly me to the States. Sent one of our own guys after me. A Rover. It didn't go well for him. Anyway, I knew then that I had to disappear. I had to be dead."

"How?"

"The car bomb? It's Beirut. I knew who to contact, how to get it done. The hardest part was making sure that someone saw me get in before it went up."

"Okay, but tell me one thing. Whose body was in the casket I watched lowered into the ground?"

"A bad guy," said Mac. His tone made it clear that it wouldn't pay to ask any further questions.

Ava's phone shook and rattled on the table. "Yes, *boychik*," she answered. Her eyes flashed at Mac. She shook her head. "I see. Well, do your best."

"Itzak?"

"Taking longer than expected."

Mac slid to the edge of the banquette. "Another coffee?"

Ava laid her hand on his arm, squeezed. "I have a better idea."

CHAPTER 27

Baur au Lac, Zürich

The room was on the top floor of the hotel, with French doors giving way to a balcony and a view of the hotel's lush lawn and, beyond it, the Zürichsee. The decor was modern classic, perfect for Louis XIV if he were alive today, or any king for that matter.

"Since when does the Baur au Lac rent rooms by the hour?" asked Mac, feeling out of place.

"They don't," said Ava. "I'm betting you're worth it."

"Expensive bet."

"I've been saving for eight years."

"A long time," said Mac. "That's a lot of pressure." He took Ava into his arms. He kissed her, tentatively at first. Was this really happening? She sensed his timidity, and kissed him passionately, pressing her body into his to dispel any doubts. Yes, he thought. It is.

"It doesn't seem to be affecting you," said Ava, coyly.

Mac opened the top button of her blouse. "Eight years."

"Up there all that time?"

And another button. "Every goddamn day."

"Never came down?" she whispered.

"Too many trip wires. NSA's gone crazy."

"Big Brother."

Mac kissed her neck. "Only way it would work. Total radio silence."

"Alone all that time."

"Yep. Just me."

The blouse fell to the carpet. Ava stepped back and unclasped her brassiere, letting it fall too. "I'd better be careful with you, then."

"Extremely," said Mac. "You're like a loaded firearm."

"Hair trigger."

"Bang, bang."

———

They lay on the bed, the sheets barely disturbed. They had always been neat lovers, finding their favorite spots, settling in, enjoying each other. Ava rested her head on his chest, running a hand over his ribs, fingers tracing his scars as she always had.

"What did you do all that time?"

"Made cheese," said Mac. "Don't laugh. It's good."

"Friends?"

"Acquaintances. Just a few. Not the baker."

"What about the baker?"

"Charged too much," said Mac.

"You and money."

"Four francs for a couple of croissants," said Mac. "Come on."

"News flash," said Ava. "Prices have gone up while you were dead."

"There was a nice kid at the dairy," Mac continued. "Martin from Eritrea. Barely got to know him."

"I didn't realize Zinal was such an international mecca." Suddenly she sat up. "What's this one?" Her finger ran up and down a pink scar shaped like a bolt of lightning.

"Shrapnel," said Mac. "Mogadishu. We weren't as quiet as we should have been. Someone chucked a grenade at us."

"I imagine he regretted it," said Ava.

"Oh yeah," said Mac. Enough about him. "What about you?" he asked. "When did you retire?"

"Retire? I'm chargé d'affaires."

"You know what I mean."

"I lost my rating."

"You? I don't believe it."

"I'm forty-eight."

"You look—"

"Forty?" said Ava. "Thank you." A gracious nod to accept the compliment. "My scores went to hell. Eyesight too. Rules and regs. Mossad is as bad as anywhere these days."

"Their loss," said Mac.

"I'll make sure you write my next fitness report."

Mac sat up, taking a moment to study her. To marvel. The feminine form. He had missed it. "And you? No one else? I mean, look at you. You're smokin'."

"You still don't understand," said Ava, propping herself on an elbow and looking him in the eye. "It was you or no one."

"I'm sorry," said Mac.

"No, don't. No apologies." Ava laughed, but without humor. "This business."

"This business," said Mac.

"And you?" she asked, playfully, now on the other side of it.

"In Zinal?" It was Mac's turn to laugh. She didn't know about the hair and the beard and the phony limp and the bad posture.

"Why not?" It was, after all, a legitimate question.

"You still don't understand," said Mac. "It was you or no one."

They kissed. Suddenly, Ava broke away. She sobbed. A tear ran down her cheek. "Hey," said Mac, taking her shoulders.

"No, no," she said. "I'm all right. These are happy tears." She wiped her cheeks, gave a shake of her head. She kissed him to prove it. "We're back."

CHAPTER 28

Zürich

Ilya awoke with a cry.

One moment he was dead asleep, the next, wide awake, sitting upright in bed, eyes open, his voice echoing in his ears. Light filtered through the blinds. The clock showed the time as either 11:43 a.m. or 1:45 p.m. He couldn't focus. His mouth was dry as chalk. A pulse at the base of his skull grew and grew until he was sure someone was pounding his cranium with a lead pipe. He closed his eyes. Please make it stop.

A quick peek.

No good.

Ilya turned his head as the bile erupted from his stomach. The stream was brief, hot, and violent, landing on his nightstand, splattering his phone and wallet. He wiped his mouth with the back of his forearm. At least that was taken care of. Let the day begin.

Ilya threw his feet onto the floor. One landed on something cold and hard. By the grace of God, he looked before standing. He stooped to pick up the bottle of Stolichnaya and put it to his lips. Empty, dammit. He tossed it onto the bed, offering a halfhearted salute to the dead soldier. It was then he saw the splash of blonde hair. No, not blonde, silver. Or, to be honest, gray. A naked shoulder. A faded tattoo. Tiger?

Lion? He glanced down and noted the scratches on his chest, still scab-
bing. A memory of nails digging into him. An urgent moan.

No . . . he hadn't.

Ilya stumbled into the bathroom and made it to the toilet in time
to aim his stream into the bowl . . . more or less. No sharpshooter
badge for him. He filled the sink with cold water and dunked his face
into it. The events of the night came back to him, slowly at first, then
all at once.

He looked in the mirror and was sick again.

Yes, he had.

———

The drive to Zürich had passed in a blur.

The highway was deserted. Even so, he'd avoided the main thor-
oughfares. He opted for the mountain roads, braving the Grimsel Pass,
the tortuous switchbacks leading to the shores of the Brienzersee, then
the sprint to Zug and down the Limmattal. He was distracted the entire
journey. Only half his mind was on the road. The other was on Mac
Dekker.

Mac had always been the tactician, the planner, the one to pause
before acting. "Wait," he'd say. "Why don't we try this instead?" There
was always a "plan B." Ilya was a "plan A" type of guy. He relied on
instinct, speed, and surprise. As for "plan B," if things went south, cross
your fingers and improvise.

Mac had taken Will's phone. His next step, therefore, was to exploit
it; to find a way to mine its contents. Or, more accurately, to find someone to do it for him. No easy task, even if you were a gifted hacker. Mac
would require the services of a professional.

But who?

The question was spinning in Ilya's mind when his phone buzzed.
A look at the screen. His sphincter tightened. The caller was a stern,

upright woman in a Russian military uniform. Who else would track him down at 1:30 a.m.? "Good evening, Colonel. It's late, even for you."

"Do you have it?"

"Soon."

"Not the answer I wanted," said Alexandra Zaitseva. "Sadly, it was the one I expected."

"What can I do for you?" asked Ilya.

"We've taken possession of Hercules."

Not the answer *he* wanted. "I thought you might wait," said Ilya. "Given the circumstances."

"What circumstances?" said Zaitseva.

Ilya knew better than to reply. Zaitseva never saw an obstacle she couldn't overcome. Or force others to overcome for her.

"I can rely on you, can't I," she said. It was not a question.

"Of course," said Ilya.

"I thought so," said Zaitseva. "The team leaves in the morning. It's only a matter of how quickly they can reach the target. Twenty-four hours at the soonest. No more than thirty-six. I wanted to make sure we're all on the same timetable."

"Twenty-four hours earliest," said Ilya. "Thirty-six at the outside."

"Precisely."

"Well, then," said Ilya. "That's that."

"Yes," replied Colonel Alexandra Zaitseva. "That is that."

Ilya ended the call, shaken. It wasn't the first time he'd faced a deadline. The consequences of failure, however, had never been so extreme. "Do or die" summed it up nicely.

He'd arrived in Zürich at 2:40 a.m. He'd decided to check out the Langstrasse en route to the safe house. The clubs were closing for the night. Patrons stumbled out of doorways. It was hardly the time to carouse. Zaitseva couldn't have been clearer. The good ship *Hercules* had sailed. Damn the torpedoes, full steam ahead. Like it or not, Ilya was aboard. Every moment that passed without his gaining possession of Will Dekker's phone and whatever information it might possess was a moment closer to Mac discovering it himself.

The clock was ticking.

Do or die.

And so Ilya, he did what he always did when he absolutely, positively, could not fuck up.

To his right, a garish neon red sign flashed a last time and went dead. He yanked the car to the curb and jumped out. The door to the establishment was closed, the stool taken inside. The platinum blonde of a certain age was nowhere to be seen. He gave the door a pull. Unlocked.

Good news, at last. He walked inside. The house lights were up. Music played from the sound system, if at a lower volume.

The blonde was behind the bar, washing glasses. In the harsh light, she looked her real age. Somewhere between Jurassic and Cretaceous. She saw Ilya, and her face brightened. "You," she said, slurring her words. "Buy me a drink."

Ilya did as he was told. In fact, he'd bought her a bottle.

———

That was seven hours ago.

Ilya closed the door to the bathroom and walked to the bed. He threw some towels on the nightstand, careful where he stepped. The woman was snoring. He could smell the booze wafting from her skin, overpowering her treacly perfume. For the life of him, he couldn't remember her name. *Suzy? Sylvia? Sonia?*

He went to the dresser and retrieved a flask. A long pull lifted his spirits. His eye fell upon the photo he'd taken from Mac's house. He looked at the striking woman. Those eyes. That body. That voice. "Ilya."

After all this time, he still had feelings for her. Unrequited feelings. He hated himself for it. He hated her too.

He closed his eyes, and there she was. Standing on a corner in Tel Aviv. Ava Attal.

———

Simba.

A joint US–Israeli operation. Goal: Decapitate ISIS. Identify, target, and liquidate the leaders of the Islamic State. Long term with a quantifiable metric of success. Dead bodies. What could be clearer?

Ilya had arrived from Germany earlier that day. He was not a fan of the Middle East, or, to be honest, of the Israelis. They were too arrogant, too cocksure, too pushy. It was their way or the highway. No questions, please. Differing opinions were not tolerated.

It was late in the afternoon. He'd left his hotel for a walk through the old town. Ten steps and he was already hot and sweaty and itching to get on the plane back to Ramstein Air Base. Ah, Germany. Schnitzel, beer, and barmaids in dirndls.

"Good flight?"

Ilya turned to face a woman standing beside him. Tallish, with tawny chestnut hair pulled into a ponytail, green eyes.

"In from Europe, right?" she said. "I'm Ava. I'm with the Office."

"Hello, Ava from the Office." The Office: what locals called the Mossad.

Definitely not a German, thought Ilya. Her accent was more French than Israeli, her voice scratchy in the best possible way. He let his eyes run over her. She looked like she'd never taken a bite of schnitzel in her life.

"Coffee?" Her eyes indicated it was an order, not an invitation.

The light turned in their favor. She walked ten paces ahead, not so much out of operational security, he decided, but habit. She liked to lead the way. Fine by him. Ilya appreciated the chance to appraise her figure. Jeans, tank top, sandals that might have belonged to Delilah herself. And fit. Very fit.

She entered a coffee shop. A look over her shoulder to make sure he was following. He took his time and entered a half minute later. She sat at a table in the rear corner, giving her a full view of the room. Ilya took a seat facing her. "Well," he said, hands splayed.

"Well what?"

"Where's my Americano with two extra shots?" he asked. "Since you already know so much about me."

A humorless smile. This one was all business. "Welcome to Tel Aviv, Mr. Ivashka."

"I've been before," said Ilya. "Shouldn't you say 'welcome back'?"

"Welcome back." A tilt of the head. He would pay for that.

"Thank you," said Ilya.

"Like it?"

"Not really," said Ilya. He could play the "no bullshit" game too. "Not the city. It's nice enough. Like San Francisco, but with better weather and fewer homeless people."

"We don't do homeless," said Ava.

"It's something else," Ilya continued. "Bad things always happen after I visit."

"I don't see you as the superstitious type."

"Not superstitious. Experienced. Ask Lev."

"I knew Lev," said Ava.

No need then for Ilya to remind her that Lev had been killed a month after his visit, a Syrian bullet ripping a gaping hole through his chest.

Not superstitious. Experienced.

"The Office thought it might be wise for us to get to know each other a bit," said Ava. "Beforehand."

"We'll be working together?"

"Simba," said Ava, coolly. "Didn't Mac tell you?"

Ilya shook his head. Mac had come through a few weeks earlier, the first one up to bat.

He'd exfilled to Diego Garcia straight after. They hadn't had a chance to talk. Maybe, Ilya decided, Mac had wanted it that way.

He leaned across the table, looking at those green eyes, the tan, muscled arms, all the rest of her. He was still the insecure, hypercompetitive kid who'd free-climbed that rock in the White Mountains of New Hampshire. Okay, Mac. If that's how you want it.

He smiled. "Am I allowed to ask a question?"

"About weather, politics, or sports, be my guest," said Ava. "Anything else, you'll have to wait."

"How long?"

"Forever."

"And about you?"

"My name is Ava Marie Attal. You know who I work for. I'm from France originally. Divorced. Twice, actually. No children. I'm a Scorpio. I like tropical beaches, long walks through the forest, and a Glock 18."

"What else is there to know about a woman?" asked Ilya.

"Exactly."

Those eyes. That voice.

"Screw this place," said Ilya. "Take me somewhere we can get a drink."

———

The bar was called Uzi's. No kidding. It was up the hill in Florentin, one of the city's hipper neighborhoods. At 6:00 p.m., the place was filling up. Lots of blond hair. Suntans. Springsteen blaring on the speakers. Ilya could be in Ocean City on the Delmarva Peninsula. Well, almost. Ocean City didn't have security guards with machine guns strapped to their chests. You only got that in Israel.

Ilya was on his second vodka, double Stolis with ice and a big chunk of lime. To her credit, Ava was keeping up. They'd talked about *Survivor* and *Love Island*. He liked the first, didn't watch the second. And vice versa. Her passion, though, was true crime. How, she'd asked him, were ordinary people capable of such extraordinary acts? "Extraordinary" as in heinous, cold blooded, and altogether inhuman. No comment on what she thought about people like . . . well, them.

"Office hangout?" asked Ilya.

"This is my place," said Ava. "No one from the Office allowed."

"Been in long?"

"Long enough to know Lev."

"Come on," said Ilya. "Tell me. *Allez.*"

Ava eyed him askance. "Is that your best French accent?"

"Like it?"

A laugh. Finally. "Sixteen years," said Ava. "After college I did a year in the Ministry of Foreign Affairs as a translator. A recruiter spotted me at a UN conference in Geneva. They're always on the lookout for someone who can pass."

"Pass?"

"ABI. 'Anything but Israeli.' I fit the bill."

"Question," said Ilya.

"Another one?" A smile to say any irritation was feigned.

"Why do you know so much about me and I don't know anything about you?"

"We're calling the shots on this one," said Ava. "You're a hired hand. You and your partner."

"Mac? We're not partners," Ilya shot back, his irritation all too genuine. "Not anymore."

"We were made to understand that you're a team. Dekker and Ivashka."

Always Mac first. It was time that ended. Ilya smiled to show he was a good sport. "That was a while back."

"Regardless," said Ava, "you were selected. Both of you."

"Because?"

"Because," said Ava, in a tone that brooked no dissent.

Because he and Mac were the best at what they did. Liquidating the opposition. Taking out targets. Posting numbers on the scoreboard.

More accurately, putting a Black Hills 250-grain slug into the skull of a man (or woman) at a thousand yards with a twenty-mile-per-hour crosswind and an altitude differential of two hundred feet.

Ilya accepted the compliment. He was getting that warm, fuzzy feeling in his belly, and a little lower. A fire-eater, he thought, looking at her. He liked the sound of it. In fact, he decided, he liked everything about her.

Time to switch from vodka to Red Bull, he decided, before all restraint was lost. It wasn't a pleasure trip, no matter how much he might wish it.

"I'm glad we met," he said, taking her hand. "I mean, I'm glad the Office ordered you to get to know me."

"Me too."

"I haven't felt this comfortable with someone . . . this, I don't know, relaxed . . . with someone in a while."

"Ha, ha," said Ava. "Now I know you're joking."

"I mean it," said Ilya.

"Ilya, come on. Don't even go there."

He held her hand more tightly. "I thought we were supposed to get to know each other."

"Not in the biblical sense."

"I'm not religious," said Ilya. "So, it wouldn't count."

"I am," said Ava. "It does."

Ilya kissed her hand. "Ava Marie. Nice name. *Très jolie.*" So much for restraint.

Ava's manner changed in a heartbeat. One moment he was getting somewhere, losing himself in those bottle green eyes. The next she was looking at him like he was one of the guys in her true-crime shows. "That's quite enough," she said, freeing her hand.

"I'm sorry," said Ilya, pulling himself together. "I got carried away. I haven't slept. The alcohol. Really, I apologize."

"It's my fault," said Ava. "Don't take this the wrong way. Under different circumstances, who knows? But come on. You know. We're going to be working together under stressful conditions. These things never end well."

"You're right," said Ilya, wondering if Mac had gotten the same treatment. "I couldn't agree more. This kind of thing doesn't end well."

"Dangerous," said Ava. "Let's just forget this."

"Deal," said Ilya.

But even as they left and walked out into the warm, sultry night, he couldn't forget something she'd said.

"Under different circumstances, who knows?"

———

Liar.

Ilya tore the photo into pieces. As he did so, it came to him who Mac would seek out to get into Will's phone. It was her. Ava Marie Attal. Who else?

And so Ilya knew exactly where Mac was going.

He sat down on the bed and pulled back the sheet. The woman was seventy if a day. Still, he'd never been one to say no, certainly not to a woman lying naked in his bed.

He placed a hand on her breast. The implant was hard as rock. He squeezed it anyway.

The woman moaned. Ilya felt himself stir. Why the hell not? He took another drink.

In for a penny, in for a pound.

CHAPTER 29

Chernobyl Exclusion Zone, Belarus–Ukraine border

Alexandra Zaitseva's excitement was palpable.

Alone in the passenger compartment of the Ilyushin Il-62, she sat upright in her seat, fingers dancing on the armrests, eyes peering through the window at the expanse of forest rushing up toward the aircraft. She was as giddy as her first trip away from home. It was not by plane but by train: an eleven-hour journey from her home to the Young Pioneer Camp in Odessa. Alexandra—everyone called her "Sasha" back then—was fourteen, tall, athletic, and madly in love with the Communist Party and her squad leader, Adam Mishkin, a strapping six-foot-tall Jew from Krasnoyarsk. Rapidly maturing, physically and intellectually, she was eager to prove her devotion to both in every possible way.

Zaitseva smiled at the memory and felt a certain warmth between her legs. A moment later, the plane hit an air pocket and dropped precipitously. All impure thoughts vanished. She spun to check on the stainless steel suitcases strapped into the seats across the aisle. Both remained firmly in place.

"Five minutes until landing," announced the captain over the loudspeaker, as the plane bounced again. Zaitseva yanked her seat belt tighter. The Ilyushin was carrying five passengers: the captain, the copilot, Zaitseva, and the two canisters of Zeryx packed in protective foam-lined cases. "Conquest" and "Death," she'd named them, after her favorite horsemen of the Apocalypse.

It was a two-hour flight from Moscow to the four-hundred-square-mile ecological preserve on the Ukrainian border. The preserve was not officially part of the Chernobyl Exclusion Zone but had remained sparsely populated since the disaster, all the same. The airstrip, unmanned and largely unused, was kept in working condition for occasions such as this.

The plane lurched once more. Below them stretched a carpet of pines, close enough to touch. She welcomed the high-pitched thrum of the landing gear being lowered into place. The sooner they touched down, the better. She closed her eyes and returned her mind to the trip to the Crimean seashore forty years before. The time since had passed in a heartbeat. Too many milestones to recall.

Her studies at Moscow State University, where she had hoped to earn a doctorate in physics.

Her subsequent recruitment by the KGB during her third year, followed by her induction into the secretive "Sparrow" program. Four years at a compound in the Caucasus. Training in languages, culture, spy craft, seduction, and sexuality. Nothing in the bedroom could be allowed to shock her. Sadly, her own tastes ran to the mundane. The missionary position and masturbation, some light domination—on her part, not his—though not necessarily in that order.

As was her nature, she preferred to be in charge from beginning to end. Her academic adviser from university, Professor Josef Rostov—the man who'd recommended her to the service—had been first to judge her training. He called it his "droit du seigneur." Zaitseva poisoned him a dozen years later. She called it her "droit du revanche."

At age twenty-two, her first posting to London, followed quickly by Washington, DC. Her target: the FBI. Her mission: to seduce agents attached to the counterespionage division. She was charged with nothing less than keeping the KGB's sources safe. It was an easy job, often pathetically so, men being men the world over, despite their profession.

American men were wildly different from the men at home: open, confident, and most of all, trusting. She found their naivete to be an aphrodisiac. And women being women the world over, she fell in love with one of those men, despite her profession. He was married, of course. A father of four. A devout Catholic. Balding. Overweight. A mediocre lover. And yet . . .

Of course, she became pregnant. He paid for an abortion at a back-alley clinic in Baltimore and unceremoniously dumped her, never the wiser to her true profession. The procedure left her unable to have children.

She chalked up her broken heart to experience. A rough bit of training. Nothing more. She had a more difficult time coming to terms with her ruined uterus. For that, she blamed him. She blamed the FBI. She blamed America. Her hatred for the West had only grown since.

And so, Alexandra Zaitseva gave her heart to her country and to the KGB, and—when the wall came down and the Soviet Union split apart—to its successor, the SVR. Her rise was steady, if slower than she would have liked. Lieutenant. Captain. Major. She was a woman who could be trusted to follow orders. A woman who could be as ruthless as the situation required. A woman with cold blood in her veins. A proud, unquestioning daughter of the Rodina.

For ten years now she had carried the rank of colonel. She had little hope of reaching general. It was Russia, after all. Hercules was her chance to earn the medal awarded to her grandmother and namesake: hero of the Soviet Union . . . even if the Soviet Union was no more.

The runway rose up to meet them. Zaitseva squeezed the armrests. A breath as the Ilyushin touched down. The plane struck the tarmac violently. This was not, she was reminded, a commercial carrier. The pilot braked hard. Zaitseva pitched forward. A minute to turn the plane around and return to the landing tower.

A dark automobile waited near the entry gates. Two men stood beside a dark SUV.

Zaitseva disembarked through the forward doorway. No uniforms. No salutes. They were not Russian intelligence officers. For the record, they were not here now, nor had they ever visited. She instructed them to remove the cases and place them in the car.

It was a brief drive to the staging area. Zaitseva regarded the forest, the dense, verdant landscape. She was less than thirty kilometers from the Chernobyl Nuclear Power Plant, where in 1986 Reactor 4 had melted down. A magnitude seven nuclear accident, the most severe imaginable. Untold radioactivity escaped into the atmosphere, poisoning the surrounding area. Even today, rumors persisted of giant wolves and feral hogs wandering the woods. Zaitseva saw no wildlife at all, which was even more frightening.

A call interrupted her thoughts. She glanced at the phone. Moscow area code. A prefix reserved for the Kremlin. And after it, nothing at all.

"Yessir," she answered, shoulders pinned to the seat, eyes raised to the horizon.

"An exciting day," said the premier, his tone relaxed, almost jovial.

"I agree."

"Everything is in order?"

"It is," said Zaitseva.

"You sound confident."

"My confidence comes from our country."

"And your country is grateful," said the premier. "Of course, there must be no ties to us."

"Of course. None whatsoever."

It had been her idea. A way to secure victory from defeat. A plan to sear the image of a superior, brutal Russia into the minds of the Ukrainian vassal state.

A simple plan with devastating consequences.

Poison gas was Zaitseva's speciality. It was Zaitseva who'd masterminded the attack on the Dubrovka Theater, later known as the "*Nord-Ost* siege," in Moscow in 2002. A false flag operation pitting Islamic insurgents fighting for a free Chechnya against a young, inexperienced Russian president. The terrorists were Chechen in name only. In fact, they were trained SVR agents. Negotiation was a ploy of the weak. In the end, poison gas was used by the strong, decisive president to clear the theater. One hundred fifty persons perished, most importantly all of the "terrorists."

During the following years, Zaitseva spearheaded research into the development and weaponization of more powerful nerve agents. Novichok. And now, Zeryx, the first VX agent soluble in water. The timing coincided with Russia's special military operation into Ukraine. An embarrassment. Worse, a humiliation.

And so, she'd spotted her chance.

"Report back as soon as you have news," said the premier.

"It will be an honor."

Zaitseva ended the call.

Two panel vans waited in a copse of fir trees near the border. According to markings on their sides, both belonged to the Kyiv Municipal Water District. Four women dressed in navy jumpsuits stood nearby. They were members of Kommando 14, a secretive wing of Directorate 6 of the SVR. All had grown up in Ukraine of Russian parents. All worked under NOC—nonofficial cover. It was essential no ties to the SVR could be found, now or ever.

Zaitseva supervised the handover of the canisters. There was no need for instructions.

Everything had been rehearsed a dozen times. Two dozen.

She kissed each woman on the cheek. "Godspeed."

CHAPTER 30

US embassy, Bern

"He's here," said Jane McCall as she stormed into Cal Thorpe's office. "Hiding in plain sight."

Thorpe sat at his desk, glasses perched on the tip of his nose, pen in hand, engrossed in whatever lay inside the sheaf of papers in front of him. If he was hungover, Jane couldn't tell, unless the cologne was to cover up the alcohol sweating out of his body.

"This is a United States government office, Ms. McCall," said Thorpe, eyes locked on his precious paperwork. "It's customary to ask if you may come in."

"I'm sorry, Mr. Thorpe," said Jane, not missing a beat. "Would you like me to go back out and knock three times?"

Thorpe removed his glasses and motioned for Jane to sit. "As a matter of fact," he said. "But since you're already here, feel free to continue."

Jane dropped the photographs of Ilya Ivashka entering the Russian embassy onto Thorpe's desk. "Check the time stamp. Yesterday and two days before. Walking through the front gate for everyone to see."

Thorpe glanced at the photos, then pushed them back toward Jane, as if they were some kind of affront. "Whatever he's up to must be important for him to be so cavalier."

"Cavalier? He knows we keep an eye on the embassy. He flat out doesn't give a shit."

If Thorpe heard the accusation in her voice, he ignored it. "Do we have a bead on him?"

"I asked Hannah Irving to run a check on his plates. The car was last spotted a kilometer from one of their safe houses in Zürich."

"When?"

"Six a.m."

"It's already eleven," said Thorpe.

"I can be there in an hour."

Thorpe frowned. An idea not to his liking.

"We can bring in Swiss intel," Jane went on. "Get a real-time feed off their cams. If he moves, at least we'll know where he's headed."

"I'd prefer to leave them out of this."

"Too late."

"How so?"

"I spoke with Peter Kleiner ten minutes ago. A second body was found on the Zmutt Glacier. Marina Zhukova."

Thorpe cleared his throat. "They're certain?"

Jane nodded. "She was killed by a high-caliber rifle. It was messy. We have twenty-four hours until he releases the news. Everything is going to get out. *Everything*. If we nail Ivashka before, at least we won't look like total schmucks."

"Jane, please."

"What's going to happen if the Swiss find him first?" she demanded. "He'll keep his mouth shut and sit in one of their five-star cells until he's traded back to Yasenevo. Any chance of our stopping Hercules will be over."

"Will you close the door, please?" said Thorpe.

Jane jumped out of her chair and gave the door a shove. "This is our last—"

"Quiet."

Jane folded her hands in her lap. For a minute, Thorpe stared out the window, his breathing deep and measured. The Yale Law grad was making a case for and against. And, to Jane's impatient mind, filing an appeal while he was at it.

"Cal," she began.

"Don't bring him in," said Thorpe.

"Pardon me?"

"Don't bring Ivashka in. I don't want any wrangling with the Swiss. Too messy."

"Cal, if you can't—"

"Shut up, Jane," barked Thorpe. "I'm giving you what you want. You told me you could do the job. So do it."

"Sir?"

"You want it in writing?"

Jane shook her head, reeling. She hadn't expected this.

"Get out of here then. Do your job."

———

Jane popped her head into Jimmy Chen's office. "Suit up," she said.

Chen glanced up from his laptop. "What's going on?"

"We got the green light."

"That green light?"

Jane nodded. "He's in Zürich."

Chen bolted to his feet. He opened a drawer, removing a holster and a Beretta nine-millimeter pistol and strapping it to his ankle faster than she would have thought possible. "You don't mean it," he said, blousing his pant leg over the weapon. "Really?"

"What?" asked Jane.

"'Suit up,'" he said with concern. "This is all I have." Chen gestured to his casual clothes: khakis, polo shirt, tennis shoes.

"It's an expression, moron."

"Knew it." Chen broke into a grin, then grabbed a hoodie from behind the door and joined her in the hall.

—

The Grand Cherokee was parked on the third floor underground.

"How fast does this thing go?" Jane asked, sliding into the passenger seat.

"Fast enough," said Jimmy Chen. "I guess. It's not like I'm trying to break the speed limit."

"Guess again," said Jane. "Today we are."

Chen guided the Jeep out onto the street. He ran a red light at Rämistrasse, accelerating as he entered the autobahn. Jane looked on approvingly as he took the speed to two hundred kilometers an hour.

"Where's the artillery?" she asked.

"Side compartment," said Chen. "Hit the Lock button twice."

Jane popped the compartment and unfastened the SIG Sauer nine-millimeter pistol inside. She dropped the magazine, counted the bullets, and recharged it, chambering a round.

"I'm not sure I like the look in your eye," said Chen.

Jane held the pistol in her lap and turned to gaze out the window. She wasn't seeing the passing landscape. Her eyes were locked on a slim, tanned face and the head of blond hair worn too long.

"Payback, motherfucker."

CHAPTER 31

Zürich

"I've been texting for thirty minutes," said Itzak, throwing his arms up. "I thought you said it was urgent."

"Excuse me," said Ava Attal, crossing the basement workspace, Mac a step behind her. "When were you promoted to chief?"

"I was just—"

She drew up, fists balled on her hips. "No, no, Itzak, tell me. Did I miss the memo? 'Itzak Cohen promoted to chargé d'affaires.' Please refresh my memory."

"Of course not," said Itzak. "I only meant—"

"I received your texts," she continued. "Thank you. I can promise that we came in the quickest manner possible . . . if that is any of your business."

"Extremely quickly," added Mac. "We might have set a record."

Ava turned her head. "Not a record," she said, solemnly.

"Close," said Mac.

"On second thought." Ava screwed up her face. Perhaps, she was mistaken.

"Definitely a record," said Mac.

"Yes," Ava agreed. "A record."

Itzak looked between them. "Is everything all right? I feel like I'm missing something."

"Who are you?" snapped Ava, once again the boss. "My new best friend? We're here. Tell us. What did you get?"

Itzak sat up straighter on his work stool, which meant he was slouching only a little. He picked up Will Dekker's cell phone and handed it to Mac. "Bad news. The SIM card is married to the handset. Standard precaution to prevent tampering. I'm not sure how badly the phone is damaged. If I mess with the SIM card, I may trigger a self-destruct."

"Meaning?" asked Mac.

"All data would be lost," said Ava. "Texts, mail, keystrokes, browsing history, passwords. All of it wiped clean."

"I need to send it to the lab at Herzliya," said Itzak. "Have them run a full diagnostic."

"Can you do it remotely?" asked Ava.

"Better if I FedEx the handset," said Itzak.

"No chance," said Ava. "The phone stays here."

"You're making things harder."

"Why do you think I brought you here?" said Ava. "You're my miracle worker."

"Now we're friends again?" said Itzak.

"How long do you need?" asked Mac.

"A day. Maybe less."

"Less," said Mac, placing the handset on the workbench. "Please."

Itzak acknowledged the plea in Mac's voice. He nodded. Yes, he would try. Then to Ava: "You might try adding a little empathy to your repertoire. It's very motivating."

"I called you 'my miracle worker,' didn't I?"

Mac put his hand on Itzak's shoulder. "I appreciate your help."

"Of course," said Itzak. He brightened. "By the way, I did find one thing."

"What's that?" asked Ava.

Itzak grabbed the phone and opened the Maps app. The screen displayed a route from the US embassy in Bern to the Hotel Bürgenstock outside Lucerne. "See this? The owner of this phone visited this place three days ago."

Mac studied the map, then showed it to Ava.

"Check the drive time," said Itzak, pointing to the bottom of the screen. "One hundred thirty kilometers in fifty-three minutes."

"Fast," said Mac, with a look at Ava.

"Fast?" said Itzak. "He was flying."

But by then, Mac was making a beeline for the stairs.

———

A clue.

Finally, something to pursue. A step in some direction. Anything to combat deadly inertia.

Mac charged past Ava and entered her office on Talstrasse.

"I'm a diplomat," she protested, slamming the door behind them. "I can't go running off after bad guys."

"I'm not asking you to come with me," said Mac. "I asked if you had a car somewhere for official use."

"Me? How did you get here?"

"I stole a car in Zermatt yesterday. Fair to say it's compromised by now." Mac peered out the window into the alley. "Do you?"

"Slow down a second," said Ava. "What about you? You said it earlier. Too many trip wires."

"Too late for that. Ilya saw me. I saw him. I'm blown. It's how things stand now."

"It's been eight years," said Ava. "You can't just jump back into the game."

"Eight years, two months, and eleven days," said Mac.

"Exactly."

"I thought you said I looked better than ever."

Ava placed a hand on his chest. "Mac. Take a breath. Think rationally. You are not protected any longer. You don't belong to the Agency.

You're not even supposed to be alive. If anything happens . . . and it will . . . you're going to get caught. You'll be arrested. There won't be anyone to get you out."

"Glad you think so highly of me."

"No one has your back," said Ava. Persuasion was out. It was time for the riot act.

"What about you?"

"That's not fair."

Mac took her hands in his. "I am thinking rationally," he said. "Hear me out. Right now we have no idea if Itzak and your people can get into Will's phone. We do know that three days ago, Will broke some kind of speed record to make it to some fancy hotel at 3:00 p.m. Less than twenty-four hours later, he was dead. I'm betting it wasn't a social visit."

Still, Ava shook her head. "Please, Mac . . . no."

"Listen to me. Ilya Ivashka has taken everything from me. My career. My family. You. And now, my son. This is my chance to make things right."

"You mean to get even," said Ava.

"Damn straight."

Ava looked at him. She stopped shaking her head. "Jesus," she said, sighing. "Okay, then."

Ava opened the top drawer of her desk and removed a pistol, tucking it into her waistband. She picked up a set of car keys from a glass tumbler and tossed them to Mac. "You're driving."

CHAPTER 32

Zürichberg, Switzerland

The city of Zürich divided itself into sections called Kreis, more or less districts. Ilya Ivashka's car was last seen by a camera on a street in Kreis 4 on the northern edge of the city. The Russian safe house was located at an address four hundred meters away.

Chen slowed as they passed the house, a modern two-story concrete design set back from the road and tucked among old-growth aspens and firs. A gravel walk led to the front door. No sign of the Land Rover parked anywhere nearby. And then, they saw it: a driveway feeding into a subterranean garage around the side of the house, its black steel door lowered.

"Safe house," said Jimmy Chen. "For who? Vladimir Putin?"

"Not quite like our huts in Kandahar," said Jane.

"Only missing the mud and manure fires. The good ole days."

Jane pointed out a place to pull over a hundred meters down the street.

Of course Cal Thorpe was right, she realized, as they pulled to the curb. It was getting messy.

There was no place for animosity, personal or otherwise, in her job. Less for conceits like revenge or payback. Spying, and everything that went with it, demanded the opposite of emotion. It was all about calm and calculation and cooler heads prevailing. An instructor at the Farm had stated it simply: an agent must divorce her ego from the objective. To illustrate his point, he'd written the word "Ego" on one side of the blackboard and the word "Objective" on the other.

In between, he'd drawn a line. The ego must never interfere with the objective. At all costs, an agent must remain dispassionate. The moment temperatures rose, emotions were stoked, and the stakes became personal, all was lost.

And yet, here was Jane McCall, GS-17, seven years in the saddle, navigating the narrow, winding roads of a wealthy suburb in a country not her own, a semiautomatic pistol carrying fourteen rounds of nine-millimeter Parabellum ammunition clutched in her lap and cold-blooded murder on her mind. Her heart was racing, her emotions stoked. The stakes couldn't be more personal. In contravention of all her training, her ego and the objective had become one. It couldn't be any messier.

And yet, for all that, Jane didn't care. Ilya Ivashka was in her sights. She planned to blast him to kingdom come.

Chen killed the engine as Jane slid a tablet from her workbag. She activated a mapping app maintained by the NGA—the National Geospatial-Intelligence Agency. Basically, Google Earth on steroids. More powerful zoom. Higher resolution. Images snapped by a satellite 130 miles above the earth and capable of reading the license plate on a car in Times Square. She punched in the safe house's address. In seconds, she had a bird's-eye view of the home. She zoomed in close enough to count the lawn chairs in the backyard. She rendered the image in 3D and held the tablet so Chen could see it.

"See the path behind the houses?" he said. "No fence. Plenty of trees. Takes us ten meters from the back door. Cakewalk."

"Don't say that."

"What?"

"'Cakewalk,'" said Jane. "You know better than that." She didn't consider herself superstitious, but still.

Chen shrugged. "Okay . . . I take it back."

"Thank you." Jane returned the tablet to her workbag. "Remember who we're dealing with. This guy was a Rover for a lot of years. He wrote the book on taking out HVTs."

"And what are we?" asked Chen. "Chopped liver?"

Jane rolled her eyes. SEALs. "Just saying, it's smart to think he's expecting us."

"Roger that." Jimmy Chen paused, one foot out the door. "Oh, and Jane, one day you're gonna tell me why you hate this guy so much."

"It shows?"

"Only a little."

"Let's put him down," said Jane. "Then I'll tell you everything."

The two left the car and cut in between two homes to the path meandering through the foliage. There were plenty of footprints. No one would be surprised to see a man and a woman out for a walk.

Jane wore a drab raincoat and her sensible shoes, her hair pulled back into a ponytail. Chen's attire was more problematic: tight slacks that barely concealed the pistol on his ankle, a form-fitting hoodie, Adidas court shoes. He was the picture of athleisure, a style of dress too casual for continental Europe.

They neared the house. Two windows on the second floor. Sliding glass doors leading to the living area downstairs. Another door to the left, probably to the kitchen.

Chen raised his Zeiss monocular to his eye and scanned the residence. "Looks quiet."

"Sound."

Chen held his phone in the home's direction. The phone contained a souped-up listening device able to detect a vocal signature at a range of thirty meters. "Quiet," he said, touching his hand to his earpiece.

"Okay, then."

Jane took a closer look at the house and made her final assessment. Go or no go.

The key to breaking and entering was speed and assurance. You moved fast, and you acted as if you belonged there. No second guessing. No looking over your shoulder.

There was no way to know if Ivashka was at home, if the Land Rover was parked in the garage, or if he was armed and expecting any kind of unfriendly visit. Worse, there was no way to conceal their approach, not at 11:00 a.m. on a cloudy day. Sometimes you had to go with your gut.

Jane stopped when they were perpendicular to the back door. "Ready?"

CHAPTER 33

Lake Lucerne, Switzerland

Ava and Mac had left Zürich an hour earlier. They'd passed Zug and the Zugersee and transited Lucerne, passing the Spreuer Bridge. The sky had darkened. Cloud and mist hovered over Lake Lucerne, its water as green as ivy, its surface smooth as ice. The highway followed the contours of the lake, long languid curves at the water's edge. To their right, foothills grew to mountains, hillocks yielded to sheer rock faces.

The car was a VW Golf R, sixteen valves, four hundred horsepower, dual exhaust, a wolf in sheep's clothing. Mac drove fast but with caution, never allowing the needle to drift past 160 kilometers per hour. He didn't mind if a radar caught him. He couldn't allow a policeman the same courtesy. Ava was right. No one had his back.

"Do you know it?" she asked, craning her neck to look at the hillside rising in front of them.

"Know what?"

"The Bürgenstock. It was originally built for the first real tourists, mostly Englishmen who came to hike in the Alps."

"I don't think Will went there to hike."

"Let me finish," said Ava, consulting the hotel's website. "These days, the hotel is popular for conferences. Doctors, lawyers, engineers. Know what group is there now?"

"I'm afraid to ask," said Mac.

"Annual meeting of the International Association of Research Chemists. The keynote speaker is Dr. Ashok Mehta."

"Should I know him?" said Mac.

"We all should," said Ava. "Listen to this: 'Dr. Mehta first gained notoriety as one of the pioneers of modern chemical warfare agents and is widely credited as the cocreator of ethyl S–phospholi-debenzene.'"

"I love it when you talk dirty to me."

Ava didn't smile. "Better known as VX gas."

Mac looked at Ava, the bottom dropping from his stomach. So much for caution. He pressed his foot against the accelerator. In seconds, the needle touched two hundred kilometers per hour, a buck twenty in the States. "Guy like Mehta has to have something on him," he said. "He didn't decide to make VX gas for the hell of it."

"How do you mean?"

"Someone was pushing him. Paying him on the side. Funding his research in exchange for the take. Either way, he has contacts with the wrong people."

"Let's find out."

Within minutes, Ava was speaking with a superior in Israel. Her tone made it clear she expected an answer in the quickest possible way. "They're checking," she said.

Mac's fingers tightened on the wheel. "Damn you, Ilya, you bloody bastard."

"You think this is about VX gas?"

"I know as much as you," said Mac. "Whatever it's about, Ilya was in the middle of it. Will was trying to stop him." He looked out the window, memories of his son overtaking him. "He was a good boy."

Ava put her hand on his. "Like his father."

They left the highway and began a gradual climb through the forest, leading to the crest of the Bürgenstock.

Ava's phone buzzed. She shot Mac a glance. *Them.* Mossad.

The conversation lasted a few minutes. She spoke Hebrew. Even the most cordial conversation sounded like a bare-knuckle brawl.

"Well?" asked Mac, when she'd finished. He did not like her sour expression.

"Officially, Ashok Mehta is what he says," Ava began. "Tenured chair in organic chemistry at Cambridge University. Pillar of the research community. Benign genius. No proof he's ever engaged in any kind of trafficking of information or matériel."

"But," said Mac, keying onto her skeptical tone.

"His file is green tabbed," she continued. "Meaning we conduct an annual review on him. Someone at Mossad is suspicious he's not as clean as he likes to appear. There are questions about his political leanings. He has an older brother, a member of the Indian parliament, who maintains close ties to the Russian Communist Party. There are also questions about Mehta's finances. Cambridge isn't known as a generous employer, yet Mehta lives in a five-million-pound estate, drives a Mercedes, and vacations at the Kulm Hotel St. Moritz."

"Family money?"

"Anything's possible," said Ava. "But . . ."

"He's dirty," said Mac. "Will didn't race all that distance for a lecture on covalent bonds."

"Of course he didn't," said Ava. "Mehta's dirty."

CHAPTER 34

Zürich

Still as the grave.

Jane McCall slid into the kitchen of the safe house, gun raised to her cheek, hands on the crosshatched grip, index finger brushing the trigger guard. Jimmy Chen followed a step behind, closing the door with care. They waited a few seconds, motionless, listening. Jane queried Chen with her eyes. *Anything?* A shake of the head. Not a whisper.

Jane placed her back against the refrigerator, allowing Chen to slip past and duck his head around the corner. He moved fluidly and without hesitation. God knew how many houses he'd cleared. In Afghanistan. In Iraq. In all the other places no one but he knew about. After a moment, he glanced in her direction, left hand raised. Follow me.

The dining room was a minefield of parquet flooring. She did her best to advance stealthily. Step heel to toe. Shift your weight evenly. It had been a long time since she'd been in the field. The hallways at Langley, however long, were hardly adequate to keep battle ready; the cafeteria, even less so.

Chen drew up at the far wall. Beyond was the front door and an airy two-story entry hall with a staircase running up one wall. He screwed up his face and touched his nose. She smelled it too. A treacly, cloying scent. Women's perfume. Not a brand she was likely to find on the first floor at Bloomingdale's.

Chen darted his head around the corner. Again, he motioned for Jane to follow. He put a finger to his mouth. Church mice. They stood shoulder to shoulder, ears trained for the slightest noise.

Chen rounded the corner into the entry hall, checked the living room, then climbed the stairs, broad strides, two at a time. He kept his pistol raised, raking the walkway that wrapped around the foyer. He reached the second floor, then rushed to the head of the corridor. A look told Jane that he wanted to check things out. One moment he was there, the next he was gone.

Jane advanced up the stairs with caution—one at a time was fine by her—shoulders bunched, awaiting an outburst of gunfire. Time passed. Ten seconds. Twenty. Sweat rolled down her back. Where was Jimmy?

A door slammed. She threw her back against the wall, pistol at the ready. "Clear," called Jimmy Chen, finally reappearing. "Place is empty."

Jane reached the second floor. "Someone was here."

"The real housewives of Zürich?"

"Not hardly."

The first room at the head of the corridor was the master. The king bed was disheveled, sheets and duvet a tangled mess. An empty bottle of Stoli stood on the dresser next to an ashtray filled with cigarette butts, all ringed with lipstick.

"What the hell?" Chen pulled a face, jumping away from the night table.

Jane saw the towel draped across the surface, the vomit dripping onto the carpet. The odor hit her a moment later. She turned the bottle of Stoli upside down. Not a drop spilled.

"Russian work ethic," said Chen.

A pair of trousers lay by a love seat, underwear caught up in the legs. Jane lifted them off the floor with her shoe. "Looks like our man was in a hurry."

"Coming or going?"

Jane pulled a face. "Your guess is as good as mine."

Chen touched the pillow. "Still warm."

———

Ilya Ivashka climbed into the driver's seat of the Land Rover and hit the garage door opener. He slid an arm through the safety belt, one foot balancing on the rocker panel as he ran his hands over his jeans searching for the key fob. He felt better than he did an hour before, which meant he only vaguely wanted to puke. What was her name again? *Rita? Renee?* One name Ilya hadn't forgotten was *Ava Attal.* He knew several people who could help him find her. One of them was likely to be quicker than the others. He put his phone to his ear and hit speed dial. So what if he was using his private phone? It was not the time to think about consequences.

"Gotta be kidding me," said Cal Thorpe. "Calling me here."

"Emergency," said Ilya. "I need some information."

"I'm at work."

"I damn well hope so."

"He's alive," said Thorpe.

"So you know."

"Hospitals have cameras."

"A surprise, isn't it?" said Ilya, his casual tone a prod. "Who'd have thought it?"

"Tell me you know where he is."

"I have an idea."

"Well?"

"I'm on it," said Ilya.

"You?" Thorpe laughed. "You're a drunk."

"I'm your drunk, remember?" said Ilya. "Or is it the other way around?"

"I'm going into a meeting with the ambassador. The shit is hitting the fan. I'll call you in an hour."

"Don't keep me waiting."

"One hour," said Thorpe.

Ilya ended the call and went back to checking his pockets for the fob. He shouldn't have called Thorpe, not without giving him the usual warning, certainly not on his mobile. To hell with that. He was beyond caring about Thorpe, or anyone else for that matter. Thorpe was his best chance at finding Ava. There was nothing else to be done. All that mattered was Hercules, or more accurately, stopping Mac Dekker from discovering the information Marina Zhukova had stolen about the imminent operation. Ilya wasn't afraid of Cal Thorpe. He was very afraid of Alexandra Zaitseva.

Ilya finished patting his pockets. No fob. Dammit.

He stepped out of the car and jogged to the stairs leading into the house, wondering where he'd left it. The bedroom? The bathroom? In a fit of clarity, he recalled dumping his pockets in the study upstairs, if only to make sure that Rita—yes, that was her name, *Rita!*—didn't steal them. He had no illusions about his choice of company. He opened the door to the living room and put his lips together to whistle, an old habit.

At that moment, he heard a man shout, "Clear."

Ilya stopped dead in his tracks—pistol drawn, safety off in the space of a second.

Instinct.

An American. Then a woman's voice too. Two people.

Here, in the safe house. Looking for him. For Ilya Ivashka.

Ilya refused to be surprised, yet still . . . *how?* And if they were Americans, why didn't he know about it? There were too many dark alleys to go down at the moment, too many unwelcome implications.

He peeked around the corner. Voices drifted from the bedroom. One man. One woman. No one else. Probably the two who'd tried to chase him down the day before. Friends of Will Dekker. Spies.

A disturbing thought came to him as he started up the steps. In his mind, he heard an educated voice. Male. Far too educated. Brimming with false outrage. *"I'm going into a meeting with the ambassador."*

Oh yeah, it was you, you sonuvabitch, thought Ilya. In this business, you never saw it coming.

"Scour the place," said Jane. "Closets. Drawers. Bathroom."

"What are we looking for?"

"Anything that can tell us why Ivashka is in Switzerland and why he killed Will. If you see something marked 'Hercules,' holler. You take the other rooms. If he left his pants just lying around, I'm betting we'll find something."

"Better not be more puke," said Chen.

Jane picked up the trousers and pulled them right side out. She ran her hands through his pockets. There was a receipt from a bar on the Langstrasse in the amount of four hundred francs at 3:38 a.m., eight hours earlier. Another from a gas station in Sierre, time-stamped at 22:58 last night. A hundred-franc banknote, which she tossed onto the floor. Blood money.

She entered the walk-in closet. A few suits. Russian labels. Pockets empty. A parka.

Mountaineering pants. Climbing boots caked with mud. And there in the corner, a rucksack and ice axe.

Jane covered her mouth.

Urgently, she crouched to open the rucksack. Gloves, scarf, goggles, gaiters, sunscreen. She unzipped the outer compartment. Chapstick, Swiss Army knife, a well-creased map. This she unfolded. A topographical map of the Matterhorn and the surrounding peaks.

It was you.

You killed him.

Jane drew a breath. No amount of training could stifle her shock, the jolt of emotion.

Angrily, she wiped at her eyes and looked more closely at the map. A route from the Italian side up the Lion Ridge marked in Sharpie. No further witnesses, Your Honor.

It was you.

There was more. A US passport, expiration date six years past. Tucked inside was a faded photograph of Ivashka with his arm around the shoulder of an attractive dark-haired woman standing outdoors in a desert landscape. Ilya was carrying a sniper's rifle with a massive scope, a camouflage scarf around his neck. The woman had an Uzi hanging off her shoulder. The developer had stamped the date on the back: August 18, nine years earlier.

Finally, a piece of ivory-hued stationery—quality stock—folded in quarters. She opened it. EMBASSY OF RUSSIA, BERN, SWITZERLAND embossed in gold lettering across the top, and the national blue, white, and red tricolor below it. Several handwritten lines in Cyrillic rambled unevenly across the page. Jane read them with difficulty. "Zaitseva to Borodin Laboratory. Dr. L. Mirin." And then, the magic word: *Hercules*. To her credit, she did not holler.

A different pen had been used to write additional notes farther down the page. "Solvay Hut 0600. MZ/GH." And two phone numbers, one with a Russian country code, the other, Swiss. The second belonged to Will. It was his Agency number. Not something available to the general public. Jane assumed the first was Marina Zhukova's.

Her eye dropped to the bottom of the page. A date. She forgot her grief. An all-consuming concern took hold of her. "That's tomorrow," Jane whispered.

———

Fifteen feet below her, kneeling beside the living room wall, pistol in hand, Ilya Ivashka surveyed the entry hall and the second floor walkway. The smart move was to return to his car and leave the area. Cal Thorpe would call in an hour. Ilya would get the information he needed. With luck, his hunch about Ava was correct. He could take one step closer to finding Mac. That was the smart move.

Or was it?

The Americans had used the same tricks to find him as he'd used to locate Mac. To leave would only be postponing a confrontation. If they'd found him once, they would find him again.

He couldn't outrun them forever. For the moment, he held the advantage of surprise. Eliminate these two, and he'd gain a measure of freedom to continue his pursuit of Mac Dekker.

There was more to it. A personal dimension. Ilya wanted to show the Americans who they were dealing with. He was still *the Ilya Ivashka*. He needed to remind them of what they'd lost when he'd gone over to the other side.

The ego, he realized without shame, had an insatiable appetite. Decision made.

Ilya rounded the corner, still in a crouch. At that moment, the man strode from the bedroom and crossed the open walkway. Buzz cut, big shoulders, pistol at his ankle. Ilya froze, ready at the slightest glance his way to raise his pistol and fire. By some miracle, the American didn't look Ilya's way. A second later, he'd disappeared into the study.

Ilya vaulted up the stairs. He paused on the landing, eyes darting in both directions. Take the man first.

CHAPTER 35

Zürich

Jimmy Chen stood at the doorway of the study. The warmth of the pillow radiated in his fingertips. It was his imagination, of course, or as he'd tell you, his radar. Instinct honed by twelve years' active duty as a US Navy SEAL. "SEAL" standing for "sea, air, and land." He'd done time with most of the teams. Teams 1 and 3 in Coronado and Team 5 in Virginia. His last assignment was with Team 6, the bad, bad boys also known as DEVGRU, or Naval Special Warfare Development Group. He'd risen from seaman third class to senior petty officer while seeing action on four continents. A jihadi's bullet had ended his career. SEALs had to run, and that was damn near impossible after your kneecap had been shattered and your calf muscle obliterated.

The Agency welcomed him with open arms the day he signed his separation papers. He had too much experience fighting the Global War on Terror, or GWOT, in short, to be let go. It wasn't the same, not by a long shot. No incursions in the dead of night fifty miles inside enemy territory. No humps across twenty klicks of marshland carrying a fifty-pound ruck and an M4.

No offshore drops in six-foot seas with the water running below fifty degrees.

The job was a lateral move into force protection, bodyguarding, site inspection, and light intel. He did a year in Langley before his posting abroad. Mr. Thorpe called him a "dogsbody," whatever that meant. Still, the salary was decent, the work interesting, and every once in a while he had a chance to put his skills to use—the ones he wasn't allowed to tell anyone about. Most importantly, he was serving his country, which for the son of immigrants from Shanghai meant everything.

Chen surveyed the study. It was a small room, twelve by twelve, desk against one wall, bookshelves, sofa, all very minimalist: "minimalist" to his mind meaning it might break if you breathed on it too hard. He started with the desk. Pens, pencils, a stapler, rubber bands. On to the larger drawers. Empty. All of them.

Chen picked up the pace. Downrange in Helmand Province, the team would collect everything in garbage bags and bring it back to base for people like Jane McCall to inspect and evaluate. He knew better than to linger on enemy territory.

He looked over the bookcase, checked behind the couch, under the desk. He was staying too long. He was lingering. If Ivashka was half as good as Jane claimed, he could sneak up on him and pop him in the head before Chen knew he was there.

Chen rose from the floor, feeling more flustered than he would have liked. "Amped" was the word. He spun, sure someone was watching him. The hall was empty. It was his radar getting hinky. He opened a dresser drawer. Empty. Closet. Empty. The place was clean. Time to skedaddle. The voice in his head was practically screaming. GTFO. He took a step toward the door and stopped.

It was then he saw it.

A sliver of paper peeking from behind the floor lamp where it had fallen off the bookshelf. He picked it up. A letter of some kind. He unfolded it. UNITED STATES EMBASSY, BERN was written across the top. It was an internal document stamped with all manner of classifications. A sitrep of a static post set up in Lugano to monitor a suspected money launderer for Hamas. The report was issued by the CIA station chief and dated a week earlier.

If he wasn't mistaken, he'd just discovered a mole. "Hey, Jane. You gotta check this out!"

Jimmy Chen rushed into the hall. His hand dove for his gun. Too late.

CHAPTER 36

Bürgenstock

There were two hotels, not one. The first to come into view as they crested the plateau was the Palace, an old-school Victorian structure, five stories tall, a grand white hostelry with wrought iron balconies and a slate mansard roof complete with the Swiss flag flying over its cupola. A hundred meters farther down the road was its newer, glitzier grand-daughter, all sharp angles, flat planes, and amber-hued glass. Nothing if not five stars. Six, even, if there were such a thing.

"That's the one," said Ava, studying the screenshot of the route taken by Will Dekker earlier that week. "Keep going."

Mac left the car in a space for guests. A liveried *huissier* asked if they were checking in.

Mac ignored him, walking side by side with Ava into the hotel.

The lobby was sleek and modern, darkly lit and scented with lavender, soft music playing from hidden speakers. He pulled up at the concierge's desk.

"We're looking for the chemists' conference."

"In the grand ballroom," said the concierge. "But I'm afraid it's over. The final dinner was last night. They're just packing up."

"Which way?" asked Ava.

But Mac was already charging across the foyer. A broad hallway ran the length of the ground floor, mirrors to either side, crystal chandeliers dangling overhead. He followed signs to the ballroom. Silver banners flanked the double doors, all emblazoned with the logo of the International Association of Research Chemists. A young hotelier in uniform exited the ballroom, hefting boxes up to her chin.

"Dr. Mehta," said Mac.

The woman slowed, balancing her load. "I'm sorry."

"The keynote," said Ava.

"Perhaps you can ask the event planner," said the hotelier, with a nod behind her. "Frau Schmid."

Mac held the door for Ava. The staff was busy cleaning up. A woman dressed in executive attire stood on the raised dais, gathering papers while talking on her phone.

"Excuse me," said Mac. "I need a word."

The woman shot Mac a dirty look, raising a hand for him to be quiet as she turned her back. Mac hopped onto the dais and touched her shoulder. "Please."

The woman spun, anger coloring her face. She spotted the one-hundred-franc banknote in his hand. Her features softened as she plucked the note from his fingers. "Yes?" She smiled as she abruptly ended her call.

"Ashok Mehta," said Mac. "It's important I find him."

"He spoke yesterday evening. The conference is over."

"When did he leave?"

The woman tucked the bill into her pocket. "I didn't say he'd left. Room 615. But you'd better hurry. We have a car coming for him in thirty minutes."

The elevator was fifty paces down the corridor. Mac and Ava rode in silence, Mac tapping his heel nervously.

"Go easy," said Ava. "We don't know for certain he was the reason for Will's visit."

"Tell me you believe that, and I'll go easy." Ava didn't respond.

The signs for rooms 600 through 615 pointed to the left. They ticked off the numbers as they walked. "Of course," said Mac. "He has to be at the end of the hall."

They turned a corner, nearly running into two guests in more of a rush than they were. Men. Dark suits. Short hair. Pale. Fit. One brushed Mac's shoulder, not slowing. "Hey," said Mac.

Neither man gave him a second look.

Room 615 was, in fact, the last room on the hall. Ava knocked politely. "Housekeeping."

Mac put an ear to the door. He shook his head. Nothing. "Move."

Ava cleared out of the way in time for Mac to drive his heel into the door an inch below the handle. The wood splintered. He kicked again, and the door burst open. Ava barged in first. "Dr. Mehta?"

It was a large room with a generous sitting area. A suitcase lay open on the bed. A window was open, sheer curtains billowing in the midday breeze. A glass of orange juice had spilled onto the carpet next to a pair of horn-rimmed glasses.

"Dr. Mehta?"

A woman's anguished scream rose from the grounds below. Mac hurried to the window. "Found him."

Ava placed a hand on the sill, craning her neck. Six floors below, the body of a diminutive man wearing only a terry cloth bathrobe lay splayed on the flagstones, blood spreading from his head.

"Are we in agreement?" said Mac. "Will came to see Mehta."

An attaché case sat open next to the television. Ava plucked a business card from the pocket. One look and she handed it to Mac. WILL DEKKER. VICE PRESIDENT. VEVEY, SWITZERLAND. A private number was written on the back.

"Grab the case," said Mac.

Ava closed the case and thumbed the locks closed.

"It was them," said Mac. "The two in the hall."

"How do you know?"

"Because I know," said Mac. "They had the wrong shoes. Rubber soles, not leather."

"You can't be sure."

"You see anybody else?"

"What are you going to do?"

Mac freed the pistol from his waistband and chambered a round. "Ask me when I find them."

Mac ran back to the elevator, Ava at his heels. The panel above the door indicated the car was on the second floor and descending. Mac turned, looking this way and that. "The stairs."

A carpeted staircase wound around the elevator shaft, three flights per floor. They reached the ground floor as the elevator doors were closing. Mac looked in the direction of the lobby and main entrance. No sign of the men. He turned to his left and right.

"There." Ava pointed to a glass door leading to a garden.

Mac rushed to the door. He opened it slowly, peeking out. A ramp led into a large rose garden, gravel lanes winding among the dormant bushes. At the far side of the garden, there was a lawn with iron tables and chairs overlooking Lake Lucerne far below and the city of Zug. Past the lawn, a footpath ran at the cliff's edge, a hedgerow planted beside it as protection against tumbling over the precipice.

And there, walking on the path, the two men who had killed Ashok Mehta. Mac removed his pistol, holding it next to his leg.

"You're not the police," said Ava. "You're not anyone. You have no authority."

"I'm Will's father," said Mac. "Authority granted."

CHAPTER 37

Zürichberg

Ilya entered the hall as the American agent called out to his partner. He knew what the man had found. Ilya was not at fault. It was a safe house. There was no cause for him to hide anything. He had no reason to expect to see anyone other than his own people here. Moreover, he'd been promised sole occupancy. The house was his to use and his alone. He was Ilya Ivashka, after all.

Ilya laid his finger against the trigger, blood pumping, eyes bright. This is what he did and did well. It had been too long. He marched down the hall, pistol held at arm's length. The American appeared in the doorway holding the "communication" in his hand, a look of astonishment plastered on his face. *Look what I found! A traitor in the embassy.*

Ilya shot him in the chest. The man took a step back, but remained on his feet. The look was no longer on his face. He appeared stunned, eyes already glassy, getting more vacant by the second. He was strong. No question. Not many people stayed upright after taking a nine-millimeter dumdum smack in the middle of the torso at ten paces.

Ilya shot him again. The bullet struck him above his left eye. His brain splattered on the wall and the windows. Ilya preferred up-close work, just not the mess or the smell.

He turned, waiting for the woman.

Three . . . two . . . one.

She dashed into the hall, pistol drawn—a SIG Sauer with an expanded magazine—making as large a target of herself as might be possible given the circumstances. Essentially committing suicide. It was the blonde from the car that had nearly run him over yesterday. He'd been moving too rapidly to get a good look at her, not to mention he'd been half-concussed from the fall.

He raised his pistol, drawing a bead on her chest. Then he saw her.

He noted the blue of her eyes, her straight nose, the set of her jaw. But it was the anger in her face that convinced him it was really her. Something dropped inside of him, robbing him of his breath. Wasn't it his day to be surprised?

Ilya fired off two rounds, both high. The woman dove into the doorway of the guest room. He kept the gun aimed at the doorway, all the while fuming. What business did she have gaining entrance to a Russian safe house? Or pursuing an experienced operator, for that matter—especially one of his value? Frankly, it made him mad.

A moment passed. She ducked out and loosed three rounds. Ilya had stepped back into the study and peeked from behind the wall. Anyone can get lucky. The shots struck the dresser at the far side of the study: a tight grouping. Bravo. The girl could shoot.

Ilya fired off five rounds, raking the doorframe. Wood, drywall, cement exploded everywhere. Cordite hung in the air. He fired off six more. The sound was deafening, beating the hell out of his eardrums. The house had been soundproofed, or so they said. He hoped so.

Otherwise, they'd be able to hear the racket all the way to the German border.

The woman darted her head into the hall. Ilya put a bullet into the doorway an inch above her, close enough for her to have felt it. There. Now you know who you're dealing with. She disappeared again.

Ilya replaced the magazine. Thirteen shots fired at her inside of a half minute. A miracle if she wasn't shell-shocked. He damn well was.

He ran to the window. One last shot for posterity. Uncle Ilya says bye-bye.

He was on the street seconds later and around the corner before she dared poke her head into the hallway again.

No chance he could take the Land Rover. Even if he changed the plates, it was, in and of itself, a rarity. They'd find him in a New York minute.

Dammit.

That was a bitchin' ride.

CHAPTER 38

Bürgenstock

Mac took Ava's hand, and they moved through the garden and across the lawn. A signpost at the head of the footpath read **HAMMETSCHWAND LIFT—200 M**. The path led down a gentle slope, curving to the right. Ashok Mehta's killers walked briskly but with no apparent urgency. Mac and Ava steadily closed the gap between them. Ahead stood a white gazebo. To its right, a path led at a ninety-degree angle to the edge of the mountainside and from there across a narrow wooden walkway to an elevator running up and down the vertical cliff. The Hammetschwand Lift. The lift was housed in a crisscrossed metal carapace supported by horizontal struts drilled into the rocky cliffside and climbing seven hundred feet from bottom to top. A peaked roof at the top of the elevator housed the machinery and lent it a rustic, old-fashioned appearance.

The men stood with their backs to them, waiting for the car to arrive. It had begun to sprinkle. A band of cloud and mist blew across the plateau.

"Can't let them get in," said Mac as they passed the gazebo and turned onto the path to the elevator.

"What are you going to do?" asked Ava. "Shoot them?"

"Just have a word."

"Good luck with that."

The elevator doors opened. Several men and women exited. The killers slipped past them and entered the car.

Mac dropped Ava's hand and broke into a run. The killers turned and faced him. "Hotel security," shouted Mac. "Please step out of the elevator."

The men made no sign they'd heard him. One raised his hand to the control panel. "Stop," said Mac, without conviction. He was too far away. Or was he? It was an old elevator. *Maybe . . . just maybe.*

The door closed slowly. Not slowly enough. He reached the elevator a moment too late.

Mac slammed his fist against the door. They know, he told himself. They know why Will rushed to meet with Ashok Mehta. Why else would they kill Mehta except to keep him from talking?

For the briefest moment—the blink of an eye—he felt Will's gaze upon him, shared a kindred sense of purpose with his son.

All sense left him. There was action. Only action.

Above the closed doors, there was a gap of six or seven feet to the peaked roof that hid the elevator's working machinery. Mac leaped and pulled himself to the top of the doorway.

With difficulty, he threw his legs over the transom and dropped onto the roof of the car as it began its descent.

He landed unevenly, his ankle buckling. He reached for something to regain his balance. Anything. His hand found the steel cable, its frayed wires as prickly as a cactus. He recoiled. Not that. He stood, knees bent, arms raised for balance.

The car picked up speed, rattling mightily, the craggy granite face to one side, the lake to the other, far, far below.

The first bullet passed close enough to his cheek that it felt like a bee sting. He jumped to one side of the car, back brushing the slats of the carapace. Three more shots followed, forming a triangular pattern in the center of the roof. Mac considered that enough of a provocation.

He fired into the car six times. He heard a man cry out. He noticed that the cliff face was much closer than it had been, barely an arm's length. A groove carved into the rock permitted the elevator's descent. He glanced over the edge of the car. They were almost at the bottom. A shaft had been carved into the rock below, dropping into a grotto at the base of the mountain. Any moment, he'd be surrounded on all sides.

He tucked his gun into his waistband. Timing it as best he could, he grasped on to the metal slats with both hands. The car continued its descent without him. In seconds, it had entered the mountainside, cables squealing as it came to a halt.

Mac slid through the carapace and climbed onto the mountainside. Using trees and shrubs as handholds, he traversed the face, heading toward the footpath that guided visitors to the Hammetschwand's entry inside the grotto. The mountainside was no longer vertical but sloped to the flat ground below. He saw one of the killers exit the cavern, walking with a pronounced limp, and follow the footpath until he was no longer in view.

Mac slid down the hillside, the heels of his shoes furrowing the dirt and loose rock. He was moving fast, without control. He managed to slow himself before leaping the last few feet onto the footpath. His momentum carried him into an elderly woman. She shouted in alarm as he wrapped his arms around her, nearly knocking her to the ground. Mac apologized and set off after the killer, first taking a moment to look toward the grotto and ensure the second man was not following. There was a commotion near the entry. A young woman emerged, waving her arms wildly, calling for police.

The second man would not be coming.

With renewed purpose, Mac continued down the hill. The footpath entered a glade of birch trees, leaves turning, fluttering in the wind. Men and women walked leisurely in either direction, enjoying the crisp fall day. He jogged easily among them, not wanting to stir concern. Farther along, he noticed a sign with the letter **P**, for parking. He rounded a bend and saw him. The killer was walking beside a young family—husband, wife, two children—darting glances over his shoulder.

Mac kept his distance. The man was armed. Mac couldn't risk endangering the family. It was not the place for a shoot-out. He stopped to take stock of his surroundings. Nearby an automobile could be heard, engine downshifting. He spotted the car fifty meters down the hill to his right. There was no choice but to wager it was headed to the parking lot.

Mac abandoned the path and cut down the hill, pushing aside branches, dodging the foliage. His foot caught on an exposed root. He tripped and fell headlong into a carpet of dead leaves. When he stood, he had an unobstructed view of the road. His wager was correct. The road dead-ended into the parking lot. Brushing himself off, he continued down the hill, careful to avail himself of the camouflage.

The killer emerged from the path at the far end of the lot. Mac crouched, watching the man thread his way through the cars. He dug his keys out of his pocket and raised a hand in the air. The beeps of a car alarm sounded. The killer stopped beside a late-model Audi. He put a phone to his ear and for a moment turned his back.

Mac left the protection of the hillside and dashed across the lot. There were maybe ten cars parked helter-skelter. The killer ended his call. He opened the door and turned to get in. Immediately, he spotted Mac. He hesitated. Should he use his gun or make his escape? He climbed into the car and slammed the door. The engine roared to life. The sedan backed out of its space, braking violently before turning and accelerating toward the exit.

Mac took a knee and fired. The front-left tire exploded. The car jerked to Mac's right. He fired again, missing, and a third time, splintering the windscreen. The Audi halted. The killer jumped out of the car, pistol in hand. Instead of shooting he ran back toward the footpath.

Mac saw the family emerge from the glade. For a moment, the father did not notice the man running at him. He was preoccupied with his daughter, who had taken hold of the dog's leash. The mother saw the assailant first and rushed forward to protect her child.

"No," shouted Mac. "Don't."

The killer pistol-whipped the father. The man collapsed as the killer shoved the mother to the ground. "*Bleibst-du da*," he shouted in German. "Stay there."

The dog bared its teeth and lunged. The killer shot the dog dead.

He scooped up the little girl, clutching her to his chest, and advanced toward Mac. "I know who you are," he said. "Ilya's friend."

"Once," said Mac. "Not anymore."

"Give me your car keys."

"I don't have any."

"Bullshit."

"Someone drove me."

The killer looked over his shoulder and ordered the father to throw him his car keys. "Which one?"

"The Volvo," said the father, weakly. "Please . . . leave her."

The killer retraced his steps through the lot. The girl was crying now, struggling to free herself. He tightened his grip on her. "Throw down your gun."

Mac had a bead on the man's head. All his experience came back to life. His finger brushed the trigger. His breathing slowed. Twenty yards separated them. He could make the shot. The problem was the pistol. He had no idea about its accuracy. At this distance, the slightest error could prove catastrophic.

The killer jabbed his weapon into the girl's ribs. "The gun."

"Don't," said Mac.

"Up to you, tovarich."

Mac dropped the pistol onto the asphalt.

"Kick it to me."

Mac kicked it, but weakly. The pistol traveled a few feet. "Again."

Mac took a step and kicked the pistol, harder this time. It skidded beneath a vehicle. The killer unlocked the Volvo. "You killed Sergei," he said, setting the girl down, whispering for her to go back to her parents. "Now it's your turn." He stepped toward Mac, raising his pistol.

Shots rang out.

The killer flinched as a screen of blood and gore erupted from the back of his head. He dropped to the ground.

Mac spun.

Ava emerged from the hillside, pistol still trained on the Russian. "I thought you didn't qualify," said Mac.

"I lied."

CHAPTER 39

Moscow

They came for her at 2:00 p.m. Perhaps they wished for her to enjoy a last lunch in her hospital room. One last cup of borscht, a slice of stale black bread, and a few sardines. She didn't believe them to be humorous men. More likely, they'd timed their visit for the nurses' afternoon break.

They entered without knocking. One was tall and dark, the other short and fair. Both were dressed in gray suits with neckties and wore scuffed, thick-soled shoes. The short man carried a bouquet of flowers. The tall one locked the door behind him.

"You are Svetlana Smirnova," said the tall man. He was pale with black hair pasted across his scalp. It was not a question. It was a sentence. A pronouncement of guilt.

Svetlana did not answer. What was the point? She knew who the men were and for whom they worked. They were functionaries attached to some secret unit of the government she had probably never heard of. They had come because of Marina Zhukova.

Svetlana had known about Marina for a long while: months, if not years. The apartment on Tverskaya Ulitsa was a tad too nice for a low-ranking government official. There were too many luxury items. The Swiss coffee maker. The new television. The designer clothing.

And of course, the travel. The sudden trips. The calls in the middle of the night to please come and look after her daughter. The lack of explanation of where she was going or even when she was coming back. The dark looks telling Svetlana she dare not ask.

No, Marina Zhukova was not a low-ranking government official.

Finally, there were the things Marina said. Comments she made as they watched the news. Remarks made upon her return from her trips to the West—Svetlana could never think of Europe or America as anything but "the West"—expressing her unhappiness with Russia's state of affairs and the country's leader.

Over time, Svetlana had allowed herself to imagine who Marina really was and, more dangerously, who she really worked for. The letter was the final piece.

"What do you want?" asked Svetlana.

"Where is the girl?" asked the black-haired man.

"I don't know."

"Katya Zhukova, daughter of the traitor," said the other. "Please."

"I don't know," Svetlana repeated.

"You will tell us."

"Never."

The short, fair man leaned closer, so close she could smell his lunch. Herring and sour cream. "We have your daughter," he said. "Nadia is in our care."

Svetlana stared back, stifling a grim smile. The fools. They were lying. Nadia was with Katya. She had taken the little girl out of Moscow. Svetlana would do nothing to place them in jeopardy. It would be her final testament.

"No," she said. "You do not."

A long moment as the men eyed one another, engaged in some sort of silent conversation. "You will come with us," said the black-haired man. "Get up."

"I am still recovering," said Svetlana. "Have you spoken with my doctor?"

"We do not need his consent," said the shorter man.

"I refuse," said Svetlana.

The shorter man set the bouquet on a chair and approached the bed. He flung back the blanket and grabbed her arm. Svetlana shouted for help. The man struck her across the face with a closed fist, then dragged her from her bed. Svetlana struggled. He slugged her in the stomach. She tried to cry out but had no air. The man wrenched her arm behind her back and marched her around the bed.

Only then did she see that the other man had opened the window. At first, she didn't understand why. She was still reeling from the blows to her face and stomach. She had expected a visit from men like these. She'd prepared her statements. Of course they would threaten her. A large fine. A lengthy spell in jail. But not this.

By now, both men had their hands on her. Svetlana fought them as best she could, thrashing her shoulders side to side, trying to jerk herself away from their grasp. It did no good. They were young and strong, and she was old and weak.

They lifted her off her feet as if she were a feather. And then, suddenly, she was falling.

She felt cold air rushing past and a drop of rain on her cheek. Svetlana hit the pavement before she could scream.

CHAPTER 40

Lake Lucerne

"Look at you," said Ava. "You're a mess."

Mac brushed the dirt from his jacket, wincing. His palms were scraped and bloodied.

He'd torn the knees of his trousers. His shirt was untucked, damp with sweat. "Yeah, well, could have been worse."

"Much," said Ava.

The Bürgenstock was behind them. They were back on the autobahn, moving north toward Lucerne, the long, dark lake beside them a calming presence. He cracked the window. The smell of the water flooded the cabin.

"You're out of practice," said Ava.

"More than I'd thought." Mac glanced in her direction. She was visibly upset, cheeks flushed, eyes red. "Hey, it's all right. I'm okay."

"Yeah, you're okay," said Ava. "Nothing to worry about."

"I am."

"Screw you."

"Ava, come on. It's what we do."

"'What we do,'" she said. "Come off of it. This is me you're talking to. I've been there. I've done 'what we do.' We do not jump onto moving elevators. We do not chase down armed men. You're out of your mind." She shook her head, her fury palpable. "Gone eight years and I almost lost you again inside eight hours."

"I'm sorry."

"I can't do it anymore," she said. "I just can't."

"I understand."

"Of course you do." Ava scoffed. He had no clue. She laughed disgustedly, looking everywhere but at him.

"What do you want me to say?" asked Mac. "'That's it. I'm done. Thank you for saving my life. Now we can retire to the mountains and live happily ever after in Zinal.'"

"Would that be so bad?"

"We can't," said Mac. "Not now. Something's happening."

"Something's always happening."

"You know what I mean."

"I'm a diplomat, Mac. I don't do"—Ava searched for the right word—"*this* . . . anymore."

"You were never a diplomat," snapped Mac.

Ava rolled down her window and angled her head into the wind. Every now and then a word escaped her clenched lips. She was talking to herself. It was an argument, as far as Mac could tell. He knew better than to take a side.

Ahead, a column of flashing lights approached. A half dozen police cars sped past, sirens blaring. High. Low. None, it seemed, were interested in a silver VW Golf with diplomatic plates.

"Where's the briefcase?" Ava glared at him.

Mac pointed to the back seat.

"Well?" said Ava. "Something's happening. Get on it."

Mac retrieved the case and opened it on his lap. Inside were several folders, tabs labeled with the names of indecipherable chemical compounds. At the bottom lay a copy of Ashok Mehta's keynote address. Mac read the title aloud.

"'Optimum Dispersal of Polyorganic Compounds in Waterborne Ecosystems.'"

"Nice," said Ava. "From the man who invented VX gas. You know what I think it is? It's a step-by-step guide to poisoning a municipal water supply."

"He was helping the bad guys," said Mac. "Will found out."

"And they told Ilya to kill him."

Mac nodded, finding it difficult to speak. Ava took his hand. "I'm sorry."

"I know. It's just—" What was there to say?

"We'll do this," said Ava, taking his hand. "You and me. Together."

Together. A word Mac hadn't dared dream of for years. He looked at their hands, fingers interlaced.

Together. Nice word.

Mac looked at her. "We need Will's phone."

———

They stopped at the bakery long enough for Mac to grab an éclair and a strawberry tart. At some point on the drive back—probably when the last of the adrenaline had petered out—his appetite had returned and with a vengeance. He wolfed down the éclair before he reached the bottom of the stairwell and the tart several steps after that. Ava sipped a coffee, eyeing him as if he were mad.

Itzak sat on his work stool, transfixed by something playing on his laptop.

"What is it?" asked Ava.

"Shh." Itzak pointed to the report live streaming from the Hotel Bürgenstock. "They're looking for a man and woman, both foreign—possibly British or American—in connection with the murder of Dr. Ashok Mehta and two unidentified victims."

"Thank God they didn't say 'Israeli,'" said Ava.

Itzak swiveled on his stool. "This is Switzerland, not the West Bank."

Ava stepped closer and slammed the laptop closed. "Thank you for your editorial comments," she said. "Next time, keep them to yourself."

Itzak swallowed, nodding. Only then did he look at Mac. "Everything okay?"

Mac said he was good. Then: "What do you have?"

"Good news and bad news," said Itzak, picking up Will's phone. "Good news is that the handset is functional. It works. The bad news is that I have to power it up with its original factory settings."

"Will you lose anything?" asked Mac.

"Everything should be backed up to the cloud," said Itzak.

"Passwords?"

"Passwords too."

"So," said Mac, reaching for the phone. "Let's turn it on."

"Not so fast," cautioned Itzak. "When we power it up, the handset will ping a tower. If anyone is looking for you . . . for this particular handset . . . you're nailed."

Ava met Mac's gaze. Someone would be looking. "Suggestions?" she asked.

"Drive," said Itzak. "If you keep moving, it will be harder to track you. With any luck, there will be a degree of signal lag between towers. It will be difficult to draw an exact bead on your location. As soon as you power up, I'll send over our malware."

"Pegasus," said Mac, referring to Israel's proprietary hacking software.

Itzak said, "Something newer. Faster. Harder to detect. Call it whatever you want. I can have the phone mirrored in two minutes."

"Two minutes?" Mac shared a look with Ava. It sounded okay. They could keep away from anyone for two minutes. Right?

"Maybe three," said Itzak.

CHAPTER 41

Zürich

The VW was out. If the police were looking for the man and woman who'd asked about Ashok Mehta prior to his plunge from a sixth floor window, they'd no doubt learned that the suspects had arrived in a silver VW Golf. Instead, Ava commandeered Itzak's 1997 Fiat Uno, essentially a red panettone tin with a Vespa's motor.

Ava and Mac left the office and drove up Talstrasse to the lake, crossing the Limmatbrücke to Sechseläutenplatz and continuing along Seefeldstrasse, never hitting a red light the entire way.

"What do you think?" asked Mac. "Can they find us out here?"

"They can find us anywhere if we stay on the grid for too long."

"I thought Itzak was your miracle worker."

"You've had your miracle for the day," said Ava.

Mac sighed. True enough. "Two minutes," he said. "I'm pulling for Itzak."

"Count on three."

They passed the Tiefenbrunnen train station, the road narrowing to two lanes as it followed the banks of the Zürichsee. The city was behind them. They had entered the wealthy, bucolic suburb of Küsnacht. The lake lay to their right, barely a mile wide, choppy, a stiff wind blowing whitecaps. Far away, past the end of the lake, stood the Alps, massive and domineering, an early snow dusting the peaks.

"Fire it up," said Ava.

Mac pressed his thumb to the On button. He stared at the screen, waiting for a flicker of activity, something to indicate that Itzak the miracle worker was correct, that the handset was functional.

"Nothing," he said.

Ava darted a glance at the screen. "Wait."

Mac pressed his thumb harder against the button. It was akin, he realized, to punching the Walk button at an intersection repeatedly, believing it would make the light change more quickly.

"Now?" asked Ava, not bothering to hide her concern. "Anything? Mac?"

Mac couldn't answer. Itzak had made good on his promise. Miracle worker, indeed. The phone had powered up. The time was 4:11 p.m.; the date was correct. But it was neither the time nor the date that had caused the lump to form in his throat and his hand to tremble. It was the vividly colored screensaver Will had chosen. At that moment, Mac was looking at an image of him and his son taken fifteen years earlier on the summit of the Matterhorn. They stood shoulder to shoulder, arms interlocked, hands raised in celebration of their accomplishment. Mac remembered the moment as if it were yesterday.

"Mac?"

"Five bars," he said, showing her the phone. "We're good."

Ava called Itzak. "Go."

CHAPTER 42

Zürichberg

This is bad, thought Jane, doing her best to keep her act together. This is beyond bad. This is catastrophic.

She stood on the sidewalk outside the safe house, hands in her pockets, her spirits as low as she could remember. Nothing mattered but finding Ilya Ivashka, and that, she knew, was not going to happen.

The place was a circus. Uniformed police officers swarmed in and out of the house.

Marked and unmarked vehicles crowded the street, light bars on, strobes flashing. The Russians were present, too, if more discreetly. A dozen of their men lurked about in overcoats and poorly fitting suits.

Jane had called in the incident as soon as she'd found Jimmy Chen. Thorpe ordered her to stay put until a team arrived to remove the body. She didn't like the order, though it hardly mattered. She could already hear the first siren approaching. It was Ilya's doing. He'd called the police. He wanted Jane sidelined, one way or another.

There had been a tense period when she was cuffed and thrown into the back of a cruiser, made to lie flat, hands behind her. At some point, instructions were issued to free her, either from Thorpe or, she preferred to presume, from Kleiner.

Cal Thorpe had arrived an hour later. She watched him conferring with his Russian counterpart, Yuri something, the two of them hunched in the doorway, looking more like coconspirators than sworn enemies.

Thorpe shook hands solemnly with Yuri. Jane could practically lip-read the apology. "I'm sorry. One of our agents went off the reservation. I had no idea they were violating your space. You know how it can be. Let's not make this an international incident. We'll owe you one."

No, Jane wanted to shout, as Thorpe broke off and walked in her direction. The Russians are planning an attack. It's called Hercules. Will knew about it, so they sent Ilya Ivashka to kill him. She looked down at her jacket, at the dried blood stiffening its hem. Jimmy Chen gave his life trying to stop it too. How dare you make nice with these bastards? Confront them. Tell them what we know. They're terrorists.

"A plane's waiting," said Thorpe, drawing near. He had on a Chesterfield overcoat with a black velvet collar and wing tip shoes, never shinier. This was as close to the front lines as he was likely to get. He wanted everyone to know Calvin Thorpe had arrived to tie up the loose ends. Silk was on the scene.

"Give me some time," said Jane. "I can find him."

"That's what I'm afraid of," said Thorpe. "And then what? You're lucky not to be going home in a body bag too."

"Ivashka did this. Why aren't you calling them out?"

"Correction. Ivashka confronted two armed individuals in his private residence who he believed posed an existential threat. Jane, this is a Russian safe house. It is practically sovereign territory. He had every right to protect himself."

"He shot Jimmy dead before we could even talk to him."

"You didn't come here to talk."

"My priority was to get information to stop a planned terrorist attack."

"If there really is one," said Thorpe.

Jane laughed bitterly. And so it begins. The excuses. The obfuscation. The denials. "I want to talk to the DDO."

"You'll have every opportunity when you're back in the office." Thorpe smiled easily, as if they were having a different conversation. "With any luck, traffic on the Beltway won't be too bad when you land. We're laying on a private jet for you, Jane. You've arrived."

"Don't patronize me, Cal."

"Not my call," said Thorpe. "Per the director's orders. Feel free to have a word with her, as well. Wheels up by 1800."

"This is bullshit," said Jane.

Thorpe stepped closer, and she saw the fire in his eye. Just as quickly, it died out. He stepped back as a hush fell over the area. Jane turned to watch two EMTs bring Jimmy Chen's body out of the house.

"Happy?" said Thorpe as the body was loaded into the ambulance.

"You're a son of a bitch." For once, Jane could say anything she wanted. Her career was over. Done and dusted. It was time to complete her studies in French literature. Back to Williams. Back to the Massachusetts countryside. Dig out her copy of *Remembrance of Things Past*. The very thought made her ill.

The ambulance drove off, strobe spinning, siren muted. Jane wiped away a tear. It was all so awful.

"I respected Will," said Thorpe. "If he decided to keep his meet with Marina Zhukova off the books, I don't doubt he had his reasons. If he told you he expected to take possession of valuable intel, I believe him."

"Blueprints of a bioweapon."

"So you say."

"That might be deployed at any moment. I showed you the paper I found. Ilya Ivashka wrote tomorrow's date on a piece of embassy stationery. This is happening now."

"It could be for his flight home," said Thorpe.

"He knew about the meet. Someone tipped him off."

Thorpe pulled a face. "Come off it. Her own people were on to her. Marina was already blown."

"Then why did they allow her to leave the country with sensitive information?" Jane fixed him with a stare. "No, Cal. They only found out after she was gone."

Thorpe met her gaze. "Ilya also had Will's Agency number on that stationery."

"What are you saying?" demanded Jane.

Thorpe didn't answer, content to allow her to fill in the blanks herself.

"No, go on," said Jane, combatively. "Are you suggesting that Will was working for the Russians? That it was Will who tipped Ilya off to a meeting with his own agent?"

"They go back a long way."

"Ilya betrayed Mac Dekker. He betrayed all of us. Will hated him. If there was a leak, it was on our side."

"I don't like your tone," said Thorpe.

"Deal with it."

"We're done, Ms. McCall." Thorpe held out his hand, palm open. "When you're ready."

Jane handed him the pistol.

"Be on that plane," said Thorpe.

CHAPTER 43

Bern

Hannah Irving poured herself another cup of coffee, her tenth of the day, if she was counting. It was a mistake. She was already on edge. Everyone was. Even all the possums belowground in the ops center.

Will Dekker. Dead.

Marina Zhukova, his agent. Dead. Now poor, lovely Jimmy Chen. Dead.

These were not the kinds of things that took place in a neutral country. In a war zone, yes. In a hostile nation, once in a long, long while. But in Switzerland? No.

Hannah returned to her desk and reluctantly sat down. She had plenty of other work. A warning had been issued from the Swiss Federal Police about a demonstration this weekend in Geneva. Climate change, the war in Ukraine, the plight of the Rohingyas . . . she didn't know, and she couldn't care less. It was her responsibility, however, to pass on the information to the embassy's consular officer, who would in turn issue an advisory for US citizens in the country and those planning on visiting to avoid Geneva this Saturday at 3:00 p.m. It took all her concentration to bang out the interoffice message and press Send.

She finished her coffee and considered having another. Suicide would be healthier. She took off her glasses and pinched the bridge of her nose. Officially, none of this was her mandate. She was a techie. All things cyber were her bailiwick. Still, she had identified Ilya Ivashka entering and exiting the Russian embassy. She had tracked down his car to the safe house in Zürich. And everyone knew that she was pals with Jane McCall. Hannah was involved, however peripherally. She'd worked long enough for the Agency to know that shit flowed downhill, and that when things went south, everyone involved, no matter how "peripherally," paid the price . . . even the possums in the ops center. In some small way, blame would be apportioned to her.

At that moment, her computer dinged, indicating a newly arrived internal email. It was a request from personnel, asking her to choose an entrée for the office Thanksgiving dinner. Fish, vegan, or turkey. The only choice she'd had growing up at Thanksgiving was pumpkin or pecan pie. She chewed on her pencil, deciding.

At that moment, all hell broke loose.

A red light on her console began to flash, accompanied by a quiet but insistent buzz. Her monitor filled with a map of Zürich. A pulsating green dot traveled south on the Seefeldstrasse. A ten-digit phone number appeared in a rectangular box at the bottom of the screen, along with an associated name. "Will Andrew Dekker."

Without the slightest hesitation, Hannah picked up the landline and hit speed dial. Her training kicked in. Twenty years' experience won the day. This was what she did.

"Sir," she said when her superior answered, "we have a hit on Target Alpha."

CHAPTER 44

Zürich

Calvin Thorpe kept an eye on Jane McCall walking to the Jeep, escorted by two plainclothes marines he'd borrowed from the embassy. He took his phone from his pocket, then put it right back. He was late returning Ilya's call, but now was neither the time nor the place.

He remarked that he was breathing harder than usual, not quite laboring, but close. He shot his cuffs, taking a moment to ensure that one inch of white Egyptian cotton extended beyond the sleeves of his jacket. No more, no less. A discreet glance confirmed that his pocket square was in place. Folded crisply, one half inch visible. He ran his fingers across his necktie. A double Windsor. Also just so. Normally, these fastidious tics served to calm him. A few moments to gather his thoughts and remind himself of his well-earned position. Not today. He felt his lungs tighten, his throat catch. He'd been breathing this way ever since Mac Dekker had showed up in the Sion Kantonsspital the day before.

Messy. That was what he'd told Jane. Things were getting messy.

It was hard to imagine how things could get any messier. He hadn't signed up to be a murderer, even if one step removed. He was a conduit for the free flow of information. The more both sides knew about the other, the safer the world was. God knew America couldn't be trusted.

Iraq, Afghanistan, before that Vietnam. He, Calvin McWhorter Thorpe, was a guardian of peace. He was helping balance the scales.

Will Dekker was a smart, capable, devoted agent. Winning his confidence had proven a challenge. As Jane had pointed out, he had trust issues. But Thorpe had persevered, even accompanying him on a weekend trek to a remote alpine hut past the back of beyond. The sweat. The dirt. The exertion. In the end, it all worked out as Zaitseva had promised. "The boy wants a father," she'd said. "We all do."

Thorpe considered it a moment of professional pride when Will revealed to him that Marina Zhukova was traveling to Switzerland with the intent of turning over classified, time-sensitive information.

And there Thorpe's involvement ended. The steps taken to remedy Zhukova's actions were not his concern. Neither was Hercules . . . whatever it might be. Will Dekker and Jimmy Chen had both willingly put themselves in harm's way when they swore their oaths of allegiance. What befell them, for better or, in this case, worse, was not on Calvin Thorpe.

He was a conduit. A guardian. He was not a murderer.

So, why then was he finding it so hard to draw a breath? Why was he sweating profusely when it was a chill fifty degrees outside? Why was he so damned frightened?

Just then, his phone buzzed. Lord God, not Ivashka again. He checked the screen. Not Ivashka, but possibly something worse.

"Yes, Hannah."

"Sir, we have a hit on Target Alpha."

"Come again?"

"Will Dekker's phone pinged a tower forty-five seconds ago."

"Dekker's phone? You're kidding?" Thorpe regretted the words immediately. He should be excited about the news. "Nicely done, Hannah. Where? When?"

"Zürich. Real time. Somewhere in the Seefeld district, currently heading south near the lake."

Thorpe vaguely knew the area. Hilly, residential, lots of winding roads. He knew who had the phone. The man who'd beaten Ivashka and Jane McCall to the hospital. Mac Dekker had the phone.

Messy. This was getting messy.

Thorpe rubbed the bridge of his nose, deciding on the appropriate response. He turned to find Jane McCall storming toward him, her marine escorts trailing close behind.

"What is it?" Jane asked. "What's wrong?"

Thorpe looked at the marines, then back at Jane. "Will's handset just pinged a tower here in Zürich."

"We have him?"

"Real time."

"Contact Kleiner," said Jane. "Loop him in to our feed. Tell him to instruct the Zürich police to make a stop."

"This is an American matter."

"Two men are dead on Swiss soil. It's their matter too."

Thorpe averted his gaze. The weight on his chest was growing heavier by the second. He needed a little wiggle room, just a little. He looked back at Jane and knew he had none.

"Right now," she said, "whoever has that phone is loading malware to mirror its contents. Get the phone, and we have a good chance of learning everything Will was up to. There's a good chance he has the information Marina Zhukova smuggled out of the country."

"Let's not get ahead of ourselves," said Thorpe.

One thing Mackenzie Dekker would have, Thorpe knew, was the email Will had sent him providing details of his meet with Marina Zhukova. Details Thorpe had claimed to know nothing about. Thorpe knew when he was boxed in. He had to do as Jane said. He put Hannah Irving on hold and contacted Deputy Director Peter Kleiner, who agreed to help as best he could. Thorpe then instructed Hannah to loop in Swiss intelligence.

"The police are on it," Thorpe told Jane after ending the calls. "I'll let you know as soon as we find out anything."

Jane remained rooted to the spot. "Whoever has Will's phone is one step ahead of Ilya Ivashka and two steps ahead of us."

"I'm sure that with the help of the locals, we will take possession of it," said Thorpe.

"And I'll be here when you do."

A firm smile. No, she most certainly would not. "Your plane is waiting, Ms. McCall."

Still, she did not budge. "The hell you say. I'm staying."

Thorpe maintained his composure. He motioned for the marine guards to approach. "I knew it was a mistake to bring you over," he said. "You and all your baggage. I did as I was told. I cooperated. I listened to you. I gave you plenty of rope. I expected you to take care of Ivashka, not hang yourself." He turned to the marines. "Escort Ms. McCall to the airport. See to it she boards the plane, and do not even think of leaving until you see it take off. Are we clear?"

The marines nodded, turning their jailers' gaze on Jane.

"You can't," said Jane.

"Goodbye, Ms. McCall."

CHAPTER 45

Zürich

"Now what?" asked Mac, studying the phone for some sign that Itzak's software was doing its job.

"Don't touch anything," said Ava.

"The software is uploading to the handset," said Itzak, over Ava's speaker. "Give it time."

Time, thought Mac, is the one commodity we do not have.

Ava had left the Seestrasse and started a climb into the foothills surrounding the lake, doubling back toward the city. The road wound through private vineyards, fields of saffron, and tilled earth. Traffic in either direction was light. Good. Mac was in no mood for company.

"How far along are we?" asked Ava.

"Forty-eight percent," said Itzak.

"Almost there," said Mac, allowing himself a measure of relief.

"Another minute and we can get started," said Itzak.

Mac cocked his head. Something wasn't right. "'Get started'? You said two minutes."

"No, no, no," retorted Itzak. "Two minutes to upload the software. Let's say ten minutes to mirror the handset's contents."

Ava nodded in agreement. Clearly, only Mac had misunderstood. First two minutes, then three. Now ten. He checked the wing mirror. Any moment he expected a police car to barrel up the road behind them, officers hanging out the windows, pistols drawn, awaiting the order to open fire.

He had taken Itzak's warning to heart. One ping and "gotcha." He knew full well that at this very moment someone was actively looking for Will's missing phone. If the Agency's relationship with Swiss intelligence was as strong as he recalled, the local shop would loop in the domestics and enlist their law enforcement to track down and capture the guilty parties.

Mac tapped his foot on the floor, feeling increasingly anxious. Ten minutes for the authorities to pinpoint the location of a certain handset as it pinged one tower, then another.

Ten whole minutes.

In cyberworld, an eternity.

They entered the town of Zollikon and slowed at a stoplight. It was a commercial intersection, with office buildings on all four corners. A pharmacy, florist, and a Migros at street level. The car in front of them stopped, turn signal blinking. Mac cracked the window. The smell of grilled bratwurst wafted into the car. Nearby, a boy held his mother's hand. Just another day.

Everything felt too calm. Too normal.

"He said three minutes for the whole thing," Mac blurted out.

"Once he has it mirrored, we'll power off," said Ava, her calm countering his unease. "We don't ever have to turn it on again."

Mac smiled tightly, lips pressed against his teeth. There was no point arguing. What choice did they have, anyway? They had to access Will's phone at any cost and at any risk. He told himself to think positively. It could very well be that the Agency and Swiss intel were at each other's throats. Sure, the Agency had them on its radar—he'd read it was possible to triangulate the location of a phone to within nine meters—but the Swiss might not be in any mood to help. Yeah. And pigs could fly.

"When is this joker going to turn?" he said, staring daggers at the car blocking their path. Ava patted his leg. "*Geduld*," she said. Patience.

"Thank you," said Mac. "That helps." Finally, the car turned.

There it was. Like a vision from a bad dream. A police car approached in the oncoming lane. A BMW 5 Series. White with fluorescent-orange flashing light bars on the roof. A lone driver.

"Eyes front," he said as Ava accelerated through the light. Another second and the car had passed them. Mac breathed easier.

"We're in," said Itzak. "The handset's loaded. Almost a terabyte of data."

"What are you pulling first?"

"Doesn't work that way," said Itzak. "The software cycles through a series of exploits to take control of the operating systems. Some work. Some don't."

"Just tell it to hurry," said Mac, watching the police car recede in his wing mirror.

"It's a computer," said Itzak. "The chip processes instructions at the speed of light. It can't hurry."

"If you say so," said Mac.

The police car was nearly out of view. False alarm. Still, he kept his eye on it.

Going, going . . .

The BMW's brake lights flashed. It pulled a hard U-turn. Strobes flashed blue and yellow.

Mac's stomach fell. "Company," he said.

Ava checked the rearview mirror. "Itzak, tell it to fucking hurry!"

Already, the police car was closing the distance. It was the tortoise versus the hare, or *il tartaruga* versus *der Hase*. The Italian one was losing.

"Tell me this car's a decoy," said Mac. "It really has a four-fifty-four under the hood. Twin carbs. Five hundred horses."

Ava's answer was to downshift into third and punch the gas. The Fiat lurched forward and picked up speed. They rounded a curve and descended a hill. The road widened to two lanes in each direction, tram tracks in between. Traffic grew heavier.

The BMW rounded the bend behind them and in a burst of acceleration narrowed the gap to a single car length.

"*Bitte fahren-sie das Auto zu dem Seite,*" ordered the officer over his loudspeaker. Pull the car over to the curb.

"You feel like pulling over?" asked Ava.

Mac's grip on the phone tightened. "Will's orders. No pulling over allowed."

The policeman continued to broadcast his instructions, his voice loud enough to be heard in Italy.

"You buckled up?" Ava sped through the Römerhofplatz, a roundabout circling a tram stop and kiosk, the Fiat listing perilously.

"We're barely doing eighty kilometers an hour," said Mac as they exited the circle and shot onto the straightaway. "What does it matter?"

"Don't say I didn't warn you."

In front of them, a city tram approached. It was close enough for Mac to read the number and the end station. Line 8. Albisgütli.

"Ideas?" said Mac.

"One," said Ava. "Hold on."

She braked. The Fiat skidded. Mac was thrown forward, hands slamming onto the dash.

The BMW reacted too slowly, its bumper nudging the Fiat, before the police car stopped entirely. Ava downshifted into second gear and pulled the car violently to the left, crossing the tracks. The tram rang its bell. *Clang. Clang.* Mac braced for impact. The Fiat cleared the tracks, the tram missing it by feet. There was a gap in oncoming traffic, though whether Ava had seen this or not Mac knew better than to ask.

She raced across all lanes and cut down a side street. She continued one block, then turned right and pulled the car into a narrow lane separating two large brick buildings. They came to a halt in the *Hof* between the two.

"I thought you didn't qualify," said Mac.

"Get out," said Ava.

Mac jumped out of the car. A sign on a wall read **RESEARCH INSTITUT MAYER**. He and Ava entered the rear door and walked across a brightly lit alcove smelling of pine disinfectant. The far door opened onto the Asylstrasse, the boulevard they'd just abandoned. A look in both directions. The tram was no longer in view. No sign of the cop car.

"We need to move," said Mac.

"Where?" asked Ava.

"Anywhere."

It wasn't the Fiat the police were following but the handset, its location derived by triangulating its signal from the towers it constantly pinged. Still, the car was officially *vehicula non grata*. They had no choice but to abandon it. Making a go of it on foot was also out of the question. Speed was their ally. Like Itzak said, their best hope was exploiting the signal lag as the handset was passed from one tower to the next. They had to outrun the police until they received the green light to turn off the phone.

They paused at the door and peered through the glass. A late-model Mercedes sedan pulled to the curb. Black. S-Class. The driver stepped out and opened the rear door, offering a hand. An elderly woman stepped onto the curb. The two exchanged words.

Mac noted that the man was dressed in dark livery. Maybe forty years old. Heavyset.

Unimposing to look at, but you never knew.

Ava brushed against his shoulder, taking a closer look. "I already shot someone today. Why not add grand theft auto?" She raised her phone. "Itzak, how much longer?"

"Six minutes."

"I'll handle the chauffeur," said Mac. "You drive."

He threw open the glass door and crossed the sidewalk. He slid his pistol inside the chauffeur's coat, jamming the barrel into his ribs. "I'm taking your car and your phone."

The chauffeur winced, looking at the pistol, then at Mac. "This type of thing is not done here," he said calmly.

"Times change," said Mac.

"An American," said the chauffeur as he handed Mac his phone and the key fob. "I should have known."

"Take the lady inside the building," said Mac. "Tell her to count to one hundred."

Ava escorted the elderly woman across the sidewalk. She hurried back, brandishing the woman's phone. No calls to the police allowed . . . at least for a minute or two.

Within seconds, they were in the Mercedes. Ava pulled a U-turn and headed north on Asylstrasse. It was 4:30 p.m.: the beginning of rush hour. A steady stream of cars traveled in both directions. They stayed with the flow of traffic, passing the Kunsthaus, turning left down the hill to the Bellevueplatz.

"Itzak," said Ava.

"Still six minutes."

Traffic slowed. They came to a halt, one in a long line of cars. A police car sped past in the opposite direction, lights flashing. Mac knew how this story ended.

"Move," he said.

"We're blocked." Ava checked the side view mirror. The police car was making a three-point turn. She edged out of traffic and drove down the tram tracks.

Bellevueplatz was an outdoor Grand Central Station, a nodal port for the city's trams, its central island servicing seven different lines, all coming and going in different directions.

A number 8 tram left the terminus and climbed the grade toward them. Twenty seconds until a head-on collision. To the left, an unbroken line of vehicles sped past in the opposite direction. Ava forced her way back into traffic moments before the tram zipped by.

Mac looked ahead. A number 4 tram was entering the Bellevueplatz from the north.

Another tram—number unseen—was stopped, disgorging its passengers. A third tram, a number 12, approached from the south. Spokes converging on a hub.

"Do your thing," said Mac.

"My thing?"

"Get us the hell out of here."

"And I thought you liked me for my nice ass."

"Think again."

But Ava was already edging her way out of traffic, accelerating down the tracks, dodging in and out of the trams. "Snaking" wasn't the word. More like zigging and zagging, horn blaring as the tram drivers yanked their bells, raising holy hell. *This type of thing is not done here.*

Ahead, the Limmat Bridge crossed the confluence of the Limmat River and the Zürichsee.

"Go right," said Mac.

Ava cleared the Bellevueplatz and ran a red light, and like that they were doing sixty down Utoquai. Freedom.

"Itzak?" It was Mac's turn to ask.

"Four minutes . . . *no, three!*"

"Four minutes," said Mac, erring on the side of caution. "We can do that."

The Café Bar Odeon passed to their right. The street narrowed to two lanes. Fifty meters ahead, traffic had come to a halt. Ava braked. Suddenly, they were stopped.

To their left, a broad asphalt walkway ran beside the river. Zürich was a pedestrians' town. Men and women, most in business attire leaving their workplaces, crowded the path. A second later, strobes from a police car lit up their mirrors. The cop turned on his siren. Across the river, another police car shadowed them.

"Ideas?" said Mac.

"One."

A tram was approaching. She gave him a look.

"Not again," he said.

"I'm starting to get the hang of this."

"What about them?" asked Mac, motioning toward the pedestrians.

"What about 'em?" said Ava.

The policeman was on his loudspeaker again, ordering them to pull over and exit the automobile.

Ava concentrated on the oncoming tram, lips mouthing some interior countdown.

Without warning, she slammed her foot on the gas and spun the wheel. Tires squealed. The Mercedes leaped ahead as if fired from a cannon, bounding across the tracks, snapping the chains that bound the walkway. Mac looked over his shoulder. The police car followed them. A mistake. The tram crashed into it, the collision as loud as a bomb.

Ava leaned on the horn, swerving in and out of the pedestrians. Most scattered at once. But not all. A man wearing headphones belatedly peeked over his shoulder. His eyes widened. Mac waved him out of the way. Without hesitation, the man vaulted the stone railing and fell into the river.

Twenty kilometers per hour was as fast as Ava dared drive. She eased the car to the right side of the walkway. Seeing a break in traffic, she regained the street, driving across both lanes of traffic and across the Bürkliplatz. Another turn. Up a bumpy alley. Could it be narrower?

Mac winced as the chassis scraped buildings on both sides, sparks flying.

They emerged from the alley onto a broad cobblestone street, the Niederdorf, Zürich's old town. Faster now. Past bars and boutiques, even a sex shop. Then right onto the Universitätstrasse, finally free of traffic.

"Itzak?" said Ava. "Please."

"Got it," he said. "Go dark."

Mac powered down the handset. Somewhere, someplace, he imagined a blip disappearing from a screen. "We're good," he said.

"Not yet," said Ava, throwing a look over her shoulder.

Mac spun in his seat. A police car was in hot pursuit. "How well do you know this town?"

"Six-years well," said Ava.

"Get us somewhere we can ditch the car," said Mac.

Ava narrowed her eyes. "I know a place. We just have to get rid of them first."

"I can't help you there."

Ava eyed the pistol. The Israeli solution.

"No gunplay," said Mac. "It's gotta be on them."

Ava turned sharply, fishtailing into a right turn. Small apartment buildings lined the street. Cars were parked in designated spots. Four on one side; four on the other. Orderly parking in an orderly nation. She carved a line between them, and God help anyone coming in the other direction.

"The Zürichberg," she said. "It's a maze up there."

The Zürichberg. A wealthy residential neighborhood on the slopes of the hills overlooking the city. An enclave of mansions and villas.

"Your call," said Mac. He spun in his seat. The police were a few seconds behind.

Happily, they were no longer stuck in a tin can with a Vespa's engine. They had a high-performance automobile at their disposal. No traffic. No pedestrians. A look to Ava. She was thinking the same.

"Faster," he said.

Ava bit her lip, both hands on the wheel. She accelerated. The engine roared. Mac grasped the armrest. Another look behind. To his chagrin, the police had not vanished. If anything, they'd narrowed the distance. He and Ava weren't the only ones with a high-performance automobile. He returned his attention to the road as they reached the top of the hill. Ahead, a fork. Ava turned left as a dump truck rounded a bend, blocking their path.

"Look out," said Mac.

She swerved right. Past an Italianate villa and a gurgling fountain. The road flattened out for a short distance, then dove down a steep grade. She braked. It was too late. The Mercedes caught air. Mac's stomach dropped. He braced for impact. The car landed ten meters down the hill, nose slamming into the asphalt, seat belts locking up. Ava's head struck the wheel. Mac lost his breath.

Ahead, barricades. Large plastic barrels. A triangular sign read BAUSTELLE. Construction site. Next to it stood a tall pile of aggregate and dirt. Beyond that, the road ended. A sheer precipice.

Ava braked hard, spinning the wheel to the left. The Mercedes spun out, the right-rear panel striking the aggregate, further slowing it. The Mercedes ground to a halt, facing up the hill, right-rear wheel over the ledge.

Mac gathered himself in time to see the police car barreling down the hill. The cop braked too late. The white BMW crashed through the barricades, continuing over the precipice and sailing through the air. It collided with a century-old pine. A stout branch pierced the windscreen and fractured the rear window, skewering the automobile. The branch cracked loudly, then a second time, more slowly, a protracted groan. It snapped from the trunk. The car plummeted to the ground.

Ava eased the Mercedes forward until the rear wheel found purchase. "You okay?" asked Mac, fighting for his breath.

"Am I?" Ava blinked repeatedly, then ran a hand over her forehead and gingerly touched her nose. No blood. "Guess so."

Mac climbed out of the car and peered over the ledge. "We can't leave him."

Ava killed the engine and got out. With caution, they made their way down the hillside. The BMW looked like an accordion. Mac smelled gas. The policeman was conscious behind the airbag. Mac unclipped his safety belt and asked how he felt.

"My legs," said the policeman, visibly in discomfort. He was young, maybe thirty, with short blond hair and a cleft chin. "I think my ankle is broken."

Ava shone her flashlight into the footwell. The officer's ankle canted at a ninety-degree angle. The left leg was broken midcalf, blood dripping onto the floor. A compound fracture. "He needs a doctor," she said softly.

"Someone will be here soon enough," said Mac. "Help me get him out and away from the car." He tore away the airbag. "Can you wiggle your toes?"

"I think so," said the policeman. No paralysis. Thank God.

He addressed the policeman. "What's your name?"

"Fritz."

"Of course it is," said Ava.

"Fritz, I'm going to pull you out of the car," said Mac. "It may hurt, but you can't remain in the car."

"You are a doctor?"

"Not exactly," said Mac.

Fritz took hold of Mac's forearm. "Why the hell is everyone looking for you?"

"What did they tell you?" asked Mac.

"Wanted by international authorities. Consider armed and dangerous. Stop at all costs." At least Mac now knew where relations between Swiss and American intelligence stood.

No reports of pigs flying yet. "How good a read did you get on our phone?"

"Within fifty centimeters."

A little more than a foot. "Any signal lag between towers?"

"Of course not."

A look to Ava. "Remember to tell that to Itzak," said Mac. "No signal lag. Accurate to within fifty centimeters." He positioned his arms behind the injured policeman. Then to the officer: "Take a breath. One, two, three."

240

The officer didn't make a sound as Ava and Mac freed him from the car and laid him on a bed of pine needles a safe distance from the car.

The sound of an engine drifted from the top of the hill. Doors slammed. Raised voices. "Do me a favor, Fritz," said Mac. "Tell them you didn't see where we went."

"I cannot do that," said Fritz.

"Good on you," said Mac, patting his shoulder. "I couldn't either." He stood and looked at Ava. "Let's roll."

CHAPTER 46

Bern

Hannah Irving sat at her console, eyes glued to the green beep transiting the city of Zürich. The whole of the ops team had gathered around her. Gossip was as bad in the CIA as anywhere else. Worse, probably. After all, it was their business to traffic in secrets. The Agency kept a small shop in Bern. Word of Jimmy's murder had spread like wildfire. No agent had died on Swiss soil in fifty years. Now, two had been lost in one week.

Hannah broadcast the Zürich police chatter over the speakers. Two suspects. A man and a woman. First in a red Fiat Uno, then spotted in a black Mercedes sedan. The chase had continued for ten minutes. Zollikon. Asylstrasse. Bellevueplatz. Last seen climbing Universitätstrasse toward the Zürichberg. *And then . . . gone.*

One second the green beep was there; the next it had vanished. "Where did they go?" someone murmured.

"They turned off Will's phone," stated Hannah loudly and for the record.

"Who did?"

Hannah had no answer. None of them did.

Still, it wasn't over yet. One policeman remained on the suspects' tail, his fevered voice barking his position. There came a cry and a bang.

Then, his communications stopped too. Over and over, the watch commander asked him to come back. Silence.

Hannah was forced to make the only logical conclusion. With trepidation, she contacted Calvin Thorpe.

"Yeah, Hannah," said Thorpe. "Where are they?"

"Sir, the police have lost them."

CHAPTER 47

Bahnhofstrasse, Zürich

Where the hell was Cal Thorpe?

Ilya Ivashka walked down the Bahnhofstrasse, content to blend in with the midafternoon crowd. Shoppers, tourists, bankers playing hooky from work. The Zürichberg was behind him, the safe house a distant memory fading like an early-morning dream. A loud dream, though. One that left your ears ringing for an hour afterward.

He kept his eyes to the storefronts, admiring the clothing in Grieder, the watches at Bucherer, slowing to check exchange rates advertised in bank windows. He checked his phone every ten steps. A habit. The ringer was on. Volume set to eleven.

Where was Thorpe?

An hour had passed since Ilya had called. Maybe two. In that time, his world had been turned upside down. There was no need to ask how they'd found him. These days there were a hundred ways to track someone down. Similarly, there was no need to ask why they'd come after him. He was a traitor on neutral ground. Enough said.

The only question was, Why hadn't he been told? Yes, that was the question. Why had Ilya Ivashka been hung out to dry?

Ilya decided he didn't like the question. Not one bit. Better not to think about it . . . at least not now.

He crossed the Paradeplatz and stopped at a vendor's stand hawking hot chestnuts. It was early in the season, not really cold enough out, but why not? Five francs for a cornet sounded like a bargain. He ate a few, then tossed the rest into the trash. His mouth was too dry. The nuts tasted like mulch. He didn't need something to eat. He needed something to drink.

Ilya ambled down the Augustinergasse and ducked into Kropf, a decidedly old-school eatery. *Lüftlmalerei* on the ceilings. Pleasantly plump servers in aprons. The smell of wurst redolent. He ordered a Hefeweizen and drank it in a single go. Lunch and a beer rolled into one. He belched loudly, threw a ten-franc note on the table, and left.

Ilya zipped up his jacket and glanced up at the sky. Gray. What had he expected? He headed toward the river. The ringtone of his phone made him jump.

Thorpe. Finally.

Hurriedly, he freed the phone, shooting a look at the screen. Not Thorpe. Her. Zaitseva.

Dammit.

Ilya allowed the call to roll to voice mail. Whatever she had to say took too long. Finally, the phone buzzed. Message ended. He played it.

"I just had a call from the embassy," said Alexandra Zaitseva. "There's been a shooting at our safe house in Zürich. An American diplomat is dead. A former SEAL, which means he was a spy. What do you know about this, Ilya? You stay at the house. Did they find you? Of course they did. Dammit, pick up the phone. There's more. Roman and Sergei are dead. You'd sent them to deal with Ashok Mehta. I was under the impression you were in Switzerland, not Bakhmut.

"What is going on, Ilya? Hercules is underway. Our team is nearing its destination. We cannot allow anything to interfere with its success. Anything or anyone. I pray you are not drinking. If so, it will be your last.

"I knew it was a mistake to send you out again. You promised me. Stop the Americans, Ilya Alexandrovich. I don't care how. Stop them." Zaitseva hung up.

Ilya winced. He took her words to heart. There was only one American he needed to stop.

Mac Dekker. Yes, Colonel, I will stop him. Promise.

Ilya knew how to find him. Mac had Will's phone, which meant Mac needed to hack the phone. Therefore Mac was at the same place Ilya would go if he needed technical support. The same place everyone in the West went these days. Israel.

Of course, Ilya didn't really think Mac had flown to Israel. He had done the next best thing. He'd contacted his favorite Israeli in Switzerland. *Her. Ava Marie Attal.* Chargé d'affaires, last Ilya had looked.

Ilya walked to the river and put his hands on the railing. He stared at the water lapping at the shore. For a few moments, he wasn't looking at the Limmat. He was back there. In Israel.

With Ava and Mac.

———

Night fell on the cusp of the Mediterranean Sea. The sun had dipped below the horizon an hour earlier, but in the western sky, a dusty orange cast lingered. Closer, the lights of a dozen fishing boats—some going out, some returning to port—flickered uncertainly.

The place was called La Playa. It was a typical beach café in Eilat. Tables placed too close to one another. Sand on the concrete floor. Fairy lights strung overhead. Customers seated cheek by jowl, so close that Ilya considered asking the guy next to them for a bite of his kebab.

Simba. Round two. The change of the guard.

Ilya, Mac, and Ava sat at a table close to the water. They were hiding in plain sight.

Spies in a country full of them. Mac was on his way home after his second tour. Per usual, the op had gone smoothly. If the rumors were true, he'd set a record for his longest shot. Just over 1,750 yards: a few shy of a mile. Not that Mac would brag. He let Ava do it for him.

"Really, Mac? How did you hit someone from so far away?"

Ilya was in from Langley, where he'd undergone a hostile debrief by his boss and a new guy from legal affairs, Calvin Thorpe. Per usual, Ilya's op had not gone smoothly. One small problem: collateral damage.

Ava had tracked the target, Sheikh Abdullah Whatshisname, to a citadel in the northwest Syrian desert. According to her, every night at 9:00 p.m.—no earlier, no later—the sheikh took his coffee and dates onto the uppermost terrace. He was smart enough not to show his face during daylight hours. Bin Laden had taught them all that lesson. Abdullah waited until night and the false safety of dark to step outside. Satellites, however, don't care about the dark, and neither did Ilya's night vision scope. It was heat that mattered—in this case, the thermal body signature—and on that night, Sheikh Abdullah might as well have been on fire, his image a blazing white silhouette against the fuzzy green-and-black background.

Ilya spotted the sheikh easily enough, accompanied by three others, all more or less the same size as he. No doubt a chapter meeting of the local ISIS brain trust. Ilya thought of it as four for the price of one. Who didn't love a bargain?

He needed less than two seconds to take out all of them. Not from 1,700 yards but 800. Respectable all the same. It turned out two were his sons, ages fourteen and fifteen. The third was his wife, as tall an Arab as Ilya had come across. How was he supposed to know?

Still, bad guys were bad guys, even to the Agency's finest legal minds. Thankfully, there hadn't been any witnesses. In the end, Ilya received a slap on the wrist and a mild "try not to do that again."

He adjusted his chair and sat up, tuning back in to the conversation.

"I'm from France originally," Ava was saying. "Lyons. Daddy was a chef. My mother taught elementary school. One day he saw an ad in the *JPost* for a spot at a restaurant in Jerusalem. At the time, Israel wasn't exactly known for haute cuisine. He jumped at it."

"Which place?" asked Mac.

"Trois Couronnes."

"You're kidding."

"You've been?"

"Two years ago," said Mac. "*Canard presse*. Better than the Tour d'Argent."

"I'll tell him you said so," said Ava, raising her glass. "You get around."

"R and R after a prolonged stay in an unnamed destination. Mess halls get old."

"*Tu parles francais, alors?*" asked Ava.

"*Un petit peu*," said Mac, eating up so much attention.

"I think more than that." A long, admiring look before Ava turned her head and put a hand on Ilya's arm. "And you? Are you a foodie too?"

A foodie? Was she serious? "You bet," said Ilya. "*Le cheeseburger royale*. Better than the Quarter Pounder. Supersize the fries, *s'il vous plaît*." He leaned closer to Ava, to those hypnotic eyes. "Ask him if he speaks Russian? Or Ukrainian? Go on, Ava. Don't be shy."

"Nyet on both counts," said Mac, good naturedly. "That's your wheelhouse. Besides, that part of the world is off limits."

"Maybe one day," said Ilya.

"How old were you," asked Mac, "when you moved to Israel?"

"Fifteen," said Ava. "It wasn't a popular decision. None of us had ever visited. Israel was where car bombs went off and someone was always fighting someone else."

"Still is," said Ilya, downing the rest of his beer, signaling for another.

"The job wasn't the only reason we emigrated," said Ava. "My father had been feeling more and more uncomfortable there. There is an undercurrent of hate toward our people. It's rather subtle, until it isn't. I never noticed, or maybe I didn't care to. I was a teenager. There were more important things."

"Was your father originally from France?" asked Mac.

"Our family, yes. For hundreds of years. But he was born in a camp for displaced persons in Poland after the war. His mother survived. His father did not."

"Why didn't they emigrate earlier?" asked Ilya. "I'd have gotten the hell out of Dodge."

"We're French, first," said Ava. "My father still doesn't have an Israeli passport."

"And you?" asked Mac.

"The moment I set foot here, I knew I was at home," said Ava. "Really home. For me, being a Jew isn't a matter of religion. It's about blood, history, country. Turns out I'm a bit of a fanatic. What about you?"

"Me?" asked Ilya.

"You," said Ava, pointing a finger at both him and Mac.

"Us?" said Ilya. "We just like to kill people."

Mac looked away, rolling his eyes. He was all too familiar with Ilya's shtick. The bloodthirsty philistine devoid of morality.

"You don't mean that?" said Ava.

"I do," said Ilya. The beer arrived. He quaffed half.

"He doesn't," said Mac. "We share the same feelings for our country as you. An obligation."

"Speak for yourself," said Ilya. "I'm past that. I do it because it's the only thing I'm good at."

"Oh, bullshit," said Mac, under his breath.

"It's true," said Ilya, feeling irked, maybe more than that.

"Now, now," said Ava. "Partners should get along."

"I told you," retorted Ilya. "We're not partners."

"I'm sorry," said Ava.

"I do my thing. He does his." Ilya glared at Mac. "Seventeen hundred fifty yards. For real? I'm calling bullshit."

"Cool it, man," said Mac, calmly, always the arbiter. "She didn't mean it as an insult."

"Of course I didn't." Ava smiled consolingly and placed her hand on Ilya's arm. A squeeze. Calm down. We're all friends here.

It was then that Ilya caught her giving Mac a look. Something passed between them.

Something private, intimate. It was them versus him. Ilya saw it and knew. She'd picked Mac.

"Dangerous," he said, feeling something stinging inside him.

"Pardon me?" said Ava.

"That's what you said that night at Uzi's. Remember, the place you and I went for drinks. 'We're going to be working together under stressful conditions. These things never end well.'"

"Tone it down," said Mac. "Where is this coming from?"

"I'm only telling you what she told me." Ilya raised a finger at Mac. "I know why you exfilled to Diego Garcia. You didn't want me to know."

"Ilya, what's wrong with you?" asked Mac.

"You tell me," said Ilya, then turned to Ava. "Or you?"

"Ilya, please," she said. "Stop."

But Ilya was just getting going. Aggression was always the best antidote to hurt. "I can see it, plain as day. *Hello.*"

"Lower your voice," said Mac.

"What, are you my boss now?"

"Look around," said Mac. "This is not the place."

"You afraid people will find out?" asked Ilya, throwing out his arms. "Don't want anyone to know you're fucking her. Ava from the Office." He laughed boisterously. "Did she pull that one on you too?"

"Shut up," said Mac.

"Mackenzie Dekker, protector of the poor and downtrodden, steals his partner's girl."

"Jesus, you're an ass," said Mac.

Ava was staring at him.

"Sorry," said Ilya. "Did I say something offensive?"

"Stand up," said Ava.

"What?" Ilya shot her a glance, confused.

"Up," she said, pushing her chair back, standing. "On your feet."

Ilya stood. "Yeah?"

Ava slugged him in the face, catching him just below the jaw. It was a good, clean shot.

Ilya went down and stayed down.

"I'm not your girl," said Ava. "I never was."

At least now Ilya knew for sure. She'd chosen Mac.

———

Ilya blinked. The recollection passed. Strangely, the emotions didn't. Ilya, odd man out once and always.

He turned and walked down the cobblestoned path that followed the river.

Goddamn it, Thorpe. Where the hell are you?

CHAPTER 48

Kloten, Switzerland, near the Zürich Airport

Jane rested her head against the window.

It was all hitting her now. Her brother's death. Jimmy. Her failure to accomplish any of the objectives she'd set out before leaving Langley. Two men dead. Her career in tatters. All for naught. She wasn't one step closer to learning more about Hercules. What a clusterfuck.

And worse . . . *far worse* . . . Ilya Ivashka was still out there. Hercules—whatever evil it might be—was happening, and Jane was powerless to stop it.

She glanced up as they passed beneath a sign for the airport. Flughafen—10 km. *"Wheels up by 1800."* Thorpe's smug, cowardly voice felt like a barb in her ear. *How could he?*

Jane laughed to herself. The real question was, How could he not? Cal Thorpe was twenty-plus years in. He was a survivor, maybe even a star, which meant he was a creature of the Agency. Rule number one: CYA. Cover your ass. There was a reason he was where he was, and Jane was, well . . . out on her ass.

She had no illusions about what awaited her. Removal from her position. A letter of reprimand. A posting in administration. A cubicle in one of those god-awful outstations in Tysons Corner. She wouldn't be fired. No one was ever fired. Firing meant the Agency had made a mistake. But she'd never be promoted again. She'd gone as high as she could. Any chance of reaching SES—Senior Executive Service, the pay grade reserved for the top 10 percent of government employees and all the perks that went with it—was gone.

She'd never get a shot to be a station chief or an adviser to a cabinet official or an aide to the National Security Council. She had lost her chance to make a difference. Jane McCall no longer mattered. Her dreams had been put to the torch.

She felt her eyes well up and slammed a fist into her thigh.

You will not cry.

Jane clenched her jaw and sat up straighter.

"Everything all right, ma'am?" The marine in the front passenger seat looked at her as if she were a criminal.

"Dandy," said Jane. "Just dandy."

She forced a smile, then looked out the window. The sky had fallen, the sun lost behind a sea of pewter clouds. A fat drop of rain struck the windshield. A grim sky for a grim day.

She looked at her phone and scrolled through her contacts to see if she had Jimmy's number. She would have to contact his parents. The Agency wouldn't give them any details. They'd receive a call in the next few days from some bot in personnel relaying the news. A letter would follow. She wouldn't stand for that. They deserved to know what had happened. He was their youngest son. He'd given his life for his country. He was a hero. To hell with secrecy.

Jane shut her eyes, overwhelmed. The heartbreak. A tear rolled down her cheek. Jimmy's death was her fault. No one else's.

One day, she vowed, she would kill Ilya Ivashka.

Her phone rattled. She looked at it. An incoming text message on WhatsApp. *Who now?*

She glanced at the screen. A picture of her brother. From Will Dekker.

Jane looked up. The marine was checking her out. She smiled. "It's private," she said. "Do you mind?"

The marine looked away.

Heart racing, Jane opened WhatsApp and accessed the message. It was a photograph showing some kind of wooden statue. The picture had been taken in low light. No flash. She enlarged the image. A rustic carving of a priest in a cassock, hands raised to offer benediction. She noted that the statue appeared to be standing in snow with gray rock behind it. And in that instant, she recognized it. Of course.

She checked the time stamp. The message had been sent three days earlier, Monday at 6:50 a.m. local time. The hour corresponded precisely with reports given to the police of gunfire coming from the Matterhorn.

For some reason, the message had never been sent until now. Until Mac Dekker powered up the phone.

"Stop the car," she said.

The driver gave her a look. "Ma'am, I have my orders."

"Stop the goddamned car," Jane repeated. "I'm going to be sick." The marine glared at her. She glared back.

"Not in the car," he said, signaling to change lanes. "I ain't cleaning it up."

"Hurry up."

The driver guided the Jeep onto the shoulder of the highway. Jane threw open the door the moment they'd stopped and climbed out. The second marine exited the vehicle. She kicked him in the balls. He doubled over, grunting ferociously. Jane freed the pistol from his shoulder holster and slid into the front seat.

"Give me your weapon," she said, the pistol aimed at his cheek. "Get out." The marine didn't move.

Jane fired a round through the roof, well away from his face. The marine handed her his pistol.

"Phone too."

The marine handed her his phone and exited the vehicle.

"Tell Thorpe I had a second gun," said Jane. "He should have made you search me. It was his fault."

"Yes, ma'am."

"And stop calling me 'ma'am.' I'm ten years younger than you."

"Yes, ma'am."

Jane slammed the door, hit the lock, and slid into the driver's seat. She drove west.

Toward the mountains.

CHAPTER 49

Restaurant Kronenhalle, Zürich

It was early for dinner, but Calvin Thorpe was tired, hungry, and in no mood to get back to the embassy. The embassy meant Langley; an appointment with his masters on the sixth floor; hours on the secure line in the SCIF. The embassy meant questions to which Thorpe was not ready to provide answers.

He sat alone at a table in the center of the main dining room of the Restaurant Kronenhalle. White tablecloth, heavy silver cutlery, black leather banquette. Thorpe was in his element.

And of course, there was the art. The Restaurant Kronenhalle was as famous for the paintings hanging on its walls as its impeccable cuisine. Where else could one savor the beauties of a Miró sunset while sipping a fine Haut-Brion and enjoying a veal steak with morels?

The server proffered a bottle for his examination. A look at the label. A '75, no less.

Thorpe nodded his approval, and a second time after tasting the vintage Bordeaux. Six hundred francs a bottle, and he intended to polish off every last drop. Thorpe was splurging, but why not? It might be a while before he had another chance.

With care, he arranged the napkin in his lap. Damask cotton. You didn't find quality like this everywhere. The server offered a menu. Thorpe gave it a look. Strangely, he had difficulty concentrating.

No one asked questions when you notched a victory. If Ivashka were dead, it wouldn't matter how loudly the Russians howled and the Swiss police protested. Let them. The boys on the sixth floor at Langley would close their ears and give Thorpe a well-deserved pat on the back. "About time someone took out Ivashka," they'd say. "Cal, we need more men like you. Men willing to take a risk. Proactive. Well done."

But when things went in the other direction, watch out. Thorpe had two dead agents on his turf inside of five days. People would be calling for his blood. He could lay much of the blame on Jane McCall. He'd deny having given her a green light to take out Ivashka. In fact, he'd say he forbade it. She'd gone rogue. She was half-insane, motivated by vengeance. The story told itself. Thorpe needn't worry about Jane.

Will Dekker's death was a different matter. The boys on the sixth floor were already demanding an explanation for Thorpe's failure to know about the meet with Marina Zhukova, recognized by all as an invaluable source. After all, it was Thorpe's primary responsibility to supervise all agents in his territory. So far, he'd put it back on Will. On his "trust issues," as Jane McCall had so adroitly pointed out. If word escaped that Thorpe had known about the meet . . . and lied. Well then. As Colonel Zaitseva liked to say, "That was that."

Which brought him to Ilya Ivashka. In the space of a few hours, the Russian had gone from his bane to his savior.

On learning Mac Dekker was alive, and most probably in possession of his son Will's cell phone, Thorpe's initial reaction was to take out Ivashka. He had two reasons.

Dekker had seen Ivashka. He would know that Ivashka was responsible for his son's death. Dekker would find him and exact punishment. Thorpe had little doubt who would prevail in that confrontation.

Dekker had always been first among equals: "Primus inter pares," as they said at Yale Law. In the event, there was a strong chance Ivashka would talk. And talk. And talk. The man was a raging alcoholic. Functioning, perhaps, but raging. Calvin Thorpe's name would come up in a most unflattering way. Dekker would remember him. How could he not? Once, not so, so long ago, they'd spent the best part of three days together locked inside the consular annex in Beirut. It was Thorpe's testimony that had damned him. Oh yes, Dekker would remember Calvin McWhorter Thorpe. It would not be a fond reminiscence. From there . . . Thorpe did not care to imagine.

The second reason he'd wanted Ivashka eradicated was more long standing. The man was a liability. His drinking aside, he was the only person besides Alexandra Zaitseva who knew of Thorpe's role as the SVR's longest-serving mole in Langley. Ivashka was a time bomb. A walking, talking, drinking time bomb. The mere possibility that Jane McCall might successfully take him out had been too attractive to pass up.

Alas, that had not come to pass. Mac Dekker had the phone. Most likely, as Jane McCall had pointed out, he had mirrored it. Soon enough he'd know all about Will's work with the Agency and his relationship with Thorpe. Yet Thorpe was not without hope.

He placed a call. An impatient voice answered. "That was a long hour."

"I just supervised the removal of the corpse of a fine young American from a certain Russian safe house," said Thorpe.

"You mean to say you didn't know they were coming?" stated Ilya.

"Jane McCall had her own agenda."

"So you say."

Thorpe patted his pocket square. *When in doubt, lie.* "It wouldn't behoove me to sign off on that," he said with steely calm. "We need to find Mac Dekker. Both of us."

"I'm glad we're on the same page," said Ivashka.

"Are we?" said Thorpe with sarcasm.

"What does that mean?"

"It's not like you to leave anyone breathing," said Thorpe. "Scorched earth has always been your play. How was it that you missed her? I mean, she's not exactly on your level. Or were you overcome with sentimentality?"

"Watch yourself," said Ilya.

"Well?"

"She's better than you think."

"I'll take your word for it," said Thorpe.

"I need an address," said Ilya. "Ava Marie Attal."

"Israeli chargé d'affaires for Eastern Switzerland," said Thorpe. "Her office is on the Talstrasse. Next to a travel agency, if I'm not mistaken."

"Her home address," said Ilya.

"Can't help you. You're talking about Israel. They protect their own."

"Find it," demanded Ivashka.

"I have no reason to ask my colleagues at the Israeli embassy for the address of a ranking diplomat," said Thorpe. "Especially as she may well end up dead by the end of the day."

"Time for caution is long gone."

"For you, maybe. You can hop on a plane and be back in your Rodina before the police come anywhere near you. Me, I have to face the heat."

"I thought we both wanted to find Mac."

Thorpe bit his lip. It was a messy situation. Damn if there were only messy solutions. "The Israelis maintain a bolt-hole beneath a bakery on Selnaustrasse," he said. "A miniature ops center of sorts. Ms. Attal gave me a personal tour. It's behind the counter and through the door marked 'WC.' Maybe you'll find someone there who can tell you where she lives. Maybe she'll be there herself."

"Selnaustrasse," said Ivashka.

"Try the linzer torte," said Thorpe.

"Maybe next time."

"And Ilya . . . *next time*, call me on a burner. I don't like having to erase the mobile number of our country's most-wanted traitor."

"Tell you what," said Ivashka. "Next time I'll come inside and let you buy me dinner. I hear the grub in this place is damn good."

"Excuse me?" Thorpe spun in his chair and stared out the restaurant window. There stood Ilya Ivashka, his face nearly pressed to the glass.

"Remember, Cal. I know how to find you."

———

Thirty minutes later, after his green salad and veal steak, his bottle of Haut-Brion and chocolate soufflé, Cal learned that Jane McCall had run away. Clearing his throat, he folded his napkin and placed it on the table. By now the restaurant was full. All eyes were on the handsome Black gentleman in the finely cut suit as he crossed the dining room floor. It took all his power not to run to the lavatory. He only just made it into the stall and locked the door behind him before he vomited his dinner into the toilet. All of it. Salad, steak, dessert, and wine.

Messy.

Very messy.

CHAPTER 50

Erlenbach, Switzerland

Ava Attal lived in a renovated farmhouse above the lakeside village of Erlenbach, ten kilometers south of Zürich. The farmhouse sat in a grassy swale fifty meters off the main road. A large oak offered shade in summer. The previous owner had grown grapes, and the vines remained. There was a shed to park the car and an old water fountain near the side door, a hollowed-out log fed by a plain pipe. Ava and Mac were sweaty, dirty, and desperately in need of a shower when they arrived. A shower could wait.

Itzak's software had worked. It had successfully mirrored the contents of Will's phone.

All 1.1 terabytes of it. Texts, emails, documents, photographs, even three thousand songs and the entire last season of *Game of Thrones*. Most importantly, passwords to unlock every app Will had ever downloaded.

Ava brewed a pot of coffee and pulled a plate of leftover chicken from the fridge. She put her laptop down on the dining room table and sat down.

"We saved everything to the cloud," she said, entering a long password. "Our cloud. Don't worry."

Mac brushed a few leaves off his pants as he sat. It had been a long walk down the hillside and back to town, keeping to the shadows, avoiding sidewalks, dashing from cover to cover, until they were a safe distance from inquiring eyes. A cab ferried them home. Mac demanded the driver go faster until the driver pulled over and told him he could take the wheel himself if he was in such a hurry.

Ava tapped an icon labeled "WD iPhone." A moment passed, and they were looking at Will's home screen. Twenty-four apps, four to a row. All the usual suspects: weather, banking, maps, news sites.

"Where to start?" said Ava.

"Telegram." Mac pointed to a red-and-white icon on the top row. Telegram was a secure texting app popular in Europe and the Middle East with robust end-to-end encryption, safe from just about anybody except Itzak.

"Fingers crossed." Ava double-clicked on the icon. The last message had come from Marina. Mac scrolled up to read the exchange chronologically.

Marina: Request crash meeting. Hercules

Will: Developments?

Marina: Obtained blueprints of weapon. Target: Kyiv.

Will: Timing?

Marina: Imminent. Five-day window. Zaitseva in charge.

Will: OK. Prato Bornum. Time?

Marina: 0600. Solvay Hut.

Will: Confirmed. 0600. Solvay hut.

Marina: Ego Ama Te.

Will: Love you too, baby.

Mac turned his head. It was not what he'd expected to find.

"What is it?" said Ava. "You look, I don't know, out of it."

"It was her," said Mac, only half out loud, coming to grips with his assumption, all of its implications. "Marina was the mother of his daughter."

"I didn't know he had children."

"He had a picture in his wallet of a little girl. Katya was her name. It was written on the back of the picture. She's an orphan now."

"Poor thing," said Ava. "How old is she?"

"Three or four, if it's a recent picture."

"We have to find her," said Ava.

"We will," said Mac, making a promise to his son. "After."

Ava leaned her head against his and took his hand. "Yes, after."

Mac returned his attention to the screen. This was about the mission, and the mission came first. "Prato Bornum is the Latin name for Zermatt. It refers to the source of the Matter Vispa, which begins below the mountain. The Solvay Hut is halfway up the Hörnli Ridge. It's a refuge for climbers."

"So they did have a meet," said Ava.

Mac agreed. "To hand over the information she'd collected about Hercules, whatever that is."

"Hercules," said Ava. "I don't like the sound of it."

"Check the directory," said Mac. "Will already knew something about it."

Ava typed "Hercules" into the query bar. A host of hits across a dozen apps appeared.

Mac's eye locked on to an email from "Col. A. Zaitseva—Directorate 6" to "Major I. Ivashka," the word "Hercules" highlighted in yellow.

Mac laughed. "They made that jerk a major. Five to one he hasn't been promoted since."

"Directorate Six," said Ava. "Foreign covert ops, assassinations, terrorism. The nasty stuff. I'm guessing Zaitseva is Ilya's boss. Ever hear of her?"

Mac said he had not. Espionage wasn't his vertical. He read the note aloud: "'Hercules is a fast-acting neurotoxin of the VX class causing respiratory distress, paralysis, blindness, and cardiac arrest. One liter is sufficient to kill one hundred thousand persons. Preferred delivery mechanism: Municipal water supply.'"

"Thank you, Dr. Mehta," said Ava.

Mac remembered the title of his keynote speech—"Optimum Dispersal of Polyorganic Compounds in Waterborne Ecosystems."

"Mehta was killed because Will was onto him. With an attack imminent, he'd become a liability. It was time to tie up the loose ends."

"A five-day window," said Ava.

"Four days ago," added Mac.

"If everything is proceeding as planned," she said, "and we have no choice but to assume it is, the attack will take place within the next twenty-four hours."

"Kyiv," said Mac in disbelief.

"Kyiv," said Ava. "Bastards couldn't defeat them in combat, so why not poison the civilians instead. It's the only victory they can claim."

"There's more to this," said Mac. "Marina didn't just bring out details of the nerve agent but about the coming attack. She believed it was sufficient proof for Western intelligence to stop the Russians from going through with it."

"It must be here somewhere," said Ava, meaning in Will's phone.

"I don't think so," said Mac. "For some reason, Marina didn't want to send it to his phone even if it was encrypted."

"It wasn't secure," said Ava.

"Evidently," said Mac, meaning "look what happened afterward." Someone betrayed the meet. Someone, he deduced, from Will's side. "She had to give it to him another way."

"A flash drive."

"Or something like it," said Mac. "Ilya didn't come to the hospital for Will's phone. He wanted the flash drive."

"We don't have it," said Ava. "Ilya doesn't have it. Will didn't have it either."

A vague picture of what had transpired three days earlier formed in Mac's mind. "The news stated that Will fell from the summit," said Mac. "I don't buy it. He was too good a climber. Don't you see? Will knew he'd been betrayed. Whatever happened, he couldn't allow Ilya to gain possession of Marina's evidence. It would be the same as giving up and allowing the attack to take place. Will would never do that."

"We don't have it," said Ava deliberately. "Ilya doesn't have it. So?"

"Will hid it," said Mac. "It's up there. Somewhere on the mountain."

CHAPTER 51

Zürich

The bakery was a ten-minute walk.

Ilya crossed the Limmatbrücke, lowering his eyes to avoid the glare of headlights. Swans cruised in pairs in the lake below. He crossed the Bürkliplatz, hands in his pockets, a look toward the paddle wheel steamships docked nearby. It was windy. Leaves danced over his shoes and against his trousers. The air smelled of wood fire. Fall.

Cal Thorpe was lying. Jane McCall had not acted on her own. No one wiped their ass in the Agency without asking which stall and how many squares of bath tissue. Thorpe wanted Mac dead not because he threatened Hercules but because he threatened Thorpe. It brought to mind a maxim. *The enemy of my enemy is my friend.* Or something like that. For the time being, Ilya and Thorpe shared a mutual foe. The part about Thorpe betraying him would have to wait.

He turned right down Talstrasse, passing the Baur au Lac, wanting desperately to stop in the warm, brightly lit bar for a quick drink, actually two. No time. A check of his outstretched hands. Steady enough.

Fraumünster Church was tolling 7:00 p.m. when he arrived at the bakery.

A woman passed him as he entered, folding her apron. The shift was over.

"Guten Abend, Fräulein." Ilya held the door and closed it behind him, deftly sweeping the lock. The display was nearly empty. A young man—an apprentice, to look at—removed the unsold pastries with a pair of tongs, placing them one by one onto a cart. There didn't appear to be anyone else in the store.

"I'm sorry, sir, we are closed." The apprentice showed Ilya the cart. A few tarts, éclairs, finger sandwiches. "If you'd care for a dessert, please. On the house."

"May I have a look?" asked Ilya, sliding the stiletto from his trousers.

The apprentice rolled the cart to the counter. Ilya bent to examine them. What was it that Thorpe had recommended? "Any linzer torte?"

"I am sorry. Our specialty. Gone by midday."

"Pity," said Ilya. "And this?" He pointed at a blackberry tart. The apprentice leaned closer, tongs at the ready. "One or two?"

"One." Ilya patted his waistline. "Mustn't overdo."

"With pleasure." The apprentice picked up a tart and placed it on the packing shelf behind him. Ilya vaulted the counter. Arm around the neck. Stiletto between the third and fourth ribs. Razor-sharp tip angled upward. A bit of resistance as it punctured the ventricular wall. A final thrust to finish things.

The apprentice gasped violently. He was dead before he hit the floor.

Ilya extinguished the lights and passed through the swinging doors into the kitchen proper. Empty. Not a soul on the premises. His luck was holding.

He located the door marked **WC**. He placed his fingers around the knob, then froze. *Israelis protect their own,* Thorpe had said. Ilya scanned the walls. There it was. A camera high in one corner pointed directly at him. Turn the knob, activate the camera. *Ding-dong.* You have a visitor. He knew how these things worked. There was probably another downstairs. Ten to one a steel door, as well, guarded with a biometric security system.

No question of breaking in. Ilya had to force them out.

A look around the kitchen. He stepped to the stove. A Gaggenau. Six burners. He turned on the gas, then found a roll of confectioners' paper and threw it on top. Ilya, the Iron Chef. The paper caught at once. Ilya took a bottle of kirsch from a shelf and doused the fire. Flames shot to the ceiling. He took a swallow to steady the nerves for what was to come. There.

Ilya waited for the smoke to gather and the alarm to go off. It was taking too long. Must he do all the work himself? Finally, he banged on the WC door while turning the knob. "Fire!" he shouted. "Help!" He retreated and ducked behind the stove.

Ten seconds later, feet pounded up the stairs. The WC door opened. A heavyset man, shirt untucked, tousled underwear hanging over jeans, stormed into the kitchen. He waved away the smoke, searching for the person in need.

"Hey there," he said. "Are you all right?"

Just then, the fire alarm went off. Water coursed from the sprinklers overhead. "Here," said Ilya, weakly.

The man turned the corner. He saw Ilya. He recognized his intent, if not his identity. He turned to run. Too late. Too slow.

Ilya grabbed his collar and spun him around, throwing him against the wall, once, twice. Stunned, the man gave up all resistance. No veteran of Shin Bet, he. Ilya dragged him toward the fire. He had three minutes before the fire department arrived. Not a second more. It didn't pay to underestimate Swiss efficiency.

Ilya thrust the man's face into the flames and yanked him clear. The scream was unholy. "Where is Ava Attal?" asked Ilya. "Tell me, you live. Otherwise, it's the fire."

The man shook his head. Ilya dragged him back to the stove. "No, no," cried the man. "Please."

"Where?"

"Erlenbach. Outside the city."

"Address?"

"I've never been."

Ilya muttered under his breath. He wanted to believe the fellow. Still, he had to be sure. Enough with the face. The smell of his singed beard sickened him. He took hold of the man's forearm and shoved his hand into the flames. The Israeli didn't like that. Not one bit.

One. Two. Three.

"A farmhouse," said the man, regarding his blistered hand. "Pflugsteinstrasse. I don't know the number. There's a water fountain in front."

Ilya threw him to the floor. Erlenbach. Pflugsteinstrasse. *Ein Wasserbrunnen.* Ilya was getting a crash course in German along with the information he needed.

He knelt beside the man. "What is your name?"

"Itzak Cohen."

"Thank you, Itzak Cohen. I am Ilya Ivashka."

"You're wel—"

The stiletto cut short his words and his life.

Ilya left by the back door. He was in time to see a fire truck round the corner. He headed in the opposite direction, wiping the blade on his pant leg.

"Taxi!"

CHAPTER 52

Erlenbach

Mac lifted his eyes from the laptop and gazed out the picture window. The view looked across the Zürichsee toward Kilchberg and Thalwil. He made out the royal blue factory of Lindt & Sprüngli on the far shore. An intercity train emerged from a tunnel traveling southbound toward Rapperswil and Sargans. The sun dropped below the mountains, its last rays dancing over the hillside. To the naked eye, all appeared as it should in this safe, orderly country. An idyll.

And yet . . . Mac knew otherwise. He saw only danger and the risk of imminent disaster.

"If he hid it, he had to let someone know," said Ava. "Nothing more on Telegram?"

Mac scrolled through the messages. "No."

"Check his call log," said Ava.

Mac opened the phone app. The last call Will placed was at 11:46 p.m. the night before his death. Country code: Switzerland. Area code: Bern. Mac noted that Will called the number frequently. "It's the office," said Mac. "Who runs things these days?"

"Station chief?" said Ava. "New guy. Arrived last year. Very slick. His first overseas posting."

"Numbers guy, right? We were always trying to sneak into Swiss banks."

"A lawyer. We had a joint meeting a while back. Kleiner, Thorpe, and me."

The name landed like a brick. "Thorpe? That's his name?"

"Calvin Thorpe. Drinks coffee out of his Yale Law mug. Smart and not afraid to let you know it."

Cal Thorpe. There was a name he hadn't thought of in some time. Could it be? "Good-looking guy? Tall, gambler's mustache, nice suits? Always fiddling with his cuffs."

"Yes?" Ava eyed him uncertainly.

It was him. It was that Thorpe. "We have a history," said Mac.

"You know him?"

"You can say that. He was a member of the team that crucified me after Ilya went over."

"Thorpe? In Beirut?"

"He questioned me about the banking stuff, the falsified documents Ilya and his Russian controllers planted to make me look dirty. Three days. No sleep. No food. Believe me, I'll never forget him."

"How could you? It must have been awful."

Mac thought back to the interrogation. Hours upon hours of asserting his innocence. The naive and wholehearted belief that since he was telling the truth, everyone had to recognize it.

But no. Things hadn't worked out that way.

"It came down to a signature on a trust document," Mac explained. "Thorpe claimed that a notary never would have affixed his seal unless I'd signed it in his presence."

"But you didn't."

"I've never been to Liechtenstein. The notary was in the Russians' pocket. But, you see, I happened to be in Munich on that date, so I was nearby. Some very nice planning on the bad guy's part. Theoretically, I could have made the three-hour drive to Vaduz. In their eyes, that proved it. The bogus notary's seal won out over the word of an agent with twenty years' meritorious service to his country."

"How could they?" asked Ava.

A question Mac had asked himself countless times. "They needed a scapegoat," he replied. "I was the unlucky guy standing at home plate. Strike one: no one believed Ilya could have pulled off the murder and theft on his own. Strike two: I was Ilya's oldest friend and work partner; therefore I had to have known he was planning something. Strike three: no way the Russians would deposit five million dollars in an account just to frame somebody."

"Against your word?"

"I never stood a chance."

"You poor . . ." Ava left the word hanging. Fill in as needed. "And now Cal Thorpe's here. Small world."

Mac stared at the phone number. "Call it."

"We don't know if it's Thorpe."

"Even better. If not him, then someone who Will talked to all the time. Including a three-minute call the night before he died." Mac pointed out the call log. "Got a burner?"

"For real?"

"What are you scared of? The Agency knows I'm out here. Who do you think ordered the Swiss cops to bring us in?"

Still, Ava appeared unconvinced. "What's the point, Mac? He's not going to talk to you."

"I just want to ask him one question: If Will hid Marina's proof, why didn't he tell Thorpe where to find it?"

"Maybe he didn't have time," said Ava.

"Maybe," said Mac, much too agreeably. "Let's find out."

Ava eyed him suspiciously. "What are you implying?"

Mac recalled the hot, stuffy room in the Beirut consular annex all those years ago. The feeling of growing helplessness. The noose swinging at the end of the hall, hungry for his guilty neck. He remembered thinking that Thorpe wanted it too badly. It was as if he were obligated to nail Mac. Ordered, even. But why the animus against him . . . against someone he'd never met? "Just saying."

"Yeah, you are." Something changed in Ava's regard. Now he was speaking her language. Suspicion. Deceit. Betrayal. The rank scent of vermin. She stood up from the table and returned a minute later, tearing open a cheap flip phone. A burner. Use once, then toss. "Here you go. It's only got fifty francs on it. Don't chat too long."

Mac powered up the phone and dialed the number on Will's call log. "Ringing," he said, giving her a thumbs-up.

Someone answered. "Thorpe."

"Hey there," said Mac. "How are ya?"

"This you, Ivashka? Finally using a burner, I see. You find that address?"

"Still looking, actually." Mac held his breath.

"Who is this?" demanded Cal Thorpe.

"This is Mac Dekker."

"How did you get this number?" Surprise. Fear. Anger, most likely at himself. Thorpe had just committed a cardinal sin.

In that instant, Mac saw a trim man in an impeccable suit, neat hands tugging his cuffs, wiping the sweat from his forehead with his pocket square.

"How do you think?" asked Mac.

"Some chase you led us on," said Thorpe. "It's time you came in from the cold."

"Not yet," said Mac. "I like it out here."

"We know what you're doing. Let us help."

"I'm good," said Mac. "But thanks anyway."

"You're still a traitor," said Thorpe. "You killed Frank Logan in Syria. You gave secrets to the enemy."

"In fact, I didn't," said Mac. "You know that."

"This won't end well," said Thorpe.

"For both of us, I imagine," said Mac. "At least now I know."

"What's that?"

"Everything," said Mac.

There was no reply. It was Thorpe's turn to see that noose swinging at the end of the hall, awaiting his guilty neck.

"See you around, Cal. Sooner rather than later." Mac hung up.

"What just happened?" asked Ava.

Mac swallowed. He wasn't sure how he felt. Not better, not worse. Just different. He discovered he had a hard time speaking. "I think I found the man who stole eight years from my life."

"Thorpe?"

"He said, 'This you, Ivashka? Finally using a burner, I see. You find that address?'"

"He said Ilya's name?"

"I've been at this too long for anything to surprise me."

"Still," said Ava, "I didn't have him pegged as a traitor. Now we know why he wanted to fry you. He was in on it. The Russians already had their hooks in Thorpe."

Mac ran a hand across the back of his neck. Suddenly, he felt tired, defeated even. "How many of them are there?"

Ava put a hand on his shoulder. She knew what he meant. How many moles? How many men and women willing to betray their country? "Stay here a sec," she said. "I have something for you."

Mac forced a smile. "Sounds ominous."

Ava disappeared down the hall. Mac rose and got himself a glass of water. He needed something stronger, but it wasn't the time. He returned to the living room as Ava emerged from the hall. She held out a black velvet pouch. "What is it?" he asked.

"Take a look."

Mac untied the strings and looked inside. "Really?"

"Really." She kissed his cheek.

Mac removed a battered wristwatch. His old Casio G-Shock. He knew that she must have claimed it before he—or whoever it was that had taken his place—had been buried.

"Classy as ever," said Ava.

"I'm a field guy, remember."

"My field guy," she said, then sternly: *"Remember."*

Mac studied the watch. It had been through a lot. He slipped it onto his left wrist, gave a shake. He liked the feel of it. Mac Dekker was back.

"Thank you," he said. "For this." He stepped closer, wrapping his arms around her, hugging her. He was tired of being alone. She was all he had and all he wanted.

"We're not done," said Ava, with conviction, and pointed to the screen.

Mac retook his seat. No, they weren't. Not by a long shot. "Forget Thorpe," he said. "He's not going anywhere. We need to move on Hercules."

"Go back to Telegram," said Ava.

Mac accessed the app. For ten minutes, they scrolled through the communications between Will and Marina, then between Will and an assortment of individuals whose names meant nothing to him, probably sources he was running. He saw nothing related to Hercules or offering any clue about the pending attack.

One messaging app remained. WhatsApp, owned and operated by Meta, the parent of Facebook. As such, there was no question but that it had been penetrated by the NSA. For that reason, Mac hadn't bothered checking it. No intelligence professional would use it. You might as well talk in the clear.

Ava double-clicked on the green-and-white icon. A list of names appeared. Mac recognized several of Will's high school buddies. He was right. WhatsApp was for Will's friends. Mac was interested, however, in the last person Will had messaged. The name was listed as "Jaycee." The message had been sent the day Will died.

"That one," said Mac.

Ava opened the message. A photograph appeared. It showed a slim, dark, weathered statue of what appeared to be a monk. The words HI BERNARD were carved cheekily on his cassock.

"Saint Bernard," said Mac, at once.

"What?" said Ava. "You know it?"

"Patron saint of alpinists. It stands just below the summit of the Matterhorn."

"Sent at six fifty," said Ava.

"After he hid it." Mac looked at Ava. "He did have time to tell someone."

"Who's Jaycee?" asked Ava.

Without answering, Mac closed the laptop and pushed his chair back. He had a funny feeling he'd learned not to ignore: a disconcerting sensation akin to something crawling on his skin. A certainty that there was another set of eyes on him.

Something . . . somewhere . . . was wrong.

"Hey," said Ava. "Check the number. There should be more details."

"Later," said Mac.

"Do you know him?" asked Ava. "Jaycee."

Mac dismissed the question. "Has Cal Thorpe been here?"

"Excuse me?" Ava tucked her hair behind an ear. "What about Thorpe?"

"Has he been here?" said Mac, growing impatient. "To your house. Dinner. Some interservice function."

"No," said Ava. "We don't do that kind of thing."

"He doesn't know where you live?"

"He does not."

"Who does?" demanded Mac.

"A few friends," answered Ava. "Um, Itzak."

"Give him a call. Ask if anyone's been nosing around."

"I don't need to. The answer is no. He'd tell me immediately."

"Thorpe knew Itzak." It was a statement more than a query.

Ava nodded hesitantly. "We do work for the embassy. We harden their phones. We hardened Will's. Thorpe may have been to the workshop."

"Has he or hasn't he?"

"He has."

Mac stepped closer. "Please. Itzak."

Ava placed the call. "No answer," she said.

"Is that like him?"

"I don't know," said Ava, shaking her head. "No. He always takes my calls."

"We need to go," said Mac.

"Yes," said Ava. "Yes, we do. Let me grab some clothing, overnight stuff."

"Jacket. Cap. Gloves. It's going to be cold."

"Sure."

Mac went to the window. "Hey . . . any firearms?"

Ava stopped at her bedroom door. "Like what?"

"An Uzi would be nice. If not, an M4. An AK. I'm not picky."

"Switzerland is an Uzi-free zone," said Ava.

Mac smiled nervously. "Thought I'd ask."

CHAPTER 53

Erlenbach

"Is there a back door?"

Mac followed Ava through the kitchen. She scooped her car keys out of a sundae dish, then opened the door and let Mac continue outside. "Stay here," he said. "Let me take a look."

The sun had dipped below the horizon a while earlier. A crescent moon sat low in the sky. He walked to the corner of the house and waited for his eyes to adjust. He dropped to a knee and darted his head around the corner. A quick look—a mental snapshot—then back.

It was ten meters to the car shed. There was a water fountain and a sturdy oak tree, who knows how old, with a swing hanging from a branch. A gravel track led from the shed maybe fifty meters up a gentle slope to the main road, nothing but grass in between. Bordering the road was forest, cloaked in darkness. An ideal spot to lay up. Sniper's heaven.

"Anything?" asked Ava.

"Hard to say." Mac retraced his step. "Give me the keys."

"Forget it," said Ava, tossing the keys in her palm, heading to the shed. "My car. Bet you can't even drive manual."

"Wait," said Mac.

"You're in luck," she said, looking over her shoulder. "I filled it up this weekend."

Two things seemed to happen at once. Ava's knees buckled, and a shot rang out. *Crack.*

Mac registered a vivid orange bloom somewhere in the tree line across the road. In the time it took to seek it out, Ava had fallen to the ground. She lay motionless behind the water fountain.

"Ava, can you hear me?" he asked.

"I hate it when you're right," she answered, her voice weak, hardly a whisper.

"Where are you hit?"

"Chest, I think. I'm a little shaky."

"Don't move. I'll get help."

"Mac . . . I'm scared."

Mac called 111 and reported a gunshot victim in critical condition and gave the address.

Five minutes, said the operator.

Mac broke cover and fired at the tree line. He had little chance of striking a target. It didn't matter. He needed to know if it was Ilya or one of his colleagues, or maybe a bunch of them together. Gunfire erupted from the tree line. Shards of concrete and wood exploded from the house inches from his head. It had been worth the risk.

One gun.

One shooter.

Ilya.

He crouched at the corner of the house. He extended a hand and withdrew it immediately. More gunfire. A rifle, by the punch of its velocity. A Heckler & Koch M27 or something similar.

"I'm coming," said Mac. "Stay still."

He drew a breath, then moved, firing continuously at the tree line, throwing himself to the ground beside Ava. A volley tore into the fountain. The wood was old and solid, three inches on each side of the trough.

"Hey," he said, taking her hand. "I'm here. It's going to be okay."

Ava winced. "Probably not."

"Optimist."

A patch of crimson the size of a grapefruit stained the area between her shoulder blades.

The bullet had passed clean through. He touched the exit wound gingerly and could feel the warm blood spilling out of her. She was bleeding out. Not good. He turned her onto her back, then ripped a T-shirt out of the backpack, folded it into quarters, and pressed it to her chest.

"Keep applying pressure," he said, placing her left hand on the T-shirt, holding it in place.

"I thought you weren't a doctor," she said.

Two more shots rang out. Splinters flew from the log.

"Ambulance is on the way," he said. "Five minutes. You can hold on. I'm right here."

"You can't stay," said Ava.

"Bullshit," said Mac. "I'm not going anywhere."

"Get him," she said. "Get Ilya."

Mac put his face close to hers, staring into her eyes, sharing his love, his hopes for their life together. Despite all of it, the mission came first. "Do not fucking die," he said.

"I love you too."

Mac kissed her. Her lips were dry, already cold.

"Go," she said.

Mac dropped his magazine. Seven rounds left, plus a spare in his back pocket. He looked back at Ava. Her eyes were half-closed, her breath choppy. He took the car keys from her hand and slid them into a pocket. She carried her pistol in her belt. He slipped it free and checked the magazine. A Glock 18. Capable of full automatic fire. One burst. Nineteen bullets a second. Not an Uzi, but it would do.

It was five strides to the tree and another five to the shed. He slid to the far side of the log. A glance toward the forest. Ilya was out there, maneuvering for position. He'd lie up opposite the shed, prone position, hugging the tree line. It was as clear a field of fire as a sniper could want.

Mac could already imagine Ilya thumbing the fire control lever to full auto. Fish in a barrel.

Except that it was Ilya.

Ilya didn't like return fire. Mac always liked to keep a hand on Ilya's shoulder when the bad guys didn't roll over and play dead. A hand on the shoulder to steady him and, likewise, to caution him that running was not an option. And another thing . . . Mac wasn't the only one out of practice. He'd lay even money Ilya hadn't been in the field since Syria. He'd grown soft. He didn't have Mac lying beside him, keeping him cool, advising him on how best to take out the enemy.

Conclusion: Ilya was alone and afraid.

Two knuckles rapped the tree trunk. Knock on wood. Mac damned well hoped so.

Suddenly, he was up and moving. He fired Ava's Glock at full auto. It was a wild burst.

Bullets flying high and low and wide. The noise itself was enough to kill someone.

Mac saw the muzzle flash from the tree line a second late, felt the bullets whiz past like angry wasps. Too late. By then, he had reached the oak tree.

Mac felt safer here, tucked into the shadows, a shadow himself. Despite the cool, he was sweating, beads sliding down his forehead into his eyes. He dropped Ava's gun and inched his head around the tree.

"Very nice," shouted Ilya. "You remembered. I hate automatic weapons fire. You were an 0331. Heavy machine guns. The fifty cal was your best friend. Me, I was an 0341. A mortarman. They thought it was funny. Give the skinny guy the fifty-pound baseplate. No wonder we slotted for sniper school. Screw the heavy stuff."

The voice took Mac back. All their times together. Good and bad. That first day supervising Ilya's high school class in New Hampshire. Their climbs in Yosemite. Years in the Corps. And then, the Agency. *How could you?*

"You gave me a scare in the hospital," said Ilya. "It took me a moment, but I knew it was you. The hair, the beard, you didn't fool me. It's the way you walk. Like a duck."

And I knew it was you, thought Mac. One look. The hair worn too long. The careless swagger. You were always an asshole.

"I'm sorry about Will," Ilya continued, his voice strong and clear, without a tinge of regret. "I gave him a chance. He's stubborn like you. He didn't have to die. It was his choice. Do you hear me? His."

The man hasn't changed, thought Mac. Nothing was ever his fault. He was always the wronged party. The persecuted one.

"He stepped off," said Ilya. "I didn't touch him. You know I'd never hurt him. He's like a son to me too. He just . . . stepped . . . off. No doubt to prove himself to you, the grand taskmaster. To be worthy of the great Mackenzie Dekker. You know what he said: 'It ain't gonna get any easier just looking at it.' Sound familiar? That was it. Then he did it."

Mac bit down on his lip. He didn't trust himself to talk. He had too many things to say, so he said nothing. Words would only lessen his son's sacrifice, anyway. Ilya had killed him, one way or the other. Mac would never forget or forgive.

There remained only action. That which must be done. And now, for Ava too.

"Listen to me, Mac. This is a domestic matter. Ukraine belongs to Russia. It always has. Leave it alone. You don't think we'd use Hercules on you? On the West. Give us some credit. Let Hercules go. Tell me where Will hid it, and I'll walk away. It ends here."

"I can't do that," said Mac.

"Of course you can, you stubborn mule. You'll never change."

"The only smart thing you've said tonight."

"How long were you up there?" asked Ilya. "All of the time? Eight years? In Zinal? For what? They betrayed you. Your own people. Our people. Everything we did for them, and how do they repay us? The promise of some chintzy pension? A few medals. A citation from the president we're not allowed to show anyone. Hah! You know what your problem is? You believe."

"I do."

"God . . . and proud of it."

Mac was. Unabashedly. Enough nonsense.

Mac picked up a large stone lying at his feet. He tossed it into the fountain. It landed with a plop and sent a column of water skyward.

Ilya fired at the fountain.

Mac dashed to the shed, tumbling to the earth halfway there, turning a somersault, as Ilya redirected his fire . . . aiming too high, clipping the tree . . . then got to his feet, opened the door, and slid inside.

The car was a BMW M3. Silver. Twenty years old. Manual transmission. And yes, Ava, I know how to drive a stick.

Mac climbed into the driver's seat and started the engine. A bullet tore through the garage door and impacted the rear window. Mac put the car in reverse and revved the engine. He released the emergency brake and slammed his foot onto the accelerator. The engine roared. The car shot backward, smashing through the wooden garage doors. He spun the wheel, his head poking above the dashboard. The car made an arc until he was facing the gravel track.

Ilya emerged from the forest. He ran down the grass slope, stopping when he reached the track and raising the rifle to his shoulder. Mac punched the gas, turning on the headlights, flashing the brights. Ilya fired. Here comes the full auto. Bullets peppered the windshield. Mac closed his eyes. Shattered glass could blind a man. He felt nothing. He opened his eyes. The windshield remained in place. A dozen stars formed a circle directly before him. A tight grouping.

Bulletproof glass. Mossad. I love you.

Mac drove the car down the center of the track, gaining speed. Ilya fired again, then dropped the magazine. Out of ammo. He tossed the rifle to the ground. He leaped a moment before Mac struck him and landed on the hood, sliding all the way to the windshield. Inches separated them.

Christopher Reich

Their eyes met.

Never had Mac been filled with so fierce an anger. Revenge. The desire to inflict pain.

He reached the top of the slope and turned onto the road, braking violently. Ilya careened off the vehicle and into the grass. Mac stopped the car. He grabbed the pistol from the passenger seat while reaching for the door. He pulled the handle. Locked. He fumbled with the release. Where was it? *There.* He unlocked the door and jumped from the car.

"Ilya!" he shouted.

Ilya was on his feet, sprinting toward the forest. Mac took dead aim, the sights in the center of the man's back. For the woman I love and the son you took from me.

Mac pulled the trigger. A dry pull.

A jam.

He tapped the bottom of the magazine, racked the slide, and the bullet dropped into the chamber. By the time he raised the pistol again, Ilya had disappeared into the forest. A shadow, then a phantom.

Mac started after him.

A siren approached, and a second. Ambulance and the police. No time.

Mac ran back to the car.

He passed the emergency vehicles as he descended the main road. He slowed to type in his destination.

Zermatt.

Five hours and fifteen minutes. To the mountains.

CHAPTER 54

Kyiv, Ukraine

Night fell as the van entered the outskirts of Kyiv.

The assault team numbered four: all women, all Ukrainians, raised in the Donbas, the country's eastern border provinces. All were trained soldiers, members of the elite brigade, a female Spetsnaz, if there were one, before joining the SVR. All had another thing in common.

They were children of native-born Russians. There was no question as to their allegiance. The blood of Mother Russia ran through their veins.

The van left the highway in Vetansk and drove to a gated garage in the commercial district. The location had been selected months earlier for its isolation and the fact that its owner had served in the SVR. They parked on the third level underground. No other vehicles were present.

The women allowed themselves thirty minutes to stretch, use a bathroom, and smoke a cigarette. None carried a phone. There was to be no record of the trip. Each had a carefully defined excuse for their absence. One was on a trip to Vladivostok. Another at a refresher course in Perm. Of course, there were witnesses willing to attest to their presence. Not that any questions would be asked.

After the allotted time, the women climbed back into the van. They sat in a circle. One last run-through to ease their nerves.

The Kyiv Municipal Water Authority was located at the mouth of the Dnieper River at the south end of the city reservoir. Every day, two hundred million gallons of water passed through the filters and pipes, providing water for four million households, nearly ten million persons in Kyiv and the surrounding oblasts.

It was not a large building. The women had long ago memorized its layout. Staff of twenty. Six engineers, two guards, the rest: administration. Entry to the facility was made through a manned gate. It would be a lightning run. They would dump the poison before anyone thought to stop them. Once in the water, it would be too late.

The women reviewed the plans calmly, smiling now and again, laughing at the audacity of their actions, already prideful of their coming victory. But their easygoing manner was a false front. They had no illusions. They would be on enemy territory and surrounded by enemy security personnel. In their heart of hearts, they knew better than to expect they would return home, tomorrow or ever. There was a reason none carried phones or passports, or any piece of identification whatsoever. They would be caught. They would be killed. No one would publicly claim them as their own. Any success would be celebrated privately and in secret by their fellows in conspiracy and subterfuge. Patriots like them.

The hour grew late. The women lay down to sleep as best they could. "Remember," a voice whispered. "Whatever you do, don't drink the water."

CHAPTER 55

Hauterive, near Bern

Home.

Thank God.

The mantel clock struck midnight as Cal Thorpe opened the door to his apartment.

Exhausted mentally and physically, he set down his briefcase and hung up his trench coat. For the first time all day, he felt safe.

The apartment took up the second floor of an eighteenth-century French nobleman's residence—a *grande maison*, not quite a château—in the commune of Hauterive, a village on the shores of Lake Neuchâtel. Stone floors, lead-framed windows, a *Kachelofen* that took up half the kitchen. Thorpe almost felt like a nobleman himself.

For the second night running, he made a beeline for the drinks trolley. He poured himself a scotch—a double, a triple . . . right up to the lip—and drank greedily. He caught a glimpse of himself in a hall mirror and lowered the glass. A hunted man stared back. Hunched. Quivering. On the run. Shaken, he took another gulp. The man vanished. He saw himself: the real Calvin McWhorter Thorpe. Tall, confident, in command. That was better.

He wandered into the living room, dropped into a plush chair, and kicked his feet up onto an ottoman. Off came the shoes. Next, the tie. He was feeling markedly improved. It came to him that he was due good news. It was high time his bad luck came to an end. He pulled out his phone and called Ivashka. Tell me you found Dekker. Tell me you killed him and the Israeli too. Attal. He'd never liked her much either.

The call went through.

A moment later, a phone rang in the study, just down the hall. Thorpe sat up, his breath gone like that.

The phone rang again. Someone picked up but said nothing.

"Hello," said Thorpe. "Ilya? Are you there?" He cocked his head.

Footsteps advanced down the hallway. He saw the tall, slim figure. The thick blond hair. Ivashka.

So much for good news.

———

"Hello, Cal," said Ilya Ivashka. "I told you I could find you."

"You're here," said Thorpe, "so I don't have to ask how things went."

"Humor me," said Ilya. "Ask anyway."

"I should be glad you're not Mac Dekker," said Thorpe.

"He doesn't do this kind of thing," said Ilya.

"What's that? Breaking and entering?"

Ilya smiled. Not exactly, my friend. "You didn't tell me they were coming. Jane and the other one."

"I told you that I didn't know about it. It was her decision."

"Save it," said Ilya. "I worked for the Agency too. Even when I was in the field, I needed a green light to take a shot. I know Jane from way back. She might have a bone to pick, but she wouldn't go rogue. Not in her blood."

"I wouldn't know."

"'Don't know this.' 'Don't know that.'" Ilya threw up his arms in exasperation. "How did someone so stupid become head of station?"

Thorpe glared at him. For once, he was smart enough to keep his mouth shut.

"Shouldn't you offer your guests a drink, Cal?" Ilya picked up a bottle from the trolley. "Or should I call you 'Silk'?" He glanced at the label before guzzling it from the bottle. "God, I hate scotch," he said, pulling a face. "Give me JD anytime."

"I can offer you vodka."

"Nyet, spasibo." Ilya dropped onto the couch adjacent to Thorpe and patted his knee. Old buddies. "Ask me what happened? Go ahead. Ask."

"What happened?" said Thorpe.

"I found Ava Attal. Mac was with her. He got away. She didn't."

Thorpe smirked. "You got the wrong one," he said. "What about you? You're limping."

"Nothing serious," said Ilya, rubbing his knee. "But thank you for your concern." He leaned forward. "So listen. I found the house. I was right. He was with her. I could see them through the front window. Then suddenly Mac freaks out. Goes into survival mode. Out the side door, armed and dangerous, looking everywhere for his pal, Ilya. If I didn't know better, I'd swear he knew I was coming."

Thorpe didn't flinch. He met Ilya's gaze. He swallowed the accusation. He didn't defend himself. Maybe, thought Ilya, he hadn't told Mac.

"We have another chance," said Thorpe. "Jane McCall. I think she knows where it is."

"How is that?" asked Ilya.

"I wanted her out of the country," said Thorpe. "We all did. Orders from the sixth floor. She made a run for it on the way to the airport."

"Where to?"

"Anybody's guess," said Thorpe. "Apparently, she received a text immediately prior to making her break. One of the marine guards said it appeared to affect her."

Now he had Ilya's attention. "I'm listening."

"One second she was all weepy and crying," said Thorpe. "The next she's alert, upright, adamant about being carsick. The guard pulls over. She throttles him in the nuts and takes off. Maybe she isn't the good girl you think she is."

"Maybe," said Ilya, without conviction. Throttling a guard in the nuts was one thing. Executing a man without orders was something else entirely. But nice try. "How can we find her?"

"I have her number. A real-time trace."

"Do it."

"I can't," said Thorpe. "I'm out of the game. I just spent three hours explaining to Langley how we lost two agents inside of a week, not to mention one of our best Russian sources. I am officially ordered to stand down."

Ilya wasn't sure if he believed him. At this point, it didn't matter. "What's her number?"

"Here's an idea," said Thorpe, perking up. "Take a hike. Outside. Get going. I'll send it to you in fifteen minutes."

"A little strange, no?"

"I know why you came," said Thorpe. "It wasn't a social visit."

At some point, Ilya noticed, he'd pulled a pistol from his jacket. A Walther PPK. He probably thought it was slim and elegant, just like he was. The real question was, Did it have any stopping power?

"I don't ever want to see you again," Thorpe continued, emboldened. He held the pistol too close to Ilya, aimed at his gut, not his heart. "Not here. Not anywhere. Get out of my house. And my country."

"It won't do either of us any good if you shoot me," said Ilya.

"You less than me," said Thorpe.

Ilya played along. "Just give me the number," he said. "Otherwise Zaitseva will have my ass."

"I'm sorry, Ilya. It's my ass I'm worried about."

"Fine. I hear you." Ilya patted his knees and exhaled dramatically. "You win. I'm leaving. Fifteen minutes, okay? Not a second longer."

Thorpe nodded. Fair enough. "Fif—"

Ilya knocked the gun out of Thorpe's hand. It clattered onto the stone floor. Before Thorpe could react, Ilya stabbed him. He slid the stiletto between his third and fourth ribs. When the hilt touched Thorpe's beautifully tailored jacket, he angled the blade upward and gave it a good solid thrust. Maybe a little harder than he should have.

Thorpe's jaw fell. Blood poured from his mouth. Yes, definitely too hard. "You . . ."

"Me . . . what?"

Thorpe coughed and went still.

Ilya snatched the phone from his hand and held it to Thorpe's face. Like that, he was in.

He jumped up from the sofa and walked to a corner. Thorpe had two numbers for Jane McCall stored in his phone. Ilya recognized the area code and prefix for the Agency. The other number—US country code, Northern Virginia area code—was her cell phone.

Ilya called the Russian embassy. As luck would have it, Mike was on duty.

"I have a number for you," said Ilya. "I need to know where she is right now. At this very minute."

CHAPTER 56

Zermatt

Mac pulled into the lot behind the station at 2:55 a.m. He slid Ava's car into the space belonging to the Porsche he'd stolen the day before yesterday. The cover lay where he'd tossed it. No sign that anyone was the wiser. He threw it over the BMW haphazardly, concealing the license plates.

Five days to the operation. Five days ago.

Mac jogged to the main street. A look in both directions. The town was still. Far away, a dog barked, then was quiet. The only noise was the hushed passage of the Matter Vispa through town, south to north.

A last look at his phone. No calls. No texts. Ava, where are you?

During the endless drive, he'd contacted every hospital in the canton of Zürich. No one had an Ava Attal, Israeli national, shot in the chest. He was more upset than disappointed. He knew the drill. Ava was still a member of Mossad, active or inactive.

Instructions had been issued to embargo any information about her condition. Mac could be anyone, including the shooter looking to finish the job. But he wasn't. He was the man who loved her. He needed to know her condition. Had she made it? Was she dead or alive?

Mac set off up the main street at a jog. It was a kilometer to the trailhead, and another five up the hill to the Schwarzsee, the halfway point, a gain of two thousand feet. He hadn't had time to fetch his gear.

No walking poles, no ice axe, no gloves, no crampons. He only had what he'd picked up at an all-night service station: a knit cap, fitness bars, and a can of Red Bull, which he'd polished off en route.

He ran past tourist shops and sporting goods stores and grocers and bakers. All were shuttered. October was shoulder season. Hotels were closed until the first snow arrived in December, restaurants likewise. The place belonged to the locals, and the locals were asleep.

The road narrowed to a cobblestone lane, ambling up and down gentle rises. No stores here. No kiosks selling Toblerones, Rivellas, and little Swiss flags. To his left, down a slope: Hinterdorf, the old town, a confused lattice of weathered wooden huts, stables, and barns, most dating back a hundred years, some five times that age. The cloying scents of damp wood and hay filled his nostrils. A cat dashed from a loft, stopping in the center of the street to stare at him.

Mac veered left down the hill and crossed the Matter Vispa. The river was low, passive, awaiting the fall rains. Then past the Furi gondola, cars locked away for the season. The town was behind him. The asphalt ended. No more streetlamps to light his way.

He jogged up a steep grade, the knee-high autumn grass obscuring the trail. Finally, Mac was moving uphill. He worked his muscles, pumping his arms, concentrating on the placement of his feet, mastering his breathing. A look to the sky. Clouds and more clouds. No sign of the stars. The peaks hidden behind the woolen carpet.

He'd always liked the walk in, the approach to a climb. It was a chance to empty his mind, to get a feel for his body, to concentrate on the work ahead. Not this time. His mind was a war zone: anger, anxiety, and fear battling one another. It was all too much. The death of his son, the events of the past days, Ava, and now his new, impossible responsibility: a five-day window . . . *five days ago*. He was thinking about everything but the climb.

He entered the woods. Firs, larches, and pines blocked all light. The trail disappeared. He could not see his knees, let alone his feet. For a while, he managed by feel alone, snaking through the trees, pretending he knew which way to go. The slope grew steeper. He was forced to slow. His eyes adjusted. Wildlife skittered away, unseen phantoms cracking twigs, rustling foliage. Deer, squirrels.

And then, like that, he emerged from the forest. The trail widened and joined a fire road that climbed the flank of the mountain. There was wind where before there was calm. It was a desolate landscape, even in the dead of night. Dirt. Talus. Scrub.

Mac adopted a marching stride. He'd hardly slept the past two days, yet he felt strong, capable, energetic, even. His thoughts calmed. He was doing exactly what he should at this moment. No question of him doing anything more. There was only the sound of his boots scuffing the dirt, the rhythmic huff of his breaths—in, out—and the forceful beating of his heart.

He looked up. For a moment, the clouds parted. He saw it. The Matterhorn, larger than he remembered, towering above him, a dark, brooding presence. But only for a moment. The clouds drew together again. It was gone. Waiting for him.

The trail flattened, and he broke into a jog, crossing a brief plateau. A hill rose up before him, an imposing slope. No jogging here. He spotted a building high above on the crestline. The Hotel Schwarzsee. He left the trail and walked up the incline. Was it always this steep? He reached the top and bent double, hands on his thighs. Gut check: he was not the man he used to be.

He raised his eyes. The hotel was shuttered until winter. No lights anywhere. He gathered himself and continued. The Schwarzsee itself, a small oval lake, black as obsidian, lay to his left, cradled by a steep stony hillside. The outlines of the gondola station and, farther along, the Furi chairlift crouched in the shadows, a stone's throw distant.

There was a fountain next to the hotel. Mac put his mouth to the spigot and drank his fill.

He cupped his hands and doused his face. There. He felt renewed. Well, almost. He rolled his shoulders and gazed skyward, studying the route ahead.

From here the trail grew steeper, several modest climbs, one false summit after another, before marching across a maze of steel-grate platforms drilled into the escarpment, cables set for handholds. Then a traverse across rocky talus, before the last climb, a series of switchbacks up a vertical escarpment to the Hörnlihütte at the very base of the Matterhorn. All told, 2,300 vertical feet. A three-mile hike. Ninety minutes if he pushed it.

He found a bench set against the side of the hotel. He'd been moving for two hours. His shirt clung to his back, suddenly cold and damp. He sat down and removed his boots, turning them upside down, giving them a shake to empty any bothersome pebbles. He took off his socks and waved them like a boy with his pennants to dry the sweat. He put his socks back on, then his boots, taking care to lace them tightly.

He closed his eyes and drew a few breaths. Footsteps.

A flashlight.

Mac pinned his shoulders to the wall. He opened his eyes in time to see a figure cross in front of the hotel, flashlight in hand. A man clad in black, a watch cap, tall. Just as quickly the man was gone, round the corner.

It couldn't be.

There was no chance Ilya could have gotten here faster, if he even knew where Mac was headed. Then again . . . why not? Ilya seemed to know everything.

Mac stood. With care, he removed Ava's pistol from the rucksack. He walked to the corner of the building and peeked around.

The man stood twenty feet away, back facing him, studying what appeared to be a map.

Or was it a guidebook? A caretaker, maybe? At 5:00 a.m.? Doubtful. Then who?

Mac raised the pistol. It would be easy enough to shoot him. Two bullets in the center of the back. Ask questions later.

No. That wasn't his way.

Mac approached, mindful of the gravel-strewn dirt—slowly now, heel to toe—guarding his breath. The man was not as tall as he'd thought. And slighter. Not Ilya.

Mac shoved the barrel into the man's back. "Hands up," he said, in German. "Turn around."

Before the words were out of his mouth, the man spun, knocking the pistol from his hand. A roundhouse kick connected with Mac's jaw and sent him sprawling to the ground. Mac landed on his back, dazed. The flashlight blinded him.

Mac rolled to his side, raising a hand to shield his eyes. "Please," he said. The light went dark. Mac blinked madly, unable to see.

Out of the darkness, a hand extended toward him. He grabbed it and was yanked to his feet.

"Jesus, it's really you." Not a man, after all.

Mac looked at her, his vision returning. Blonde. Blue eyes. It couldn't be. How had she changed so in only eight years? "Jaycee?"

"Dad."

CHAPTER 57

Hotel Schwarzsee, Zermatt

They stood facing one another. More than strangers; not quite father and daughter. "It was you," said Jane. "Outside the hospital."

"I couldn't really stop," said Mac.

"Didn't you see me?"

"I was moving pretty fast. I just saw a woman wearing sunglasses, the suit. Sorry. I was kind of preoccupied."

"I didn't want to believe it at first," said Jane. "The hair, the beard, the dark eyes. *Who is this crazy old man? Could it be . . .* well, you? You're dead. Or you were dead. Still, part of me knew. I felt it. Then, later, I saw you on the hospital security camera. I knew."

"I had to see Will."

Jane nodded. Her shoulders slumped. Her chin fell. "Daddy."

"I'm here, sweetie."

Jane rushed into his arms. "He was such a good kid."

He hugged her, felt her head against his shoulder. It was something he'd never expected to enjoy again. "The best."

"I should have done something," said Jane.

"No, don't," said Mac. "These things. They're never one person's fault. You couldn't have known."

Suddenly, Jane shoved him away, slugging him in the arm. "You sonuvabitch. You left us."

Mac saw the anger in her eyes. He understood. "Had to."

"How? Why?" Jane demanded. "And now . . . you're here. You're alive." She took a step back, never taking her eyes from his. "What the . . ."

"Later," said Mac.

"Always later."

"Jane. Come on. Not here."

Jane considered this for a moment. "Just tell me what they said about you isn't true."

Mac shook his head. "Not a word of it."

"It was him, wasn't it?" said Jane. "Ilya. There were rumors that you were set up."

"Yeah, it was him. He played me. Maybe I let him." Mac tossed her his bottle of water and waited for her to drink. "I saw the message Will sent you," he said.

"Saint Bernard," said Jane. "You mirrored the phone."

"I had help."

Jane nodded. Of course she knew that. Ava and Itzak had hardened the American agents' phones. The Israelis were always the go-to when it came to surveillance tech.

"We almost got you," she said.

"I had a good driver."

"Was it her? Ava? I know she's in the country."

"You remember?"

"Just at the end," said Jane. "You mentioned there was someone."

Had he? He didn't remember. By then, the kids were grown. He saw them three times a year, if that. In truth, he'd left them even earlier than Jane believed.

"About Thorpe," said Mac. "He's dirty."

"Dirty? How?"

"On Ilya's side. He knew about the meet. He betrayed Will."

"Thorpe," said Jane. "No. He said he didn't know about the meet. He was upset I'd signed off on it without telling him."

"He was lying," said Mac. "He's the one who told Ilya, or Ilya's boss, whoever's running him."

"Thorpe?" Jane's face fell. "My God."

Mac nodded.

Jane appeared to come to terms with the news. "Will never stood a chance."

"That's the way they like it," said Mac. "Just know it's not your fault. It was Thorpe."

"This business," said Jane.

Mac nodded grimly. This business. He looked at his daughter. A grown woman. A life of her own. A career serving her country. There was so much to be said, to be explained, to understand. There would be time. "We'll talk."

"I'd like that," said Jane. Then: "Sorry about the punch."

Mac grimaced, rubbing the spot. "That hurt." He gestured to the pistol lying on the ground. "May I?"

"Sure I can trust you?" Jane eyed him warily. It was, Mac decided, a look that could convince the toughest man to talk. She laughed. "Dad. Joking."

Mac scooped up the weapon. "We need to move."

"Is he coming?"

Mac turned to stare down the mountain. The lights of the village twinkled far below. He angled his ear away from the wind. He heard only the tinkling of the water fountain and the inconstant wind. Still, he knew.

"Count on it."

———

The Hörnlihütte sat on a slab of gneiss and granite the size of a football field, hugging the northeastern flank of the Matterhorn. It was, in fact, two buildings. The original hut, constructed in 1897, was a two-story, flat-faced concrete structure, bland as bland could be, its name written in block letters across its white facade. Directly adjacent stood its younger brother, a modern reimagining of the staid alpine hostelry, stainless steel and glass and exposed spars. Both had kitchens and dormitories and catered to day hikers as well as climbers from around the world, who visited between the months of July and September.

Several picnic tables fronted the older hostelry. All were stacked against the front door.

Mac pulled down a bench. Jane collapsed on it, gasping for breath. The last hundred steps were a killer.

"See anything?" she managed, still cradling her face in her hands.

Mac stood nearby, gazing down the mountainside. It was 5:30 a.m. Nearly dawn. A band of violet rose in the east. The North Star and Ursa Major twinkled in a clearing sky. "He's close."

"How do you know?"

"I can feel it," said Mac.

"Come on."

"It's Ilya. We were like brothers once."

"What happened?"

"Ask him," said Mac, bitterly. It was the best he could do.

Jane stood and stretched her arms, taking stock of her whereabouts. "We can hide. Ambush him."

"He'll be ready."

"But there's only one way up."

Mac stepped to the edge of the terrace. A set of stairs built into the escarpment descended to the path below. There was never only one way up. "He knows that."

Mac walked to the side of the building. He found a faucet and filled up his water bottle.

He scanned the area, stopping now and again, listening.

"You want to beat him," said Jane. "You want to get there first."

"Have to," said Mac.

"Don't you ever stop?"

Mac disliked the edge to her voice, the latent accusation. "Do you know what Marina Zhukova brought out? What Will hid up there?"

"Only a little," said Jane. "She called it Hercules. Some kind of high-casualty WMD. Will was afraid it might be used soon."

"A VX-based water-soluble nerve agent," said Mac. "Target: Kyiv. Sometime in the next twenty-four hours. Marina believed that providing the West proof of the planned attack would prevent Russia from going through with it."

"Take away their deniability," said Jane.

"The US would put them on the list of terrorist states. Other countries would follow." Mac pointed to the mountain. "Will gave his life so we might find that proof. Damn right I want to beat Ilya up there."

"I'm sorry," said Jane. "I didn't mean it like that."

"It's okay. You're not entirely wrong."

Jane put on her rucksack. "I'm coming."

"Not a chance."

"I can climb, you know."

"You were a damn good climber," said Mac. "When you were twenty-one."

"Meaning?"

"Look, Jaycee . . . Jane," said Mac, quietly, matter-of-factly. "We don't have any ropes. No headlamps, no harnesses, nothing. This isn't a little scrambling on loose rock. It's four thousand vertical feet to the summit, exposed every step of the way." He gazed at the rock—immense beyond description—towering over them. "Look at that. It's a beast. One misstep. One stumble. Anything . . ."

"Dad, I can."

"No," said Mac.

"You always have to do things alone."

"Not always," said Mac. "Sometimes."

"For the last eight years."

"Yes," said Mac. "It was my decision. Right or wrong."

"We needed you," said Jane.

Mac stared at his daughter, searching for an excuse. Something. Anything. He didn't have one. His children had needed their father, and he had not been there. That's all they knew. It wasn't their job to question what had happened. They didn't know what he did for a living. Or that he had put them in jeopardy, however inadvertently. Resentment was the price they'd paid for their survival. He was sorry about that, but there hadn't been any other way. If he'd run, the Agency would have used them as bait. Mac wasn't sure how. It didn't matter. He only knew that it wouldn't have ended well. The Rovers did not leave loose ends.

"Find a way inside," he said, hoisting the rucksack. "There's a dorm on the second floor. Lock the door behind you. Be ready."

Jane stood in his way, hands on her hips. "If I were Will, you'd—"

"You're not," said Mac. "You're my Jaycee. You're all I have left."

He set out, full of indignation. Kids. They never change. He made it ten steps before turning around. "And when I get back," he said, matching her defiance, "you're going to tell me why in the hell you and your brother joined the Agency."

"Dad," called Jane, as he disappeared around the back of the building. "We always knew you weren't an inspector."

CHAPTER 58

Matterhorn

Ilya hugged the rocks immediately below the Hörnlihütte, listening to Mac converse with his daughter. He didn't miss a single gut-wrenching word.

It was apparent Mac had gotten into Will's phone. He knew about Hercules, about Kyiv.

About Thorpe. (Well, thought Ilya, at least that's one problem taken care of.) As he suspected, Will had hidden Zhukova's stolen information somewhere up there. But where? "There" was an entire mountain.

Mac was right about one thing. Ilya would be ready.

He waited until the voices grew distant, adjusted the pistol in his waistband, and free-climbed the rock. It was nothing difficult. More or less vertical but with plenty of footholds, a fat crag to wedge his fingers and toes into.

He'd gotten rid of his suit as soon as he arrived in Zermatt. A pit stop at a sporting goods shop left him better equipped than in his heyday. The price was better too. He only wished they'd had a different color of jacket in his size. Orange was not an ideal choice. Once it was light, he'd stand out like a fluorescent Post-it Note.

Ilya reached the top of the cliff and peered over. The sky was growing lighter. No sign of Mac or Jane. He freed the pistol and hauled himself onto the ledge, ducking beneath the safety cable. He heard the creak of a door opening and then slamming shut. He ran to the corner of the building. Were they both inside? Not Mac. He wouldn't stop now.

Ilya approached the door, pistol raised, finger brushing the trigger. Thorpe was right about one thing. Ilya had suffered a bout of sentimentality upon seeing Jane Dekker. *Jaycee.* Maybe even nostalgia. How could he not? He was, if he recalled, her godfather. They had spent considerable time together over the years. It turned out that she did not share his warm, fuzzy feelings.

Ilya tried the handle. The door opened, creaking as loudly as before. *Thank you*, he mouthed silently. So much for the element of surprise. He placed a foot inside, gazing up a gloomy stairwell leading to the second floor. Out of the corner of his eye he caught a flurry of activity. He stepped back. It was Mac. He was already at the base of the mountain, climbing the first fixed rope.

Ilya looked back inside. She was there, upstairs in the dormitory. Jane, his unsentimental goddaughter with the trigger finger. He weighed his options. He could be in and out in a minute, maybe two. Settle matters once and for all. Then again . . . there was Mac, already ahead of him. Never the fastest climber, but the best.

There was no question.

Ilya closed the door and ran past the building, up the slope to the mountain. Game on.

———

Ilya took hold of the fixed rope with both hands. Stout, coarse, like the ropes at Parris Island. He looked up. The wall was maybe seventy feet high, vertical, a messy slag heap, a few footholds but not many. He ascended the rope masterfully, one hand over the other, his feet propelling him.

He reached the top and took hold of the rock near him. He stood on a ledge maybe a foot wide, three feet long. All the room in the world.

He scooted sideways before spotting the first of the iron stanchions that served as route markers to the summit. Metal poles drilled into the rock, three feet in height, an inch in diameter, used by climbers to fix their ropes to guard against a fall.

No ropes today. Hands, feet, thirty years' experience, and the knowledge that if he didn't beat Mac to the summit, his life was over.

Ilya began the climb in earnest. The first part was easiest: a broad convex face, crumbling gneiss and granite. Not climbing really but scrambling. Up, across, zigging and zagging, never slowing, eyes constantly searching for the next handhold. It was like climbing a tower of messy blocks, some big, some small, some sharp, some not so. All the while the distance below him grew. Five hundred feet. A thousand. Not the best time to slip.

The wind picked up, cutting into his clothing, knifing down his back. Ilya shivered. He liked the cold. It instructed him to pay attention. He was in Mother Nature's world, and she was in charge.

He moved rapidly, at once feeling at home on the rock. He didn't worry about the exposure, the wild drops all around him. Danger wasn't a concept to him. It carried no real meaning other than some vague fear. Risk, yes. Risk, he understood. Risk could be measured, calculated, and accepted. If anything, Ilya felt relaxed. In his element. The bracing air, the whipping wind, the endless tower of unyielding rock. He was precisely where God wanted him to be. Well, kind of. Ilya didn't believe in God.

"Mac, you sonuvabitch," he shouted, seeing his old friend above him. "I'm coming for you."

Two hundred feet separated them. Ilya had closed the gap considerably. The young guns—the "speed climbers"—could make it to the top in seventy minutes and down even faster. Not quite running, but damn near close to it. And they didn't even have guns pointed at their heads.

Faster, dammit.

Ilya willed himself to move more rapidly. He came to a series of steps, carved by nature as neatly as if by a carpenter, so perfect he could skip up them. He skirted a jagged outcropping, bulging like an oversize potbelly, crossed his feet one over the other, and was past it.

Mac had stopped just below the Solvay Hut. He stood looking down at him. The air was exceptionally clear, making the distance between them appear shorter than it was. Ilya noted with alarm that Mac was pointing a gun at him. He glanced down at his orange jacket. A blind man could hit it at fifty paces. He drew his own pistol, thumbed the safety off, and aimed it at Mac.

He's daring me, thought Ilya. He wants me to shoot first. Have it your way.

Ilya fired off a round. It was a lousy shot. He couldn't see where it hit, no flurry of dust or fractured rock. He took better aim and fired again, but by then Mac had crouched and was no longer a target.

Ilya crouched too. He was no prideful fool. And just in time. Rock splintered inches from his head. A second round struck the rock behind him. He didn't wait to see where the third bullet hit.

Ilya traversed a section of rock, taking cover behind an overhanging slab of gneiss. He waited a moment, then hazarded a glance. A shot struck to his right. He heard a shout. He looked up. Mac had slipped. He slid on his side a few meters before grasping on to the rocks, scrambling to safety. A close call, the fool. He'd lost his pistol too.

It was Ilya's chance. He stood and fired. This time he saw an eddy of dust swirl a foot away. He adjusted his aim and got off two more shots. Both misses.

It was useless. He remembered that altitude played havoc with a bullet's trajectory. The air at fourteen thousand feet was a lot different than at sea level. There was wind too. Cold temperatures. And all that on top of his own fatigue. His heart rate had to be north of 150.

He steadied himself, laying an arm on the rock, closing an eye. He sighted on Mac's back. *This time.* He squeezed the trigger.

At that moment, Mac took a step, moving higher and to the left, not to the right as before. Another miss.

Ilya fired again. He was out of ammunition.

Ilya felt in his pocket for his stiletto. Present and accounted for. He chucked the gun down the mountain and began to climb.

It had to end this way.

———

It was catching up to him.

Mac gathered his breath, struggling to ignore his discomfort. His knees bled from slipping and scraping his legs. His fingertips were raw. Any second his muscles would start cramping. And now this: he'd lost his pistol. Worse was to follow. He hadn't even reached the hard part.

Mac was over fifty. No matter how much he'd trained over the past years, how many push-ups he'd done, how many miles he'd rucked, he was getting older. He hadn't felt it till now. Till he was doing something he had no business doing.

There was hiking, and there was climbing. He could hump a thirty-pound rucksack from dawn till dusk, cover twenty miles and bag two peaks. This was climbing. It wasn't just strenuous physically, but mentally. Once, he might have charged up the Hörnli Ridge, all piss and vinegar, oblivious of risk, daring the grim reaper to take him. Just try it! That was no longer the case. He'd seen death up close. He'd lost friends. He'd escaped with his life when he should not have. He had no illusions about what awaited. He preferred living.

Mac looked down. In the space of fifteen minutes, Ilya had cut the distance between them in half.

There was no time to rest. He sucked down a breath and set off. A short traverse, a steep staircase of loose rock, and he was at the Solvay Hut.

He pulled himself onto the terrace, barely an arm's length wide. The hut was a one-room wooden cabin built on a perch hardly larger than the cabin itself. He paused, leaning against the cabin, a little light headed.

From here, the aspect of the climb changed dramatically. Earlier it was a question of ascending the face, a broad convex wall with plenty of room to find a path, not too, too steep, always the possibility of moving right, left, diagonally. And all the exposure at your back.

Above the Solvay Hut, he'd be climbing the mountain's spine, navigating the narrow ridgeline separating the north and east faces. A band of uneven, jutting rock three feet wide, with exposure on every side. A vertical drop of three thousand feet.

He hurried to the back side of the hut. Another fixed rope up a fifty-foot cliff. He took hold and began to climb. Without warning, his hand slipped. He threw out a boot for purchase. Nothing. He fell to the terrace, landing on his back, protected only a little by the rucksack.

When he stood, Ilya was there, jumping much too spryly onto the ledge, advancing toward him.

"You never could shoot a pistol," said Mac.

"Yeah, well, I didn't drop mine like a greenhorn," said Ilya.

Ilya charged, shoving him against the rock. Mac kneed him and brought his forehead down on Ilya's nose. It was a glancing blow. Ilya stumbled, shaking it off. By the time Mac saw the blade, Ilya was swinging his hand in an arc. Mac blocked it with his left arm, but only partially. The blade punctured his chest. Mac weakened. Ilya drove it home, then pulled it clear.

Mac gasped, his knees buckling. He waited for Ilya to strike again, but Ilya stayed back.

He was waiting too. Waiting for Mac to drop dead.

Mac ran a hand beneath his parka. His fingers came back painted a dark crimson. He felt weak, light headed, not from fatigue this time, but something else. There was no pain, just his body telling him that something was wrong.

So, he thought, this is it.

He leaned against the rock. "You never told me why."

"For my country," said Ilya.

"You were raised in Bethesda, Maryland. You lived on burgers and fries. The only music you listened to was Springsteen and the Stones."

"The Stones are English."

"Whatever," said Mac. "They played 'em on the radio. WWDC."

"That makes me American?"

"Your favorite TV show was *Walker, Texas Ranger*. That makes you American."

"My father was born in Russia," said Ilya.

"He became an American citizen," said Mac. "So why?"

Ilya rocked on his feet, figuring out his answer.

Ilya wants this, thought Mac. Ilya has to explain. Not so that Mac might finally understand, but so that he, Ilya Ivashka, might feel better about the decision himself.

"To say, 'fuck you,'" Ilya shouted. "To the marines. To the Agency. Mostly, to you. All that bullshit about being better than everyone. More moral, more righteous, the world's policeman. The arsenal of democracy. Come on. I know what side I'm on now."

"The wrong one."

"We don't lie."

"You just poison a city's water supply and kill ten thousand civilians."

"Ten, a hundred, a thousand, what's the difference?"

"You really mean that."

"As much as I mean anything."

Mac was seeing patterns at the corner of his vision. Diamonds? Clubs? He blinked, and they went away. "You said, 'You don't always get to win,'" said Mac. "Aleppo. Before you killed Frank Logan. What was that about?"

"You know," said Ilya.

"Tell me."

"She loved me."

"*She?* Ava?"

"Before you showed up, we were together."

A surprise. Something Mac hadn't seen coming. "She was our liaison. You had a few drinks. Dinners. It was her job. Like she did with everybody who came through her office."

"She told you."

"Of course she told me. You said she liked you. As a colleague."

"No," said Ilya. "There was more."

There's no arguing, thought Mac. He was too tired anyway. "So you shot her."

"About time," said Ilya. "Now neither of us can have her."

A woman, thought Mac. It's about a woman. "You are way gone."

Ilya stepped closer, twirling the blade in his hand. "Don't make this harder than it has to be."

This is what he's always wanted, thought Mac. One final victory. Mac Dekker does not always win.

A look over his shoulder. Craggy rocks. A snowy couloir. Then air. A long fall to the glacier below.

He scooted back an inch, his heels hanging over the edge. That was all the room he had.

The wind swirled at his back, pushing him, pulling him. He squared his shoulders. Something caught in his chest. He felt something warm stream down his abdomen.

Mac raised his hands. An invitation. "Come and get me, brother."

Ilya brandished the stiletto. "It's been fun."

A gunshot shattered the calm. A bullet struck the hut, inches from Ilya's head. Then another, closer, spraying wood splinters. Ilya ducked, covering his head.

Mac saw Jane, her eyes above the ledge, pistol in her outstretched arm. He shoved Ilya against the cabin, pressing a hand against his neck, fingers clawing his throat. Just a little more and he'd have the larynx. But no. He was too weak, too light headed from the exertion, the loss of blood.

Ilya knocked the hand away, spinning him around, and pinned an arm around his neck, touching the stiletto to his carotid artery.

Jane faced them, breathing hard, eyes rimmed with fatigue, one hand on the cabin for support.

"Your move," said Ilya.

"Let him go," she said.

"I have a better idea," said Ilya. "Throw away the gun. Tell me where Will hid the flash drive. We all live to fight another day."

"Shoot him," said Mac. "Don't worry about me."

"Jaycee," said Ilya, reasonably. "This is me. Ilya. I didn't hurt you earlier. I don't want to hurt your father. We're family."

"You killed my brother," said Jane. "Some family."

"You have my word."

"Don't listen to him," said Mac. "You know where it is. Do what you have to do. Take your shot."

Jane raised the pistol. Ten feet separated them. She had two choices. Go for a headshot and risk killing her father. Or shoot her father dead and pray the bullets passed through and killed Ilya too.

"Do it," said Mac. "Screw him."

"Dad, no."

"Jane, be reasonable," said Ilya. "You are not going to kill your father."

She pursed her lips, her hand steady. Mac sensed a current passing through her body, and she seemed to stand taller, more confidently.

"Your choice, young lady." Ilya nicked Mac's neck. Blood flowed freely.

"Jaycee, don't," said Mac.

Jane tossed the pistol over the ledge. "The statue of Saint Bernard," she said. "He hid it here."

"Was that so hard?" Ilya lowered the stiletto.

And then in the next instant, he grabbed Mac by the shoulders and threw him off the ledge.

CHAPTER 59

Solvay Hut, Matterhorn

"Dad!"

As Jane rushed forward to look for her father, Ilya slammed her against the cabin. "Next time," he said, "I won't be so understanding."

"Neither will I," said Jane.

Ilya threw her to the ground and rounded the corner of the hut to begin his climb to the statue of Saint Bernard.

Jane scrambled to her feet and rushed to the far side of the cabin, then dropped to her belly, craning her neck to see over the edge. The east face of the Matterhorn was a sheer, featureless wall, an immense granite plane coated with ice and rime, rising from the Zmutt Glacier over four thousand feet to the summit. Directly beneath her was a steep, snowy couloir bounded by rock, and then oblivion.

It was a few minutes until sunrise. A band of orange hugged the horizon. The sky had cleared. The silhouettes of all the nearby peaks grew in definition. The Zinalrothorn, Monte Rosa, and closer, Castor and Pollux.

Jane could see no sign of her father. After a minute, she retreated, pressing her back against the hut. It's not over, she told herself. Not yet. She had to believe that.

She crossed to the back of the hut. Ilya was making his way up the mountain, easy to follow in an orange parka. A fixed rope led up a short, sheer wall. Past that, the route narrowed and climbed at an unforgiving pitch.

Jane touched her head to the rock. She felt overwhelmed, unable to process all that had happened. It would be so much easier to stop here. She'd done her best. No one could fault her. No one could say she'd given up.

Live to fight another day.

Jane shook herself. No. That was what Ilya wanted. He wanted Jane to put herself first.

He wanted Jane to forsake her duty, just as he'd forsaken his.

Sometimes there wasn't another day.

Jane took a bottle of water from her rucksack. She drank half, already feeling more herself.

"Jay—"

The voice was halted and distant. "Jaycee."

It was him. Mac.

Jane ran to the east side of the hut. She dropped to her knees, looking down the couloir. She saw what she'd missed a minute before. Her father clung to a climbing stanchion at the base of the snowfield, hands wrapped around a bent, rusted metal rod extending horizontally from the rock, only the top of his head visible.

"Dad. I see you. Hold on."

"Inside the hut," he said. "There's a rescue locker. Get a rope."

The door to the Solvay Hut was unlocked. Jane spotted the locker in the corner. She opened it. Inside, neatly arranged, were several coils of rope, carabiners, climbing harnesses, gloves, crampons, and a first aid kit. She grabbed a coil of rope, carabiners, and harnesses and ran outside. She tied one end of the rope to a stanchion beside the door, then slipped on a harness and tied herself in. She rappelled off the ledge, descending the couloir until she was beside her father.

"I'm going to slide in behind you," she said. "I'll tie a length around your waist, then we'll walk up together. Can you do that?"

"Not sure," said Mac. "He got me with his knife. Something isn't right."

"Do what you can," said Jane. "I'm here."

"I guess I'd better," said Mac.

Jane pulled an extra length of rope and tied it around her father's waist, fashioning a belaying knot. It was more cosmetic than functional. It was up to her not to allow him to fall.

Step by step they climbed the couloir. Their boots disappeared into the deep, rigid snow.

Her posture was more horizontal than vertical, wholly reliant on the rope for their safety. Her father was not a small man. She felt every pound on her as she muscled her way to the top.

Once on the ledge, she led him into the hut and helped him lie down. She unzipped his jacket and pulled up his shirt and sweater. There was a puncture wound between his third and fourth ribs.

"He was going for your heart," said Jane. "You're not bleeding anymore, but I can't be certain what the blade did."

"It hurts when I take a breath," said Mac. "He nicked something. Maybe my lung."

Jane applied sulfa and iodine before covering the wound with a bandage. There was nothing else, really, that she could do. She rose and opened the box containing the emergency phone.

"What are you doing?" asked Mac, awkwardly getting to his feet. The pain had lessened, or maybe he refused to acknowledge it.

"Air Zermatt," said Jane. "We'll helo you off the mountain. You need to get to a hospital."

"Later," said Mac, opening the hut door.

"Are you kidding me?"

"He'll go down the Italian side once he finds it."

"We'll call the authorities," said Jane. "They can stop him."

"We are the authorities," said Mac.

"Dad, you're hurt."

"Once he gets the drive or whatever Marina brought out, he'll destroy it," said Mac. "There will be no proof. No way for us to figure out exactly what they're planning."

"You can't."

"I have to," said Mac. "We have to. A lot of people are going to die otherwise."

Jane looked at him. "Yeah," said Jane. "Okay. We have to."

Mac walked to the back of the hut and took the fixed rope in his hand. "You can climb," he said.

"Told you," said Jane.

Mac moved aside and handed her the rope. "And so?"

"Beat you to the top," said Jane.

CHAPTER 60

Matterhorn

The statue was four feet tall, a bit crude, carved out of some kind of dark wood; a monk in a cassock, wearing a cross around his neck and with a face like William Tell. There were some words inscribed above him, but damn if Ilya knew what they meant.

He sank into the snow, exhausted. Tradition demanded a climber touch the statue for good luck. The story was that a thousand years ago Bernard had been a priest living somewhere in the Alps. He'd devoted his life to building refuges to protect travelers crossing the mountain passes. That was it. Not exactly like bringing people back from the dead or seeing the Virgin Mary, but Ilya guessed it would do. He kissed his fingertips and patted good old Saint Bernard on the top of his head.

Who, he wondered, is the patron saint of spies? He owed him a kiss on the forehead too.

Ilya took off his rucksack, desperate for a drink of water. He should have brought something stronger, given how things had worked out. He lifted the bottle into the air. Cheers to Saint Bernard! Cheers to Mac Dekker! Cheers to Ilya Ivashka!

He sat taller and examined the statue. It stood on a stone pedestal anchored onto the slope by stout cables and sturdy screws. Beneath it, between the pedestal and the mountain, was a gap of about four inches. It was, Ilya decided, as good a place as any to hide a flash drive.

He downed the water and chucked the empty down the slope. He dropped to his knees, took off his gloves, and cocked his head to look into the space. He saw a few small rocks. That was about it. He activated his phone's flashlight and shined it inside. It did little to help.

Moving closer to the statue, he bunched his sleeves to his elbow and thrust his forearm into the space. He probed the area blindly, fingers tap, tap, tapping all over the place. He wasn't exactly sure what he was looking for, except that he'd know it when he found it.

"There!"

Ilya touched something smooth and hard. Something man-made. Just out of reach. He leaned down to peer inside. It was too dark to make out anything. He withdrew his hand and waggled the sleeve of his parka higher, just a little so he could maneuver more adeptly.

The sun was up. It was a bluebird day. Not a cloud in the sky. All the peaks were on full display. The Zinalrothorn, Monte Rosa, Castor and Pollux. His eyes wandered down the snowfield. It was about as long as a football field and about half as wide, a pitch of forty degrees, similar to an Olympic ski jump.

Two climbers appeared above the upper shoulder and started up the snowfield. A man and a woman. Ice axes, crampons, ropes. Ilya squinted. *Could it be?* It was them. Mac and Jaycee. He had no time to wonder how, not even a moment to be pissed off.

Ilya peered into the space. A ray of sunlight lit up the farthest recess. He spotted something dark and shiny—possibly circular, possibly metallic—behind the backmost cable. It had to be the flash drive.

Ilya thrust his arm deep into the space. To his elbow. Past it. He wriggled his fingers and touched the flash drive. It was in the shape of a ring. He forced his arm deeper still. His fingers clutched the drive. He had it.

He glanced over his shoulder at Mac. Too late, my friend. You lose.

Ilya gingerly slid his hand out of the gap. He didn't want to drop the ring. He encountered a little resistance, as if he'd snagged something. He gave it a tug. Something hard and sharp stabbed his hand. He screamed and yanked his arm free. A piton had impaled his hand. The steel spike had gone all the way through, a few inches visible on either side. Blood spurted everywhere.

Ilya jumped to his feet and spun away from the statue. He grabbed his wrist, the pain excruciating. The ring fell to the snow. He dove for it and lost his balance, tripping over his boots. One moment he was up. The next he was flat on his back, sliding headfirst down the snowfield. He threw an arm out to stop himself. Even in his distress he knew he had to act quickly, that he had only a second or two to arrest his momentum. His hands bounced off the hard surface. He tried again, clawing his fingers into the snow. Nothing. Maybe the piton? Yes, it would dig into the ice. He tried again with his injured hand. The piton skidded against the hard surface, ripping open his hand further. Agony. He struggled to turn over. The parka was too slick and too smooth. He went faster still. Everything was a blur. He began to spin. His feet faced downhill. He banged his boots repeatedly against the snow. It was no good.

He saw Mac and Jane coming up rapidly on his right. One last chance. He stretched out his hand, straining, straining to reach them. He lifted his head.

"Help! Mac! Please! Help!" Neither made a move to assist him. "Help me, dammit!"

And then he was past them. The snowfield grew shorter and shorter. Beyond it, an expanse of blue. Air. A sheer drop of four thousand feet to stone and ice below.

Ilya screamed.

———

Mac found the flash drive lying in the snow at the foot of the statue. He dropped to a knee and peered into the space. With care, he reached his hand inside and retrieved a length of twine, not unlike the hunting snares he kept upstairs on his table.

"What is it?" asked Jane.

"Old trick," he said. "Booby trap. Will was an Eagle Scout." He handed Jane the flash drive. "For Will."

"For Will."

Mac sat down and gazed at the magnificent panorama. It was one helluva view.

CHAPTER 61

Belarusian–Lithuanian border

Nadia spotted the yellow, green, and red tricolor of Lithuania flying above the border-control station, snapping smartly in the early-morning breeze. Finally, they were safe.

A look in the rearview mirror. The black SUV that had been following them for the past three hours was still there.

Not safe yet.

Nadia pressed the accelerator. Another mile. Please, God.

"Where are we?" Katya rubbed the sleep from her eyes, uncurling herself from her sleeping position.

"Almost there," said Nadia, then quietly: "Another hour."

"Is my mother here?"

Nadia glanced over her shoulder. The little girl's hair was a mess, her eyes rimmed with fatigue. She was no longer the bundle of optimism and energy Nadia had met a few days earlier. At some point, all that energy had left her. She looked wary and frightened.

Nadia searched for an answer. Sometime soon she would have to tell Katya the truth.

But not yet. "I hope so," she said. "We must keep looking."

"But where could she be?" asked Katya.

Nadia offered a smile, nothing more.

———

The drive from Minsk had taken seven hours. Twice they'd stopped for snacks at a roadside café. Katya demanded borscht, which was her mother's favorite. She settled for cheese sandwiches and chocolate milk.

Their stay in Minsk was all too brief. Pyotr was not so much a friend of Marina's as a fellow conspirator, probably a spy too. He was a short, fidgety man, forever looking this way and that. A bundle of nerves and not afraid if everyone knew it. It was apparent that he was in some way beholden to Marina. A debt owed: one he wished to repay as rapidly as possible.

"You cannot stay," Pyotr had said, early yesterday afternoon. "People are looking."

"Who?" Nadia had demanded.

"People."

A hundred questions fought for her attention. How did Pyotr know? Who were these people? Were she and Katya safe? Nadia held her tongue. Pyotr was not the type to answer freely. Or maybe Nadia was afraid he'd answer too freely.

"Where are we to go?" she'd asked.

"You have a car. Money. I can give you more. It is up to you. No matter. You must leave Belarus. Here we are in Russia, only with a different name."

"Who will take us?"

"Anyone, I suppose," replied Pyotr. "The world is at war with the Russian government, not its people."

"But—"

"You must go."

Nadia had decided there was one person she could ask. The one person she had always relied on to guide her. Her North Star. She placed a call to the hospital in Moscow.

"May I speak to a patient?" she said. "Svetlana Smirnova."

"One moment."

Nadia waited as one moment turned into two. A minute passed, then another. She began to worry. She had little experience with hospitals. Were they always so brusque?

"Who is this?" A male voice, less than accommodating.

"Who is this?" Nadia fired back.

"You are looking for Svetlana Smirnova?"

"Yes." Nadia had already said as much. Did he expect her to change her mind?

"We have no one here by that name," said the rude man.

"Of course you do," said Nadia. "She checked in four days ago. She had an operation for acute pancreatitis and an inflamed gallbladder. I spoke with her afterward."

"You are mistaken."

"This is the Novgorod hospital?"

"It is."

"Then I am not mistaken," said Nadia. "Dr. Kerensky operated on her. She did not like him. Please connect to my mother."

"You are Nadia Smirnova?"

Nadia bit her lip. A mistake. Oh well. "Yes," she said, pridefully. "I wish to speak with my mother."

"Where is she?" asked the man, his voice softer, cajoling. A trickster. "Where is Katya Zhukova?"

"I do not know," said Nadia. "Give me my mother."

"We will find you," said the man. "Make no mistake."

"What have you done with her?"

"Goodbye."

Nadia started to dial again. Pyotr grabbed the phone from her hands. "No," he said. "They will track the phone. That is enough."

"But my mother is at the hospital."

"No," said Pyotr. "She is not."

"What do you mean?"

Pyotr handed Nadia his own phone. An article from the evening edition of the *Moscow Gazzetta* filled the screen. In horror, Nadia read the headline. Patient Jumps From Window of Hospital. It continued: Svetlana Smirnova, age 63, jumped from the fifth floor window of her private room yesterday at 3:00 PM . . . suffering from mental distress after a routine operation.

There was more, but Nadia could no longer read. Tears clouded her vision.

She returned the phone to Pyotr. "She was sixty-two," said Nadia, in some kind of shock. "They made a mistake. It would have upset her."

"I am sorry," said Pyotr.

Nadia felt ten years older than she had just a minute earlier. A cold settled about her shoulders. Dread. There no longer could be any doubt. Marina Zhukova was dead. "We must go," she said.

They'd left as soon as it was dark. The highway west was crowded. It seemed everyone wanted to go to Lithuania too. Soon they left the city and its outskirts. The countryside was dark and featureless, fields waiting to be planted. She rolled down the window. The air smelled of loam and home fires.

At the first rest stop, Nadia parked and rummaged through her purse. There remained one avenue yet to explore. She found Marina Zhukova's letter and reread it, searching for the name of Katya's father. There. William Dekker. Geneva, Switzerland. She had not thought of calling him until now. She had no desire to talk to an American spy. There was another reason. Nadia did not speak English.

Seated in a booth, buoyed by the customers around her—people no different than she and Katya—she dialed William Dekker's number. The call rolled immediately to voice mail. The phone, Nadia knew, was not turned on. "Allo," she began in halting English. "We are—"

Katya snatched the phone from her. "Hello," she said, speaking clearly and confidently. "I am Katya. I am your daughter. We are looking for my mother. Please help us. Thank you. *Spasibo bolshoe.*"

Six hours had passed since. William Dekker had not yet called back. The black SUV had been with them the entire time.

The flag grew closer and closer still. It was not the prettiest flag Nadia had ever seen, but at that moment, it was her favorite. She slowed and pulled into the right lane. The black SUV moved closer. She noted that its windows were tinted and that it rode low to the ground. If it wished to stop her, it must do so now.

At that moment, the SUV accelerated, its aggressive grille filling the rearview mirror. Nadia spun and looked over her shoulder. The SUV veered into the adjacent lane and stopped at the checkpoint. The driver's window rolled down. A woman her own age was at the wheel. A blonde girl no older than Katya sat beside her, clutching their passports. The guard waved them through without examination. The SUV pulled out of the checkpoint and entered Lithuania.

A minute later, Nadia and Katya followed. They were safe.

At least for now.

CHAPTER 62

Kyiv Municipal Water Authority, Kyiv

The panel vans bearing the name of the Kyiv Municipal Water Authority arrived at the gates of Pumping Station No. 1 at 12:00 p.m. exactly. The time had been chosen with care. Twelve noon signaled the beginning of the lunch hour. Government offices kept to a strict schedule. A majority of the staff left the premises to dine at home or at one of the reasonably priced cafés nearby. A single engineer oversaw the control room. Security around the facility was likewise temporarily depleted.

Across the country, the weather was fine. It was as clear and warm a fall day as could be remembered. In Kyiv, the streets teemed with pedestrians. Lovers held hands. Children filled the parks. Lines formed for tables at the many outdoor cafés. On such a beautiful day, all agreed, in spite of the war, life must go on.

The guard at the gate of Pumping Station No. 1 diligently checked all identifications. He signaled for the gates to be opened and waved the assault teams through. The drivers guided the vans to the main pumping facility. It was a large, windowless building, essentially a concrete bunker. A prime example of Stalinist architecture. The state as monolith.

The vans drew to a halt.

Inside, the women checked their pistols. They chambered rounds, replaced the weapons in their holsters, and zipped up their jumpsuits. One by one, they opened the suitcases carrying the VX nerve agent. Zeryx. They freed the canisters from their protective restraints. They took special care to unscrew the caps, leaving the caps affixed but loose. They placed each canister in a standard-issue workbag, an over-the-shoulder canvas satchel issued to all personnel.

A last confident look among them.

"To Russia," they said, each offering her own prayer for the mission's success.

And then, they were moving. The doors slid open. The women alighted. They walked to the main entrance of the pumping station. No one stopped them. No one questioned their presence. All was proceeding according to plan.

Clockwork.

The door to the pumping station was locked. A look among them. Less confident now.

The main door was never locked during working hours.

The women regarded the entry area. It was too quiet, even for the lunch hour. No cars were parked nearby. No vans like theirs awaiting dispatch. Not a person was to be seen.

"Leave," said one of the women.

"Leave," the others agreed.

They turned and retraced their steps to the van. They never made it.

A squad of Ukrainian Special Operations Forces, newly trained by NATO, rose from their hiding spots and opened fire. Their orders were clear. Stop the attack. Confiscate the VX nerve agent. Take no prisoners.

There was no desire for lengthy interrogations. The authorities had all the information they needed. A rogue Russian colonel. An operation named Hercules. A blown network reaching as high as the US embassy in Bern, Switzerland. The fewer questions asked, the better.

Seventeen soldiers—men and women—armed with American M4 machine guns emptied their magazines: 450 rounds, give or take.

Take no prisoners.

In Kyiv, few people paid attention to the clatter of machine-gun fire. "The war," they said, if they said anything at all.

And then, they returned to their lives. Wasn't it a beautiful day?

CHAPTER 63

SVR headquarters, Yasenevo, Russia

They were coming for her.

Colonel Alexandra Zaitseva sat proudly at her desk, hands clasped, back straight. She wore her finest dress uniform. A row of medals hung from her chest. Seven in all. Not, it turned out, her lucky number.

The pounding at her door grew louder. Men shouted her name. "One moment," she called out.

Zaitseva very much wished she had some pictures to look at before she said goodbye.

Husband, children, a lover, even: there were none. She had only her parents, and they had gone long before.

With ceremony, she poured herself a shot of vodka. Moskovskaya, her favorite. Sadly, there had not been time to chill it sufficiently. Oh well. She raised the glass and offered a toast. But to who?

To the Rodina? No. She had done her best for her country. In this last endeavor she had failed. But didn't duty, loyalty, sacrifice count for something?

To the Service? Again, no. If there were any justice, she should be running the place.

Then who? To herself? Why not? She had tried. She had given all of herself. That was enough.

Alexandra Zaitseva drank the vodka.

She pushed back her chair and stood, paying the heated voices no heed. Let the wolves bay.

One last thing. She took her lipstick from the drawer and applied a fresh coat. She wanted them to know that she was a woman too.

And so, it was time.

Alexandra Zaitseva unfastened her holster and drew her Makarov pistol. It was an old gun. Small and heavy for its size. It had belonged to her grandmother, the Angel of Stalingrad, during the Great Patriotic War, or so they said.

The doors to her office burst open. A half dozen uniformed men stormed in.

With her right hand, Zaitseva saluted. With her left, she placed the pistol to her temple. It was surprisingly easy to pull the trigger.

CHAPTER 64

Zinal

"So this is it?" asked Jane McCall.

Mac guided the new station wagon up the driveway to his chalet. He'd put in some work over the past weeks. There were fresh flowers in the window boxes. He'd touched up the paint. He'd mowed the lawn one last time before winter arrived. All things a younger man would do to keep his home in good repair.

"Be it ever so humble," said Mac, sharing a proud glance.

"Or remote," said Jane.

"Better be."

Mac put the car in park and killed the engine. It was a postcard day. Blue skies, light breeze, a bracing forty degrees.

They sat for a moment in silence, listening to the engine tick down. There was an unsettled feeling between them. Was this the end of something, or maybe the beginning?

"You've decided," said Jane.

"It was easy," said Mac.

"You're not coming back."

"Nothing's changed."

"Everything's changed. You prevented a mass-casualty event. You killed the worst traitor in thirty years. You cleared your name."

"No, Jaycee. You did all that. Mackenzie Dekker . . . he died eight years ago."

"Dad, please."

He patted her arm. "Best let sleeping dogs lie."

Jane nodded, fighting back tears. "I understand."

"And you?" he asked, a sprig of hope in his voice.

"Me, what?"

He gestured toward the chalet. "Plenty of room at the inn."

Jane gave him a side glance. She wiped a tear. "You don't think I could live here . . . with Heidi."

Mac shrugged. "Clean air. Not too many people. Cheese is good."

Jane turned to face him. She took a breath. News. "I got a promotion. Deputy chief of station, Berlin."

"Berlin. The big time."

"Like you said: Ilya, Hercules, Thorpe. I did it all myself."

"That's my girl." Mac took her hand. He'd been wrong not to want his children to follow in his footsteps. The Agency needed good people. The country did. Ilya was right all along. Mac still believed.

"Come for a visit," said Jane.

"Risky," said Mac. "But if you need me."

"An emergency."

"Something like that."

"Just promise me one thing: you won't grow that beard again." Mac laughed. He'd liked that beard.

"Shh," said Jane. "You'll wake her up."

Mac unbuckled his safety belt and looked over his shoulder. Katya Dekker was asleep in her car seat, blonde hair covering her eyes. They'd tracked her from Moscow to Minsk to Vilnius. The Lithuanian government was only too happy to assist with her return. They knew a thing or two about parents and children being separated.

Mac got out of the car and opened the rear door. Jane helped Katya out of her car seat and carried her to the house.

"Were three-year-olds always this big?" she asked.

"Tell you the truth," said Mac, "I can't remember."

"This time," said Jane. Challenge issued.

"This time," said Mac, with conviction. Challenge accepted.

"Sure you're up to it?"

"Is anyone?" Mac walked to the front door. "Hey," he shouted. "We're home."

The door opened. Ava Attal stepped out. She used a cane and had difficulty moving her left arm. The doctors had not promised a full recovery. She and Mac promised to prove them wrong.

"See," he said. "I have help."

Ava kissed Jane on the cheek and took her arm. "Come in. All of you. Let's eat."

ABOUT THE AUTHOR

Photo © Katja Reich

Christopher Reich is the *New York Times* bestselling author of *Rules of Deception* and many other thrillers. His novel *The Patriots Club* won the International Thriller Writers award for Best Novel in 2006. He lives in Newport Beach, California.